New Canadian Speculative Fiction

Tesseracts 7

edited by
Paula Johanson
and
Jean-Louis Trudel

TESSERACT BOOKS
an imprint of
The Books Collective
Edmonton

The translations in this book were made possible by a generous grant from the Canada Council. Thanks to the Canada Council Block Grant programme for overall publishing support. Thanks to Screaming Colour Inc. (a division of Quality Color Press Inc.).

Cover art copyright ©1998 by Gerry Dotto.
Inside design and page set-up by Jason Bartlett. Printed at Houghton Boston, Saskatoon, on 50lb. Offset White with softcovers of Cornwall Cover and hardcovers in buckram with Luna Gloss dustjackets.

Published in Canada by
Tesseract Books, an imprint of the Books Collective,
    214-21, 10405 Jasper Avenue, Edmonton, Alberta, Canada T5J 3S2.
    Telephone (403) 448 0590, facsimile (403) 448 0640.
Tesseract Books are sold/distributed in Canada by the Literary Press Group/General Publishing. Mail orders from anywhere in the world to the press.

Canadian Cataloguing in Publication Data

Tesseracts

 ISSN 1486-0805

 1. Fantastic Fiction, Canadian--Periodicals 2. Canadian fiction--20th century--Periodicals.
PS8323.S4T47   C813'.087608054   C98-901492-4
PR9197.35.S33T47

Τ⁷

TABLE OF CONTENTS

ALIEN POETRY

Carolyn Clink

Jumble word sounds
Buzz-saw images
Pulse odd rhythms

Purple vertigo
Perfume rose kiss
Understanding

Foreword

Jean-Louis Trudel

In olden days, people would wait every year for the first ships to sail up the Saint Lawrence, bringing news and goods from foreign shores. There would be a buzz on the docks as the ships were unloaded. Among the leisured classes, one of the most sought-after commodities was a new book, from Paris or London as the case might be. And especially a new work of fiction, alive with dramatic situations and characters as yet unmet.

Did these fortunate readers of yesteryear ever wonder what would happen if the ships stopped coming?

Every year, I suspect the editors of the newest volume in the *Tesseracts* series have wondered if they might run short of worthwhile manuscripts coming in from all over Canada. When Judith Merril edited the first *Tesseracts* anthology, it seemed insanely ambitious to think there might be enough interesting Canadian SF stories out there. Before starting to read for the anthology, she had resigned herself to including perhaps a couple of older SF tales in order to reach a reasonable page total.

In the end, she didn't need to. She found all she needed, and more. Still, a Canadian SF anthology edited every year or so might exhaust the inspiration of Canadian SF authors…What if it has all been said already? (Editors will fret over such things.) Could there be nothing left to say?

Happily, it turns out the only one who'll have trouble finding something new to say is the editor required to come up with a fresh hook for this foreword to the eighth volume in the *Tesseracts* series! As usual, our authors will have you range far and wide, gentle readers, from Victoria to Moscow and beyond. Cyberspace lovers and vampires will make you forget the saucy maidens and daring swordsmen of a bygone era's novels. Whether you receive a letter from your dead mother or miss your chance to live life in the slow lane, you won't have to pursue scraps of paper into the bowels of the Earth to get to the end of this book.

But we may hope that you'll have found the trip too short…

In olden days, if the ships had stopped coming, mayhap Canadian authors would have started writing stories of their own much earlier. Now, the ships carry Canadian stories and they keep coming…

Altered Statements: #1
Addendum from The
Department of Depth

M.A.C. Farrant

We realise that the public's impatience with life is due to their lack of success during this season's egg hunt and we take full responsibility for the hunt's failure. Many citizens have complained that the eggs were not only too cleverly hidden but were disguised as well and we regret, therefore, the confusion that the giant babies caused. The eggs, of course, were hidden in the babies' fists. But because the babies were hideous, deformed and mindless, as well as being giant, the public refused to approach them. We apologise for the distress and the deaths that subsequently occurred—the public wailing, the suicide epidemic. The giant babies, we believed, were a clever foil for the eggs and we'd hoped that the public would be more enterprising in searching them out. We know that many citizens feel that something important has been left out of their lives and consequently devote much time and frenzy to the egg hunts in order to recover what they believe they have lost. It is regrettable that this season so few eggs were discovered; each egg contained a drop of wisdom in the form of a printed message imbedded in hexagonal prisms on the egg's surface. The failure of this season's egg hunt has left the public's imagination in a dangerous state of flux.

In order to calm wide spread agitation several of our staff will be on the road during the month of March. As a gesture of good will, the department has initiated a replacement search, one which should not be too difficult for the public to grasp and which offers citizens an opportunity for levity.

Workers will be appearing incognito at public gatherings and the department is pleased to issue two clues as to their identities:

Clue #1 - They will be alone, aloof, and bemused, indicating by their manner an overwhelming lack of need.

Clue #2 - During the course of conversation they will be imparting three new insights.

The job of each citizen is, first, identify the field worker and then engage him or her in conversation during which time the insights will be revealed in full. The three insights are about death, bagpipe music and balding men and will be imparted in a lively and amusing manner. We are confident that these new insights will create in each citizen a feeling of joy.

A caution, however. The joy will be temporary, lasting only until the department's next event, the annual giraffe sightings, when the public's mood will change to one of awe. Already several hundred giraffes are being groomed for the event, their long necks craning above their enclosures in anticipation of the sweet geranium plants which many citizens shyly place for them on their apartment balconies.

SHELF LIFE
Michael Skeet

Benny Sanfernando wakes from a dreamless sleep knowing that he has to fly to London. While the kitchen builds him a cup of NuYu coffee-flavoured beverage, he has his apartment remake itself into the gourmet foods section of Fred's ÜberMart. Coffee in hand (the cup is a reproduction styro disposable accurate down to the teeth marks nibbled into the rim), Benny paces up and down the aisles, thinking about this unusual certainty with which he's awakened.

It could be a spirit guide, he thinks, leading him on. In that case, he'll know why he has to go to London once it's necessary for him to know. Or he could be having a psychotic episode, in which case he'll never know why, and when he comes to his senses again he'll feel like a complete jerk. But that's not a very interesting option, so Benny ignores it. The spirit guide is the one he'll go with for now. It's always nice to be under the influence of powerful beings who want everything to work out for you in the end. Benny takes his travel case from the shelf beside the bonito-flavoured fried chickpeas, and drops it into his shopping basket, wondering as he does how he should handle the drive from Stansted into London. There's a cashcard in the case's outside pocket; he buys a ticket to London, complete with car rental, from an anonymous-service broker whose terminal appears amongst the Moroccan goods, between the brik pastry and the harissa sauce. Benny finds the ÜberMart a peaceful place, now that he's been released from the need to choose from its impossibly extensive selection. The colourful, exotic packages, jars and pouches are of theoretical interest only now, since his NuYu digestive system doesn't allow him to digest anything but NuYu's patented paste and liquids, and you can't buy them at Fred's. Not that he has any complaint against NuYu. They've kept their part of the contract: Benny is slim and trim; he looks fabulous, and with next to no effort on his part.

Except that as he thinks this his stomach begins to swell and bloat. This doesn't hurt, except for the emotional stress brought on by memories of a fat childhood. But Benny's pajamas pop open as his belly distends. Good thing they close with snaps. Equally fortunately, he still has his fat clothes. They look freaky to him, but then again so does being fat. He'll have a talk with his NuYu rep when he gets back, but right now he has a sudden craving for lunch on Pall Mall. Even if it is just NuYu paste. Benny thinks he hasn't been to London since he was a kid, but he dreams about London so much he can't really be sure of that anymore. Somehow he knows that he'll rent a car and follow a route into town that he'll recognize because he sees it every other dream or so. He hopes the buildings will look as interesting as they always do at night with his eyes closed. He decides the spirit guide has told him they will. Great. With a last longing look at the fruit salsas and tubes of love-apple sauce, Benny switches off the ÜberMart. He calls his friend Josie to ask a favour. Josie's hobby is inserting herself into media; occasionally she does the same for Benny. He has a great disk of himself in every one of Howie Mandel's early films, the good ones. Benny asks Josie to plug him into Field of Dreams. He doesn't want to take Costner's place; he never does that. He wants to be along for the ride, a passenger in the back while Costner and Jones talk about dreams and visions. If you build it, they will come. If you go to London, you will know why. Josie says of course she'll do it. She's a pussycat.

The scramjet to London is pretty much empty, so much so that they hold it for Benny while he explains to the boarding-lounge sniffer about his stomach. (The NuYu DNA is human-compatible, of course, but it still sets off sniffers and scanners in a lot of places.) There are faster ways to London, but nobody pays attention to scram passengers anymore, and that suits Benny's spirit guide just fine. He stays awake, watching media, the whole two hours of the trip. He's just had a fine, dreamless sleep, after all. It's early morning when he steps into Stansted's arrival arboretum. A butterfly offers to have his bag carried to customs, but Benny likes to keep his travel case with him. The butterfly flits away, disappointed. It looks pretty, though. Benny always likes flying into Stansted. Flowers open and close in a pattern he recognizes as coming from Busby Berkeley's work with actresses in 42nd Street. A brilliantly coloured tree frog hops onto a leaf beside him; once it thinks it's caught his eye, it shifts colour as its smooth, cool back displays the logo of first one, then another, of the car rental firms with outlets at the jetport. Benny enjoys the colour without regard to the content; he already knows where his car is waiting. When the mannikin at customs asks the purpose of his visit, Benny says, "Lunch" and the mannikin doesn't even blink. Looking at his girth, the belly—his belly?—swollen up like a blister about to burst all wet and slick,

Benny suspects the mannikin wouldn't blink even if it could. Has the NuYu digestive system failed that dramatically? He occasionally dreams about this happening, but it's far more disturbing to live through it. He keeps bumping into things he ought to be able to avoid, and because the nerve endings in the stretched belly-skin haven't fully adjusted to the expansion, each inadvertent contact feels as though it's happening to someone else.

His spirit guide offers no solace, not until Benny's through customs at any rate. Then he knows that a visit to the washroom is necessary. That's a strange way for a spirit guide to manifest itself, but these things follow definite rules, and so, therefore, does Benny. Benny's good at following rules. Inside the cubicle, his stomach shrinks with a series of noises that embarrass Benny so much that he sits on the toilet, miserable, for ten minutes, listening to people come and go outside the cold grey universe of the cubicle. He'll have to change his clothes, of course; the fat clothes are ridiculously big now. He packs them in the travel case, careful not to disturb the other contents in their padded receptacles. Before he leaves the washroom, he puts on his driving glasses. He never drives in LA; the public transit system is so good he never has to. But when he travels he likes to drive, especially in London where the world is still so close to the roads that you can look inside peoples' windows as you pass by.

The main roads into the centre of the city are busy, but Benny finds himself taking a route that's much less heavily travelled, even if it does mean occasionally driving in all directions save the one he wants. He's feeling more like himself now; seeing the buildings as he drives has awoken memories of other trips here, maybe even recent trips. He's taken this route before, he suddenly knows. He's also pretty sure now that there's more to this trip than lunch.

He finds the garage without difficulty, and swaps cars as his spirit guide tells him to. The new car is a small electric, perfect for fitting into parking spaces most drivers would fear to attempt. He's got a lot to do this morning, he realizes now. Benny tucks the spirit guide away in a part of his mind he seldom goes to, and drives into the City. There's a small gap between two cars right in front of the ÜberMart, and though it's marked off with a double yellow line, Benny angles the electric into the space anyway. He's not going to be here long. He finds the imported foods section immediately, thanks to FredCo International's policy of using the same layout in every one of its ÜberMarts. The data's on a gallium arsenide flake sitting amid the crumbs at the bottom of a bag of bonito-flavoured fried chickpeas; Benny knows the instant his hand touches the right bag. It costs him three pounds fifty, which is a ridiculous price, especially since the ÜberMart doesn't even know about the gallium arsenide and what's on it. Benny doesn't know what's on it, either, but that's not the point.

He's getting into the electric when he realizes that someone has followed him to the ÜberMart. He has no way of knowing how far back the tail picked him up, but there's nothing to be gained by chastizing himself for that now. Closing the door, he puts his purchase on the floor in front of the passenger seat, and busies himself with his travel case. The tail walks past, no doubt to take up a watching position down the block. He's the perfect tail: a nondescript middle-aged Asian man with large, watery prosthetic eyes protected by TufKote spectacles. Benny smiles, impressed; the eyes have no doubt been modified to resemble those defective HocusFocus peepers that caused such a scandal a few years back. When the tail turns the corner, Benny flips open his travel case. The handgun is tiny, a child's toy, and it nestles into his palm like one of those teacup chihuahuas. Benny steps back into the street, and follows the tail. The thing he likes best about London is how neighbourhoods of wildly differing quality can exist side-by-side without attracting any attention. Take this place, for example. He's in the middle of the City, the wealthiest few blocks in England if not the world today; and right around the corner from the ÜberMart is a dismal little parkette and a grime-encrusted church that has to be three hundred years old if it's a day. The building looks abandoned; the parkette is definitely empty, save for the tail, who still seems to be looking for a vantage point—though he's getting further and further from the street.

That's fine with Benny. He pops open a chill can, masking his body heat so infrared sensors won't notice him. Then he switches his clothes to dazzle mode, to scramble any video cameras that might be watching, and enters the park. Walking quickly, he closes in on the tail, raises his hand. The tiny gun clicks as its cute little baby electromagnets drive a carbon-tipped, crystalline needle through the side of the tail's skull, at a point just behind his ear. Still moving forward, the man turns his head, lifting his hand to scratch behind his ear. The hand never connects; he sinks to the paving stones, then slides sideways onto the damp, funky smelling grass. He slowly tips face-down, as though trying to breathe in the scent of mingled growth and decay.

Benny stoops over the man, whose breathing is shallow but steady. The crystal needle is dissolving, releasing enzymes that will savage the mitochondrial DNA of the nerve cells in the tail's brain. He won't die, not for a while anyway. But he'll be about as functional as anyone in the terminal stages of Alzheimer's. Only the carbon tip will remain as evidence, and then only for someone who knows what to look for. Benny knows he should be looking for something. He takes the man's wallet, pulls the cashcard and a couple of data-caddies and tosses the worn leather folder into the bushes. That's good, but it's not enough. There should be something else. He goes through the man's pockets, looking carefully at everything he finds. When he eyes the notepad, a receptor in his head chirps. He pockets the notepad and walks back to his car.

Benny drives the electric back to the garage, swaps it for his rental and locks the garage. Time for lunch. He finds a pub on a small street perpendicular to Pall Mall, and orders a pint and a steak and kidney pie. He knows he's at his most vulnerable now, with his memories fully restored and his mind rich with as much knowledge of the job as he's ever allowed. This would be a bad time to be taken. But the window of opportunity for a real meal is a narrow one, and he's determined to exploit it to the full. His memories aren't deep enough to explain his love for English pub food, but he doesn't really care. The pie's crust is flaky, unlike that of the last pie he ate, in a shiny plastic corporate pub in Hampstead six month ago; the kidneys have been properly cleaned and every last shred of membrane removed. The sauce is rich, the kidneys squeaky-firm and with just a hint of acridity. It's all he can do to resist the urge to lick the ramekin clean. In the pub's washroom, Benny locks himself into a cubicle, drops his pants and sits down. He places notepad and data-caddies into a sterile pouch from his travel case. It occurs to him to wonder whether the man he shot was in fact tailing him. He certainly didn't look like a pro—which could have been deliberate. But in his search of the body, Benny found no evidence of any augmentation other than the eyes. Perhaps Benny was at the ÜberMart because the man was going to be there. Or perhaps he's thinking about this to avoid what he knows he has to do. After a moment's hesitation, Benny swallows the pouch. The modified NuYu digestive system purges itself, and Benny says good-bye to the pie and beer. When the pouch is secure, the receptor in Benny's brain chirps again. A little unsteadily, he gets to his feet, flushes, and leaves the washroom.

He knows something's wrong before the door has closed behind him. A policeman is nosing around Benny's table, looking for telltales that Benny has not left there. The cop is in mufti, but with his mind running at full strength Benny can sniff out the law in the next time zone, let alone the next room.

Benny ducks back into the washroom. There's a window, which is just big enough for him to squeeze through. But it might be watched, and Benny can't think of any reason why he should have to suffer any more discomfort than he already has. The only people who've looked at him remotely carefully are the barmaid and waiter, and the barmaid won't be able to see him if he goes directly from the washroom to the front door. Benny pulls a length of fibroptic cord from his travel case, snakes one end through the crack between washroom door and jamb, and inserts the other into a slot in his left ear. The picture that fills his mind is a kafka dream because the cable is having trouble compensating for the low light level, but Benny is still able to see when the waiter steps through the kitchen door to pick up an order. Disconnecting the cable as he moves, Benny slides out of the washroom and walks to the front door. The policeman doesn't even look up as Benny steps out onto the sidewalk. Hiding in plain sight is always best, Benny thinks.

It's with some regret that he leaves the rental where it's parked. He has no way of knowing whether the policeman was making a routine check, or whether the odds have massively conspired against him and he's being looked for; but Benny hasn't lived as long as he has by taking chances. He walks to Harrods, changes into his fat clothes in a public washroom, and wills his stomach to bloat itself. A fat man again, he takes the tube to Stansted. Three hours later, Benny visits one last washroom, in LAX. He retrieves the pouch, shrinks his stomach to California flatness, and changes back into his thin-wear. Then he calls Josie. They meet in a cafe in Inglewood, and while Benny stands guard Josie cracks into Stansted's security system. She locates every image of Benny picked up by the cameras, and begins to play. The images of his arrival she removes entirely. The images from the customs check she re-maps so that it is Kevin Costner from Field of Dreams who says the single word, "Lunch." For amusement's sake, the final shot of Benny at the boarding lounge she replaces, with deliberate clumsiness, with a different shot of Benny, one she's appropriated from an LA subway security camera. Finally, she maps a random selection of anonymous Angelenos onto the images in the system, so that her work on Benny will be lost in the noise. Nobody admits to trusting video anymore—it's too easy to manipulate—but there's still a residual need in most people to believe in what they see. Josie's just made it a little bit harder for anyone who gets past that need to believe.

Benny interrupts his subway journey home in order to drop the pouch and package of chickpeas into a garbage bin at a station four stops from his own. He wonders if they will be picked up for analysis by his mysterious employer, or whether the package, notepad and data-caddies were simply a pretext, and the mental crippling of the Asian man was the true goal of the journey. He does not want to know. Wherever his memories go at night, it is clearly in both his and his employer's best interests if Benny remains a little bit ignorant of just exactly what it is that he does. Back home, Benny opens the hidden compartment in his livingroom wall and places the travel case in its shielded, shockproof cradle. His stomach has reached the end of its reserves, and hunger is giving him a headache. Benny imagines that it is his memories of the day's activities, anxious to leave him. He squeezes some NuYu paste down his throat, and rubs some analgesic on his temples. The cold penetrates and soothes his head, and he begins to feel a bit better. Benny strips and crawls into bed.

As he lays waiting for sleep to take him, he considers his other self. Would that Benny want to know what this Benny does to keep them both in NuYu paste? It would be easy to leave a record of what he's done today. Benny tries to decide if he's unhappy with his double life, but thinking about this only brings back his headache. Then his spirit guide reappears. It reminds him that he goes through this exercise every time he does a job, and every time he ends up deciding not to bother leaving a record for his other self—who probably wouldn't understand it anyway. Better to save the mental energy and just not start down that particular path. Benny smiles and settles his head deeper into the pillow. The spirit guide is a good friend. As he drifts into unconsciousness, the limbic system of Benny's brain takes over. Artificial synapses transfer the day's memories across a vapour-link to a communications chip, which encrypts and sends them across the blood-brain barrier and through the port in his left ear. The earport uploads them into his pillow, where they mingle with billions of bits of his life, being stored against the day when they might prove necessary.

ᚱ

Benny Sanfernando wakes from a sound sleep. As the kitchen builds him a cup of coffee, Benny sits up in bed, smiling. He's had the London dream again. The dream never progresses beyond the drive into the city, so he never gets to have his dream lunch in London. But it's always better to travel hopefully, he thinks, even if you never arrive.

In your places of power
(Transmogrifications)

J. Marc Piché

Lamia, eyes of three colours, I was unfamiliar with your rites that first held me in your places of power, the recipes hidden in the journal where you collect used dreams of caves and lost children,

: feed him a basil leaf in the presence of a black dog
: walk him through a graveyard where the artist lies
: take him to see the evening tide turn and take back what it has left
: lead him along the seacliffs in a half-moon that reflects the waves as bracelets
: keep silent, keep silent, keep silent, and feed your Change
: share with him a potion of herbs steeped in history
: and then, only then decide your shape and taste your Change.´

He must follow.

You placed my finger on your third eye but I wouldn't admit I could feel it. On your ceiling you had painted a spider's map of concentric visions and the colours mixed my senses so that I was enthralled by the taste of your cries, cries I had never heard before:

> the howl of the Were´
> in a night that smelled of burning
> driftwood.
> This was your night for Turning.

But you are older in this lycanthropic skin; my own nakedness was like a stretched suit, my legs twisted in the slough. The change was unequal for me

> the moon
> was only half.

In the morning
the three circles of colour in your eyes
revealed the shapeshifter
in between
skin and skin and skin

Moscow

Jan Lars Jensen

The executive slumps in his chair, as if he's been struck. His head rolls back, and he stares up at the ceiling, saying things under his breath, jihad, holy war, embargo. The footage has sent him spinning.

On the flatscreens surrounding us, we were watching images from a marketplace in Hebron. A crowd of angry Muslim shoppers captured media attention this evening, their rage articulated by one outspoken caliph. "Are we to walk on the name of God?!" the man shouted, turning the sandal he was brandishing so a worldwide audience could see what had sparked the incident. "Allah Footwear," read the logo pressed into the sole. And one other name molded in rubber: Bialkin.

Here in the situation room, we know it's impossible for our corporation to have put a word holy to Muslims on the bottom of a shoe; none of our subsidiaries has an interest in the manufacture of footwear—or the creation of international incidents. But it must seem possible to the shoppers in that Palestinian bazaar. As possible as the overturned tables and knocked-down stalls to follow, and a dance of angry feet over a Bialkin sign, and sudden bonfires built of piles of rubber sandals. Oily smoke gradually erased the Muslims from view, but the hooting continued, the curses, beneath the solemn voice of a newscaster reporting that the U.S. Special Envoy to the Mideast had been made aware of the incident. The screens gave us one final shot of Bialkin's good name, melting in rubber goo, before the flatscreens left us with darkness.

"This," said Mersey, "is a disaster."

It's suspect, I told him. We need to look carefully at what happened.

"By tomorrow morning," the executive continued, "they'll be canceling trade pacts.

There will be harsh criticism from Islamic holy leaders, talk of heresy…."

This is where he began free-associating uncontrollably, a characteristic of Bialkin executives. The polite response is to keep quiet, let him talk his way through and maybe reach a surprising and profitable conclusion. But I am impolite, and logical.

"Some other party must be responsible for Allah Footwear," I tell him. Mersey blinks, seeing me again.

"Someone is trying to smear Bialkin in the Middle East."

He nods.

"Could it be internal?" I ask.

"No," he says, surfacing from his thoughts. "Unlikely."

I motion to the secretary sitting beside us, and she begins inclining her head, typing.

$ $ $ $. Four keys marked with symbols for currency, and she strikes each frequently. The keypad runs to a latex appliance covering part of her head, something adapted from the helmets of fighter pilots, responsive to both hand and head movements. As she moves, the flatscreens light up again around us, one by one, fencing us in amber text and graphics. Profiles of fellow corporate citizens.

They march around us in an amber carousel, from which I select STP, the corporation currently wooing the Saudis for an export processing zone, where Bialkin has previously been favored. Added to what might be called a tradition of lobbing economic bombs our way, I have the logic-steps necessary to draw a conclusion from Mersey.

"STP," he says. "STP is responsible for Allah Footwear."

I am silent.

He says, "This can't go unanswered."

My cue to leave. I prefer to get out of the room before the executive can say anything incriminating. But before I reach the exit, Mersey calls me back. His eyes are dreamy again.

"Were you pleased when you saw the news?"

"Why would I be pleased?"

He shrugs. "Empowerment."

"Nobody likes a messy situation."

"Not even if it reinforces your world-view?"

"What would you know about my world-view?"

He leans back, closing his eyes. "Call it intuition."

I call it his mental condition, and leave, not wanting to hear its spin on my world-view.

⌐

In the white-collar labour pool, the smell of poverty almost overwhelms me. Somehow all the designer scents worn by unemployed accountants and market research analysts combine to one recognizable aroma, the smell of upper-middle-class desperation. The visual experience is also difficult to bear. Navy blazer, cotton shirt, conservative tie—the symbol of recession is repeated so often in these pools it's dizzying, it's like an Escher trick made real and is difficult to walk through, the whole crowd sitting up straight as I come by, each of them trying to muster dignity and stand out against their peers in unemployment.

It might be easier to ruin STP, totally.

In private moments I have imagined how this could be accomplished with a reasonable amount of capital and few breaches of enforceable laws. But in the upper floors of Bialkin such ideas are unwelcome. The upper floors, like every other component of the free market, fears more than anything else instability, which an open fight would entail. Only after taking a blow as flagrant as the one landed against Bialkin in Hebron will the corporate heads agree to retaliation, and even then it must be a measured response.

I leave the labour pool with a small army walking behind me. Former employees of STP, mostly specialists in Middle East markets and international trade, a good number of them no doubt displaced by the last STP/Bialkin mêlée. They make no complaints, of course: they're happy to be allowed onto Bialkin's private compartment of Skytrain. They're pleased to be given spaces in a mezzanine of our flagship building, even though they have to assemble the pressboard workstations themselves. They bubble with gratitude, and only after they've been inside and caught a glimpse of the amenities available to full-time employees do I reveal why they've been hired.

Show me the weak spots in STP's campaign to create an export processing zone in Saudi Arabia.

The former employees brainstorm, I mobilize Bialkin resources accordingly. A measured response. Conservative stratagems.

Days later, we are chasing up land prices in Saudi Arabia with Bialkin venture capital, and using Arabic translators in an overseas marketing office to perfect innuendo about STP, suggesting it will pressure the Saudi government to give more freedoms to women once ensconced on their soil.

We could do worse.

Ten days after initiating the counterpunch, one of the former employees calls my attention to her monitor. "I noticed a whole lot of paper being dumped in the bond market," she tells me. "I recognized the issues from when I was with STP accounting. It looks like the rainy day fund."

"The what?"

"STP had a contingency fund of easily liquefied capital. I think they're finally cashing it in."

"Emergency cash? What for?"

"Cash is a useful thing, I'm led to believe."

"Maybe STP is purchasing something big."

"If that were the case, they'd finance it through the usual channels. We'd see signs of the leverage. This is their special fund, and it looks like they're making it accessible. We're seeing ripples around a bank in the Netherlands."

"Money…"

"Is the way of this world," she says.

The comment lingers with me after I leave the building.

Skytrain slides right through at the 34th floor—Bialkin's private stop. Only one car in the train opens doors here so only Bialkin employees can get on or off. I enter the private car, settle into a foam rubber seat. Directly across from me is a polarized window, so I'll spend the ride staring at my reflection.

No wrinkles in my skin, no lines, and I am fifty-nine. I stopped showing signs of aging at twenty-five, for no reason. For a long time this pleased me, but then I went so long without aging it became unsettling. Every morning, I warily approached the mirror, knowing I would see my smiling youth had lasted another day. When my wife and I married, people sometimes remarked that we looked so alike we could be sister and brother. Time went on, and unlike me, my wife aged properly, rapidly it seemed, and people started to say we looked like we could be mother and son. Or at least, she thought people said that.

Whispered it.

Which only seemed to age her faster, until at last, she passed away.

No, that isn't right, she didn't die—I see my reflection shaking his head—she didn't die, she just went away and never came back.

Sometimes I forget she is probably still alive.

Alexa.

I look over my shoulder to the building as Skytrain pulls out. Nowhere is the word Bialkin yet that is all the structure says: day-glo orange, angles hanging over the impossibly slender stem of the structure. I can't look at the building and not imagine the secret sum of STP money being used against us.

This is my world-view.

As the building turns from sight, I sit back, resume the staring contest with 25-year-old me, wondering what he wants.

ᵣ⁊

Days later. I move through office-space, a honeycomb of cubicles in simulated wood-grain supporting hundreds of Bialkin employees—and not one of them sees me, not one. They look away just in time, or cover their eyes, or stand their briefcases to shield themselves from view.

"Am I in the doghouse?" I ask Mersey when I reach the situation room. "What's happened?"

He looks like flu symptoms feel. "Bialkin wouldn't associate with anyone," he says, "with even remote ties to the IRS."

"What do you mean?"

He leans over to tap his secretary's head; flatscreens light around us. "Footage from this morning," he announces.

It is of six or seven plain brown sedans screeching over a sidewalk and around a piece of public art. They brake in a semicircle before the ornate entrance to a building; STP, reads the frieze above the doors. Beneath the iron scrollwork march a dozen IRS agents, carrying something in sterile plastic that looks like a robot jaws-of-life. It is clear from the way they walk, this is a raid. Later they emerge with the robot and cardboard evidence boxes no doubt holding small components of memory physically extracted from STP computers.

"You couldn't resist," Mersey says.

"Am I connected with this?"

"Be subtle, we told you. Be boring."

"Maybe this is just our luck."

"This," he says, "is nothing one corporate citizen would wish on another."

A long silence.

He says, "You have no sense of corporate etiquette."

"I learned something about STP last week. Money they're trying to keep secret."

"You can't resist going for the kill."

You, you, you. It goes against what I know of Mersey for him to be so linear. Not like him to be so focused. Not without coaxing.

He seems to reach a decision. "There's someone I want you to meet."

In comes a man who looks as if his features have been changed to protect his identity, unlikely hair, plastic nose. But this is his real face. When he approaches me, body language gives him away.

I ask Mersey if the upper floors of Bialkin know he is consorting with schizophrenics.

"Mister Gora's network is proven stable and effective," he retorts.

To corporations like Bialkin, the supposed appeal of networked people is their ability to interact with multinational entities, on hundreds of fronts at once. The pauses, the strange slowness I notice when Mister Gora raises his hand, these derive from being the tip of an iceberg, one member of a network of people scattered around the globe. Such networks have gained legitimacy recently thanks to a public image overhaul, but they are really still just a subculture of netheads as old as this century. Cochlear implants allow them to communicate with one another constantly, so they may observe a multinational entity at every major point in its operations, world-wide, and assemble a comprehensive real-time picture. They are connected to the point where individual identities are submerged. Gora has taken no offense to my comment about schizophrenia.

"A real pleasure," he says to me.

I'm surprised his hand is warm.

"STP may retaliate for your stunt with the IRS," Mersey informs me. "So we have contracted Mister Gora's network to monitor the corporation at major points of concern."

"You should have run this past me, first."

"All we're doing is providing another tool."

I nod.

"What's the weather like in the Netherlands?" I ask Gora.

"The Netherlands?" He pauses, then gets back to me. "Sultry," he says with a grin. "Why ask?"

I inform them both of STP's contingency fund, then suggest the network move one member to the bank where the money currently resides. Maybe Gora's associate in the Netherlands can spot someone who works for STP, someone to follow, someone whose portfolio might hint at what they have planned for all that cash. Gora closes his eyes and speaks beneath the level of ordinary hearing, relaying my instructions to members of his network in various time zones.

A good way to keep him from interfering with real work.

ᚱ

I platform down to the mezzanine where our battle is being won. Our rumours about STP have trickled into Saudi Arabian media. With the same woman who spotted the secret fund, I discuss ways to keep up the momentum. We're discussing paying off some Saudi professors to make a damning comment about STP, when she suddenly goes quiet, staring past my shoulder.

Gora.

"Interesting," he says. "How things fit together."

There is a half-grin on his unlikely face.

"What are you doing down here?"

"This is interesting: how one can toy with European stocks, and make a bank collapse in Russia days later."

"I'm not well read in chaos economics."

"I was referring to your personal role in the workings of the world."

I stare at him.

"You shouldn't let yourself be seen around here; it's considered indiscreet."

"You and I have met before," Gora says. "I mean, you and an associate of mine have met before."

"Unlikely."

"It was Kazakhstan, around 2010, 2011? You were visiting on behalf of the Treasury Department."

"Also indiscreet are wild speculations about another person's past."

"Or maybe on behalf of Langley, Virginia. You were facilitating unwanted free market reforms."

"You've been putting ideas about me into Mersey's head," I say slowly. "You're the one."

"My associate in Kazakhstan recognizes your face," Gora insists.

"What's going on? Is this some kind of investigation?"

"The mystery is how little your face has changed, after all these years."

"The mystery is what you're really doing here."

A staring contest. Looking into the eyes of a networked person feels like looking into a live news camera. The former employees are silent. But the woman beside me breaks in, rescues me.

"Money just left the Netherlands," she says. "It's gone to Brazil."

Substantially smaller than before.

ך

Gora is describing a monster to Mersey. Apparently neither of them realizes I've stepped into the room.

"...he single-handedly undermined a currency, putting the country at risk to external forces...created bread riots, black markets...years of fiscal instability, the effects of which continue to this day..."

They're sitting in a ring of images. One member of Gora's network has positioned herself outside a bank in Sao Paulo. This is where the secret STP money currently resides. She is wearing a camera smaller than an earring. The feed is relayed to flatscreens here, providing a view of the green glass building and traffic passing through its front doors. But Gora and Mersey are too engrossed in conversation, not paying attention. I stand back, listening, opening and closing my hands. At first Gora was just channeling fragmented observations from around the world to Mersey, who sewed them together in free associative mode. But talk eventually turned. To me. Dark talk.

"Maybe," Mersey says, "we have brought too much into this fight."

And then, something onscreen compels me to step forward.

I surprise them. Mersey's voice falls off, he leans back, eyes rolling. "Anger," he says. "Indignation, retribution…"

"Relax," I tell the executive.

But I clamp my hands over Gora's ears. He doesn't resist.

"What do you want?" Mersey says.

"Look at the flatscreen. I know him."

Coming out of the bank in Brazil. An older gentleman, hair slicked to his skull. He wears frameless glasses, tinted red, and his arm ends above the wrist and continues in a chromium ball joint, currently locked to a suitcase.

"Him."

The gentleman is ex of the army, formerly of an economic division that specialized in leveling the field between the U.S. and trade rivals who didn't play fair. The unit would surreptitiously organize and support trade union movements in the nation creating the problem, raise production costs, whatever was necessary; in second-world nations, his unit was a silent champion of human rights. But in recent years the group had splintered, gone private.

I believe the suitcase clamped to his prosthetic contains the difference between the sum of STP money arriving in Brazil and the sum leaving. I believe it contains cash, and he is collecting payments, taking a discreet amount at each stopover point. Walking past the network member in Brazil, the gentleman tosses a coin, accepting her disguise as an accountant down on her luck. She snaps her head at the gesture, then lowers her face into camera's view.

The coin between her teeth. She swallows it.

"A friend from the past?" she says to me.

I twist Gora around.

"Is he a friend from the past?" Gora repeats.

"Listen," I tell him. "We need a member of your network in Myanmar. Is anyone in Myanmar?"

Mersey says, "What's going on?"

It takes little time for Myanmar to appear on the flatscreens, Yangon, a city that seems all factory, one after another, joined at the hip and repeated to the horizon. Paintings from Buddhist mythos adorn their surfaces, leftover from an effort to ease the presence of foreign capital, but soot and corrosion have transformed these images into something more contemporary, and all an observer could read off them is that this is the fourth world, where manual labour comes irresistibly cheap. Cheap enough to matter to Bialkin: these factories are an offshore Bialkin city.

I instruct the network member there to determine the labor climate.

"We won't assist you in anything," she tells me via flatscreen.

"Me?"

"You meddle in foreign affairs," she spits. "You fuck us up."

I ask Gora directly, "Why does your network care about me?"

He turns up empty palms, smiling.

In Myanmar, the member says, "You thrive on foreign strife."

But I'm no longer listening to the network's accusations.

Mersey in the meantime has made an associative leap and figured out what the economic unit implies for Bialkin Myanmar. He is working on my request, instructing his secretary to go through the necessary motions, and she returns news of an incipient labour movement, widespread unrest, anti-Bialkin sentiment, trade unionism.

Calling cards of the economic division.

"Sociopathic fucks!" The network member in Myanmar shouts at me.

We cut off the feed but a moment later her anger blurts out of Gora's mouth. "You thrive on transnational unrest! You live off it!"

He continues ranting even after security arrives and manipulates his slack body into a submissive hold. They drag him out by the ankles and he shouts into the carpet. Mercenary, provocateur…

Mersey and I do not discuss these words—we avoid talking. The news from Myanmar unfolds around us in our circle of live feed, software translating news for us in a neutral voice: a factory floor tragedy in Yangon, someone killed on the job. A body is produced, wrapped in orange tarp and carried into the street, and his coworkers are quick to follow, en masse, some of the world's lowest wage earners draining from their factories for the rest of the world to see.

Thousands of clenched faces clot the streets, but one in abundance: the face of the sudden hero, the dead man and alleged martyr. His employee ID has been photocopied and posted throughout the city, an easy image for the rapidly materializing forces of the media to capture.

"Give the workers whatever they ask for," I tell Mersey.

But over the next forty-eight hours, they ask for nothing. They seem content to sit in the baking sun, drawing media scrutiny of what has happened. We watch Bialkin stock prices tumble and slide.

Eventually I turn to Mersey. "Tell me something."

"Yes?"

"Did you ask Gora's network to investigate me? Hire it to research my background?"

"The network came to us."

I sit back, puzzled. "I don't know why it was so interested in me," I tell him. "Or how much it said. But none of that matters. In Myanmar we've got a PR disaster; Bialkin is going to get globally stung, if I don't act now."

Still he is unresponsive; I stand, walk toward the exit, and tell him what the corporation must provide if it wants me to act on its behalf. A chartered flight, a suitcase full of hard currency. Mersey does not say yes or no. But whatever he thinks of me, whether or not he supports me, I won't allow the situation in Myanmar to further degenerate.

Even if it means returning to old battlegrounds.

ר֖ז

There is a Bialkin aircraft waiting for me, but it's a cargo transport with few provisions for passengers. I get into the cold aluminum hold, sockets in the floor for cargo pallets and tethered webbing hanging throughout. I tie myself in, along with the suitcase. It slides back and forth throughout the long flight: thirteen hours before the aircraft tilts into a return to earth.

Through the window I can see airport, the lights showing derelict craft pushed off runways. After the cargo transport touches down I open the suitcase, remove an inch of bills. When the hold opens, a forklift operator peers inside and raises his eyebrows when he sees me. I show him money, and he does what I tell him.

Ferries me over to a cut-out section in the chain link fence, avoiding the terminal, bathed in a haze of sodium arc lamps.

I walk about a mile before flagging down a cab. I offer the driver good solid pesos but he says "No Camels?" and looks disappointed. He's wearing an elasticized web-belt holding about a dozen packs of foreign cigarettes. Grudgingly he accepts the pesos and drives me through the night. The city comes together out of darkness, piece by piece. We pass old rosebushes once shaped like a big red star, now just dead bushes shaped like nothing. On the slope of an overpass is a flower bed spelling out a welcome in withered tulips.

Welcome to Moscow.

Much is the same. The domes are eternal; lit through the night, they rise in carnival-tent colors from the decrepit building supporting them. Brick buildings have been patched together with more brick, all rhodonite red. In the brick walls I can see brackets where icons were once mounted; patterns of offset brickwork suggest old faces, old symbols, old slogans. Moscow. The taxi rocks along uneven cobble streets. A cordon of soldiers marches past with PCs strapped to their backs. They're accompanied by a jeep with a huge spotlight in its trailer and dented file cabinets. This must be the militia of the biznysmen, the Russian entrepreneurial class.

"War was over before we got here," a superior once told me, somewhere along this street. "And we won. We bankrupted them before they could bankrupt us."

Nobody even heard the shots fired, I said.

He shrugged. "The Cold War was always economics. Generals knew it a long time before they decided to train you and me."

When I get out of the cab I can smell sweet smoke, a scent carried by the Moskva from an old cake factory upriver. The street is enclosed by soot-stained buildings with warnings scraped into their facades, declaring them under protection of biznysmen militia. In this quarter, free enterprise is vigorously enforced, but further off I can hear the squawk of acoustic wave weapons as the militiamen flush out nouveaucrats, maybe even some anarcho-syndicalists.

It doesn't take long to find the address, but at this hour in Moscow every door and window is shuttered in steel mesh. I'm not tired. I'm immune to jet lag. I live outside time zones—maybe between them. Not far away is a hole in the sidewalk, the work of street people who tap the city's old but still functional communal heating system. Steam rises, and I position myself nearby, less for warmth than the billowing cover.

Better to be a ghost here. Here I have done things.

One of them opens around nine am Moscow time.

A heavyset man unlocks the door, huffing. I give him a few minutes. On my way inside, I pass a tarnished plaque no one has gathered the energy to remove.

SOVIET DEPARTMENT OF HYDROMETEOROLOGY.

⌐¬

Fifteen minutes later the deal is done. I come out of the office, having left the suitcase with the manager. Outside, the morning is brisk, Moscow emanating mist, resisting efforts of purification by a far-off sun. I step to the edge of the street and look both ways for any sign of a cab.

I see her instead.

Her face is masked in wrinkles but still I'm sure. Standing across the road. Dressed like a Muscovite. String bag full of vegetables in one hand. The other raised, pointed at me.

Her.

I turn, walk.

She moves on the other side, keeping pace with me.

Her strides are calculated, mechanical. Key movements are slow.

I am sure it's her. But how can I be sure? Her face has changed so much. I could probably tell from her voice, it will have survived the years. But when she opens her mouth to speak, her voice is buried in many voices. "You came back." When I walk around the corner I see what is happening.

Marching down the street, dozens of network members. Gora must have kept track of me and alerted his associates to my journey, word must have spread. And so they've flown in, rode in, trained in, from points around Europe and the former Soviet Union. They've gathered here, so many of them they impede traffic. They move as a unit and speak in unison.

"You couldn't resist coming back," says the network. "Returning to the scene of your crimes."

I keep staring at the old woman. "Alexa." Could she really be one of them? It would explain how the network became interested in me. How Gora knew things about my past he should not.

I turn around, walk the opposite way. The congregation follows, stepping in stride. Other Muscovites stare. This is not how to be discreet in a fractured city.

I walk faster.

"See how many people you have ruined?"

I run. Behind me I hear the tromp of them increase speed. Group footfalls echoing across brick edifice, the dead faces of the buildings all around me. I run down an alley, hopefully losing them, but even if I'm far ahead I can still hear. You are a transnational mercenary, you thrive on the misery of millions. I am shaking my head. People are stopping, staring. Everyone in Moscow must be able to hear the giant shout: "What do you plan to do to the workers of Myanmar?"

"Rain," I whisper. "Only rain."

Pilots have been dispatched from Vladivostok. Vintage MiGs screaming toward Myanmar, where they'll saturate the clouds with silver iodide, seeding them, and it will rain on everyone in the streets.

"The people of Myanmar," says the giant.

They will go back inside. They'll realize their factories have better roofs than their huts; the rain will remind them. The people of Myanmar can return to work without further strife, and the puddles in the street will be rain—not blood. Hydrometeorology is useful, maybe the best company we made from remains of the soviet military, so many years ago.

"What will happen to the people of Myanmar?"

"Only rain," I tell myself again.

Squealing around the corner is the militia jeep. Even though it's morning, they turn the spotlight on me. The jeep brakes hard, blocking my path, and the old soldiers want to know what's going on.

"Socialists," I say. "Socialists!"

Perfect Russian, and the magic word. The jeep squeals off toward the source of the giant footfalls and I'm free to find a cab, jumping inside before it can stop.

Socialists. That's a stretch. Some kind of collective conscious, maybe. But it doesn't take much to put militiamen on the offensive.

The cab gets me back to the fence around the airport. I run, looking for the hole. Unable to find it, I climb the wire mesh. And then I stop, still hanging on. In the daylight I can see just how littered the airport is with Russian surplus. Not much room for a takeoff, but somewhere within the junk, turbines are screaming, and I spot a tail sliding between old Aeroflot fuselages, then up, up, rising above it all, the Bialkin cargo transport lifts into blue sky, as easily as an idea.

Moscow.

A good place to dump me off. I can almost imagine the free association in Mersey's head, the leaps of logic. Too risky to continue retaining me, too likely my services would eventually embarrass Bialkin. As a former soldier, I know very well the process leading to such a decision, the decision to make a necessary sacrifice.

I think briefly of Alexa.

A truck is racing over from the terminal, full of airport security and kalashnikovs. I jump from the fence, momentarily airborne and strangely elated. I probably couldn't have stayed away from here even if I wanted. The market has a way of matching services with demands; this is where I belong.

Seven Things
I Know About Green

Eileen Kernaghan

1. When I was nine I had a velvet dress the colour of green apples
   with twenty-eight gold stars around the hem.

2. Green is the colour of hope, and inexperience,
   and envy.

3. In Fife, if the youngest daughter marries first,
   her sisters wear green garters.

4. These belong to Venus: the number seven, the swan, the dove,
   the element copper and the colour green.

5. In Egypt, green (Akdhar) is inauspicious.
   The evil eye is prevalent among green-eyed women.

6. It is unwise to wear green near the habitat of fairies.

7. At eighty-five, my mother still has secrets.
   To this day, she will not wear green.

Millennium Songs

Gerald L. Truscott

The paper boy rang the buzzer as Joseph Klein was washing his breakfast dishes. Over the intercom, the boy's voice contained no trace of apology. Joseph grumbled, "You're late", then pushed the button to let him in. He waited scowling in his doorway for the boy to come round the corner. But it was not the regular paper boy. A young man smiled at Joseph, said "Happy New Year" and handed him a paper.

"Where's…ah…" Joseph stammered, trying to remember the regular boy's name.

"David? He quit yesterday. He and his family went to some mass gathering over in Abbotsford. I'm just looking after his route until they find someone else."

"He won't be coming back?"

The boy shrugged. "He's a doomer." He carried on down the hall, dropping papers at the doors of subscribers.

"He's a bloody fool," Joseph grumbled, backing into his room. He returned to the kitchen, where his little radio blurted out another song about the millennium. He turned it off and sat down with the paper and the last of his morning coffee. The headline said:

FIRST NIGHT OR JUDGEMENT DAY?

Beneath it was a picture of a crowd of apocalytes—most people called them doomers—on the steps of the Legislature, placards raised pronouncing the end of everything. Joseph sat at the kitchen table and sipped his coffee as he read.

GOD DELIVER US, said one placard in the picture. Another said JESUS IS COMING. ARE YOU READY? And another announced the usual: THE END IS NEAR! Joseph read the list of recent disasters on a large sign in the middle of the photograph:

> BORNEO RAPED
> BANGLADESH DROWNED
> SUDAN STARVED
> YUCCA'S POIS

Heads and bodies blocked out the rest of the sign. Yucca's Poison, Joseph guessed, and probably more disasters were submerged in the crowd. The Yucca Mountain calamity happened only last month. A major earthquake in Nevada killed fewer than a hundred people. Luckily, the centre of the 'quake was in a remote part of the desert where few people live. Unluckily, the place was Yucca Mountain, where the US government had been storing nuclear waste since the 1950s. The mountain had split like a melon, spilling irradiated pulp onto the desert. They would be cleaning up the mess for decades, and they were still looking for a new storage site. There was a follow-up story at the bottom of the front page: U.S. N-Waste Still Homeless.

Joseph shook his head and looked back at the photo. The large sign was humanity's scorecard, he thought. According to the doomers, the disasters added up to: THE END IS NOW!

"They're bloody fools," Joseph said aloud. The end is not now, not even near. It's a long way off after an agonizing descent.

Besides, he thought, today is not the last day of the second millennium. There is still another year to go. AD started in year 1—there was no year 0—so the new millennium starts on January 1, 2001. All these people singing their millennium songs are dead wrong. They'll soon realize it and sing them all over again next year.

Joseph flipped to the second section where a space shuttle lifted off. The headline read:

UN launches assault on stratosphere
The war on ozone depletion began in earnest today with the launching of the Discovery space shuttle. The six-person crew will deploy two Duschene Gunner satellites to fire laser beams into the ozone layer....

He skimmed on from there; he knew the background. Project 2000, as they called it, had been going on for more than two years. "...high-altitude bombers loaded with ozone factories...ozone enhancement...laser light is known to break down CFC molecules...critics claim the $400 billion project is already over budget...."

"*Schlimmbesserungen,*" Joseph muttered. It was his father's word for such things: so-called improvements that make things worse. Project 2000 will make people feel better, make them think something's being done, and take their minds off the real problem: too many humans, too many greedy humans.

He slapped the paper on the table and took his coffee cup to the sink. Decades ago, governments knew about ozone depletion, global warming and many other problems caused by pollution and bad resource management. They did nothing about it then, and now they applied a $400 billion bandage. Joseph's wife, Una, had died of cancerous melanoma three years ago, just a few months before the UN announced its war on ozone depletion. Soon after, Joseph confirmed his membership in the growing ranks of cynics and felt better for it.

Through the small window above the sink, he saw Peter Kusnetzov from 104 putting his golf clubs in the trunk of his car. That's all he cares about, thought Joseph. If the world ended tomorrow, Peter would end it on a golf course. The young man put his clubs in the trunk and glanced up at the grey sky. Perhaps he felt a drop of rain. It certainly was not cold enough to snow.

г⅂

Just before 8:30, Joseph fastened his tool belt and headed down the back stairway to the guest suite. He had a little bit of work to do today, but first he wanted to ask his nephew, Martin, up for a New Year's toast this evening.

Three days ago, Martin had arrived carrying only his backpack and a wooden box full of saplings. He was a graduate student in biology at UBC. All he had told Joseph was that he had come to collect some rare, endangered plants and deliver them to some remote northern area of the province. Joseph had the guest suite ready for him.

Martin was leaving tomorrow, and Joseph had not had much time to talk to him. The young man had come up for dinner on his first night here, and they talked mostly about the family. Martin was Una's sister's son, and Joseph saw so much of Una in him, the shape and colour of his eyes, the curl of his lips when he smiled, and his mannerisms: the way he gestured when he talked, the way he said "actually" with a heavy accent on the a.

The guest suite was in the basement, next to the covered parking area; its entrance was at the side of the building. Through the little glass window in the door, Joseph could see Martin moving about in the kitchen. He tapped softly on the glass, and Martin opened the door with a mug of coffee in his hand. He wore a grey-green sweatshirt with a cartoon drawing of a smiling man covered with small animals and plants; beneath in yellow letters, it said "ECOFREAK!".

"Hi, uncle." He smiled brightly. "C'mon in."

"You're probably in a rush," said Joseph. "I—ah—"

"No, I'm actually ahead of schedule. C'mon in."

Joseph stepped in. The apartment smelled of coffee and damp soil. Several boxes lay along the walls of the kitchen, the waxy brown boxes used to ship produce; green garbage bags stretched over top hid their contents.

"Can I get you a coffee?" They both looked at the nearly empty coffee pot on the counter. "There's about half a cup left," said Martin.

"No thanks, Martin, I just wanted to see—if you have no plans tonight— would you like to come up for a drink?"?"

The young man started slightly, smiled like Una smiled when she considered an offer, and said, "Sure. Yeah. Sounds great. I'm, ah —"

"I thought we could bring in the new year together, but you could come earlier—for dinner, I mean—if you want."

"Well, actually, I was going to go out for dinner with some friends —"

"That's OK," said Joseph. "You have other plans."

"No. *They* have other plans. I was just going to have dinner with them, then come back here around nine or so. I could come up then."

"You're sure? Good." Joseph smiled. "Nine o'clock, then." He moved towards the door, tapping a bottle of cleaning solution in his tool belt. "I have to start my work," he said. "Halls, today." On his way upstairs, he berated himself for that needless explanation.

⊤⅂

Oak Meadow Mansion was a small apartment building, a designated heritage house. The absentee owners had hired Joseph and Una to manage it twelve years ago. It was surely the smallest of their holdings, only 18 apartments and the guest suite. They treated Joseph well, kept up with the local salary levels and every Christmas sent him a card with a generous bonus. This year the card was from Sao Paulo. He, in turn, managed Oak Meadow as if it were his own. His tenants often complimented him on the spotless hallways and the neatly tended garden.

Joseph started cleaning, as always, at the front door, then worked his way down the halls and up the stairs. He did not meet any tenants this morning— most, he supposed, were away on holidays or preparing to meet their maker on judgement day—until the third floor. The door to 304 opened and Eva Kovaks waited patiently for Joseph to shut off the vacuum cleaner.

"Good morning, Joseph." Eva was a few years older than Joseph, energetic and independent, but a little lonely. Her apartment oozed Christmas cheer. A piny scent drifted out from behind her and festive colours lent her small body a shimmering aura of red and gold.

"Good morning, Eva." Joseph tried to look as busy as possible. He half expected to be asked to examine her faucets or some other excuse to lure him into her apartment. Her only goal was conversation, and she loved to talk. Noticing an oily smudge on the wainscoting beside her doorway, he pulled a cloth and spray bottle from his tool belt and attended to it.

"I know you're busy," she said. "I just wanted to invite you up for a New Year's drink this evening."

The invitation caught him off guard. Her invitations for tea and cookies were always immediate.

"If you don't already have plans," she added.

"Well, yes I do." He hoped his tone didn't give away his relief.

"My nephew is in town. He's coming to my place tonight."

"The young man staying in the guest suite? He seems nice."

Joseph smiled and nodded.

"You know," said Eva, "my great nephew Kyle, my niece Mary's boy, well he's in one of those doomer cults. He's off now in a retreat in the Okanagan, *preparing* for the end."

"He'll be disappointed then," said Joseph, "because nothing's going to happen."

"I hope you're right." Eva sighed, leaning against her door jamb.

Joseph fidgeted with the tools in his belt. "Well, thanks anyway, Eva, for the invitation."

"It's important to be with family." She straightened herself, smiled bravely. "Perhaps tomorrow, in the afternoon? My dear friend Lorna invited me over for New Year's dinner, but I won't be leaving until three or so."

"I—I suppose…." He could think of nothing else to say.

Now she smiled as brightly as the decorated room behind her. "About 1:30, then?"

Joseph smiled back and nodded, then resumed dusting the ledge of the wainscoting. Later, as he vacuumed the third-floor hallway, he contemplated his small victory. Eva had counted on him being alone tonight, and he couldn't help feeling a little satisfaction at her surprise and disappointment. But she recovered quickly and nabbed him for another few hours of listening to her innocuous stories about relatives and friends he didn't know or care about. Why couldn't he say no to her?

Joseph shut off the vacuum outside 306, and heard familiar music flowing softly through the door. Beethoven's 9th, choral version—Karl

Schmidt's Christmas music. Joseph paused for a moment to absorb the final verse. He sang along in a whisper:

…Über'm Sternenzelt
Muß ein lieber Vater wohnen.
Ihr stürzt nieder, Millionen?
Ahnest du den Schöpfer, Welt?
Such'ihn über'm Sternenzelt!
Über Sternen muß er wohnen.

It was one of his father's favourite choral odes—he had played it often, conducting furiously in front of the stereo and enunciating the words so Joseph would remember them. Not because the message was so important, though Gerhard Klein was a religious man, but because the words themselves were part of such wonderful music.

Joseph packed his vacuum downstairs, the joyful chorus cascading behind him.

He stashed the vacuum back in the utility room, then wheeled the blue recycling bins, one at a time, out through the covered parking and around to the curb in front of the house. He was not sure if the truck would come by on New Year's Eve. What's the point of recycling if the world is about to end? He chuckled at the thought, but took some comfort in the sight of other blue bins and boxes on the boulevard.

With each trip he passed by the guest suite. He imagined the living room full of plants, dirt-filled crates and boxes covering the floor and furniture, dirty water leaking onto the carpets. Returning from his last trip to the curb, he stopped at the door and peered through the lace curtain in the window. The apartment was too dark to see through to the living room. Along the wall of the kitchen were the dark shapes of boxes covered with green plastic, and Martin had left a few dishes on the table and the countertop. One box of saplings was also on the counter.

It was the box he had brought with him when Joseph showed him the suite three days ago. "I'll keep all the plants in the bathroom or the kitchen," he had said. "Just a few boxes. I won't make a mess."

"Don't worry about that," Joseph now regretted his words. He knew nothing of Martin's personal habits. Maybe he was a slob. Scientists often are, thinking only about their work and not the people who have to clean up after them. When he saw him tonight, he would give his nephew a strong hint about leaving the place tidy.

After a few more chores, Joseph returned to his apartment and fixed himself a sandwich for lunch. While he ate, he made a shopping list. A few groceries, and something to drink for tonight; he did not know what Martin liked to drink, so he put beer and wine on the list. After lunch, Joseph put on his jacket and backpack, glanced out the window and decided to wear a hat.

⌐¬

The grey sky pressed down on the world a slow, fine drizzle that washed colours into the earth and made asphalt, metal and glass darkly reflective. A typical west-coast winter day, but a little warmer than usual for this time of year.

The shopping village was an easy walk from the Mansion and Joseph passed only a few people along the way. He rounded the corner three blocks away from the village and saw a small circle of placards bouncing spastically in front of the bank. Joseph groaned and mumbled, "Is there no escape from the morons?"

As he approached he saw that they were cheery-faced, simple-looking folks, quietly singing, "Swing Low, Sweet Chariot". Their placards displayed their uncluttered wit: "You can't take it with you!", "No banks in Heaven", "Money is the root of all evil", "God doesn't take credit". The last one forced a chuckle from Joseph. They did not get in anyone's way, but just happily delivered their message to passers by.

Joseph walked past them into the bank, where he almost bumped into Karl Schmidt, from 306. "Hello, Joseph, *wie gehts?*" he said. Karl was a stocky man, with wispy white hair that hung to his shoulders. He always wore a cap when he went outside, to cover his baldness, though he'd never admit to being self-conscious.

"Fine," said Joseph "How're you doing?"

"*Danke, mir geht es auch gut,*" said Karl. He was watching the demonstrators through the plate glass window of the bank. Retirement allowed him time for such things. Joseph stood beside him and looked out at them. "A happy bunch, eh?" he said.

"It must be nice to be absolutely certain of death and the afterlife," said Karl. He had only a slight accent when he spoke English. "They'll be heartbroken when they find themselves still alive tomorrow."

"Are you absolutely certain they will be, Karl?"

He laughed. "Perhaps if enough people believe the world will end, it will."

"There are enough sceptics, cynics and unbelievers to hold the world together, I think. Besides, they've got the wrong year for Armageddon."

"Yes," said Karl, "but these people are anxious for something to happen. They believe the world is a terrible place and that they are powerless to do anything about it. So they want God to intervene and save them from themselves, they want the angels to come down and lead them to a new Jerusalem."

Joseph grunted in agreement, but he was thinking about Karl Schmidt standing here, pondering the motives of these people. Karl had lived in Germany during Hitler's rise and fall. They never spoke about the old country, though Joseph often wondered what Karl had done as a young man during the war—how he had survived. Was he an observer then, somehow escaping the turmoil, or a participant??

Outside, smiling faces passed before them mouthing the words to a millennium song. Happy with their faith, Joseph admitted. But that's all faith is good for: it keeps you happy in a hopeless situation.

"It's easier, isn't it, to leave it to God," he said. "If only more people would try to build Jerusalem on Earth."

Karl snickered. "But would you want to live in their *Jerusalem*?"

"Hah!" Joseph patted Karl's shoulder and moved towards the queue of the bank machine.

ᛉ

At the grocery store, Joseph bought enough food for the next few days, then he went to the beer-and-wine store. The number of people lining up to buy food and liquor reassured Joseph that there were indeed enough sceptics, cynics and unbelievers in the world. He emerged from the liquor store laden with food and wine in his backpack and a six-pack of beer in hand.

Across the street, a scuffle had started in front of the bank. The placards sank into the jostling crowd, angry shouts whipped out of the tangle of bodies. A man fell backwards out of the mêlée, spilling his cap. Joseph recognized Karl Schmidt's bleached hair and bare pate. The old man struggled to get up while the angry crowd bustled around him.

Joseph rushed across the street and pushed through a few onlookers. He helped Karl to his feet and then found his cap on the curb. The old man brushed himself off and said, "I'm okay, I'm okay."

"Come on, let's go home." He directed Karl out of the crowd and towards home.

They walked for about a block in silence before Karl offered an explanation. "I just fell over," he said. "Well, he pushed me and I fell over. I'm okay now. Thank you, Joseph."

"What was that all about, anyway?"

"I don't know, really. When I came out of the bank, one of them pointed to me and said that I'd been laughing at them. I told them that they were mistaken, just as they were about the year of the new millennium. He and a young woman engaged me in a debate about Armageddon. I should have walked away, you can never win an argument with these people. Others joined in, on both sides, and then people started pushing and shoving. Someone pushed me over. I think it was that *Typ* who originally pointed me out."

Joseph stopped abruptly. "Shit." He turned back to the village. The scrum of people still moved about in front of the bank. "Shit, shit, shit."

"What is it?"

Joseph looked at his empty hands. "I must have put it down when I helped you up. My beer."

"I'm sorry."

He turned back. "Oh, it's all right, Karl. It was for my nephew. He's staying in the guest suite. But I have wine. He can drink wine. Wine is better for toasting the new year."

"Yes. Wine is better for toasting. But let me pay you for the beer. After all —"

"No. It was my own fault for leaving it there." He quickly changed the subject as they turned onto their street. "It's better to ignore those people, you know, the doomers. If you humour them—well, you see what happens."

Karl snorted a laugh. "The world is a crazy place. You'd think we'd have progressed in two millennia."

"So you are a Christian, eh Karl?"

"What? Oh, well you can't deny your heritage, can you? Even if you don't agree with it. I don't know what I am, probably won't till the day I die." He was silent for a moment, then said, "What about you, Joseph?"

"Same as you." They laughed, then walked the rest of the way home in silence.

ר⁷

Joseph unloaded his groceries, then went back outside to retrieve the empty bins from the boulevard. Misty rain continued to drift down from the sky. Back in his apartment, Joseph ate a bowl of yoghurt and finished reading the paper. A columnist wondered if the business world had really solved the millennium bug; another contemplated the alignment of celestial bodies predicted for next spring and suggested that the end of the world might be then instead of now.

There's no poetry in that, thought Joseph. Spring is not a time for ending.

He folded the paper and thought of Martin hiking through the dripping rain forest in search of rare plants, gently lifting a seedling from the damp humus....

⌐¬

The knocking startled Joseph. He wiped his eyes and squinted at his watch in the darkened room: 4:52. Someone knocked on the door again. Joseph turned on a couple of lights and opened the door. It was Martin, wearing a fresh change of clothes, his hair wet and brushed. "Sorry if I disturbed you."

"No, no, come in," Joseph wondered if Martin had come early or made other plans. "I was just listening to the radio," he said, then realized that the radio wasn't on, so he added quickly, motioning towards the couch: "Sit down. Can I get you something? A drink? Something to eat?"

"No thanks, Uncle Joseph. I can't stay long. I'm meeting Mary and Josh in about an hour. But I'm still planning to come here at about ten or so."

"That's fine." He didn't know what to say next, and Martin seemed unsure why he had come. So Joseph offered again: "Are you sure you won't have a drink? You look thirsty. I have juice or wine. I don't have any beer, I'm afraid to say."

Martin nodded. "Juice is great. Thanks."

Joseph went to the kitchen to pour two glasses of orange juice. When he returned, Martin was standing at the fireplace looking at a picture of Una and her younger sister, Martin's mother. It was an old picture: Una was in her twenties and Ingrid about fifteen.

"You have some of Una in you." He handed Martin a glass.

"I liked her," he said, looking at the picture once again.

"So did I." Joseph held up his glass, as if to make a toast, then he changed the subject. "Sit down for a moment. Let your hair dry before you go outside."

Martin touched his hair self-consciously. He sat on the couch, on the edge of the cushion as though he were prepared to jump up at any moment. Joseph sat back in his rocker, across from him. "Where are you going for dinner?" he asked.

"A little Vietnamese restaurant downtown. I'm not sure exactly where it is. Near Mary and Josh's place—I'm meeting them there."

"All the doomers will be downtown tonight."

"Probably. The First Night festival is also going on. It will be crowded near the harbour. We were talking about it earlier. None of us likes crowds, so we all agreed to come home early. They invited me back to their place, but I told them I'd rather be here."

"Are you sure?"

"Hey, it's not often I get a chance to spend a New Year's Eve with my uncle. Really…."

Joseph smiled. "Just keep away from the doomers when you're downtown."

Martin laughed. "Victoria is pretty tame compared to some other places."

"They were fighting down at the village this afternoon, just a few blocks from here. Idiots."

"Fighting?"

"Well, pushing and shoving mostly. Karl Schmidt, from 306, got caught in the middle of it. Oh, he's okay. Just a bruise or two. I think he'll keep away from them from now on."

"It's difficult, they're everywhere."

"True. True."

"So, what do you think, Uncle? Do you have much hope for our future?"

Joseph did not want to answer. He would seem a cranky old fool. And he dared not trample on Martin's idealism—it was likely as fragile as the plants he collected, as fragile as Joseph's had been. As the world slowly comes apart, he thought, each generation loses hope sooner. He decided on an oblique answer: "Well, you and I will be here tomorrow. Even if I believed in Armageddon, I'd get the year right. The new millennium starts in 2001."

Martin laughed. "That's for sure," he said. "But what about after that?"

Joseph sighed, put his juice cup on the coffee table. "We live very comfortably here. Most other people aren't as lucky. And generations to come in Canada—in North America—won't have it so good. Technology was supposed to make things better. But it's just—we've just—made things worse, while we maintain an illusion of prosperity. Too many people. Greedy people…. Ah! I'm a doomer of the worst kind."

Martin's expression had not changed since he asked the question—it was one of detached interest, the face of student in a lecture hall. He said, "Some people think that fighting over resources may actually save the planet. By reducing the human population. But at great cost to the global environment. Others think we have a little bit of time left to make things better."

Joseph shrugged. "What do you think?"

"I don't know. It's a complex problem."

"Getting more complicated."

"But sometimes there are simple solutions. We just can't always see them. A whole bunch of small acts can add up to a positive change."

Martin's university-trained idealism, Joseph concluded, and he was unsure how to respond, so he just nodded and smiled.

Martin looked at his watch. "I should go." He put his empty glass on the table.

"Let's only talk about pleasant things later tonight," said Joseph.

"Would you like to see my plants? The Campanula—the plants I came here for. They came in today.."

On the way downstairs, Martin prepared Joseph for what he was about to see. "They came on the ferry from Port Angeles. Eight flats. Mary and Josh are taking four to the north part of the island, and I'm taking the other four to the mainland."

"You're importing plants? All this time I thought you were out in the woods digging them up."

"I've been collecting others, myself. It's just the bellflowers—the Campanula—that we've been waiting for.".."

"They must be very important." Joseph felt as though he were being let in on a great botanical secret.

"Most people wouldn't think so," said Martin. "This species is rare, found only above the tree line on some of the Olympic Mountains. They're small plants, not all that impressive to look at right now. In the summer they're quite beautiful—delicate little flowers—but in winter they're usually under a metre or so of snow."

He opened the door to the guest suite and led Joseph through the dark kitchen and into the living room. The apartment was cold. "I hope you don't mind me putting a few plants in here," Martin said. "It's only for one night."

"As long as they don't leak onto the carpet."

"I'll make sure they don't."

Martin turned on the light. Four small, nursery flats lay on a blue tarp on the carpet. Joseph saw no sign of water on the tarp or the carpet.

The young man kneeled beside the nearest flat. It was filled with pots containing small, green plants, bunches of tiny, toothed leaves lying flaccid on gravelly soil. "We weren't going to move them until next summer, but this winter has been so warm. It's global warming that's killing them. They're restricted to cold mountain tops in north-west Washington. When it gets too warm, they have nowhere to go, so to speak."

"I've seen these, or plants like them, in local gardens," said Joseph.

"Those are relatives, other blue bells or bellflowers. This one is Campanula piperi, Piper's Bellflower." He crawled over to his pack sack by the door and pulled out a book. "I have a picture of one in summer. Here. See? It's not a great picture, but there aren't many of this species."

Small, sky-blue flowers reached up from shiny, deep-green leaves. The plant grew out of a crack in a rock. He compared the picture with the sad little plants in the flats. The summertime flowers seemed so hopeful.

"Pretty little things, eh?" said Martin. "They're not doing as poorly as you might think. They usually look droopy in winter."

"Under the snow, I guess."

"Yeah. They're covered up for most of the year."

Joseph tapped the picture in the book. "Beautiful."

"Mm-hm. Soon, the Olympic Mountains will be too warm for them. These ones are going north to the Kitimats."

"You're going to all this trouble for this little plant?"

"Actually, there are a few other plants…there's a rare form of trillium that grows on mountain tops just north of here. It's Dr Herrero's project. He's my botany prof. at UBC. I'll be meeting him and another grad student in Vancouver, then we take all the plants to Kitimat. We leave tomorrow afternoon, so I'll be leaving here early in the morning."

Joseph stared at the plants. A strange feeling took hold of him. A comfortable feeling, like he felt when he listened to a great piece of music: he wanted to linger in it, here in this cold, dimly lit room with Martin and his plants.

"We think this little guy's chances are pretty good," said Martin. "Actually, it'll be a few years before we know for sure if it can establish itself in the Kitimats. By then the Olympic population will likely be extinct."

Joseph touched one of the flaccid leaves. "They are refugees," he said, and looked to his nephew.

Martin smiled. "Yeah, I guess they are."

ᴦ⁊

On his way upstairs, Joseph reflected on the journey of the bellflowers. Across two bodies of water, over land, to a safe place in the cool mountains where they could live in peace, and flourish. He could remember nothing of his flight from Germany to England, when he was five, and only snippets of the journey to Canada: the freezing Atlantic spraying over the bow of the ship, the spring sunlight on the white clapboard houses on the shores of Halifax Harbour. His mother had told him many times of the people who had helped them escape; she used to send them Christmas cards every year.

He found a plate of Christmas treats waiting at his door, a colourful paper plate crammed with Christmas cake, mince tarts, shortbread cookies and chocolates, some wrapped in coloured foil, all pressed down by clear plastic and tied with a ribbon. A note, written in shaky hand, said:"For you and your nephew. Love, Eva. P.S. See you tomorrow at 1:30."

ᴦ⅂

Joseph watched the news while he ate dinner. Celebrations and rioting all through Asia and Europe: the chaos was sweeping westward with midnight. He left the TV while he cleaned up after dinner. Nothing good was on, but the sound of voices made the room seem less empty. At nine o'clock, a news special began summarizing the events of the twentieth century, decade by decade: all the wars, disasters, scientific advancements, scandals. To Joseph it was a chronicle of human failures and it made him feel ill. He left it on, but he kept finding things to tidy up or rearrange and every few minutes he looked out the window for Martin's car—his nephew had said ten o'clock, but he could be early.

Outside, Christmas lights sparkled on the houses and dripped splotches of colour onto the shiny wet asphalt and parked cars. A horn sounded and wheels squealed on a nearby street. Sirens in the distance.

The TV show caught his attention when it got to the rise of Nazi Germany. He had seen the old footage a thousand times before, but never lost his interest in it. When Joseph was old enough to understand, his father had admitted that he had agreed with Hitler's reforms at first, but as the Nazi Party became more powerful, he realized what was happening, and fled."It wasn't just the Jews he persecuted," he told Joseph. But he had always carried a significant load of guilt for leaving some of his family behind"They didn't want to come with us," he said.

The news program contrasted post-war Germany to the reunified Germany of today. Then the show moved on to the war in the Pacific.

Shouting outside attracted Joseph to the window. A crowd of about thirty doomers marched eastward down the centre of the street. Brandishing painted signs, whooping and howling to the neighbourhood, they headed downtown, psyching themselves for the End. The crowd went quiet for a moment and Joseph heard shouting from across the street. One of his neighbours was yelling at them from his front porch. Joseph muttered,"Idiot, go back inside." The doomers slowed down; some drifted onto the sidewalk and shouted back, waving their arms aggressively. Rocks cracked against the man's porch like gunfire. The doomers weren't waving – they were throwing. Joseph's neighbour fell back into his house. Glass shattered. The doomers celebrated, crowing to the neighbourhood, and continued on, noisier than ever.

Joseph shook his head, turned back to his TV.

By 11 o'clock, Martin had still not arrived. Joseph continued watching the summary of the century, though he had lost interest, trying to put the violence of the doomer crowd out of his mind. The program marched through the post-war decades highlighting the major news stories, summarizing human violence and greed. The usual stuff— nothing new or insightful. And periodically, a newscaster would interrupt with news of rioting in some eastern city, and the rioting was stepping westward with each hour.

The minute hand of the clock on the mantel pointed to the floor. Only half an hour to go. Joseph wondered if Martin had forgotten; he was probably having a good time with his friends. He pictured briefly Eva Kovaks sitting alone in her room, and Karl Schmidt in his, both watching the same news program. Joseph peeled the plastic wrapping off Eva's plate of treats and sampled a mince tart. The clock hand began its arc heavenward, and the show carried on through the 'nineties, highlighting the schlimmbesserungens (though, of course, they did not call them that) and ended its coverage with the usual message of hope for the next century: capitalism and the technology it creates will solve all our problems.

He switched to a channel where crowds of people waited for the ball to drop in Times Square, broadcast delayed for Pacific Standard Time. Joseph slammed his hand on the arm of his chair. "He could have phoned," he muttered. "I wouldn't have minded." But part of him worried that Martin had got caught up in the violence of the night.

He went to the kitchen, opened the bottle of wine and poured himself a glass. The ball dropped, paper streamers and confetti filled the TV screen, people cheered. Joseph raised his glass and drank it down, then poured some more. The TV did its usual tour of cities in the western world. But this year it contrasted the celebrations to the riots, often in the same cities.

"To self-expression," said Joseph. He drank the wine in his glass and filled it again. Then he surfed through the channels until he came to a movie: A Night to Remember. He watched it through to the end: the band playing, lifeboats sliding away in the dark water, the great ship slipping into the deep….

┏┛

The phone startled him. An infomercial played on the TV, and the dim light of morning permeated the room. He had fallen asleep. He sat up, looked at the ringing phone, then at the floor. His wine glass lay on the carpet next to a small red stain. His head throbbed. The phone rang again and again.

"Hello."

"Joseph Klein?" A woman's voice, impassive.

"Yes, who is this?"

"This is the Royal Jubilee Hospital, Mr Klein. You are related to Martin, ah, Townsend?"

Joseph sat up, head ringing. His voice faltered only slightly. "He's hurt? Is he okay?"

"He's resting now, Mr Klein. What is your relationship to Mr Townsend?"

"I'm his uncle. What happened?"

"He was injured in the riot last night, sir, but I don't have specific information. We've been unable to contact his parents—"

"They're at Whistler, skiing. I can contact them."

"You may have trouble getting through, Mr Klein. The phone lines are overloaded."

"Can I come and see him?"

"Yes."

┏┛

Martin lay in a ward with six other patients. He was asleep, tubes up his nose and jabbed into a vein on the back of his hand, face and shoulder bandaged. They'd stabbed him, idiotic doomers or troublemakers looking for a fight. The floor nurse had told Joseph that Martin's wounds were serious but he would recover. His friend, Josh, was barely hanging on in the intensive care ward. She knew nothing about the other friend, Mary.

Joseph sat on a wooden chair beside Martin's bed. The nurse had said that he might not wake up today, and that if he did, he might not make any sense. Martin slept peacefully, his mind far away from the pain and trauma of his wounds. The attacker's knife had punctured a lung and cut him in several places. The nurse said that if he hadn't been on the perimeter of the riot, the ambulance may not have reached them. A waiter in the Vietnamese restaurant had called 911. Joseph surmised that Martin and his friends were just coming out of the restaurant when they were attacked by a group something like the one he saw on the street last night. Bad timing. Joseph shook his head, thinking that this kind of violence shouldn't happen here, not in Victoria.

According to the news reports, four people had been killed last night. Joseph hoped that Martin's attacker was one of them. Probably not, though—they always seem to get away. He touched his nephew's arm, whispered, "Martin, it's Uncle Joseph. I'm here with you."

Martin's eyelids twitched. Was he dreaming? "I tried to call your parents," said Joseph, "at Whistler. But all the phone lines are busy. All morning. They're probably out skiing anyway. But I'll keep trying."

He looked for some sign of acknowledgement on Martin's face, even the slightest movement. He might comprehend something through the haze of drugs.

"What should I do about your plants? I can water them—"

Martin frowned, parted his lips, then fell back into his passive sleep.

On the way home, Joseph decided what he would do about Martin's plants.

At home he tried phoning the mainland every five or ten minutes. Always that deep, authoritative voice: "All circuits are busy. Please hang up and try again…." He phoned the ferries. On schedule, no waiting. How strange, everyone on their phones, staying put—were they waiting for the world to end?

Joseph fit all of his nephew's plants in the back of his station wagon, except for the bellflowers, which he put in the back seat. As he carried the second flat to the car, he saw Karl Schmidt returning from his morning walk.

"Frohes neues Jahr," the older man called.

"Hello, Karl," said Joseph, struggling with the flat of bellflowers. "Can I talk to you for a moment?"

Karl hustled over and grabbed an end, helped him slide it onto the back seat of his car. "What are you doing?"

"These are Martin's plants. My nephew Martin. I'm taking them to Vancouver. Can you watch the place for me while I'm gone? Just for a day. I'll be back tomorrow." He hoped Karl wouldn't ask him why. He didn't want to explain right now.

"Are the ferries even running? All the long-distance phone lines are dead, you know. I heard that a telephone switching station was damaged last night. We could be really isolated now."

"The ferries are running."

"I suppose you heard about the riot downtown last night. Six people killed."

"I heard four," said Joseph. But more could have died since this morning. Not Martin. He would be okay. The doctor had assured him.

Karl helped him with the last two flats, all the while giving him far too many details about the downtown riot and other acts of violence around the world, as reported on radio and TV. When all the plants were in the car, Karl asked about Martin, as if Joseph's behaviour suddenly struck him as being odd. Joseph told him about the attack on Martin and his visit to the hospital, as quickly as possible, and answered Karl's questions.

"I'm sure he'll be fine," said Karl. "But it's an awful thing to happen."

Joseph nodded, "I have to go, or I'll miss the next sailing." He opened the car door, but before he got in, he turned once more to Karl. "The Ferriers in 202 were going to drop off their rent today —"

"I'll get it from them and slide it under your door. Don't worry."

"Oh, and please, can you tell Eva Kovaks in 304—you know Eva —"

"Yes, yes."

"She invited me to her place for a New Year's drink this afternoon."

"I'll tell her that you had to help your nephew take his plants to Vancouver."

Joseph sighed, placed his hand on the older man's shoulder. "Thank you, Karl, you're a good friend." Then he said, "Hey, maybe you could go there in my place."

Karl raised his eyebrows, "Maybe I will." He leaned closer. "Joseph, what's so important about these plants?"

"They're refugees."

Before Karl could respond, Joseph slid onto the driver's seat and closed the door.

Karl stepped back, smiling as if he understood. Joseph laughed aloud. In that moment, he felt he knew Karl Schmidt better than ever before. As Joseph drove out onto the road, he got that feeling again, the one he had in the guest suite with Martin and his plants. He breathed in the moist, earthy smell of the potted plants in his car. "You're safe now, Piper's Bellflowers," he said, "and on your way to a new home."

Altered Statements: #2
Disasters
M.A.C. Farrant

Field report: five households surveyed.

Household # 1 - All the disasters were pretty good but we liked the earthquake the best because of the way the freeway bridge snapped in half like it was a pretzel. We liked seeing the survivors and rescuers tell their story; they looked so beautiful on TV, so solemn and eloquent. Some even cried and we liked that; we appreciated the way the camera got up close to their faces, catching their tears in mid-flow.

Household #2 - Watching the volcano erupt and the lava flow in its slow, deadly path towards the subdivision was pretty upsetting for everyone and we were glad there was a panel discussion after the show because our fears were erupting all over the living room and we needed reassurance. Volcano experts said eruptions only occur where there's a volcano so we're glad we live on the flat lands; no lava's ever going to squish our house even though it looked nice in the TV picture, cracked grey and hot pink inside, quite lovely. What we have to worry about here is snakes and poisonous spiders and you should have a disaster show about them, the way the victims die and all that.

Household #3 - We hated the hurricane; it was so boring. No roof tops flying, no cars flipping over. You do see a couple of black kids crouched beneath a freeway overpass and a lot of severely blown glass but so what? The only interesting thing was the way the hurricane dwarfed ordinary Ranchers but we only got to see that for a couple of seconds. On the whole don't bother with hurricanes again. Not unless we get to see some real destruction, squashed bodies and a lot of blood. We give the hurricane a 2.

Household #4 - The flash flood made everyone mad. Because it served them right. There they were, a guy and a woman and her six year old daughter sitting on the roof of a pickup truck, stranded in the middle of a muddy, fast-flowing river. They shouldn't have been there in the first place, any idiot could see that. That guy was stupid (stupid!) to drive across the river. Several residents of the area even said as much. In future, if you're going to have a flash flood you'd better warn people not to drive through it. Watching that guy and woman and kid on top of the pickup for so long was really irritating. We could imagine the argument they were probably having because the guy figured he could make it and didn't. And not the kid's father, either, that was obvious—baseball cap, fat, and a beer drinker to boot, a low-life is what we figured. When the helicopter finally came our hearts went out to the Grandmother waiting on the shore with a blanket for the kid. Everyone here hopes she'll get custody because it's plain the mother has no sense when it comes to men; her choice nearly cost the kid her life.

Household #5 - We think the Department should beef up its disaster series; this month's offerings were ordinary fare and we're getting bored with the show. The freak wave was a bust: an old woman toppled like a stick doll, a screaming ambulance, cars smashing against each other, a baby howling inside a semi-floating station wagon. Big deal. In our opinion, the Department needs to have death make an actual appearance. There needs to be bleeding bodies and hysterical, mourning mothers hurling themselves over the corpses. The closest the Department came to real life disaster was during the earthquake: a car, a new Acura Integra, squashed under the freeway. The car was only eighteen inches high; the fireman said the car didn't have a chance. Now, that's a disaster!

Please add your suggestions to the preceding list keeping in mind that all disasters must be "natural" i.e. not subject to political interference and not environmentally sensitive. Forthcoming disasters will focus on "killer" insects and reptiles, collapsing mountains—mud slides, avalanches, rock slides and the like—and freak wind storms with an emphasis on toppling power lines and the spectacular profusion of life-threatening electrical sparks which can occur at these times.

The Slow

Andrew Weiner

1.

Running late, Rick Bachman tried to quicken his pace, but the dense lunch-time crowds on the avenue held him back. In just twenty minutes, he needed to be back in the office for the project team meeting. But first he had to get to the health food store.

He had felt a cold coming on all morning—stuffiness in his head, scratchiness in the back of his throat—and he wanted to squash it before it went any further. He wanted vitamin C, zinc, echinacea, golden seal, whatever was going. Because he simply couldn't afford to get sick right now, not with his projects at a crucial stage, he just didn't have the time.

"Projects," his old girlfriend, Nina, would scoff, when he would break dates or show up late. "You'd think it was the Manhattan Project or something. When actually you're just ordering new office furniture, or revamping the bookkeeping system."

That had been the whole problem with Nina: she just didn't get it. She was a grade-school teacher with a tenured job and a strong union and plenty of free time.

His current girlfriend Fiona, a marketing manager for a telecommunications company, had her own projects, her own impossible deadlines. She understood his world as he understood hers. It was an ideal relationship, in a way, except that they rarely managed to spend time together.

At last Bachman arrived at the store—or to where the store had been. The front window, once filled with a vast array of vitamins, was blank and empty except for a sign:

WE'RE MOVING

TO SERVE YOU BETTER

The sign provided the store's new address, four blocks to the east.

He looked at his watch, and began to sprint down the street.

Running fast.

Running late.

2.

Panic. Bachman had it bad, the time panic.

He'd been running for years now, scurrying hard to get it all done, but somehow he never could. The demands of his work were such that there were never enough hours in the day. Always, something had to give: friends, family, personal development, hobbies, exercise, sex, sleep. He had taken time management courses, labored over day planners, prioritized his life. But the effect was only to turn up the speed on the treadmill, to make him run even faster.

Increasingly, Bachman felt like that old comic book hero of his youth, the Flash, the fastest man alive, zipping through the city in a crimson blur. Except that this was like being the Flash in a world where everyone had super-speed.

Bachman worried incessantly about the rapid passage of time, and the paucity of his achievement. As a child, minutes sometimes seemed to him to stretch like hours, days like weeks. But now, at thirty one, everything was accelerating like a videotape stuck in fast-forward. His life was whizzing by him like a runaway train, leaving him no chance to climb aboard.

3.

Two blocks to go, and he had to face facts: he was not going to make it. Either he would be late for the meeting, or he would come down with a cold. And he could not be late. His presentation was up first, and he had been preparing for it for weeks. It was an opportunity to show senior management what he could do. Despite all his long hours and hard work, he had been stuck in the same position these past two years. It was long past time to move up.

He sneezed, took out a paper tissue and wiped his nose, then turned wearily back towards the office. And saw the sign in the window of the store right across the street:

REMEDIES etc.

He crossed the street to take a closer look. It was an unprepossessing store. There were a few small, unidentifiable brown glass bottles in the window, perched on a well worn oriental rug spread over the top of a milk crate. There was no name on the window, or above it. Bachman hesitated, then plunged through the door. There was still time to pick up a few things and get back to the office in time.

The store was dimly lit, with heavy velvet curtains and intricate tapestries covering the walls. There were no display shelves, no check-out counter, just a wood table and chair at the far end of the room, and a doorway to a back room covered by a walk-through curtain made of bright yellow fettucine-like strands. There was no one in sight.

A pile of hard-covered books sat on the table: Bertrand Russell, James Hillman, Spengler's Decline Of The West. He tried to remember when he had last read a book. Who had time to read? No one had time.

Obviously business was slow around here.

"Hello?" he called, tentatively. "Is anybody there?"

He took a step forward, feeling himself sink into the thick carpet.

"Just a moment," said a calm, clear, crystalline woman's voice. Bachman did not have a moment to spare. But something in that voice, some kind of promise, held him back.

A woman swept out of the back room, through the tendrils of the curtain. She was wearing a long black dress with red-embroidered dragons on the sleeves and a purple scarf around her neck. She was quite young, he thought, looking at her smooth, unlined face. Early twenties, probably.

"I need something for a cold," he said. "Vitamin C, echinacea, whatever you recommend."

She frowned slightly. "Actually we don't sell vitamins."

"But it says 'remedies' in your window."

"There are other remedies."

"Herbs, you mean?"

"Oh yes. Certainly herbs."

Her voice was delightful, but increasingly for Bachman it was being drowned out by the ticking of the imaginary alarm clock strapped to the back of his head.

"Well what can you give me? I don't mean to be rude, but I'm in a hurry."

"Of course you are," she said. "That's your whole problem. That's how you make yourself sick. You're in too much of a hurry."

Just what I needed, Bachman thought. Some health food store clerk giving me life management tips.

"You really need to slow down," she said. "Slow right down. Take some time to experience what you're really feeling. Stop worrying so much about the future and what you need to accomplish."

"I'm sure you're right," he said, looking at his watch. "But right now I really do have to get going."

"Wait," she said, turning towards the back room. "I'll get you something that will help."

"I'll be late for my meeting," he said, still frozen to the spot.

"You won't be," she said. "I promise."

4.

The woman in the store—"My name is Evangeline," she told him, unprompted, as he was leaving—had not lied. He was not late. And his presentation went perfectly. There was a lot of dense information to get across, but rather than rushing through it, the way he would usually have done, he was cool, calm, unhurried. He could anticipate the questions of his fellow team members even as they formed them on their lips, and was able to lead them, effortlessly, where he wanted to take them.

Afterwards his manager, Ron Ziegler, took him aside to congratulate him. "Masterful, Rick. Just masterful. You know that new AVP job that's opening up in marketing? Well of course the decision isn't up to me, but I do have some input, and you're my number one contender. Just keep getting the work out." So saying, Ziegler handed him yet another project.

Bachman didn't mind. He had time for it now. All the time in the world, thanks to Evangeline.

She had returned from the back room of her store with a small brown bottle, from which she had unscrewed a dropper. "Made from all-natural ingredients," she had assured him, confusing him with someone who gave a shit, as she counted out three drops on to his tongue.

The remedy had tasted a little like vanilla. Whatever it had been, it had made him a new man. Moving at a relaxed, unhurried pace, he found that he could focus better, and get much more done. That afternoon he accomplished more than in two ordinary days.

His cold cleared up, too.

For once, he found himself not having to take home work that night. He called Fiona to see if she wanted to catch a meal and a movie. She was able to squeeze in the meal, but not the movie, because she had to go back to her office to finish an overdue report.

Bachman was not that disappointed to go home alone. He had found it hard to pay attention to the usually fascinating details of Fiona's working day. His mind had kept drifting to Evangeline, to her crystalline voice, her mysterious half-smile.

"No need to hurry," she had called after him as he left the store. "Take your time. All the time you need."

5.

That night Bachman caught up on lost sleep. And dreamed a deep, slow dream of Evangeline.

In his dream he was back in the store, and she was leading him by the hand, into the back room. He tried to form a protest—"I don't have time"—but his lips refused to move. Although somehow she seemed to hear him anyway, because she put her finger to his lips. "Yes, you do," she said. "Now."

And it was true. Even as she spoke, the world was slowing around him. The colors of the walk-through curtain flared an unnaturally vivid yellow, and the red dragons were strobing on Evangeline's dress. Her voice sounded blurry, as though she was speaking underwater, each word taking an eternity to form and resound. "And if you join us…you will always have time."

"Us?"

"The Slow," she said. "We are the Slow."

And then she pulled on his hand again, to lead him through into the back room, and he did not resist.

Some dream, he thought, when he woke up.

It had really been unusually vivid. In his mind he could still see the big red couch with the soft cushions in the back room, and the dim red lantern hanging over them. And the luminous whiteness of her breasts. It felt almost as if it had actually happened. But of course he would have remembered. And anyway, there hadn't been enough time.

He thought briefly about dropping by Evangeline's store to thank her for her marvelous remedy, and see if she was interested in doing something one night. But on reflection, that didn't seem to be such a good idea. Really they had nothing in common, they lived in quite different worlds.

Some dreams were best left as dreams.

6.

Three densely-packed and remarkably productive days later, Bachman woke up with a headache and an aching body and a raw feeling at the back of his throat. He felt like going back to sleep, but that was out of the question. Today was the big intranet project group meeting, which he was team-leading. And he had promised to accompany Fiona to her company's benefit at the opera that night.

And so he dragged himself off to work, and then at lunch time to Evangeline's store.

"You look awful," she told him.

"I feel awful."

"You've been overdoing it," she said, disapprovingly. "You've missed the point of the remedy. The point isn't to work harder."

"The point?" He stared at her, puzzled. "You gave me something for my cold and it worked. I felt fine, I felt great. You didn't tell me I needed to take it easy."

"I'm not talking about your cold. I'm talking about your life."

Bachman began to wish that he had gone to a real health food store.

She sighed theatrically. "Come with me."

She led him through into the back room and indicated for him to sit down on the big red couch.

"Oh," he said, looking around the room, as she reached down a bottle from a shelf. He sank down into the couch, which was as soft as in his dream, and looked up at the dim red lantern overhead.

"Open wide," she said.

This remedy was sweeter and sourer than its predecessor, and tasted faintly of peppers.

"I dreamed I was here," he told her, as she sat down beside him. "In this room, sitting on this couch, with you."

"Oh?" she said. "And what were we doing in this dream?" She rested her hand lightly on his arm.

"Or was I really here? Could I have forgotten?"

"Does it matter? You're here now."

"But…"

"You're thinking too hard, Rick. And losing the moment. The way you always do."

"But…" he tried to say again. His lips, however, refused to move, and there was a buzzing in his ears, and the colors in the room were unnaturally bright.

"Just relax," she said. "Into the moment that lasts a thousand years…"

7.

Much later, after hours of lovemaking on the red couch, and after slipping into a deep and dreamless sleep, Bachman woke up.

The intranet meeting, he thought. I missed it.

He looked at his watch. It was 12.15. But that was the same time it had been when he entered the store. He shook his wrist.

Evangeline was staring at him.

"My watch stopped."

"There's nothing wrong with your watch."

Even as she spoke, he saw the second hand sweep forward.

"But it says that it's still 12.15."

"It is 12.15," Evangeline said, pointing to the flashing digital display on her own watch. He watched the seconds rush by: 12:15:11, 12:15:12…

"But what happened to the time?"

"Nothing happened to it," she said. "We just enjoyed the moment to the fullest. And if you like, we could keep on enjoying it."

Her watch stopped flashing, freezing at 12:15:29. He looked at his own watch. The second hand had stopped again.

"You can stop watches? How?"

"I don't stop watches. I stop time."

"Time?" He gaped at her. "You can't stop time."

"We can." She stretched her arms, flexed her neck. "We can do all kinds of tricks with time. Bend it, stretch it, speed it up, slow it down."

"We?" he echoed. "Who are 'we'?"

But even as he spoke, he remembered his dream. If it had been a dream. "The Slow. You said you were one of the Slow."

She nodded.

"But what does that mean?"

"We are people with a different experience of time. We don't burn it up, the way you do, but savor every moment. We live among you, but so slowly you may not always notice us."

"That remedy," he said. "It isn't a medicine. It actually slows down time."

"For you, yes."

"And that's how you do it? How you control time? By taking these drugs?"

"No," she said. "We don't need to. For us, it's almost like a kind of meditation, being aware, really aware, of the moment. Focusing on one thing at a time, noticing how you're feeling, physically, emotionally. Being present in each and every moment of your life…But you needed help. Not so much a drug as an antidote, for all the poisons you've been fed."

"Poisons? What kind of poisons?"

"The poison you put in your mouth to burn as fuel, all those sugars and starches and alchohols and animal fats. And the poison you put in your mind to whip you into a frenzy: your competitiveness, your greed, your ambition to succeed at any cost. Everything that says to you more, more, faster, faster. Everything that makes you run this insane marathon race straight into the grave."

"While you stand back and watch."

"We don't, much. It's too painful."

"What do you do with all your time?"

"Listen to music. Look at pictures. Eat delicious food. Read books. Have interesting conversations. And great sex." She smiled, showing off her small, perfect teeth. "Anything that's pleasurable, we can stretch out the moment to fully experience it.

"Get dressed," she said, "and I'll show you how we live."

8.

They stood in the doorway of the store and watched people rushing past them in both directions.

"Look at them run," Evangeline said. "Faster and faster every year. I feel so badly for them—for you—sometimes."

"Then why not try to help us?"

She shrugged. "Not everyone can be slow. For some to be slow, others must speed up. We need other people to do the running for us, so that we can enjoy our lives."

"But that isn't fair."

"Not everyone wants to be slow, Rick. A lot of people take pride in how busy they are, in not having a moment to themselves. They boast about it. They don't want to stop and experience their lives. They'd much rather get it over with quicker."

She took his hand. He felt a faint electrical tingle. And watched as the people on the street began to slow down, then came to a complete standstill.

"What did you do to them?" Bachman asked.

"Not to them," she said. "To us. I took us back into the deep time."

They began to walk down the street, past the frozen traffic, weaving around the pedestrians who stood as still as statues.

"It's like we're moving fast and everyone else has stopped."

She shrugged. "Relativity," she said.

"And this is how you see the world?" he asked.

"We move back and forth, between the shallow time and the deep. But mostly we stay in the deep, where we can slow down time, or stop it almost completely. Isn't that what everyone wants, Rick, to stop time? In the deep, you can live forever in a single day. I've lived a hundred lives already. And so can you."

She came to a halt in front of a fashionable and expensive department store. "You need a scarf," she told him, leading him inside. "Let's go get you one."

The store clerks stood frozen as Evangeline went behind a counter and began to take scarfs out, settling on a black-and-yellow tartan. She wound it round his neck.

"Perfect," she said.

She took the scarf back to the counter and expertly removed the store security tag.

"Let's go," she said.

"You want me to steal it?"

"We don't think of it as stealing. We take only what we need."

He reached into his pocket. "But I have money…"

"We don't use money. We don't need it."

"But I'm not one of you."

"You could be. I could teach you."

"You want to save me from myself?"

"I want to save you from time, Rick."

9.

They visited an art gallery and looked at the pictures for what seemed like hours. They went to the museum's cafeteria and helped themselves to sandwiches.

"Just taste those red peppers," she said. And he did, until their intensity became unbearable.

They strolled in the park for awhile. Then she led him into the lobby of a grand hotel.

"Where are we going?" he asked.

"To a party."

People stood frozen waiting for the elevators, but she took him up the stairs. They climbed three flights.

"You must get good exercise," he said. "Walking everywhere. Using the stairs instead of elevators."

"It's not like we're in a hurry."

They came to a halt in front of a door. "The people who were staying in this suite are on the way down to the lobby to check out," she told him. "The party started when they left, five minutes ago. It's been going on for months…"

"But why have your party here?"

"Because we can."

The door was slightly ajar. She pushed it open, and they walked through into the living room of the hotel suite. It was a large room, with high ceilings, and a table covered with a buffet along one wall. There were perhaps fifty people scattered around the room, standing and talking and eating or lounging on the many chairs and couches. It seemed to Bachman that all of them turned to watch him enter with Evangeline.

"Ah," said a thin blonde woman, coming forward to meet them. "Fast company. But can you slow him down, Evangeline? Can the hare lie down with the tortoise?"

"Rick, this is Moira," Evangeline said. "She's going to be nice to you, right Moira?"

"Of course," Moira said. "You know me, I adore fast men."

Evangeline left his side and crossed the room. Bachman watched out of the corner of his eye as she hugged a white-haired man.

"I dated one myself once," Moira told him. "Charming man. But he couldn't keep still. Always had to be doing something else, someplace else. Always in a hurry to go nowhere so he could get back quicker."

"Couldn't you slow him down?" Bachman asked.

"I tried of course. But it didn't take. He just didn't have the aptitude." She leaned closer, put her hand on his arm. "But I'm sure you do. Knowing Evangeline. And we all know Evangeline."

"I don't know her, really. I only just met her."

"Then you need to spend more time with her. Much more time."

10.

Later, much later, Evangeline appeared at his side and announced that it was time for them to leave.

They went back to her store and made love several times. They read poetry to each other. They fell asleep.

And when he woke up, it was still 12.15.

"I should go," he said.

"Why?"

"Because I can't stay here forever."

"Actually you could."

"But I have work to do."

"You don't need to work. Work is for other people. It isn't for us."

"But I like to work. Sure, I bitch about my job, like everyone else. But it's still a buzz, getting it done, making things happen."

"A buzz? Or maybe a rush? You're talking about an addiction, Rick."

He shook his head. "I don't know, Evangeline. To become like you…I had plans, big plans. Getting ahead, making money, making a mark."

"Stupid plans."

"Perhaps. But I'm not sure I'm ready to give them up."

"Think how wonderful it would be," she said, "how much time we would have together."

"We could still spend time together. Lots of time."

She shook her head. "You can't live in two worlds, Rick. You have to choose."

"Then I need more time to think about this."

She nodded. "Don't think too long."

11.

"…so I told him, that's really unacceptable…"

In the back seat of the limo, Bachman listened to Fiona debrief him on her latest work adventures. It seemed to take forever. Was this, he wondered, what he sounded like when he downloaded his experiences to Fiona?

After he had left Evangeline, time had resumed its normal pace. Or maybe not. The afternoon at work had dragged interminably. And now he was dreading the prospect of the opera. Even on a normal day, an opera could take forever.

"Did you ever think about stopping?" he asked Fiona.

"Stopping?"

"Just giving it up…I don't know. Going to live in a small town somewhere, living in a house with a big front lawn, raising some kids."

Fiona gave him a searching stare. "Is that a proposal?"

"I don't know."

"It's not an attractive one," Fiona said. "I hate small towns. I grew up in one. Everything is so slow. And I couldn't imagine not working. Work is what makes me feel alive."

"I know exactly what you mean. But maybe we're just hooked on an adrenaline rush which is really just fear…"

"Are you feeling all right, Rick? You don't seem to be quite yourself."

"I'm fine," he told her. "Just fine."

12.

Evangeline called him at work the next morning.

"I'm still thinking," he told her.

"I miss you," she said. "It seems like it's been forever. Let's meet somewhere for lunch. I'll bring a picnic."

"I don't know…I've got this huge report to finish."

"You'll make time. I'll see you 12.30, in the park by the pond. We can feed the ducks."

He worked away at a calm, measured pace until midmorning. He was halfway through his report when Ziegler called him into his office.

"It's looking more and more like a wrap," Ziegler told him, "that AVP position in marketing. It's yours practically for the asking. You've just got to show the marketing group what you can do." He passed over a huge sheaf of paper. "I need you to pull these numbers into shape. Bring them back at two and we'll go over them together before I make the presentation."

"But I promised the intranet recommendations on MacKenzie's desk by one."

"And I'm sure you'll meet your commitments," Ziegler said. "If you're really AVP material. This is what you've been working for, isn't it?"

"I'll get it done," he said.

Just be cool, he told himself. Be calm. Pace yourself. You can do this. You can still do this, and meet Evangeline.

But Ziegler's numbers were an infuriating mess. And when he tossed them aside to pick up his interrupted report, he found that he had lost his train of thought completely.

He poured himself another cup of coffee, emptied several packages of sugar into it. He's bullshitting me, he thought. I'm not up for AVP.

But he had made a commitment. He slogged on through to the end of his recommendations, and tossed the finished document into his out-basket. Then picked up Ziegler's numbers again, crunching and recrunching them into some sort of shape.

Even if they do offer me the job, he thought, I don't really want it. I should just walk out of here right now and sign up with Evangeline's crew…Oh Christ, Evangeline.

He looked up at the clock on the wall.

It was 1.30pm.

13.

The cab crawled with agonizing slowness through the crosstown traffic.

On his wristwatch, the minutes continued to race by.

"I'll walk," he told the driver, as the cab came to another halt. He tossed him a five dollar bill, jumped out of the cab, and began to jog up the street.

It was 2.15. He should be back in the office briefing Ziegler. But instead he had plunked the breakdown on Ziegler's desk and rushed away, pleading an emergency. He would pay for that later, if he went back. He did not plan to.

He was going to take up Evangeline on her offer. If, that is, her offer was still good.

There had been no reply when he called her store. She must be still waiting for him in the park. For her it would seem like an eternity.

Running through the crowds was like trying to run through glue. The park, just two blocks away, seemed to recede at every step as he ran onwards.

Running hard.

Running late.

14.

Evangeline was sitting on a bench by the pond, tossing breadcrumbs to the ducks. He sat down beside her. She did not turn to look at him.

"Evangeline, I'm really sorry..."

She threw the last of her crumbs into the water and stood up.

"I waited to say goodbye. Goodbye, Rick."

"I'm really sorry," he said, again. "I got hung up, I didn't notice the time."

"Too bad," she said. "You'll have every opportunity to notice it now."

She began to walk away. He got up and ran after her.

"I didn't mean to keep you waiting," he said. "I promise you it won't happen again."

"It's not that you're late. It's why you're late. You made a choice, Rick. Now you're going to have to live with it."

"I'll quit," he told her. "Just give me one more chance, Evangeline. I'll go back there and quit."

"Maybe you would. But it wouldn't take. You'd soon get restless to do things, achieve things, to run with the pack. I'm sorry Rick, you just weren't meant to be Slow..."

"But..." he said, reaching to touch her arm. As he did so, he realized that the gap between them was widening. His own pace was slowing, as hers seemed to be quickening. And then he was not moving at all.

He stood frozen, watching her walk away, for about a hundred years.

The Dishwasher

Lydia Langstaff

"Today will be the day," Ruthanne said to herself. She put her apron on, followed by her pink rubber gloves. The kitchen was noisy as always. Noisy with the sounds of the diner's patrons. Conversations and clatter wafted through the humid air to the large sink. Sound pummelled her from all sides. It never seemed to stop; the cook was always shouting; the bell ringing for each order; and the waitresses calling in their own language "Adam and Eve on a Raft"....

Sounds wrapped around Ruthanne as if to cocoon her within her own thoughts. Thirty-one and still stuck in the same little town. All the men were long gone to the oil rigs. She didn't really have much hope of marriage or anything else. She was kind of quiet and she never did meet anyone— what with being in the back of the kitchen and all. Still, today was the day. After all her horoscope was really good this morning. Ruthanne was a Gemini, and today the paper had said a chance to meet her soulmate was coming. Though she didn't usually believe in destiny or magic, this sounded so good it gave her new hope.

Ruthanne hung her head and watched the clean water flow into the bubbling lather. The white foam rushed up to meet her. She controlled it by turning off the taps, killing the rushing monster and watching it die down into the sink. The dishes were piled in through the foam and she gazed deeply into it. Then as she brought the first plate up to wash and rinse, she saw a man's face reflected on the wet surface. He had a hawkish nose and square jaw with thin black hair.

Ruthanne reeled back, startled at first. She quickly glanced over her shoulder, expecting to see this stranger in the kitchen, but was only met with a new pile of dirty dishes from the last of the breakfast crowd. The reflection reminded her of an ad she once saw on T.V., but this face had a cruel glint in its eyes. Ruthanne shivered once, then she took control again and rinsed the face away. With hesitation she pulled the next plate out of the water. There in front of her again was a face looking back at her from the plate. He was a lot nicer looking, blue eyes, blond hair and skin suntanned from construction. She did not know how she knew this, only that it was so.

"Too handsome," she whispered to the bubbles as she rinsed him off. Would this happen a third time? Ruthanne wondered. This must be the sign her horoscope spoke of. Sure enough, another man's face appeared. "This time he's too old", she sighed. Plate after plate she washed, rinsing each face from it. Until at last it was her break time. She removed her gloves and her apron. Instead of eating in the back as was her custom, she went to the cloak room and glanced in the mirror. Ruthanne looked into her big brown eyes and saw the softness that made her fear. Her vulnerability was so close to the surface. Dare she? Then she grasped her black vinyl purse and removed her hair net. She took the plastic pink comb out and combed her hair back into place. In an unprecedented move she applied lipstick.

With ten minutes to spare, she helped herself to coffee and a donut. She proceeded to sit down at a stool in the diner—with the customers. "Be brave", she whispered within herself. As one of the waitresses took a load of dirty dishes into the kitchen, she realized that people could see her from the diner. That swinging door suddenly seemed like a saviour. Miraculously this new perspective changed everything.

If only someone nice would look.

Coffee drunk and donut devoured, she walked back into the kitchen with head held high. She began to wash the dishes again but this time with a new zeal. Each plate came up through the water with a face that Ruthanne now hoped would be the one. All day the dishes showed faces, but none was right. Too old or too handsome, were mostly her reasons for rejecting them. She did not stop for lunch afraid to miss the face, his face: soon to be her one and only. On through the afternoon without a break, but she dare not stop now.

At about six-thirty, she saw his face in a spoon. All this time she had only noticed plates, yet the spoon contained the reflection of someone really nice. Ruthanne thought he had a kind look to him. He was young and his eyes were soft and brown like hers. Eyes that said I've been lonely too. She gazed into the spoon wistfully. Then as she looked up into the diner the door swung open and her eyes met his. He was reading something, but he glanced up for a moment.

Their eyes locked together like bubbles connecting diaphanously, but within seconds they had each blinked away. This is him. The bubbles seemed to say it as each popped and died away. Ruthanne had to do something. He was almost half way through his coffee and apple pie. So she took her break.

She ran to the cloak room: removed her hairnet, and fixed her hair. She carefully applied another coat of lipstick and purposefully walked right out into the diner. She took a hamburger and some coffee and sat one seat over from him.

This was a triumphant moment. She knew it, the water in the sink knew it, the spirits of the dead bubbles knew it, if only he did. But he just sat there eating the last of his pie and taking his last mouthful of coffee. He turned to leave, but Ruthanne met his eyes again. Her survival depended upon it. Dishes forever would be her fate if this moment were to end.

She was desperate, so she said, "Refills are free."

"Thanks," he replied shyly.

"So what, what are you reading?" Ruthanne asked, afraid to let go.

"Oh, just a dishwasher manual."

"A what?"

"I, I fix dishwashers. I'm a dishwasher repairman."

"That's funny, I'm a dishwasher," Ruthanne said and smiled.

Oh, Won't You Wear
My Teddybear

Judy McCrosky

Andrea heard a rustling in her bedroom. The sound brought her bolt upright, sheet clutched to her breasts, her breath tight in her throat. Had someone broken in? Maybe if she didn't turn on the light, he wouldn't notice she was there.

Don't be a fool, she told herself. There's no one here. And even if there was, you're in no danger. You're the invisible woman, remember? She reached out and flicked on her bedside lamp.

No prowler dressed in stripes and a mask, carrying a bag marked "LOOT." The rustling continued, coming from the floor.

She looked down. No man. Only a very fluffy hamster, fur trailing from its backside in two long wisps, waddling out from under a plastic bag she'd tossed in the corner.

Andrea shrieked, and then felt foolish. How could anyone be afraid of something so cute? She encountered disturbing and horrifying sights every day at work, and dealt with them with equanimity. Yesterday she'd autopsied a car crash victim, determining that it was a heart attack which sent his car spinning off the road and into a tree. Exploring his broken body had not heightened her breathing or caused her blood pressure to rise. Apparently it took a furry small animal to send her adrenaline surging. She released her grip on the sheet. "What are you doing here?" she asked the hamster.

It sat up on its hind legs and looked up at her. She bent over, put out her hand and it hopped onto her palm.

The hamster, a female, had black fur, a pointy nose, long whiskers, and black caviar eyes. She was disgustingly cute. "I think I'll call you Jasmine," Andrea said. Jasmine sniffed the air, her nose moving up and down, up and down. Her furry stomach pressed into Andrea's hand, soft and warm. Andrea smiled, the warmth spreading through her, as if she'd pulled a favorite old blanket up over her body. She lay down and went to sleep as Jasmine waddled about her bed, exploring.

When Andrea woke at her usual time, seven, there were two hamsters in her bed. The new one was tan coloured, and Andrea named him Spot. "I guess you were lonely," she said to Jasmine. "It must be nice to want a friend and have one just appear."

She got up, pulled off her nightgown and went to stand in front of her mirror. Carefully, missing no part of her body, she examined her skin for signs of cancer. She ran her fingers along one arm, gently rubbing the mole just below her elbow, checking if it was larger or if its texture had changed. She twisted her head, looking over her shoulder at her bare back in the mirror, at the wine-stain birthmark. It was no larger than the day before. There were no new marks on her face, her hands, her legs. She rotated her shoulders, took in deep breaths, and relaxed, ready to face another day. She dressed in her greens and ate cereal for breakfast. A new hamster had joined the others, this one a lovely white and tan brindle. He was even more fluffy than the others.

Still, cute as they were, Andrea did wonder where the hamsters were coming from. She went through the ground floor of her house, checking baseboards on the external walls, examining the fit of the front and back doors, looking for holes or cracks large enough for a hamster to fit through. She found only dust. There were no openings to the outside world. She watched the hamsters waddle across her kitchen floor, got out her list of things to do that day and added, 'Buy cage and hamster food.'

She put on her lab coat and slung her stethoscope around her neck. She almost never used it, as her job involved analyzing bits of people and she rarely dealt with a whole living person, but she wore it because other people in the hospital recognized it as a badge of office and treated her with more respect.

⌐¬

That evening was her weekly quilting bee, and she looked forward to telling her friends about the hamsters. There'd been five when she got home, and she worried about whether the cage she bought was too small. She poured cedar shavings on the cage floor, added the food bowl, attached the water bottle, and looked about to see six hamsters watching her with great interest.

"Where are you coming from?" she asked. The six stood up on their hind legs, front paws in the air, and looked at her. She smiled. "It doesn't matter, does it. You're here."

They readily allowed her to pick them up and put them in the cage. They rooted about in the shavings. One of them started chewing on a cage bar, and she saw with admiration that he had long curved teeth. She sighed at how cute the hamsters were, and got out her quilting bag.

"I have hamsters," she told the other quilters. They sat around a huge quilt frame. The quilt top they'd pieced together over the past weeks was done now, and they were sewing together the top, the padding, and the bottom, using their long needles to quilt in a pattern of curves and swirls. The color design was one of sun and sky, with bird silhouettes flying across the blue, and a border of leaves all around the edge. It was supposed to be what a person would see if she lay on her back in the center of a circle of trees and looked up into the sky.

"They're teddybear hamsters," Andrea added, proud of this knowledge which she'd gained at the pet store.

"I didn't know you were into pets," Marlene said. She had seven cats and three dogs, and was proud of being an animal person. "When did you get them?"

Andrea had to stop and think. "I didn't get them. They just appeared."

Edna and Lucinda looked at each other, eyebrows raised. "Andrea," Edna said hesitantly, "you know it's not exactly normal to have hamsters just appearing."

"I like them," Andrea said, feeling defensive. "They are welcome at my house."

"Be careful." That was Jane, who owned the house they were in. The bee always met in Jane's house because she had the only one with a room big enough for the quilt frame. It was the cleanest house Andrea had ever seen. "Hamster infestations can be terribly hard to get rid of." Jane sniffed. "Have you again left cookie crumbs in your living room sofa?"

Andrea wasn't sure if Jane was joking or serious. It was often hard to tell with her. She moved her needle up and down, up and down, through the quilt. "I just cleaned my sofa. And you should see them. They're so soft and warm."

"Whatever turns you on, honey," Lucinda, tall and muscular, looked around, accepting the laughs sent her way.

Andrea wrinkled her nose. "Maybe I need that in my life. There's no fluff or warmth where I work, after all. In the morgue, no one is cute or cuddly."

There was a silence, broken only by the small pops of needles puncturing fabric. Then Lucinda grinned. "You telling me I'm not fluffy?"

They all laughed. "Who's coming to my party this weekend?" Lucinda asked.

All the women except Andrea said they were. It was spring, the start of party season. All the women were divorced or never married. Andrea, at forty-four, was the oldest.

"I don't know," she said. "It seems that every party I go to, all I do is talk to all of you."

"And what's wrong with that?" Edna stopped sewing and put her hands on her hips.

"Nothing." Andrea ran out of thread, tied a neat knot on the surface of the quilt, and cut the trailing end. "It just seems that if we're at a party where there are other people, we should talk to them."

"Other people?" Marlene laughed. "You mean men."

"Men don't notice me." Andrea squinted at her needle and slid a new thread through its eye. "I'm invisible."

Lucinda punched her lightly on the shoulder. "You seem pretty solid to me."

"Men see what they want to." Andrea shrugged "They look for cute and perky and if what's there is wrinkled and saggy, they see nothing."

"Oh, don't get on that kick." Edna, sitting next to Andrea, put her arm across her shoulders and gave her a hug. "You're an attractive woman. Maybe you need to do something to get them to notice you. Wear bright colors or something."

Andrea looked about the circle, at the faces of her friends. Each one was vivid, each one beautiful in her own way. Marlene, all sharp planes and angles, high cheekbones, arching brows. Lucinda, large and strong, had a smile that, if you got it at close range, made you feel you'd been kissed by an angel. Edna, so pretty with her red hair and huge green eyes you wanted to hate her, but you couldn't. And Jane, her dark eyes so intense it was hard to talk to her one on one.

"I tried being noticed," she said. "I wore a red feather boa over a black and pink dress, and I had a black hat with a peacock feather on it."

"I remember that outfit," Lucinda said. "I loved it."

Jane wrinkled her nose. "You're not supposed to love an outfit like that. You're supposed to notice it."

"It didn't work," Andrea said. "Nobody noticed me. Older women are invisible, just like I told you. It doesn't matter what we wear. You'll all find out, when you're as decrepit as me."

No one said, "You're not decrepit." Andrea hadn't expected them to. They all cared too much for one another to say the expected.

T⁷

When Andrea got home she found thirteen hamsters playing under her living room furniture and, judging from the rustles in the kitchen, a few more in there had discovered her paper recycling box. Some were sleeping, piled together in a corner of the sofa, a fur ball coloured brown and orange. The cage, its door firmly shut, stood empty.

A chill swept up Andrea's spine. The number of hamsters was increasing for no apparent reason, just like the cells in a tumour, a melanoma, perhaps, growing with its own logic, its own purpose. She shivered and wrapped her arms about herself. Three hamsters discovered her feet. One was Jasmine, and she climbed onto Andrea's shoe and stood up on her hind legs, looking up as if trying to find her face. Andrea bent and scooped her up, pressing the soft fur against her cheek. "You can't be a cancer," she whispered. "You're too cute." She picked up the empty cage and put it in the back of her hall closet.

Andrea switched on her TV. It was tuned, as usual, to the Weather Channel. She stroked Jasmine and the other hamsters who were congregating on her lap, and waited for the Ozone Hole report.

The satellite image appeared on her screen, colored a cool blue where the ozone layer was thick and complete, gradually shading through purple to a fiery orange to show the hole. "Over Antarctica," the weatherman said, "ozone protection is ten percent of normal." The graphic shifted, its motion swift and sudden, leaving Andrea feeling as if she'd just flown through an air pocket. The continent shape beneath the blue was now the familiar full bosom and narrow waist of North America. "Over the North Pole," the weatherman continued, "the ozone layer is thinning, the hole's edge brushing northern Canada, here and," he used a red laser pointer, "here."

Andrea sat bolt upright on her couch, sending three hamsters tumbling from her chest to her lap. "Ultraviolet," she told Cherry, a fat ochre hamster who was grimly climbing back up, "is not good for hamsters and other living things."

Cherry curled up on her shoulder and went to sleep. Spot and another hamster, she thought it was Fido but she wasn't sure, as there were by now seven orange hamsters, arrived on her lap. "We," she told them, "are killing our planet's skin and there's nothing I can do about it." Spot and maybe-Fido sat up and looked at her, their round black eyes unblinking. "I'm scared."

Spot climbed up to her shoulder. He stood on his hind legs and balanced his front paws against her cheek. His tiny claws pressed against her skin, the touch oddly soothing.

The next morning, after Andrea checked herself for signs of skin cancer and found no changes on her skin, she arrived at the hospital and discovered that Jasmine had come to work with her. The hamster clung to her lab coat, a ball of fluff just above the breast pocket, her nose whuffling up and down, up and down, as she took in the new scents in the air. Dr. Baines, one of the other pathologists, passed Andrea in the hall leading to the lab. "Nice brooch," he said.

⌐¬

Andrea decided to go to Lucinda's party. "I can't just give up," she told Spot. Rover and Tibby sat on her shoulders, listening, too. "I don't mean to insult you," she continued, "you're wonderful company, and so cute, but I need human company. Maybe even male company." At her feet, other hamsters waddled about, sniffing her shoes, exploring under the furniture. She thought there were thirty-seven of them now, but she wasn't sure.

She put on a black velvet skirt and a raspberry-pink silk shirt, brushed her shoulder-length dark hair back from her face, and set off for Lucinda's. Rover and Tibby had resumed their posts on her shoulders. Walking into Lucinda's loft apartment, they stood up to take in the new place, each placing a paw on her earlobe for balance. A man she knew slightly, who worked with Lucinda in Emerg at the hospital, complimented her on her earrings.

All about Andrea, people mingled, talking, eating, laughing. Colors swirled and moved in arcs and straight lines, merging from one pattern to another. Most people seemed to be about her age or a little younger. Across the room Edna smiled and waved. Jane and Marlene stopped to talk on their way to the kitchen for fresh drinks. Other people brushed by her as if she didn't exist. Andrea wondered when she'd be invisible enough for them to walk right through her, a woman without substance as well as without an outer surface.

The hamsters were warm and soft against her neck. She scanned the room, looking for a likely prospect, determined to take matters into her own hands. A little way from her, sitting on a couch, was a man wearing a blue-striped shirt. He had a thick black mustache and his eyes reminded her of a policeman's, watchful but shuttered, taking in but letting nothing out. The place next to him on the couch was empty, and she thought he looked lonely.

She sat down beside him. "Hi. My name's Andrea."

He looked blankly at her, then back at the knots of people.

Press on, she told herself. Keep shooting until you see the whites of their eyes. "How do you know Lucinda?"

Another man came to the couch. The man she was talking to jumped to his feet, punched the new man on his biceps, and two merged into the crowd.

Andrea took Tibby from her shoulder and stroked his brown and orange fur. "What do you think? she asked. "Try, try again?" Tibby butted his nose into the space between her thumb and forefinger. She took that to be a yes.

A man stood by the window, one shoulder against the wall. His hair was long, tied at the back of his neck by a leather thong. Andrea liked pony-tails on men. "Hi," she said. She propped her hip against the windowsill. "I'm new in town and I don't know anyone. Can I talk to you?"

The man's gaze went to her face, then moved past it to over her shoulder. A smile grew on his face, and he reached to take the hand of a young woman approaching him from behind Andrea. The two moved away, talking animatedly.

Andrea held both hamsters against the front of her neck, closing her eyes and reveling in the feel of soft fur against the skin under her chin.

"I'm lonely. Talk to me." The man she said this to asked her if she knew where the bathroom was and, when she pointed him in the right direction, moved on without a further word.

She sat on the couch again, between two men. One drummed his fingers incessantly on his thigh, the other slouched back, his head tipped so he stared blankly at the ceiling. "I may be old," she said to the ceiling gazer, "but I'm a nice person. Would you sit and have a drink with me?" He ignored her.

She turned to the finger drummer. "I may be old, but I'm a nice person. Would you sit and drink Geritol with me?" He jiggled the glass he held in his other hand so the ice cubes rattled, tossed back the rest of his drink, and stood to head for the bar.

Andrea wandered into the kitchen and talked with Edna for a while, about the quilt, the hole in the ozone layer, the latest group of med students she'd taken through the morgue, and the artist who'd had a tantrum at the gallery where Edna worked, because his paintings were hung six inches lower on the walls than he'd wanted. Then she thrust back her shoulders, puffed out her chest, and went back into the party.

She walked to a man standing alone, tapping his foot to the Dire Straits music. They both gazed in silence for a moment at the people dancing, and then Andrea touched him lightly his shoulder. He looked at her, startled. "I've just learned I have a terminal brain tumour and will die tomorrow," she said. "I've never slept with a man, and it's an experience I want to have before I depart this world of tears forever. Will you—?"

A look of intense fright came over his face, and he scuttled away, looking back over his shoulder once, eyes wide, his skin pale.

"I've made progress," she told the hamsters. "He noticed me." She stuck out her tongue at the retreating man, went home and turned on the Weather Channel. The ozone hole over Antarctica, she learned, had increased slightly. Scientists were unsure of why this happened, and two men and one woman who worked for the Weather Bureau debated whether the growth of the hole was an anomaly due to unusually active sunspots or if it was the beginning of a trend which proved that human awareness of the effects of pollutants, and a genuine desire to save the planet would have no effect.

"The hole in the sky," Andrea told the eight hamsters on her lap, the three on her chest, and the one on the top of her head, "is real. People can't see it so they pretend it's not there. They don't want to deal with it. People think if they pretend something doesn't exist, it will go away. It's easier than controlling pollution. Or seeing the person beneath the wrinkled face." She paused, stroking the hamsters' soft fur. "But don't worry. I won't let you get skin cancer."

The hamsters stirred, their small claws gripping her clothing, their noses whuffling against her skin. Botticelli, the brown hamster on her head, took a strand of her hair in his mouth and tugged gently.

ᴦ⁊

Andrea's home now held sixty-one hamsters, furry balls of black, brown, tan, ochre, umber, white, and orange. She went to work every day and analyzed suspicious lumps and fluids which came to her in small containers. She did autopsies on bodies which lay on steel tables. Dead people are all surface, she thought, as she cut a Y-incision in a chest, revealing what lay inside. People use surface to control what others assume about their inner selves. The dead can hide nothing.

The hamsters accompanied her in increasing numbers, to work, shopping, other errands. She liked having them along. Their fur was soft, the warmth and slight weight of their bodies comforting on hers. They were always pleased to go to a new place, interested in exploring new scents and sights. People often complimented her, and Andrea liked the attention. One day, when she wore a sweater with a floppy cowl neck and several hamsters rode on it, three lab technicians and two doctors mentioned her lovely necklace. On a day when she'd gone downtown to do errands, and hamster enthusiasm reached new heights so that they clustered thickly on her shoulders, several people mentioned, often with envy, that they loved her shawl. She said, "Thank you," to each compliment. The hamsters gripped her clothing and hair and watched the world about them, their eyes dark, their noses in constant motion.

Andrea found no signs of skin cancer on her body. She wanted to check the hamsters, too, but it was difficult, now that there were over one hundred of them, to be certain she got to each one. Besides, they didn't have much exposed skin. "You're very sensible," she said to the ones on her lap and on the couch beside her as they watched the Weather Channel. "You know about the importance of covering up when you go out into the sun." She offered sunblock to Jasmine one day, concerned about the hamsters' pink or black bare noses, but Jasmine sneezed when she sniffed the block and backed away. "I'll keep it handy for you," Andrea said, "and you let me know if you want it."

ᴦᴉ

Andrea hadn't been to a party for a long time. There seemed no point. She saw her friends once a week at the quilting bee. She had, she told herself, enough human contact.

One evening in late June, when the sun was fierce and the ozone hole was growing at an unprecedented rate, sparking much fascinating commentary and many panels of experts on the Weather Channel, Edna phoned Andrea to tell her about a party at the art gallery.

"It's in honor of Tim Legere, of the University art department. He's retiring. Why don't you come? I know you love his work."

Andrea did like Legere's paintings. They were landscapes, done in subtle earth tones, each detail so finely and lovingly rendered that the hills or forest or lake came alive, filled with the rustle of leaves and the scent of the wind. Hidden in each scene, subtly drawn so they seemed more a part of tree or sand or sky than separate life forms, were figures. They were part of the landscape and yet not of it, they were hidden and shy, and could only be seen if the viewer looked carefully.

Andrea glanced out her window to where the sun blazed from a clear sky. All about her, on the floor and furniture, the hamsters sat up on their hind legs and looked at her. "Okay," she said to Edna. "I'll come."

ᴦᴉ

"It has been confirmed," the Weather Channel told her. "A hole in the ozone layer has opened over the North Pole. The layer has thinned in a large radius around the Pole, so that solar radiation levels are higher as far south as Baffin Island."

It was the night of the party, and Andrea was uncertain of what to wear.

She listened to the TV as she stood in front of her closet and gazed forlornly at her clothes.

"There is concern," the commentator said, "that recent droughts and unusual blights and other crop failures are due to the increased levels of solar radiation. Skin cancer rates are at a never before imagined high."

Another voice came on the TV, describing new forms of eye disease and how ophthalmologists were unable to keep up with the demand for their skills. Glancing through her bedroom doorway, Andrea saw a doctor standing in front of a phacoemulsificator used for cataract surgery. The scene changed abruptly, and now she was looking at the trading floor of the Toronto Stock Exchange. "Investors," said the commentator, "savvy enough to buy shares in companies which manufacture sunblock and other skin care products are—"

Andrea went into her living room and switched off the TV. "Our skin is being destroyed," she told the hamsters. "My skin, the earth's skin. And what's more, I have nothing to wear tonight." She sighed and sat on her sofa. Several hamsters immediately begin to climb up her legs. Their claws scratched and pinched, but the sensation was not unpleasant.

"You're smart," she said, scooping up a handful of hamsters and dumping then on her lap, "to keep your skin covered. And fur is always in fashion if you're the original owner."

She gathered another armful of hamsters and, lying back, spread them over her chest. They whuffled and poked their noses into her neck, and spread out to explore, eyes bright, whiskers twitching. Andrea suddenly knew what to wear.

She put on a slip, one which, although sleeveless, covered her from her shoulders to just above her knees. She stood between her sofa and a chair and the hamsters swarmed from the furniture onto her body, each finding a place to cling to. They were excited to be going out, moving their heads from side to side, their noses in constant action, up and down, up and down.

Andrea heard music and laughter as she approached the art gallery. Silhouettes of people talking and drinking could be seen inside, and light streamed out into the night through the building's large windows. She squared her shoulders, "Are we ready?" The hamsters stirred on her body, shifting their claws to get a better grip. Together, they entered the gallery.

Edna spotted Andrea as soon as she came in, and moved across the crowded floor to greet her. "It's so good to see you," she said, and leaned forward to kiss Andrea on the cheek. The others, Marlene, Jane, and

Lucinda came to say hello, too. Lucinda pressed a glass of white wine into Andrea's hand.

"Here," she said. "It's sweet, just as you like it." She wrinkled her nose to show what she thought of sweet wine.

Andrea held her glass by her waist, and hamsters leaned forward to sniff it.

"You look lovely," Jane said. "I've never seen this dress." She reached to smooth her hand along Andrea's shoulder, and suddenly froze. Andrea's four friends looked at each other and back at her, their eyes wide.

"Hamsters?" Lucinda said.

There was a flurry of motion around them, as people moved from one conversation to another, refreshing their drinks at the bar along one wall, admiring Legere's paintings which hung on the other walls. A man appeared at Andrea's shoulder. She recognized him as the man in the blue-striped shirt she'd spoken to at Lucinda's party.

"Andrea," he said. "It's good to see you. You're looking lovely tonight."

Another man, the one with the pony-tail, pushed his way to her side. "Hey, Andrea. Long time no see. C'mon. Let's dance." He took her hand and pulled her across the room to where a trio, two guitars and a drummer, were playing a Rolling Stones song.

The man placed one hand lightly on Andrea's shoulder. The hamsters drew back a little, and sniffed at his skin. "How," he asked, "has someone as cute as you remained hidden away for so long?" He rested his cheek against hers. "You're so soft and warm."

At the end of the dance, Andrea thanked him and moved away, even though he asked for another dance. She'd forgotten where she'd left her wine, so she got another glass and sipped it slowly, moving along the sides of the room, looking at the paintings. The hidden figures, women leaning out from behind trees, long-haired men lifting their faces above the surface of lilied lakes, women lying in grassy fields, arms stretched up to the sky, had nothing to say to her.

"His work is stunning, isn't it?"

Andrea turned and saw a red-haired man standing beside her, gazing at a painting of a sand dune.

"Every brush stroke is a brilliant statement, all on its own," he continued. "Each color is a separate jewel, glowing with its own unique light." He turned to face her. "But none of these works can compete with the beauty of your eyes."

Andrea smiled, and asked him if he knew where the women's room was.

As she crossed the gallery to find it, she was stopped three times, once by a man who told her how lovely she looked in her dress, by a second man who said he was just leaving for a really fun party, and would she like to come along, and by a third who asked her to marry him. Each time she smiled and kept walking.

Inside the bathroom, which was mercifully empty, she took in a deep breath. The hamsters on her shoulders stood up and pressed their noses against her neck and cheeks. Their whiskers tickled and she smiled.

"It's not me," she told them. "They don't see me. But it is me who can have a good time, so I will."

She splashed water on her face and went back out to the party.

She laughed and talked, she drank glass after drank of sweet wine, she danced until the soles of her feet felt numb. Wherever she went she was surrounded by an admiring group of men, anything she said was greeted with laughter if it was a joke, and respect if it wasn't. She saw her friends watching her, Lucinda's eyes filled with pride, Edna's with love, Jane's with surprise, but she never got a chance to speak to them. When the party was over she fended off seven offers of rides home and eleven offers to continue the party elsewhere, usually at the man's apartment, and took a cab home. She'd had a wonderful time and when she got back she collapsed face down on her bed, scattering hamsters in every direction, and cried until her eyes hurt and the skin of her face felt burnt.

⌐¬

The sky quilt was almost finished. If they worked hard tonight, it would be done. The five of them sat around the frame, needles darting up and down through the three layers of material. Andrea began a curve parallel to three other curves she'd already quilted, the line of stitches sliding in between the leaves along one edge.

None of the hamsters had come with her tonight. They never came to the quilt evenings. Sitting beside her, Jane reached and put a hand on her shoulder. "Andrea, are you okay?"

Andrea sighed and dropped her needle. It landed on the yellow cotton sun and bounced a few times before lying still. "No. I'm not okay."

"You've been depressed since the party," Edna said.

"It's not your fault. Don't feel guilty." Andrea picked up her needle and rolled it between her thumb and forefinger. "I had a very good time."

"Why are you so low, then?" Marlene asked.

"They only liked me because of my dress." Andrea stabbed the yellow sun, again and again. "They look for cute and cuddly, and that's what they found."

She put both hands flat on the quilt. The taut material vibrated beneath her palms. "Surface is all that matters," she said. "I can do nothing about the changes to my surface, and not enough people care about the earth's surface."

"The ozone hole?" Lucinda asked.

Andrea nodded. "We can't see what we're doing. We look and we see only what we want to see. We don't see it shrivelling, drying, dying." A tear pushed against her eyelid and she wished with passion that she had a hamster or two to press against her face. "I confirmed diagnosis of three new melanomas today."

"You're scared," Lucinda said.

Andrea nodded, fighting the burning wetness in her eyes.

Her friends sat very still. They looked at each other, eyes meeting eyes, and then they all nodded. "There's nothing that can be done to control aging," Edna said.

"There's nothing," Jane added, "that can be done to control the stupidity of those who can't see beyond the surface."

"But," Marlene said, "we can do something about the hole in the ozone layer. People who care can do wonders."

As one the four women pulled the threads, still attached to the quilt, out of their long needles, and stood. "Come with us," they said to Andrea and she followed them.

Outside it was still light, for the sun set late this time of year. Edna, beautiful tiny Edna, held her needle up above her head and passed it up and down, up and down, through the air. Lucinda, big woman, started sewing too, and opened her mouth to sing. The others joined in, and their needles wove music into the air, a high wordless song. Andrea watched her friends, each moving her needle in and out of the sky.

She lifted hers, too, her body reaching up, and plunged it through the air. She added her voice to those of the others, and the song rose up into the atmosphere. Lucinda began to bob and sway, her red dress swinging about her ankles as she took long gliding steps across the grass. The five women danced and sang their wordless song as they sewed up the hole in the sky.

⌐

When Andrea got home, the house was quiet and empty. The hamsters were gone. Only Jasmine remained, sitting like a furry statue on top of the dark TV.

Andrea knew she'd miss the hamsters, but it was good to have the extra space, floors and furniture now clear and free.

She sat on her sofa and looked at the new quilt. The women had finished it, sewing long past dark, not talking but saying much. Her friends had given it to Andrea, insisting she take it, that they would start a new one the next week. She'd spread it out on her living room floor and she looked at it, the yellow sun, the blue sky, the black bird silhouettes flying fearlessly through the air.

Andrea leaned her head back and stared up at her ceiling. It was stippled, and swirls and curves of white flowed across her sight. She had no urge to turn on the TV.

She felt tiny claws moving up her leg, and she lifted it to see Jasmine on her knee. She bent her leg, spilled the black hamster onto her lap. Jasmine looked up, and began to climb, clinging to Andrea's light blue blouse.

"Are you lonely, here by yourself?" Andrea asked. "I have friends, wonderful friends. They see beyond the surface. But," and she waved her arm, almost knocking Jasmine down, "I have to wear a dress of cute hamsters to be noticed by men."

Jasmine, still climbing doggedly, reached Andrea's chin. She stood up, reached with her paws and rested them on Andrea's mouth. Andrea felt a gentle pressure, the tiny pricks of claws, as Jasmine pushed on her lips, stretching them into a smile.

The smile grew, long past where Jasmine's short legs could reach. "I did get noticed, though." Her smile stretched further, until it cracked open and a great laugh surged out. "I went to a party wearing hamsters." Andrea held Jasmine cupped in her hands, and laughed until the sun on the quilt filled her eyes.

Old Woman Comes Out of Her Cave and Puts The World in Order

Mildred Tremblay

Old Woman shambles out of her cave,
feeling sulky, feeling troublesome.
Lifts her hand to swat the gaping moon
from the sky, flings it
like a broken egg across the stones.
Looks around for Old Man.
Love, she says. I need love.

Down by the river Old Man sits on a branch.
He has turned himself into a bluejay.
Rrrr, he says, preening indigo feathers,
eating a wood louse, hoping to fool
Old Woman. Rrrrr. He knows
she will wear him out, reduce
his delicate penis to flummery.

Jay, says Old Woman, have you seen Old Man?
Meow, says Jay, I mean rrrrr, rrrrr.
Old Man has gone into the woods;
craving truffles he has taken his spade
and…Swat! Old Woman's hand
swings through the air.
Damn liar, she swears. You are Old Man.
Now come be my lover, be brave, show me
your prickly wild thistle
that grows in the bracken.

Poor Old Man succumbs. Cannot resist
a chance to display his favourite thing!
His springboard of champions, his valorous
longboat, his Cedar of Lebanon, his Taj Mahal
his Eighth Wonder whose lift and heft
has kept him in thrall since boyhood.

Now it leaps up. O Beautiful purple,
eagerly gleaming, pin-eyed pet. And
once again Old Woman over him rolls
in a tumult of dust and crushed
sweet clover. Ravages, savages,
peels the stem, snaps the blossom,
transforms his elegant Prince of Sticks
into a miserable, shrivelled escargot.

Humming, Old Woman returns to her cave;
leaves Old Man mumbling praise in the dust.
At her door she pauses. Scoops up the streaks
of splashed moon from the stones, reshapes
the gold in her great broad palms.
Imprints it with the face of Old Woman.
Pins it back in the sky.

Altered Statements: #3
Urgent Missive Concerning the Boring White Woman Lobby

M.A.C. Farrant

Even though it is the stated mandate of this department to integrate minority groups into mainstream culture when ever and where ever possible, the department is still not willing to entertain the demands from the Boring White Woman lobby. We are not yet convinced that they constitute a minority in the classic sense despite their repeated attempts to convince us otherwise—the petitions, demonstrations, media events, and so forth. Events, we might add, which can only be described as exercises in pitiless whining. Furthermore, the department rejects their claim that they constitute a minority group because they live—happily, they insist—with men. Attendance on children is also not proof of visible minority status and no amount of mother's days cards delivered to this office in black plastic bags will persuade us otherwise. Motherhood has been known to cross all boundaries, both of gender and colour, and is not the special domain of Boring White Women. In fact, we expect a public apology from the Boring White Woman lobby because of their challenge to our declaration that the old-style nuclear family is dead; we expect nothing less than their denouncing of this abhorrent fantasy.

The aim of this department is the disbanding of the Boring White Woman lobby into more appropriate groupings—into one of the many victim groups, perhaps, or into associations for the specifically afflicted.

Staff are again reminded that fraternising with Boring White Women will not be tolerated and any department member who attends a Boring White Woman event as a guest will be immediately dismissed. (Refer to the enclosed invitation, THE BORING WHITE WOMAN REVUE) Such invitations are never harmless; Boring White Women are legend for their guile and deviously feminine ways while maintaining an outer appearance of shallowness. In truth, they are extremists and their attempts to gain minority status is an infiltration tactic, a ploy to regain their formerly privileged position.

The influence of the Boring White Woman lobby must be countered at every turn; they've had enough special attention and their access to special programmes for minority groups will continue to be denied. Do not believe the Boring White Woman lobby when they claim they are lesbians, if not in body, then at least in heart.

Effective immediately there will be a ban on Boring White Woman charity events. The Department of Diversity declares that citizens will no longer be won over by the obvious sentiment of such endeavours. Diseases and the Poor will now be championed by one of the minority groups from our approved list, crushing once and for all, we believe, the irritatingly benevolent social worker image for which the Boring White Woman is renowned. As well, the following bans continue: bridge groups; committee work; self-help groups which focus on maintaining loving relationships with men; and mindless consumerism which, we now know, is the special province of Boring White Woman.

Field workers are urged to continue in their derision of the Boring White Woman lobby keeping in mind our recent and spectacular successes in dealing with their counterpart, The Dead White Male, now reduced to whimpering on the sidelines of history.

In closing, congratulations are due to those staff members who have successfully forayed into Boring White Woman territory—the suburbs. The department is pleased to note that several of our favourite special interest groups are now operating within the public schools where they have wrested control of the parent-teacher agendas. It is cheering to see the Boring White Women lobby marginalised to the status of hot dog server where they belong. May they remain there.

Systems Crash

Scott Ellis

"Another beer, Frank?"

"Thanks, Hal. Yeah, set me up again."

"So, what's happening?"

"Saw Estelle at a party a while back."

"Oh man, when are you going to get over that chick? Lookit, Frank, she's no good for you. She's good-looking, she's sexy, she's bright enough, I guess. But she's the Queen of the Bitches. Look at how she dumped you. Everybody says so."

"Hey, chill. I just said I saw her. Well, actually, I knew she'd be there."

"Why am I not surprised?"

"Yeah, she was with her new boyfriend, Jerry Martens."

"Jerry Martens? That prick whose Dad ran the chemical plant? The one who always used to sneer at us when we did the pizza delivery to his parties?"

"Yeah, rich Jerry. His Daddy died and he cleaned up on the will. He's finishing up his Master's in Business. Got himself chopped, cloned and networked."

"Heavy gold."

"You're not kidding. Dude must have towed in five mil in parts. Fast-twitch grafts, great hair, cheekbones you could cut yourself on, bone extension so he's damn near seven feet tall, mylar contacts, the whole nine yards. He had on one of those fastpeek jumpsuits, with random transparencies so's you could scope out his manly fizzicue. Hung like a Triple Crown winner, now, too."

"Subtle."

"Well, that's Estelle and Jerry: Always go with class. He's even got four little ornamental aerials on his left temple, so you know that somewhere he's got four dedicated clones doing the mental gruntwork, making him look good. Just in case you miss the point. I take one look at him and think 'No way am I tangling with that, all on my lonesome.'"

"Now you're finally talking sense."

"But he starts in, needling me 'bout my job and him going to Dartmouth, with Estelle laughing and egging him on and I figure what the hell, so we start arguing."

"About what?"

"Kind of a question is that? These things are never 'about' anything, they're just dicksize wars and he's got me beat seven ways to Sunday."

"Oh, I don't like the sound of this…"

"Yeah, Jerry's talking rings, no, talking Dyson Spheres around me. You want facts and figures? He's got 'em, pipin' hot out of the databank. He's even wired up with one of those little Toshiba handholos, so he can do 3-D graphs, right in your face. You want literary? He's got epigrams from Molière, Sappho, Oscar Wilde, the Gilgamesh cycle, Kristeva, George Sand, I mean it's all coming at me, so fast and funny and furious all I can do is gape. I remember some of the stuff he said and now it don't mean much of anything, but at the time he sounds like a genius. The guy's in the zone, he's smoking a Davidoff Double Corona and drinking a Tidepool, with the PCP, vodka and the live crab? The fuck does he care, he's got neural cutouts, he can do that shit all night long. Smiling his great smile that cost more money'n I make in a year. Everyone's watching this post-human dirtbag access his four little flunkies to flatten my butt while Estelle giggles and wiggles like a cat in heat. Everything's going according to schedule."

"Bad scene."

"So meanwhile, Roberta and Cherysse…"

"Wait a minute. Roberta and Cherysse were there? Man, what the hell are you still sniffin' around Estelle for? Roberta's twice as smart, easy to look at and she actually likes you, Christ knows why."

"Yeah, I know. We been out a few times."

"And Cherysse! Whoa-ho-ooh-whee! That girl is a jaw-dropper."

"Down boy. And they're not there."

"But you just said—"

"Will you let me tell it?"

"Sec. I gotta get some customers. Two Becks and a Gimlet? Comin' up."

т⌐

"So?"

"So, meanwhile, Roberta and Cherysse are out in Silverwood, talkin' to these security guys at one of those secure condos?"

"Is this where…"

"Right. Where the clones are stashed. Little utility apartment down in the basement."

"How'd you find it?"

"Some hacking and cracking on my part and Roberta's. That girl can pull code apart like you untie your shoelaces. Cherysse helped with social engineering."

"I can just guess. And what are they getting out of this?"

"Well, Roberta never did like Estelle much. Calls her a parasite. Plus, she says this is going to be part of her research project."

"If Roberta ever puts whatever that is all together, the world's in for a shock."

"And Cherysse, besides being Roberta's bud, had her own little run-in with Jerry a while back. It got kind of ugly."

"OK, they're there. Now what?"

"Well, they're with the security guys and everybody's relaxed. Couple good-lookin' girls, Friday night, talkin' that sweet trash and with their own tokes. Hey, everybody's gotta loosen up sometime, am I right?"

"Ahh…"

"Yeah, just a light trank in the weed, just enough to leave Joberto and Otis in dreamland, there in the employees' lounge."

"So they're in. What now? Go knock out the clones? Take down the link?"

"Please. Leave us not be crude. No, they go knock on the door and one of these guys answers. A Jerry. Except he's not like our hero, currently hanging me out to dry, ten miles away in midtown. No, he's pudgy and shy and awkward and kind of near-sighted. And he's got all the social graces and confidence of a zit-faced fourteen-year-old whose voice is cracking and who can't help getting boners in public."

"A nerd."

"Of the first water. They're all of them nerds, sitting there at their consoles, looking through databanks, one or the other miming out Jerry 1's party talk. Oh, one's had most of the implants and grafts, just in case Jerry 1 needs a backup, but basically they never get out, they don't talk to anybody, they don't know from anything except getting Number 1 the answers and grades, while he's off living the high life."

"But aren't they suspicious?"

"Roberta's a pretty good talker. And Cherysse, well, suspicion is kind of beside the point, when she sets out to charm guys about as sophisticated as Butthead's little brother."

"So what happens?"

"What happens is Roberta gives them a survey."

"A survey?"

"We cobbled one together, out of some I found in a dumpster. A long survey, with questions that meander all over the place and that you have to think about for a long time to make sure you're giving exactly the answer you really want to give. It's about politics, lifestyles, their spiritual thoughts, their toothpaste purchasing habits. And they love it. No one's ever asked them what they think about anything before."

"So, meanwhile…"

"Jerry's losing his edge. No one notices but me, but his eyes are wandering, like he's having trouble concentrating. I come on a little stronger and start pressing him for stock tips. That gets his attention—he can handle that stuff on his own—and he starts bragging about the killing he made on the floor this morning. Then they get to page 8."

"Page 8?"

"Page 8 is where the survey goes off in different directions. Jerry 2 gets questions on his sexual preferences, 3 a bunch of Libertarian propaganda, 4 has to think about where he'd like to vacation and gamble, 5 does a long questionnaire on crop herbicides."

"How'd this play back at the party?"

"Jerry 1 definitely looks a little flustered. He keeps blurting things about Posse Comitatus, anal sex, Roundup and Atlantic City. Estelle tries to get him to leave. I make fun of his clothes. And hers, while I'm at it."

"I'm sorry I missed it."

"Meanwhile, back at the ranch, Cherysse peels off her outfit. Underneath she's got on about as skimpy a bodysuit as anyone can stick on a body like hers. She puts on a dance disc, a really fast one with a cumbia beat and gets them all jazzercising, as much as they can while they watch her bounce and stretch. All this while Roberta barks weird questions at them."

"Oh, man."

"Yeah, Jerry's jerking and twitching, trying to do a merengue and crunchies and recite the Bhagavad Gita at the same time. By this time, everybody's figured out what's happening and they're all laughing and clapping in time. Plus, it turns out Estelle and he are wired up so they're always in synch when they're dancing. Well, somehow that circuit cuts in, so they're doing this stuff in unison."

"Jeez, this is great!"

"All of the sudden, Jerry freezes. Total systems crash. Falls down on the couch, knocks over his drink. The crab gets out and pinches him on the nose."

"So, is he OK?"

"They're bringing him around slowly. Right now, he can count to a hundred and he likes to play Go Fish. They figure he'll make full recovery, but it'll take time. They're not sure if he can ever link up again. The quadruplets are fine, never better. They were in Disney World, last I heard, having a ball. The estate pays for it all."

"And Estelle?"

"Someone told me she was waiting tables at Maloney's, just off the Interstate. Could I get another beer?"

ALTERED STATEMENTS: #4
SCAPE
M.A.C. Farrant

WE ARE THE AMORPHOUS AUDIENCE NERVOUS FOR ANOTHER FUNFIX. WE DO NOT INTERACT, WE BEHOLD; WE VIEW, ARE TARGETED AS AUDIENCE, AS VIEWERS. WE ENGAGE AND DISENGAGE LIKE MOTORS. WE CLAP LIKE MORONS BEFORE SELECTED FUNNYMEN. THE FUNNY WOMEN ARE ALL UGLY. WE DISH IT UP; WE LIKE IT TASTE-LESS. WE COLOUR CO-ORDINATE OUR IDEAS TO MATCH THE PREVAILING WINDS, THIS YEAR NEON, NEXT YEAR RUST. THE ONLY RELIEF OCCURS WHEN FEAR BREAKS THROUGH THE FIFTEEN ALLOWABLE SHADES OF PLEASURE TO PANIC THE VIEWING HERDS OVER TV CLIFFS. WE'VE BECOME NO MORE THAN A CHIP OF AN HISTORICAL SOUND BYTE. NO MORE THAN EARLY BIRDS SHOPPING FOR THE ENDLESS BIRTH AND REBIRTH OF CELEBRITIES. THERE IS NO ESCAPING THE MARKET RESEARCHERS. WE ARE PIGEONS WITH A STARRING ROLE IN A VIDEO CALLED "TARGET PRACTICE". WE ARE BEING TAPED BEFORE A DEAD AUDIENCE. TOMORROW IS A POP SONG.

You Are What You Wire

Nancy Johnston

Paratrooper Tom calling Gloria-Gloria. Paratrooper to Gloria. Do you copy? Little darling, I'm high in the friendly skies. Will reach suitable altitude at 20:00 hours. Are you ready for freefall? Please respond. Paratrooper out.

To: Paratrooper Tom <paratrooper tom@consex.vrprep.com>
From: Gloria-Gloria <gloria gloria@consex.vrprep.com>
Subject: Re: Freefalling

Gloria-Gloria, here. Paratrooper. Do you read me? I copy every word.
Affirmative for the jump. Stabilize your cabin pressure. Will finish flight preparations. I'm slipping into my flight suit. Ready for rendezvous at 20:00 hours. Gloria-Gloria, roger and out.

1: Jane Prepares for Freefall

Jane held her index finger on the mouse ball a moment longer than was strictly necessary to launch her email reply. She liked the feel of the hard plastic button under her sweaty fingers. The blinking cursor spun in concentric circles across the screen while Jane thought about Paratrooper Tom. He was so much more than she expected. He was more than the ads had promised. This was a partner who could make her forget and get caught up in the fantasy. Chatroom encounters could be good in their place, there was no denying that. Even so, she often felt slightly inadequate in those murky rooms. Her computer was only a clone, an inferior clone at that, her keys sometimes stuck (usually the "s" and "x" keys), her keyboard was not enhanced, and her modem was definitely not top-speed. Even when her fingers clicked out clever innuendoes and exclamation points, she was secretly suspicious that everyone else had moved on to new personas. Sitting alone on her vinyl swivel chair, she could feel the perforated bumps puckering her skin through her cotton skirt. If things got hot, Jane rubbed her sore wrist, she could never type fast enough. The smell of her cigarette left burning in her ashtray would eventually distract her even as she conscientiously ohohohed and ahahahed with her keys.

Consexual Virtual Encounters promised to take her beyond the banal. No clever personas? No problem, Jane had just selected one and the people at Consexual uplinked her with a compatible partner. Still, Jane hesitated, taking a quick drag from her cigarette. If she withdrew, Paratrooper would have to find someone else to take into his cockpit. He, or at least his encounter parameter, seemed so virile…so masculine…so physical. Even now she can almost feel a cool wind whistling from the cargo doorway around his silhouetted body, a rush of air across her flushed face. Jane sighed and imagined what it would be like to find herself suited and already in her VR costume. To skip the zip and be launched right onto the virtual plane.

Jane unbuttoned the top of her blouse and rolled forward in her vinyl chair. She toggled on a glowing silver icon, a dollar sign floating in the left bottom corner of her screen and logged onto her Consexual Encounter account. While she flexed and rotated her wrists, Consexual Customer Service Safety Warnings scrolled down the screen to the tune of "In the Mood." Finally, a yellow happy face blinked and intoned a sexy "welcome" in four languages. Under Logbook Entry, she read a half-hour jump-time logged for Consexual client, Paratrooper Tom. Jane closed her eyes and winced, mentally calculating the per minute downtime cost. A bit steep for her, but, then, she could not imagine anything more humiliating than being prompted for a credit card number during freefall. What if she plunged to the landing site before he did? He might even turn out not to be very interactive. Shaking her head, Jane selected a pre-paid thirty minute encounter with a voice command option. At the critical moment, when it began to feel like the ground was rushing up to meet her, she need only shout the phrase, "my chute won't open, my chute won't open" and her credit card would be debited automatically for an additional ten minutes.

Logged in for the rendezvous, Jane began her preparations in earnest. From under her bed she pulled out a large plastic shopping bag adorned with the ChromArt label. Recommended by Consexual Encounters: ChromArt—The Discount Wetware Store where the motto was: "Shop where its virtually free." A tastefully airbrushed photo of a large-breasted woman floated against a background of midnight blue. The figure's right palm covered her groin and her left arm strategically concealed (most of) her voluptuous breasts. Jane turned her attention to her purchases. From inside the bag, she pulled a shrink-wrapped cardboard box about the size and weight of a 250-page package of laser printer paper. Finding the package reassuringly substantial in her hands, Jane flipped the box over and squinted over the top of her reading glasses to study the multicolored flow chart. It illustrated optimum sizing for female VR suit wearers: European sizes were marked in red, and American sizes in green. Ideal sizes for "full-breasted women" or "long-legged ladies" were coded in incremental steps of numerals and letters. To accommodate her own computer-spread, she had chosen a conservatively large Green 5-B which should enshroud her curves. From experience, she knew that it was wise to err on the side of caution; she had calculated and converted herself into metric with a generous eye. As her mother always said, it's easier to tuck it in, than to take it out.

Closing her eyes for a moment, Jane said a silent prayer before she punctured the child-proof seals with a thumb nail and snapped open the box. On her bedroom rug, she dumped out a coil of multi-coloured wire, twelve suction cups and clips, a single-use tube of nontoxic lubricant, a hefty user's manual, and a small vacuum-sealed packet. Not until this moment, when Jane scanned the contents of the box, and the tiny packet lying on her white shag rug, did Jane allow herself any pangs of doubt. The cellophane-wrapped packet resembled nothing less than an individual portion package of microwave popcorn. Before the popping. It was much, much smaller than the instruction book with its 354 pages printed in five languages (three continental and two Asian, although none in English). Holding the packet up to the light, she noticed fine print embossing the edge of the box. Words ominous to women everywhere were printed in small white letters. Panic rose in the back of her throat as she read aloud: "One size fits all. Helmet sold separately." Seizing the packet now, she ripped off the plastic and watched the VR suit spill out onto the white carpet. There, like a snake crawling through a nylon snowbank, the nylon and lycra VR bodystocking writhed and unpuckered. When it ceased its shuddering, the stocking stretched only to the length of her thigh.

A syntho-version of "Ain't Misbehavin'" played along as Jane slowly stretched the body-stocking over her naked legs, thighs, and butt. By rolling and rocking on the rug, static making the hair all over her body stand on end, she could pull the Velcro strips over her shoulders. When she held her breath she could even move her legs without too much constriction. Her face flushed and determined, Jane crawled back up into her chair to grasp the manual and the coil of multi-colored wire. She flipped quickly through the colour diagrams. Erogenous zones, erogenous zones, where are they?, she muttered aloud. Pausing over the most likely diagram: an illustration depicting a female figure dressed in the body stocking and poised in Crucifixion. Spots were numbered from one to twelve, corresponding, she hoped, with the twelve clips and suction cups. After plugging a leader cord into the VR node of her computer, she got to work untangling the twelve cables and clips. Each suction cup received a squirt of sticky non-toxic lubricant/adhesive before Jane attached them to the greyish rubber nipples sewn all over her VR stocking. With the exertion, she began to sweat copiously inside the impermeable suit. Jane aspired to emulate the illustrated woman. She clipped on her lubricated connectors with great care: one on each breast over her real-time nipples, one at her throat over the carotid artery, one over her navel, two behind her knees, two for her inner elbows, two for her gloves, one for her goggles, and a final one at the small of her back. Looking over at her mirror and herself in the lumpy VR catsuit, she was unsure for a moment that she has done everything correctly. She paused to look again at the figure. Glancing at the diagram, she counted the numbered pulse points from one to twelve before it suddenly occurred to her: the crucified woman had no genitalia. She dropped her hand down to where her own lucky thirteen should be. Her suit had no grey polka-dot anywhere near (or below) her Venus mound. A defeated Jane leaned back into her chair, wondering if it would really make any difference. There were no refunds from Consexual Encounters. Jane sighed and idly picked at a small snag in the nylon fabric stretched across her navel. The VR body stocking gasped under her fingers and began to run from her belly to the tip of her left toe.

τ⁷

To: Paratrooper Tom <paratrooper tom@consex.vrprep.com>
From: Gloria-Gloria <gloria gloria@consex.vrprep.com>
Subject: Systems Operational

Gloria-Gloria to Paratrooper. Turn on the auto-pilot. Let me come and rub your silk chute against my thighs. Stroke your ripcord. Wrestle with the weight of your parachute bundle. We'll skydive into the clouds and sink back into the fall. All systems operational. Gloria-Gloria, roger and out.

2: Todd Prepares for Freefall

Todd tapped the enter key three times before lifting his thumb. He blinked before the screen image faded from his inner eyelids. He was amazed. The advertisements had not prepared him for Gloria-Gloria. Todd had secretly thought she was too remote, even untouchable…much too glamorous to be interested in him. He had wanted to get out of the chatrooms where everyone seemed to know you. He had been lurking for months, hardly ever taking up a persona, believing that his friends were snickering behind their cursors. Consexual Encounters, with its free introductions and persona services, promised a new level of encounter. Just typing as Paratrooper Tom made him feel sexy and desirable. Taking one last sip of cold coffee, Todd jumped up from his console chair to cross to the bed.

Todd ran damp hands over his brand new padded VR jumpsuit lying across his unmade bed. His first one, and the number one choice for male-users polled by Consexual Encounters. Crisp, shiny black, and streamlined: it looked like a scuba outfits that surfers wore to protect them from the pounding waves. Dropping his greying boxers to the floor and struggling out of his faded T-shirt, "Widower95", Todd turned the suit over to crawl through the entry zipper up the spine. He popped out his head, arms and legs, quickly sliding his white feet inside soft pliable booties. Doing a set of flexes and knee-bends, he was satisfied with the snug fit. He liked the way the rubber conformed to his real skin. Patting out the seams and puckers, Todd snapped up the velcro enclosures on the boots. With particular care, he swivelled his hips to manipulate the position of his basket until he could slide himself carefully through the reinforced circular opening at the suit crotch and into a metallic mesh bag. Once secured, he arranged sensor cables so the wire tangle hanging between his thighs did not cut off circulation to his groin. Turning around to face the mirror, he could not resist taking a peek. Even though Gloria-Gloria would never see him like this, she would only see the superimposed VR personality Paratrooper Tom, Todd liked what he saw. Stepping fully before the mirror, he was Jacques Cousteau diving into cyberspace.

But he had not forgotten la pièce de résistance, his specialty mail order item from Senso-Jack for the Millennium Man. More expensive than the whole suit (but that goes without saying), he was eager to try his new toy— his power stick—in action. Stepping over various computer cables and empty takeout boxes, Todd waddled over to his bureau in his virtual snowsuit. Cracking open the top drawer he pulled out his prize: a neon-green plastic cylinder resembling a large mailing tube. This flexible plastic twelve-inch case, the advertisement had said, was lined with washable vinyl mesh and coated wires: "Enhance your pleasure and virility with virtual length. Use only as directed." Todd patted his mesh bag, already growing hard in anticipation. Quickly he scooped himself inside the tube where he could feel the attachment's smart-vinyl conforming to the width of his shaft. A snug fit, he chuckled. Clipping the safety catches to his suit, Todd sealed the final connectors, and jacked in. Accordion-like the cylinder began to whir and expand. Setup mode began on the computer screen and music, the theme from "Mission Impossible," played softly in the background.

Todd again looked into his mirror, admiring himself from the front and then in profile. Something, however, nagged at the back of his mind. Tight inside his enhancement, he felt not a tingle. Absolutely nothing from the start-up sequence. Waiting for the first sensations, he began to have his first twinge of concern. Maybe he had been a bit too eager, just plugging in without a test drive. Todd stepped back to the desk to get a better view of the ignored instruction book. He balanced the book against the computer monitor and carefully turned over the pages under his rubberized thumbs. Unconsciously, Todd swung his hips to the left and to the right, making a soft thump-thump inside the cylinder. A comforting thump-thump. On page 231, he paused. The sensors, according to the diagrams, should give him the cool touch of chrome against flesh. He felt nothing but the slightest pressure of the vinyl. Just a high-priced padded jock-strap, he thought. Pushing back from the desk, he checked to see if he was plugged into the jack. All systems were on. Springing to his toes, jumping up and down in his boots, Todd thwacked himself side to side inside the cylinder. Bang-bang, bang-bang. He sounded to his ears like the lone tennis ball in a can. Out of breath, he wondered if perhaps the attachment was too large. Worse, he might be too small. Panicked now, he turned to another page of the manual, and glanced at an important illustration highlighted in bright red block letters. He read: "Warning: apply Senso-cream before inserting member into module. Senso-cream is essential for optimum satisfaction and for protection against chafing and topical burns." Todd gasped audibly and snapped off the suit connectors. The cylinder will not come off. He whimpered. "Senso-cream is biodegradable, hypo-allergenic and not made from Rain-forest oils. Cream sold separately." Todd went flaccid inside his can.

⌐⌐

To: Gloria-Gloria <gloria gloria@consex.vrprep.com>
From: Paratrooper Tom <paratrooper tom@consex.vrprep.com>
Subject: Re: Systems operational

Paratrooper Tom to Gloria-Gloria. Paratrooper to Gloria. All ready for the leap. The air is thin and I'm panting for breath. Come, join me in the cockpit. I have the flight plans open in my lap and I'm fingering the maps. I'm zipped into my jumpsuit and buckled into my chute. Ready for the freefall on the signal from the tower. Paratrooper out.

3. "Freefall" (Scenario 13): Consexual VR Technology©

They stand at opposite ends of the cargo bay. Abandoned by the cowardly flightcrew, they must share a single parachute—their only hope for freedom—if they are to survive the jump. Gloria-Gloria is the first to step out of the shadows of the gunnery bay. Paratrooper Tom watches her from the cargo hatchway. A smile passes over his rugged features. She watches him watching her. In another step, in a surreal moment of anticipation, their eyes lock, without shame, in complete and wanton desire. Their desire consumes them like the fire in the gunnery bay that is sweeping the aircraft. The sound of the twin engines vibrates between them, throbbing with the rhythm of their bodies. The wind whistling through the open door sends shivers down their spines.

Gloria-Gloria emerges fully from the shadows. Paratrooper Tom sees her for the first time: her torn flightsuit abandoned, she is nude and assured as she walks toward him, her stride confident, her breasts high, her nipples blushed and erect. Curves and muscles are licked by her perspiration and the heat of the blaze. Her red hair frames her face in windswept auburn waves as she nears the cargo door. A length of hair blows across her mouth, open and wet. She is an Amazon of rounded flesh ready for his embrace in freefall. He wants her. More than any woman, he wants her. He wants her to caress him. She stretches out her left arm as she walks toward him. When she sways her hips, her right hand appears, then disappears from view. It seems to disappear inside her navel. No, Todd/Tom notes, it fades in and fades out right where it should cross in front of her naked stomach. He is close enough now to see how her eyes gently roll back in their sockets with each disappearing stroke of her hand. When he squints his eyes inside the visor, he can almost make out the rip in her VR suit where she has tucked in her right hand.

Gloria-Gloria watches Paratrooper Tom silhouetted against the cloudless sky. Unabashed, she rakes her eyes up and down his handsome body. His sun-streaked sandy hair sweeps back from his windburned cheeks and hangs like a mane just below his collar bone. His flesh is sculpted and flawlessly tanned. He stands erect and still before her, facing her with nearly hairless pecs and enormous Herculean shoulders that are tensed for the jump. Nothing covers his ruggedness…except a strategically held parachute bundle. He holds it, Jane/Gloria assumes, provocatively, perhaps hoping to prolong her pleasurable anticipation. He grips the bag firmly over his hips where it covers him like a large canvas fig leaf. But there is so little time for coyness, Jane/Gloria thinks. In a spontaneous gesture, Gloria-Gloria strides toward him. Standing before him, she looks him in his pale blue eyes. She reaches forward with her left hand to push away the canvas. She wants him. She must have him, only him. But Paratrooper Tom staggers backward a step. Is he coy? Afraid? Shy? Face to face, she searches his eyes for the answer and finds one. His eyes drift southward to the vanishing point of her right hand. Her right hand is locked onto pulse point #13, her handmade erogenous zone. Only somewhat distracted, Gloria-Gloria reaches out to Paratrooper with her left and tugs encouragingly at his parachute bundle. But he does not respond, at least not as she thought he would. He wrestles her for control, crushing the canvas harder against his pelvis. Suddenly, when she releases her grip, Paratrooper Tom staggers backward to the very edge of the cargo doorway. Off balance, he drops the chute and it rolls deep into the recesses of the plane. Gloria-Gloria can now fully begin to appraise him, from the top of his tanned head to where she thought she would see the root of his hard manhood. Adrenaline pumping through her veins, her eyes linger a moment over his washboard abs. Then, she pauses, puzzled. Her vision rests on a perfectly rounded hole in the middle of his pelvis. Through that hole, a hole the diameter of a small salad plate, she can see the cloudless sky behind them. Mesmerized by the panoramic view through the pelvic porthole, she stretches out her arm to Paratrooper Tom, and stumbles. They fall backward together out the cargo window. Launched prematurely into freefall, Todd and Jane link hands, and dive into the blue, blue sky.

Pascagoula Creatures

Richard Stevens

Well, we're Pascagoula Creatures;
we got no eyes or features.
Where you good ol'boys got noses
we got stubby carrot hoses;
where you got those flappy ears
we got pointy carrot spears.
We don't need no brows or peepers:
we got radar-programmed beepers.
We wrinkly-skinned rhinocers
gonna float out of our saucers,
gonna beep beep beep our way
across this moonlit bay.
Gonna nab and bag you boys;
ain't gonna give you a choice.
Gonna take you 'board our craft,
while you stare gawk-eyed and daft.
Gonna nip and probe and pry
with a long snake through the eye,
collect some human tissue,
'fore we hypnotise and issue
a few post-hypnotic orders
'bout your crossing mental borders.
Then we'll set you back to fishin'
and you can go on wishin'
you catch your limit of dolly varden
while we beg your leave and pardon
and you stare at your ol' bobbers
and forget us space hobnobbers.

Ain't no point in fanning coals
of paranoid space goals:
you had yourselves a dream
'bout some interstellar scheme.
There ain't no Pascagoula Creatures,
'cept in Friday Creature Features.
Go home and watch your Raiders;
we ain't no space invaders.

ÈVE-MARIE

Natasha Beaulieu
Translated from the French by
Yves Meynard

"I'm not like other people."

Sitting before me, at my ridiculous kitchen table stabilized by a piece of cardboard folded into fourths and stuck beneath one short leg, Ève-Marie displays the enigmatic face of a turn-of-the-century heroine. I know nothing of her, but already I adore her. All the women I've known before her have become phantoms, their phosphorescence fading little by little in my memory. Now there is only her, whose whiteness and purity have me captivated. Even the bright flame of the red candle beside her wine glass cannot gild the pallor of her skin.

I'm consumed with shame at the idea of having to serve this woman common raviolis with canned tomato sauce. But everything happened so fast I had to improvise with what I had on hand. And anyway, it's clear to me that although this is our first intimate dinner, it will not be the last. I'll have a chance to make up for this with a more refined meal. A dish fit for her. Fit for this Siberian princess dressed all in white.

"I've always found it absurd that someone other than myself should decide the date and time of my death."

I hold back the spontaneous "Why?" that almost passes my lips. How could she have guessed that death is a subject that fascinates me? I decide to let her explain. I'm curious to find out where this mysterious woman will lead me.

"I chose to die on a day when I was very happy. I climbed to the top of a building and flung myself into space."

She's said this in an ordinary tone, as if she were telling me what she did today or was planning to do tomorrow. I try to keep calm, taking on the detached expression of someone who's heard something banal, but already I'm aroused by the daring of her story.

"I woke up naked in the night, at the foot of a tree," she says in her velvety, deliberate voice.

Her irises shine like priceless rubies. Her imagination warms me. I shift nervously on my chair. Whatever this woman is about to tell me,

I'm sure it will be the most seductive scenario a woman has ever invented, just for me.

⊤⁷

It happened seven months ago, at the end of a beautiful winter afternoon. A real winter day, on a par with those we save in our childhood memories. Huge, light, lovely snowflakes fell on Montreal. Many customers' faces, usually dour, were lit by naïve smiles.

I would have turned my head anyway. I have that reflex, of checking to see who's coming in. But when I glimpsed this woman, hugging the sides of a large white fur coat against herself, I had been dazzled. Within a few minutes this stranger had reached to all my senses, one by one, evoking sweet images, childhood memories of happiness and sadness. Without knowing me.

She had stood a few seconds before the door which was closing behind her. The typical pause of first-time customers. I couldn't see her face; its upper half was hidden by the white fur hat that reached down to her eyes, the lower by the coat's collar, which she had pulled up against her cheeks. All that I saw of her was pure whiteness. A mystical purity.

In a slow, gracious movement, she'd taken off her coat. She had shaken it gently to get rid of the snowflakes that had crystallized at the tip of the white hairs. That gesture had awoken one of my favorite scenes from the film of my life, which was always playing on the screen of my memories: my mother, sitting at her makeup table, delicately sliding the powder puff sprinkled with Chanel N°5 on her smooth pale neck, then along her very slim arms. I, her only son, gazing at her, fascinated by this spectacle of beauty and sweetness she offered me every night. When my mother had finished powdering herself, she would turn to me, hold my little cheeks between her warm hands and kiss me high on the forehead, at the root of my hair. Then she would slide under the sheets of cream-colored satin, coil up against my father who was often already sleeping. Without a word, I would leave my parents' bedroom, close the door behind me and go slip into my bed, beneath the blue cotton flannel sheets.

Her heavy luminous coat over one arm, the woman who had evoked the projection of this pleasant childhood scene in my memory had gone to the table by the window. Her wool turtleneck, her short velvety skirt, her opaque tights and her laced ankle boots, all that she wore was of an immaculate whiteness. I had felt it was normal. Natural. I'd already constructed a new scenario around her, to add to my repertoire. This mysterious woman was returning from a long trip to icy Siberia. She'd gone there to meet her lover,

TESSERACTS⁷   99

whom she'd surprised in the arms of another. Rather than confront her rival, she had fled. She'd just reached Montreal, didn't know where to go, and had found herself here, in the *Café Renoir*, by happenstance. Just for me.

␡

My Russian princess has fallen silent, because of the irritating *beep-beep* from the microwave, announcing that the tomato sauce is hot.

After an apology, which isn't really necessary since I am guilty of nothing, I rise. I busy myself draining the raviolis, stirring the sauce, arranging it all in the plates, as artistically as I can. Fortunately, I've found, at the back of one of the fridge shelves, some parsley I can still pass off as fresh to enhance the visual appearance of this humble repast.

Ève-Marie remains mute while I prepare the dishes. Nervous, sweating now, I inwardly curse the microwave, vow to throw it out the window if it should have cut off my charming guest's inspiration.

I'm about to offer her a glass of plonk from the corner store when I remember I received as a gift, a few weeks ago, a bottle of excellent Italian red wine.

"May I pour you some wine?"

Her pretty pale lips stretch in a discreet smile and she nods. I feel myself melting, like a pat of butter at the bottom of a skillet over a raging fire.

Once I've laid the dishes on the table and uncorked the 1993 Valpolicella, Ève-Marie continues the intriguing story she's woven about her person.

"He who controls the date and time of people's death, the one we conceive of as the Supreme Power, brought me back to harsh reality. No more than any other mortal could I escape my fate, the power of his will. So he decided to bring me back to life and punish me by robbing me of every sense save touch. I could neither see, nor hear, nor smell nor taste anything."

I down half my glass in a single gulp and look her in the eye.

"Maybe I'm the chosen one who'll help you rediscover your lost senses."

I feel a bit guilty for tossing out this pretentious sentence. This isn't like me. But I can't help it: I want to insinuate myself into her scenario, to put across the idea that we're made for each other.

The only answer to my veiled suggestion is an irresistible smile I can't interpret, then she goes on with her scenario.

"Someone picked me up in his arms and took me away somewhere. Afterwards I spent days trying to recover my senses. I knew they weren't gone forever. I felt them, somewhere within me, recorded in my memory. But how to access them remained a mystery until I realized I had been trying to get them all back at once; it was probably a bad way to go about it. I then thought to isolate them, to concentrate on each in turn. I chose sight first. Isolating this first sense, I managed to access the billions of images held in my visual memory. I fainted. When I awoke, my left hand, against my cheek, was covered with a warm, soft, rather sticky substance. When I slid my fingertips along my cheek, I realized the substance was flowing slowly from my ear. Instinctively, I opened my eyes and coated them with this kind of cream I was producing. And thus, gradually, as I applied the substance that flowed from my ears onto my irises, I recovered my sense of sight."

⌐

She had laid her fur on a chair and moved the other so it was parallel to the window. Once seated, the Russian princess had taken off her ankle boots and laid her white-stockinged feet on top of the heater. Then she'd put her hands under her thighs, no doubt to warm them as well.

An elbow in my ribs had made me start.

"Your cappuccino's about to go past its best-before date, Simon."

I had turned to Ricardo. My face must have betrayed some of what I felt: my colleague had begun to sing one of his repertoire of Italian songs at the top of his voice; its main subject was love, of course.

I'd grimaced, but I hadn't gotten angry. I'd been working with Ricardo for a year and he often teased me about my "great emotivibility". I had at last glanced at the steaming black cappuccino: I'd poured the hot milk on the counter beside the cup.

Perhaps five minutes later, my beautiful Anna Karenina still hadn't gotten to her feet and come give her order at the counter. I'd caught Ricardo by the sleeve.

"I'll go see what she wants."

"Don't leave me alone too long behind the counter!"

I had to know what her smell was. Innocently influenced by my recollection of the powder puff from my childhood, I was convinced that from this woman in white would rise the smell of Chanel N°5, which I could recognize from among all the perfumes in the world.

She hadn't moved since she'd put her hands under her thighs. Once I'd approached her table, I'd spoken as normally and courteously as possible.

"Hi, may I get you something to drink?" I'd felt as though a fork had scraped my vocal cords when I spoke. I had had to clear my throat to regain a normal tone. "I recommend the cappuccino: specialty of the house."

It was when she'd turned to me that she'd touched another of my senses.

At first disappointed to realize her smell was no smell of powder, never mind Chanel, I had suddenly been brought back by my olfactory memory to another recollection that was just as pleasant. Two years before, I had been working at a pastry shop, where my main task was to ice the cakes. I was the one who'd write as artistically as possible "Happy Birthday Martin" or "Congratulations, Isabelle!" for special orders, with an edible ink, a mix of icing sugar and vanilla. And the same delicious smell, sweet and perfumed, came from this woman.

ⲄⲀ

Ève-Marie hasn't touched her wine, but she's eating hungrily. Between bites, she gives more details on how she regained her sight. Her imagination goes beyond my wildest hopes. And my role in this boundless scenario is becoming clear. She explains that her ears still secrete the greenish cream and that she keeps applying it to her eyes. I decide we need a bit of dialog at this point.

"When does this cream come out of your ears?"

"Anytime. But now I feel it. I know when it's about to start flowing."

"I'd like to see that. It would help me understand."

I've said this with a half smile; I thought she would answer in kind. But she's frowning, looking very annoyed.

"If you see now as well as you did before, what use is it to keep applying the cream to your eyes?"

"It allows me to see things I didn't see before. To see beyond. For example, it allowed me to see all the memories you associated with me as soon as I came into the *Café Renoir*."

Suddenly ill at ease, for I know not what obscure reason, I drain my glass of wine. I have to wipe my brow, drenched with perspiration, with my table napkin.

ⲄⲀ

"I'd like a latte. In a glass," she'd specified.

Her voice, warm, soft and low-pitched, had reminded me of the voice of the first woman I'd ever loved. A bewitching voice, like a languorous blues melody. Caressing, like a long velvet gown on a female body. Intoxicating like the voice of Marilyn singing "Happy Birthday" for John F. Kennedy. That woman who'd whispered wild words in my ear. Extravagances only passionate lovers may savour.

I didn't know whether I was coming or going, but I felt euphoric. Cloud of powder, sugar breeze, breath of ecstasy—I wanted to write her a poem, kneel down at her feet and recite it for everyone to hear.

Standing next to her, I was probably about to ask her if she wanted the cappuccino she hadn't ordered sprinkled with chocolate or cinnamon, when she'd taken off her white fur hat. Seeing her long silky hair, as white as the fur that framed it, I had thought I would faint.

When my Siberian star had raised her face to me, a white lily set with two ruby irises, I had had the conviction that I had never seen anything so pretty. She was so pale, she seemed so fragile, I had had to restrain myself with all my might not to bend down and clasp her in my arms, to protect her from all the misfortunes and dangers of life.

ᴛ⁷

"Strangely enough, I recovered hearing before taste. But in order to hear things, I had to lick them. It took me a lot longer, as you can guess, to regain hearing than sight. Imagine everything I had to lick to hear sounds once more: faucets to hear water running, my bird to hear it sing, my alarm clock to hear its ticking, the refrigerator for its purr, the television set and radio to hear actors speak—"

She's becoming more and more impassioned, even though she hasn't touched the wine. I'm up to my third glass and starting to ask myself serious questions about my guest.

"And these were things at home. Imagine when I came outside for the first time. I had to lick a bus to hear its engine, lick a shopping cart to remember its rumble, lick the washing machine at the laundromat, lick the—"

Now it's distress I'm feeling. Convinced that I'd met my living fantasy, a woman with an inexhaustible imagination with whom I could elaborate and live the most extravagant scenarios, it never occurred to me that this goddess of purity seated before me might simply be crazy. No. I don't want that to be true. I chase this horrible thought away and tell myself Ève-Marie is an exceptionally creative woman, intelligent and full of fancy. I want to go on playing to find out where her scenario will lead.

"When you say you licked things, what do you mean exactly?"

"Oh, just a brush of the tongue and I can hear."

"But how can you hear people talking?"

"I only had to lick one person, and then I could hear everyone else talking. It's always like that. A brush of the tongue on one car and I could hear all other engines purring."

"And if you lick something, now that you recognize all sounds, what happens?"

"I hear sounds made by things that should be silent. For instance, I hear someone speak on a photograph, a sheet of paper breathing, the ink in a pen"

I feel tortured. Am I really before the love of my life, or a mentally ill person? I can't contemplate uniting the two possibilities.

Ève-Marie watches me with her strange red irises. I think she guesses at my thoughts. She leans down and licks the tablecloth with the tip of her pink tongue; I can't help finding it adorable, wanting to kiss it. She sits up, this time smiling broadly and sincerely.

"I heard the threads from which the tablecloth was woven."

"And what did they tell you?"

"That they were thirsty."

When I was a child I was given a test, one question of which has always stayed in my memory. Was a stone a living thing? I had answered "yes" without hesitation.

Carried away by this memory and by my confusion, I spill my glass of Valpolicella on the white tablecloth, right where Ève-Marie heard the threads asking for a drink.

ᴦ⁊

I had returned behind the counter, surrounded by a bubble that insulated me from my day-to-day world. I was living a movie of which I was also the producer.

"Hey, Earth to Simon! It's rush hour."

In the wintertime, the crush occurred in late afternoon. Most regulars came in for a coffee before shutting themselves up in their homes for the evening.

Ricardo had remained understanding and given me time to prepare the best cappuccino in the world. Once I was done, I had wrapped the glass in the usual white paper napkin, whose touch I had found dreadfully unpleasant. I would have preferred a velvet napkin so that my Russian princess wouldn't hurt her hands.

Nervous, my legs limp, I'd gone over to her table and set the glass down, smiling without being able to rid myself of the feeling I was sporting the most inane smile of my life.

"Here's your coffee."

My voice had seemed just as horrible as before. I'd wanted to die, so ridiculous did I feel. I'd craved only one thing: to touch this embodiment of purity, to caress her, to tell her she was the most beautiful woman I'd ever seen and that I was in love with her.

Since I couldn't touch her, I had been unable to resist surreptitiously brushing the fur of her coat with one hand as I left. This had caused another memory to emerge; a sad one this time. One evening, the previous summer, walking in a park, I had seen a white patch at the foot of a maple. Coming closer, I had realized it was the corpse of a tiny rabbit, probably a baby. I had bent down, carefully picked it up, stroked its soft, still-warm fur, which bore no trace of blood or violence. The death must have been recent. I remember having felt a deep sadness. I had thought of burying it, but I hadn't, because I had been obsessed by the desire to watch the white shape it made in the night. So I had set it back down at the foot of the tree, hoping someone else would do what I had failed to.

Seeing this Siberian woman had dazzled me. Her smell had intoxicated me. Her voice had seduced me. Touching the fur of her immaculate coat had reminded me of death.

I had returned behind the counter with a new obsession: I had to "taste" this woman.

⌐¬

The wine must have contributed to my daring because I've pulled my chair right by Ève-Marie's, and I'm stroking her hands. She doesn't appear displeased by my initiative.

I don't know what to think anymore, so I've decided to push this further. I want to see how far she'll go.

"I've recovered smell and taste recently. To tell you the truth, there are several things I still can't smell and taste. Wine, for instance."

I'm not curious enough to ask her if she tasted her raviolis. That doesn't matter at all.

"But do you know how to achieve it?"

She nods.

"Do you want to tell me how?"

"I'm embarrassed."

"Now? After you've told me all the rest? Please, Ève-Marie, you can trust me."

Am I sincere when I say this? I'm speaking as though I truly believed her story. Or is it that I am, indeed, starting to believe it? At any rate, I must have been convincing, because she picks up her glass and brings it near to her face.

A few seconds later, after a surprising ritual, she looks at me, smiling, and says: "This smells good. Very good."

⌐¬

The Anna Karenina of my scenario, which played on in the set of the *Café Renoir*, had sipped at her glass of latte for the past hour, during which I'd dropped a cup on the floor and spilled a glass of water on the counter. With a fingertip dipped in ground coffee, Ricardo teased me by drawing brown hearts on my white apron.

After putting her white ankle boots back on, hiding her hair under her fur hat and wrapping herself in her long coat, the Russian princess had headed for the door. I'd have run over and asked her for her name and whether she would be coming back, but at that moment I was scalding myself with the hot milk I was once more pouring beside a cappuccino rather than in it.

Ricardo was laughing loudly. The beautiful stranger had left without paying.

Then, offended, I had taken some change out of my jeans pocket and laid it on the counter. I had taken off my apron, thrown it in my colleague's face and, after snatching up my coat, had run out.

White shape on a white background, I'd nevertheless caught up with her at the street corner. Out of breath, I'd stammered at random, "I'm Simon; I'd like to invite you to dinner. Would you like that?"

She had opened the collar of her coat, revealing her snowy complexion as well as a radiant smile.

"I'm Ève-Marie and I'd like to have dinner with you," she'd replied without the least hesitation.

⌐⌐

In my arms, Ève-Marie snuggles against my chest. I'm certain she weighs hardly more than her heavy fur coat.

I know, I understand that she's not normal. She's not like other people. Didn't she warn me herself? I'm far from knowledgeable about medicine, but I still think she must be ill. I should have thought of it sooner, instead of tangling myself up in my fantasies and selfish scenarios. The whole story she told me was nothing but a metaphor to tell me she has an incurable disease which causes sensory deprivation. I know there are such things.

Once we're in my room, I set down the mysterious Siberian princess on my bed and lie down next to her. We stroke each other's face in the shadows and slowly, before even kissing, we undress.

Her naked body suggests a piece of chalk, about to trace a memory on the blackboard of night. I suddenly realize that, blinded by the aura that Ève-Marie and her white clothes give off, it never occurred to me she might be an albino. Yet she has white hair and red eyes, but it never seemed unusual to me. Just beautiful and fascinatingly strange. And now that I realize it fully, it doesn't prevent me from loving her and wanting to keep her by me.

She lets me hold her tight.

In fact, I'm waiting for her to confide in me. I know nothing about albinos. Maybe there are diseases specific to them.

On my left shoulder, I suddenly feel an unctuous liquid spilling. I don't dare move. Is it really possible for a substance of some sort to flow out of an ear, unless it's discharge from an infection? Wouldn't the smell be unpleasant then, while this is rather sweet, fragrant?

With the tip of her delicate fingers, Ève-Marie coats my eyelids with the cream that comes out of her ear. I let her do it. I'd rather not understand. Ève-Marie then applies the strange substance directly onto her irises, and closes her lids over them. I wait for a while and ask her what "more" she sees.

"I see in you. I see that you're sincere."

Even though this experiences brushes against the irrational, a logical explanation remains possible.

Her eyes still closed, Ève-Marie takes my arm, slides her little tongue whose pinkness I remember well along it. I want to respect this poetic ritual she's initiating me into. And I ask her what she hears.

"I hear the blood flowing in your veins."

"What's the sound like?"

"A little like the sea."

I feel like I'm in the company of a fairy, through whom all the hidden things in life are revealed. I enjoy this feeling, though keeping in mind that sooner or later a painfully rational explanation will come.

Ève-Marie suddenly starts running her face all over my body. She sniffs me deeply, like she did earlier with the glass of wine. Until the blood starts dripping from her nostrils. Once her precious liquid has fallen on my body, she tells me my smell is a mix of tree bark, earth and honey. Once more I let myself be charmed by the magic of the moment, by the imagination and the poetry in her words.

A long while passes before I dare ask her a question.

"I know it's absurd, Ève-Marie, I know we've barely met, but I love you passionately. I want you to know that whatever you have, I'll take care of you." She raises her face, leaning over my chest. Once more she has that annoyed expression I saw before. This worries me. Have I been clumsy? I try to apologize.

"Look, you don't have to tell me tonight. You'll talk about it when you feel the need. Okay?"

Huge tears begin to flow down my Siberian princess's cheeks. I could kill myself. Her pretty voice broken by sobs, she says: "You don't believe me?"

"Of course I believe you, but you have to explain things clearly if you want me to really understand."

She says nothing, waves her face above my body, letting the tears patter down. Once more, I don't dare make a single move. I don't want to disappoint her even more than I have.

She then begins to kiss and lick my skin, still weeping. Her weak moans tear at my heart with their overwhelming sadness.

"Your skin tastes like that of a man who loves but has understood nothing," she manages to whisper.

"But that's all I'm asking for, Ève-Marie, explanations."

"I've spent the evening explaining everything. But you don't believe me. It's no use anymore."

She keeps on weeping on me to better taste me. Meanwhile, I fret, trying to understand. I close my eyes and rub my lids with some of the cream that's left on my shoulder. I hope I can manage to see beyond. I'm crazy about this woman and I know I have to see further than the end of my nose if I'm to keep her. Of course, nothing happens and I grow tense.

I want to clasp her in my arms again, but I grasp only air.

I open my eyes.

Ève-Marie is no longer there.

ᴦᴎ

It's snowing on Montreal again today. The *Café Renoir* is packed. And I know Ève-Marie won't be coming back.

Last night, I thought of committing suicide, in the hope that I would join her in her strange world. That I would live through exactly what she lived. That I also would regain, one by one, my lost senses. But I know that wouldn't work, because I can't decide the time and date of my death. Thus if I took my own life, my fate could not be similar to Ève-Marie's. No doubt it would drive us even further apart than we are now.

A little more and I would have believed all she told me. I find some comfort in telling myself that I'm probably the one who brought her almost completely back to life and that maybe I'll have another chance to do it.

I know I may sound insane. At first last night I thought I had dreamed all of this. But when I found a large, white, red-eyed rabbit on my kitchen counter, I think I understood. Oh, not everything of course, but surely a small part.

QUEST

Melissa Yuan-Innes

bi curious
by George
I think he's got tits.
Can we check downstairs, too?
That's why we withdrew
worn twenties spit
from the bank machine slit.
And I'm not just bi curious,
I'm tri curious
deca curious.
Alien tentacles
Angels sliding their wings along my shaft
Ants in more than my pants
Snails alive on my tongue
Orgies with knot hole tree vaginas
Nuns on a stick
Stewards washing my feet
Strawberries and bananas
exploding from yin yang
Tied up with licorice whips and a
rubber extension cord
Imprisoned with five angry gorillas
Hijacking a DJ booth to come
screaming over the dance floor
Store mannequins streaked with come
Teddy bears decapitated for my pleasure
Screaming yes until dawn breaks
the vampire suckling my throat.

Everett's Parallel Universes
or
How To Make Love To Someone Without Ever Meeting

Pierre Sormany
Translated from the French by
Wendy Greene

1. Interference

If you turn on a light source behind a screen with two pinholes and move to the other side of the screen, all you will see is two points of light, as if the light came from two closely spaced sources. However, the two lights, originating from the same source, are in phase. The result is a phenomenon known as interference. If you expose a photographic plate to the light from the pinholes, you will clearly see appear alternating bands of light and dark. This is because light is a wave. The exact same phenomenon is at work to produce the beat heard when two identical music instruments play almost the same note.

ך

As to the actual events that took place that weekend, I doubt that there would be much difference between her version and mine. But events are simply markers, unavoidable flashes of reality through which the thread of life weaves its tortuous way. Millions of possibilities inhabit every glance, every word exchanged; a multiplicity of conflicting thoughts fluttering about like mad birds swooping elusively around the simple facts of the story. The essential truth lies within this blur of interference.

The facts of our love story are quite simple. It started one starry night over supper at Jean Pierre's. It was a Friday. I had come to see Jean Pierre and two or three old friends I hoped would be there. And it was a cool summer evening that, more than anything else, had prompted me to get out and make the most of the fresh air and the setting sun. But I wasn't there for romance. In fact, I thought I was now safe from those moments of madness when I would dream of meeting Ms. Right every time I stepped onto the dance floor. Did this relative indifference to love actually make me more vulnerable that night?

But I'm already embellishing on the simple facts of the story. I'm cheating on reality. So let's go back to those markers: there was duck washed down with port for supper, a few friends, jazz playing softly in the background, and, of course, Brigitte.

Brigitte had light-brown, medium-length hair that barely brushed the shoulders of her loose silk blouse. Her nose was small and straight, her lips full. She reminded me of Monique, an old girlfriend whose face I had always found charming. But thinking it over, I realized I was completely off-track. Monique was taller, her eyes were dark and her mouth wider. Very little similarity, really. My eyes blurred. I turned my gaze elsewhere. I sat down in a free chair at the other end of the patio and forgot about her. I talked about music with Jean Pierre and sports with Gilles Philippe—the kind of small talk that always takes place, like it or not, before the evening really gets going.

I saw Brigitte again during supper. By chance, we had been placed opposite each other at the end of the long wooden table. She seemed distracted. I followed her gaze, staring off into the still-light sky two thousand kilometres beyond me. This dreaminess fascinated me: it was like feeling dizzy, being drawn into a void. I wanted to talk to her. I chatted idly, saying the kinds of things you tend to say to people you don't yet know, as if you were throwing them a life raft. She didn't answer. I thought it was because of the noise. As soon as there was a moment of silence, I asked another question. I was no more successful. The third time, I said to myself that she must be oblivious—or she was making fun of me. I felt trapped at the end of the table, facing this unreachable woman. And yet, something was already being played out between us; I felt it clearly, that indescribable vibration when our eyes met.

A friend of Jean Pierre's, whom I didn't know, was sitting to my right. His name was Cedric. He started talking, looking at Brigitte. He talked the way all men do when they're coming on to a woman. He talked about his childhood, his education, his work.... She awoke from her stupor. It looked like a sham to me: I've always thought it's really stupid the way people tend to talk about themselves the first time they meet you. It drives me crazy to see how easily others fall for that trick.

But this time, the subtle intonations of Brigitte's voice showed me that Cedric was as boring to her as he was annoying to me. And perhaps it was through this shared feeling that I was finally able to get through to that lovely woman. But ever so little! Just a few knowing glances, a few words between us, a few waves that broke the surface of Cedric's ocean of words. But that was all I needed to feel comfortable in the magic space created by Brigitte's simple presence and by the dreamy way she spoke, there yet far away. And then there was the music, the cool air, the fine wine and the delicate beginnings of drunkenness that rocked me into a stupor. There are nights when I love to just sink back into my chair and open myself up to the alpha waves of the angels, if they actually exist.

The others had started talking about politics. As the noise level rose, it created a screen of sound around our trio—Brigitte, Cedric and me. I didn't say very much. I preferred to listen to the trickle of muffled jazz that floated through the air and the melody of Brigitte's voice when Cedric let her get a word in edgewise.

After dessert, Jean Pierre moved the stereo speakers to the windows and the others started dancing. Cedric must have understood what was brewing between Brigitte and me since he slipped away, leaving us alone. I asked Brigitte to dance. She let me take her in my arms. I liked feeling her body against mine. She felt a bit cold. She asked me to hold her more tightly. And she was the one who put my hand on her breast. At that point, I no longer was the one in control.

2. Auto-Interference

If you reduce the intensity of the source to the point where the photons of light are only emitted one at a time, there should no longer be any interference. Many photons will hit the screen, others will go through the first hole, and the rest through the second. But since each photon travels alone and goes through only one hole at a time, you would expect to see on the photographic plate two fuzzy dots forming slowly, centered opposite each hole.

But this is not what happens! Even though they go through one by one, the photons will disperse across the width of the plate and you will see, slowly building up, the same pattern of alternating bright and dark fringers as if they had all been emitted at once.

This is one of the great mysteries of physics. How does a photon going through hole "A", say, manage to "know" that there is, elsewhere in the screen, a second opening and adjust its trajectory accordingly? The only possible answer is that the photon does not follow one or the other path, but that it follows both at the same time! So that it, in effect, interferes with itself.

I was in a rotten mood. But when I saw him on the sidewalk across from

Josiane's place, it perked me up a bit. Did he have an adorable kisser, or what! I don't know why I let the opportunity slip through my fingers. He was so cute with those egghead glasses of his. The usual introductions were made: his name was Cedric. He was a friend of Jean Pierre's, Josi's guy. I introduced myself without going into detail. I wasn't in the mood to tell all. I had just had one of those unforgettable fights with my sister. My soul was empty, my heart full of acid. I think all I wanted was someone who would just let me be, someone to just spend a decent evening with.

As we sat at the table, I was quite taken with the no-nonsense way he won my trust by talking about his childhood, his dreams, his life. Men who dare to expose their inner feelings are so rare. And he had such a warm voice. I could have spent hours sitting on an ice floe with him and his tone of voice would have kept me toasty. But he had to leave early—he'd told me that at the beginning of the evening when I sat down beside him in the garden. He had a friend coming in from California and had to be at the airport at eleven. I considered sticking to him like glue and tagging along to the airport, but I don't like watching reunions between long-lost friends. I don't like being a fifth wheel.

So I set my sights on another guy. It was pure laziness: he was sitting across from me. At first glance, he wasn't my type. He was taller, stronger, no doubt, but rather withdrawn. At first, his questions bothered me a bit. As I said, I'd decided to play the clam. I said whatever came to mind. I don't think he liked my answers because he acted as if I didn't interest him anymore. He was uncommunicative. A few words here, a few words there. But really, he wasn't such a bad guy.

So, when Cedric took off, I was left with the quiet one. It wasn't so bad— I won't need to say much, I thought to myself. That evening, he seemed so shy that it would have made me laugh if I hadn't felt so sad over my sister. It's ridiculous acting like children at our age. Manon and I are two tigers. I'm 26, she's 24, but we're just as jealous of each other as we were at 10 and 12. Sometimes, I say to myself that it's my fault. But what can I do if she can't see Dad without getting furious? I'm not going to burn all my bridges just to make her happy!

Whatever! I just couldn't get it out of my head. And I felt stupid feeling that way. I wanted to stop thinking about it, so I was happy when he asked me to dance.

It was a bit cool out. I let him put his arms around me. He was strong. His body was warm. When I closed my eyes, I could think about nothing, or think about other things—it was all the same. Tall, handsome bodies are good for that. And then, suddenly, he put his hand on my breast. Well now, I thought he'd gone too far. My first reaction was to slap him. One colossal smack, like in the movies. A smack that would have made a "whaaack" that all the other guests would hear. But I would have had to react right away. Two seconds later, it was already too late. My breasts are my soft spot. I went weak in the knees.

O.K., I thought to myself. After all, Brigitte, you were looking for someone tonight, someone who's not a total idiot. This one's no worse than any other. Go for it, girl.

3. When Possibilities Take Shape

There is a simple way of explaining how the path of an isolated photon obeys the laws of interference, as it intersects a screen pierced with two holes or slits.

When light propagates, it is not composed of particles, but of a wave filling all of space. This wave will therefore go through all the openings in the screen and undergo interference phenomena, just like sounds in air or waves on the surface of water. It's only when the light hits the photographic plate that it resumes its corpuscular form. In short, it will "materialize" on the plate in a given point.

The precise moment where, out of all the possible positions available to the photon, only one is given existence has been designated by physicists as the "collapse of the wavefunction".

At some point, Gilles Philippe and his girlfriend felt the urge to listen to some oldies. They took out old Beatles records and pumped up the sound. There we all were, flailing our arms together in the vaguely rural setting of a house in the suburbs. Twenty minutes of pure primitive madness, in striking contrast to the romantic atmosphere of languid jazz that had enveloped us until then. It roused me out of my torpor. I should have taken advantage of the moment to mix with the others but I was still under the charm of that nymph, her silence and her absent gaze. I was a prisoner of that breast she had granted me, that breast whose nipple moved under the damp silk every time she waved her arms.

She was sweating profusely and I was afraid she might catch cold when she stopped dancing. I suggested we go into the living room.

"No. I'm exhausted. I think I'll go home instead. I had a tough day," she told me.

I could have pressed her but she quickly looked away and I interpreted it to mean "period, over." Was it the end of the sentence or the evening? I suggested taking her home, almost hoping that she'd refuse. After all, what could I do with that girl? She was definitely attractive. But she obstinately refused to talk to me, robbing me of the pleasure of exploring, the only pleasure that adds real spice to the game of seduction.

She didn't push me away. She only lived about ten minutes from Jean Pierre's place but since she felt cold, she asked me to put my arm around her shoulders as we walked there. The chain of events had begun.

As I walked her home, we said barely anything more than we had during the evening. By the time we arrived at her door, I realized that I knew nothing about the girl and that it would be better to turn back. But she didn't even turn around to say good-night. She walked in, leaving the door wide open. It was like a vortex I couldn't escape from. It was the same as she reached the bedroom and then her bed.

I have never felt so bewitched. I was no longer master of my actions. I found myself in bed with a girl about whom I knew nothing, someone I hadn't even really begun to desire. I thought of Circe—I would have made a very poor Ulysses. And then I said to myself that I didn't have a Penelope at home spinning and unspinning her wool. The only thing I had to fear was a stray yeast infection. There were condoms on her bedside table. I didn't take any chances; she didn't stop me.

I've already talked about her charm, that magic space—but it was not until I entered the depths of her lair that I truly understood the extent of her fairy powers. She took me into the privacy of her womb as no woman had ever done before. It was an astonishing night. The way she moved her body—curling it so softly, all her muscles contracting to tighten around my penis—I had the impression of being totally sucked up. And when I came, she took me again, and again, and yet again until I saw the sun appearing through her window as I caressed her bottom. It was already past six and we were still making love.

I fell asleep, as if stunned by the prying eyes of the sun.

T⁷

We danced for a half an hour, maybe an hour. It was nice when we danced slows. His body was warm. When we danced fast, I warmed up too. But afterwards, pouring with sweat in the cool night air, with my silk blouse soaking wet, I was really cold. I was afraid of getting sick. I wanted to go home. I told him that I didn't live far, but he insisted on walking me home so I wouldn't catch cold. Is he trying to get me into bed, or what? I thought to myself. So, why not?

We walked for fifteen minutes. He put his arm around my shoulder. It kept me warm. I thought about nothing. My mind was clearly on other things. Did I invite him in, or did I simply leave the door open, forgetting to vaguely say good-bye? In any case, when I found myself in the kitchen, he was still there. Men are all alike, I thought to myself: he didn't doubt his power over me for a second. I was already conquered territory.

I wondered whether I should offer him a coffee and then send him on his way, but I didn't have the heart to wash two cups, boil the water, etc., etc. I was still upset by my sister's rage when she had left that same room five hours earlier. I didn't feel like lingering there. I wanted to forget.

In my bedroom, I looked at the man beside me. Actually, I found him attractive. I realized that I didn't even know his name.

"You asked me earlier," he answered, more amused than insulted. "My name is Alain. Alain Demers."

"I never asked you that. You must have been dreaming! Look, you can put your things down here."

I showed him the toilet, the shower, the towels if he wanted to wash up. And I watched him slowly take ownership of my home.

And ownership of me. I let myself go. He knew how to caress so well that I thought he must have been very experienced. I was afraid of catching something. I moved his hand toward the condoms on the night table. He didn't resist. Then I let him take me, ever so gently. I stopped thinking about that other fellow, Cedric. And as he made me come—with his fingers, his tongue, his penis that refused to go soft—I forgot about all the others.

The next morning—actually it was afternoon when we finally got up—I wasn't very proud of myself. I had this guy in my bed. I'd had a good time with him. He had fulfilled his function. But I really didn't need him around anymore. Unfortunately, I've never been good at asking people to leave. Maybe I'm too nice. I always want things to end without a bang, affectionately if possible. So I wait for the right time, which never comes fast enough.

I served breakfast, if you can call a meal served at that time breakfast. And then the silent man began to speak: about his job, which he couldn't stand; about jazz, which he adored; about long extinguished flames of love "which never burn again quite so brightly once you get to our age," as he explained to me although he was barely thirty and I could clearly see in his eyes that he was ready to fall madly in love!

I talked about myself too. It's hard not to when someone is opening their heart up to you. He asked his questions so insistently that at first I felt a bit uncomfortable. Oh, just ordinary questions: who I was, where I came from, what I did in life.... Usually, in response to such questions, I talk about my work. But I couldn't do that with him. I tried my best to dodge them, but he wouldn't give up. He was targeting my dreams, my plans, my soul. I ended up admitting that my dream was to become an actress. It surprised me. It's something I've always kept to myself. A no man's land. What right did this intruder have to enter here? Since when does having sex give someone the right to do as he pleases?

But you should have seen the look on his face. It could have opened up your soul as easily as opening an oyster, with a simple flick of the blade. I tried to close my eyes. He asked me if I was crying. I apologized.

"I'm just tired."

"That's why you weren't feeling yourself yesterday?"

"What do you know about 'feeling myself' yesterday?" I answered. "That's how I usually am, buddy!"

He didn't believe me. I don't know what he did, but in two minutes he had me talking about my sister. He could see it all, I'm telling you. And it gave me a strange feeling—something between the fascination of meeting someone with whom you can share everything and the fear of being violated. I didn't dare open myself up further but there was no use trying to sneak away.

The best I could do was take him back into my bed. I think it was the best way to end the emotional strip-tease he was forcing on me. I needed silence.

A bit of screwing and then, honest, I would kick him out.

But I had the feeling that it would be a serious mistake. I loved this guy, damn it! And Lord knows, that was the last thing I wanted! It was much too early to get stung. So, what could I do? There are times when you feel caught—damned if you do, damned if you don't.

ר

The next day, or to be more precise, a few hours later the same day, the sphinx started talking. She was 26. She worked as a cashier in a clothing store and dreamed of a career in the theatre. She had had a few lovers, only one of whom had lasted over three years. A period of calm in an otherwise fragmented life. She had a sister she both loved and detested. From what I could tell, they were like the two poles of a magnet: inseparable opposites.

"I'm talking about it because she's the reason I was in such a rotten mood last night. I guess you should know that."

"Oh! You were in a rotten mood?" I said. "Since I don't know what you're like on a good day, I can't really compare."

"Let's say, sometimes I'm more talkative than yesterday."

I think that's when she asked me my name again. I thought it was strange that she hadn't remembered it.

"Alain Demers," I said, adding with a slightly mocking smile, so she wouldn't take offense: "When you make love, do you often forget the name of your lover the next day?"

"It's because you never told me. You imagined it, sweetie," she said.

I didn't contradict her. I helped her make some toast and coffee, without quite being sure of which meal we were sitting down to eat. I looked at my watch: almost four o'clock. We had a few bites and went back to bed. There was still so much to do, so much to explore.

⌐¬

We screwed again until exhaustion set in and then I fell asleep with my head on her stomach and her scent to feed my dreams. Dreams perfumed with passion—you'd think that in a single night this woman had rekindled a blazing fire within me. I still feel the heat, even with the passing of time.

4. The Laws of Chance

In physics, the probability a particle will materialize here or there in space depends on the interference pattern of the wavefunction. But it's a statistical law. If the light beam is so weak that only a single photon manifests, the location where it appears seems completely random. It's only after hundreds of thousands of light points accumulate on the plate or film that the interference patterns shows up clearly.

Here is the central enigma of quantum physics. If all the photons are identical, why do they materialize here rather than there?

⌐¬

One detail is sometimes enough to change the whole course of events. When I woke up, she was already a different person. She had just picked up the receiver to call her sister. That's what had woken me up. Out of politeness, I didn't want to listen to what she was saying but I felt the rage in her voice. When she hung up, I asked her what had gotten her into such a state. All I wanted to do was open the gate so she could pour out her pent-up feelings if she felt she felt the need. She preferred to remain silent. She simply explained that when her sister called, it was to try to pick a fight. "Wasn't it Brigitte who had called this time?" I thought to myself. But it wasn't really important, anyway. She snuggled up in my arms again, affectionate once more.

It was after eight in the evening. She suggested we go to the movies to finish the day spent in isolation from the rest of the world. I wasn't keen on it. I wanted to delve deeper, not take my mind off things. Movies are a bubble of silence, a foreign body in the life of a couple. They cut off communication. I suggested we go to a bar that I hadn't been to in ages, a place where I fondly remembered having spent romantic evenings in the past. I felt ready to dream about love there again.

There weren't many people at the Bar de l'Éclair-du-soir. Not too noisy, a cozy place. But Brigitte was distant. She was nervous. I could see it by the way she nervously drummed her fingers on the edge of the table, the intolerable way her eyes darted to and fro, the way her comments floated in the air like a rudderless boat. I asked her three or four times what was wrong. She responded that she didn't feel like talking and that we would have been better off going to the movies. It probably had to do with her sister but she didn't want to say anymore about it and when I insisted, I felt I was intruding. I had to pretend not to see her discomfort.

But I was furious. How could I survive this incessant bouncing back and forth between passion and indifference? I don't like roller coasters! I retreated into my own stubborn silence.

Then Mikhail arrived. He wasn't a close friend though I used to know him in the days when I was a regular at the bar. Brigitte's muteness was making the silence painful for me, so I was happy to see him come along. I waved him over and he came and sat down at our table.

And then a repeat performance of the night before with Cedric began. When I tried talking to Brigitte she didn't hear me, or at least she pretended not to. But she came back to life with Mikhail. Her eyes opened wide. Had I been mistaken in thinking at Jean Pierre's that we had established an understanding in the well of silence she had built around herself? Anyway, this time I felt nothing of the kind and I couldn't stand it. It was because we'd screwed, because of the intimacy the act engenders, the new reality created by two beings when their bodies unite. It drove me crazy to see her treating me with such indifference. After half an hour, I took off.

When I left the bar, I hated Brigitte. But I still wasn't ready to say goodbye to the relationship.

It was around eight in the evening. We'd just finished screwing when the phone rang. It was my sister. She was still angry with me over the day before, the bitch was just calling to try and stir up more trouble. The call lasted at least twenty minutes and really upset me. His eagle eyes didn't miss a thing. He saw it all. Which got us going again for a good half-hour pouring our hearts out and once again I felt uncomfortable being so transparent with him.

It was fright, I think. The fear of going too fast. I needed some air. I felt like taking my mind off things. He suggested we go to the movies. I said O.K. I didn't care about the movie. I just needed time to think.

We went to the Lux first where he leafed through a few magazines and bought a package of Dentyne. Then, instead of going to the movies, he dragged me to a bar. I didn't make a fuss. I must have been totally out of it because I didn't even realize what was going on—we were already sitting in a fairly well-lit, quiet corner when I realized our plans had changed!

I admit it, my mind was on other things. Millions of thoughts scurried through my mind like red ants digging their tunnels. That's the way I see my thoughts sometimes: I never stop running after them, but they scurry through my neuron roots like thousands of tiny agile beasts in an ant hill you're better off not stopping to visit.

"What's wrong, Brigitte?" he asked me. "Have I said anything to offend you?"

"No, no, Alain. I'm fine. I was thinking, that's all."

"What are you thinking about? I can see in your eyes that something's wrong in there. And look at your fingers. You can't stop drumming them. Don't try to tell me nothing's bugging you."

His insistence made me uncomfortable. I looked for a way to get him talking about something else. He owned me—that's what was wrong. Honest to goodness! And when love rings the doorbell, it always makes me run in the opposite direction. It seems to me that things are going too fast, that I've made a mistake. I don't trust chance enough. That's the way I am. I didn't want to start lecturing on the topic. I should have insisted we go to movies, I thought to myself.

At one point, another guy came and sat down at our table. His name was Mikhail. One of Alain's friends, nothing to write home about. He wouldn't stop talking. I could see right away that he was a real bar-fly. But I was happy that someone was filling in the silence between us. I was starting to fear that Alain would think I was a pain in the neck when actually I was acting so badly because he troubled me.

Now that Mikhail was sitting between us, I started to relax. He talked so much—without caring whether or not anyone was listening—that all I had to do was smile from time to time and slip some "Oh yeahs" into the pauses in his incessant gibberish for the evening to flow as smoothly as water over Niagara Falls. But behind this simulated happiness, I resumed the ant hunt in my mind, hoping that I could see things more clearly and decide at last what to do about this fellow Alain who saw all, made love like a god and whose very silence disturbed me as we sat there.

And that's exactly when he stood up, that jerk, and left the bar without even saying goodnight! Shit! And here I thought this guy understood everything. What an idiot he was!

Worse yet, I still had to get rid of the other guy—he was the clingy type. When I told him I wanted to leave, he offered me a lift and I didn't think to say no. But then, no matter how hard I tried, he just wouldn't get up to go. Eventually I gave up. Too bad, I'll just take a taxi. And then he got up with me and took me to his car. It was parked across town, seven or eight blocks away. Once we got in the car, he started telling me an endless story about a friend who'd traveled around the world. I was treated to a tour of half the countries on the planet and twenty minutes later he still hadn't started the car.

It was the same thing all over again once we got to my door and I refused to let him in. Another half-hour epic struggle! So by the time I was finally alone, it was one-thirty in the morning. I was furious. I called Alain. He was probably asleep but I wasn't going to let him get away with the trick he'd pulled on me that night! If he hadn't enjoyed the sex, he could have told me instead of ditching me at the first opportunity!

On top of it all, I wanted him in my bed—I admit.

5. Multiple Universes

Why do the laws of motion, in physics, allow us to predict the behaviour of thousands of particles but not the specific path of each one?

Physicist Hugh Everett has put forward a fascinating answer to this conundrum of quantum physics—the hypothesis of "multiple universes". In our experiment with the screen and its two slits, each individual photon can, according to him, appear anywhere on the photographic plate. Therefore, he postulates that each photon interacts in every possible way, but in as many parallel universes.

In each of these universes, there would be other versions of us, observing the same experiment and watching the photon reach the plate in different spots.

Thus, if we perceive only one event, one point of light appearing on the plate, it's not because of the random behaviour of the photon, but because each observer can only be aware of one universe at a time.

⌐¬

She called right in the middle of the night. She was in tears.

"Why did you leave me alone with that guy?"

"I couldn't take your games any more!"

"Huh? Are you crazy, or what? We spend the night together. We have sex like I've never had sex before. You take me to a bar and then you palm me off on the first buddy who turns up. You must think I'm a whore!"

She was like a wild beast. Fortunately, you can't get bitten over the phone. Which didn't stop me from thinking she was being unfair.

"I didn't palm you off on anybody. Anyway, that guy's not really a friend. I barely know him. But with those pretty eyes you were making at him, it was clear as day. When I feel like I'm not wanted, I clear out!"

"Where the hell did you dream that up? I was making eyes at him! I wasn't even talking to him. You knew very well I didn't want to talk to anyone. I wanted to go to the movies. The rest is all in your head. But that Mikhail knows how to stick to a girl like glue, he's hell to dump. I just got rid of him now."

I looked at my watch. It was past two in the morning.

I heard her voice on the other end of the line: "So, are you coming to get me?" I was so ready to believe that she loved me too that I answered yes without hesitating.

It took me a while to take a quick shower, get dressed again, go out into the night air and get to Brigitte's. There were no lights on at her home. I hesitated slightly, but I didn't want to have come all that way for nothing. I rang: once, twice, three times. I waited forever in the cold night air.

Finally, I had to face facts: she'd taken me for a ride—perhaps it was her way of getting back at me for leaving her at the bar? I felt cheated, I'd been had. And I made my way back home through the moonless night, alone with my anger.

⌐¬

Perhaps I rushed him a bit on the phone when he started putting on his great show of jealousy. Men—they're all the same! He tried to make me feel guilty, as if I had tried to seduce his buddy Mikhail. Come on. I wasn't the one who had asked him over to our table and then left. And he hadn't had to spend a good two hours afterwards trying to get rid of Mikhail. It got me hopping mad and I thought I'd better to put a stop to it. When they're jealous from day one, you've got to put the brakes on big time.

I said good night and hung up. The bed seemed empty. It took me a million years to fall asleep. I couldn't stop thinking about Alain. I had him under my skin, like it or not!

The next day, I felt a bit stupid moping over this guy and not having him right there beside me. I called him. I was full of good intentions. It was a disaster. I hadn't said more than three words before he ripped into me. Honestly, I couldn't repeat half of the filth he spewed at me over the phone. I had become the worst slut, a bitch, a wildcat, half the beasts in the zoo. And I didn't even know why he had flown into such a rage.

"Who the hell do you think you are?" I said. But that didn't stop him for a second. So then I started yelling myself, just as loudly. Then, having spent all my breath and my rage, I burst into tears. That's what's rotten about women—we always cry too fast.

He said to me: "I'm on my way." I let him come. After all the horrors he'd spit out at me over the phone I wanted to get it over with. It had stopped my budding love dead! But I didn't want it to end on a bad note. I didn't want the last picture in the album of our passionate weekend to be so ugly. I wanted to make love one last time, so that both he and I could then find peace of mind. I have trouble with anger. It was like with my sister, the other night. Though with my sister I can't recover quite so fast just by making love to her! Though sometimes I think, what the hell, maybe we should try!

When he arrived, I didn't say a word. I didn't even wait for him to make himself comfortable. I dragged him into my bed. Good God, this guy knows how to screw! In barely five minutes, I was in nirvana. In less than an hour, I'd had three or four orgasms. I lost track.

ᒥᒧ

The next day, she called again. I was feeling all the more glum since I'd barely slept. The insults rolled off my tongue like an avalanche, crushing everything in their way, even what I might have cherished most about her. There are words that you regret even before having said them, words that come out nevertheless because the magma in your soul is boiling over. Once the irreparable has been committed, there's no going back. You want to rewrite history, but there you are, powerless, observing the effect of the words you just let fly as they stab the Other like swords gone mad.

I realized at a certain point that she was crying. I said, "Wait for me. I'm on my way," without knowing if I really intended to go to her or instead take revenge on her for the indifference she'd shown the previous night when she'd left me cooling my heels at her door. But fear of the disaster my words could have triggered—and love too, I admit—won out. I went to her as fast as I could.

And that is how, Sunday afternoon, without saying a single word to each other, we again threw ourselves at each other in a passionate dance. And with each wave of tenderness, a few of the marks that the ebbing tide of hate had left on the shores of our hearts were erased.

Then calm returned to the part of the universe bounded by the halo of sweat created by our satisfied bodies. She started talking to me again using the warm voice that had so charmed me the first night, the voice that disappeared as soon as she became angry.

"Why did you leave the bar last night?" she asked me again. Once again, I explained about her attitude toward Mikhail, how uncomfortable I felt seeing her so open toward him and so closed toward me. Again, she refused to recognize what I had nevertheless experienced. It was as if we'd spent the evening in two completely different universes, as if her Mikhail and mine were two different people, as if my Brigitte was not hers.

"And maybe you'll tell me that you opened the door last night when I rang?" I suggested.

"What? You rang last night?"

"Three or four times, if you please! You must have been sleeping like a rock."

"When did you come over?"

"Right after we talked, when you asked me to come over!"

"I never asked you to come over. I was much too furious. And anyway, I don't believe you. I didn't sleep a wink last night. If you'd rung, I would have heard something."

The look in her eyes, the tone of her voice, how her naked body responded to my caresses—everything seemed so sincere that it wouldn't have occurred to me to think that she was lying. In any case, there were so many possible explanations: she hadn't been aware of the invitation she'd made in a moment of intense emotion; she'd fallen asleep without realizing it as often happens; the doorbell hadn't worked…

6. Intertwined Universes

Everett's theory of multiple universes has been criticized for being impossible to test and, much worse, absurdly uneconomical!

Think about it. In every second, in every cubic centimetre of matter, there are billions of particles obeying the same statistical laws of quantum mechanics. With each interaction, Nature should be splitting itself into an infinite number of divergent universes! Where would all the energy come from to produce these boundless universes at each point in space, with every passing increment of time?

"But why should these multiple universes diverge?" responds Everett. After all, if you repeat the double-slit experiment a million times, with billions of photons each time, you will always get in time the same interference image on the photographic plate. In short, the history of each universe will differ in the specific ordering of microscopic events, but all will finally meet and merge, subject to a common fate.

On the macroscopic scale, there will only be a single universe, after all. It's only its fine structure that will be made up of an infinite number of parallel yet constantly braided timelines.

ᴦꜟ

Towards the end of the afternoon, when we'd gone out to get a breath of fresh air, I began to have my doubts about her reality—and mine, for that matter. We'd walked towards downtown and as we passed by the Lux, she went in.

"I won't be long," she said. "I just want to buy a magazine. I saw it last night when we were here."

"Huh? We weren't at the Lux together last night!"

But that didn't stop her from finding the magazine she wanted right away, without having to look through the racks. I figured she must have been there another night, that she was confused. I didn't want to let myself get upset. I bought a pack of gum. As I left, I offered her a stick. She refused, giving me nevertheless one of those loving glances that just melt my heart. I smiled at her.

We started walking aimlessly again, strolling along. We were silent for a few minutes. It was a gorgeous day. I should have felt good with this absolutely lovely girl on my arm. But I couldn't shake off the strange feeling that we were living in two distinct worlds. I thought about the phone call she'd made to her sister, the one she'd said she'd received; about our totally different perceptions of her behaviour at the Éclair-du-soir; about the rotten trick she'd played on me during the night and then denied the next morning. And now, this business with the Lux…Was she lying to me, or had we truly experienced two different realities? Is this always the way people meet, converge and separate during every moment of their lives? When you hear multiple, irreconcilable versions of the same story, is it possible that they're all true?

The further we walked, the more uncomfortable I felt in this love story. When our legs brought us back to her house, I didn't want to go in. Of course I felt as drawn to this place of passion as I was on the first night. But I felt as if I had to first understand things more clearly.

Fortunately, she didn't insist. We smiled at each other. We kissed tenderly and then she said: "Good-bye. I don't think we'll meet again, Alain." I protested, but my heart wasn't in it. It was only later, on my way home, that I started really regretting things. Passion, desire, the memory of love—they all drew me back to her. I phoned her often during the days to come but she never called back. It was as if she had disappeared into thin air!

ד

After making love, all was calm. I felt good. But then he broke the charm of that precious moment that often follows the act of love. Instead of saying to me "You're beautiful," or some other loving words, he again asked why I hadn't let him in that night when he rang the doorbell. Come on! I gave him a strange look. He was putting me on. Especially since it wouldn't have been possible at the time he mentioned. I was wide awake. I know because I kept looking at my watch every ten minutes.

He wanted to make me feel guilty—just a way to make me accept his anger that morning, justifying it with a supposedly ruined night. O.K. I preferred not to start the discussion yet again. He didn't insist either.

He proposed we go for a walk. I suggested we head for the Lux where I had seen a fashion magazine that interested me the night before. He looked at me strangely, claiming that he didn't remember having gone to the Lux the previous day. But two minutes later, as we were walking in the cool late-afternoon breeze, he reached into his pocket and pulled out a pack of gum. I looked him straight in the eye. He couldn't deny the Lux. He gave me a silly smile like a child caught lying red-handed and shyly offered me a stick.

We went on walking for a long time, talking about this and that. When we arrived at my door I said farewell to him, as I had the night before to Mikhail.

"Farewell? Why 'farewell'"? he asked.

"Because I don't think we'll see each other again, Alain. Not after what you said to me this morning on the phone."

"Listen, Brigitte. I was a shit. I was furious because of last night. The words were stronger than what I felt."

"Maybe. But there are things I just can't accept. I wanted to see you again so we wouldn't break up on that note. I wanted to make love with you one more time. I wanted to remember your body with fondness. But it's finished now. No hard feelings."

I was pleased with myself for having spoken so coolly. Because inside I felt torn. But I'm sure I was right. When I closed the door and found myself alone once again in my apartment I felt wonderful. In the final analysis, I would only keep warm, tender memories of that weekend.

ᴦ⅂

Yesterday I read a book on Everett's interpretation of quantum mechanics. I'm sure of it now—that's what we experienced! Though her version resembles mine, though a jury able to judge the facts would certainly see one single story, we nevertheless spent the weekend in parallel universes. Two worlds, admittedly entwined around the same facts, but mutually exclusive. How many other times has this happened to me before? Do two people ever manage to actually live in the same universe?

How many other similar yet different fuzzy universes did we perhaps travel through during those few days—two coloured threads intertwined on the same immutable loom of reality that nevertheless weave new designs from one tapestry to another? And would all these universes have led to the same failure? In these infinitely variable scenarios was there only one real exit from the labyrinth of facts?

Sometimes, I hope the answer is yes and that unlike the planets, the limits of reality have not condemned us to pre-defined orbits; that there is room for the unexpected at the end of a sequence of interconnecting events. Yet sometimes I find myself wishing that all these parallel possibilities would arrive at the same conclusion. That way, I wouldn't have to regret having made the wrong turn at one of those countless, unnoticed forks in the road. That way, I wouldn't have to feel that this failure was all my fault.

Stick Man

Dora Knez

An eye the size of heaven looked, and found
a human shape too vast for human eyes.
Not stars alone—whole galaxies compound
to dots connecting known to unknown skies
where he, the Stick Man, strides across the dark.
Discovered by a science most arcane,
yet he's familiar; children in the park
could use a purple crayon to explain.
The true enigma, friends, lies not with him
(exotic flesh like fruit with seeds of light),
but in the seeking gaze. Is this a limb?
If yes, then I am holding hands with Night
and watching what will put an end to fear:
Love's face from heaven's blankness coming clear.

The Knot

Élisabeth Vonarburg
Translated from the French by
Aliocha Kondratiev and Élisabeth Vonarburg

They say nothing to you, at the Center. They open the door for you, they give you drink, food: it's been a long journey. You're taken to a room: white walls, a narrow bed, and a window you go to at once, drawn to the dizzying blue of the sky, where night is settling. The door closes again, and you turn around: they haven't said anything to you, and you've only just realized it.

The next morning (you always arrive at night, it takes everyone a whole day to climb up from the last way station), you wake early. Not a sound. The walls, the ceilings, are mute. No steps reverberates in the corridors. You do know, however, that there are people around you. The Center's inhabitants are many, as are the aspiring Voyagers. Suddenly you think of the Voyagers: perhaps some of them have returned during the night, or a short while ago. You realize, then, that you are at the Center, THE CENTER, and a kind of dizziness makes you close your eyes, clutch the edges of the bed; it seems you're falling right through the stone floors, sucked down by a great void: the underground hall which houses the gate to other universes.

They didn't say anything, the next morning. Sounds of voices and smells of food guided me to the dining-hall at breakfast time. An arm raised as I entered guided me to the only face I knew, that of a tall black man with white hair but unlined skin, and merry wrinkles at the corners of the eyes: the one who'd opened the door for me, the day before. Had I slept well? Tea or coffee? Nothing more. And of course, they don't really need to talk. You're there, you've come from any one of the continents, you've had enough strength, obstinacy or just plain luck to get to the end of the road. It's enough of a definition, to start with.

Then you talk, you ask questions. And thus they learn everything they want to know about you. (And if you don't talk? But you always do: they can remain silent for a very long time.)

I first asked: "When?" and Tieheart, the black man, shook his head: "It will depend on you."

I did not say "Why?". He knew then that I was aware of the necessary steps in preparing for the Voyage. One leaves only when one is ready. The body, at least, should be ready. The mind…One prepares it as much as one can, and that's not much.

I asked: "When do we begin?"

He smiled without answering: it had begun already.

ᴦᴣ

When I went on my first Voyage, I woke up in light. I could feel it through my closed eyelids, a cruel, sharp light. I forced myself to keep my eyes shut, to breathe deeply, to go through all the exercises of waking. Listen, smell, feel. Be calm. Relax. Let the hard-won reflexes come into play, open to the new modes of perception developed through months of patient training. Gravity greater than Earth-normal; heavy infra-red; no ultra-violet. Am I underground? An underground hall which echoing voices make me visualize as high, round—artificial?

And filled with a light that made me blink several times. At first I did not see the walls of the chamber, they were lost in the blinding glare. Then the adjustment was made: the light came from the walls themselves, from the floor, the dome. Stone? It was like glass, mirrors. Looking down at my feet, I saw my image reflected from a depth that made me dizzy. I rose with the slow movements of a tightrope dancer and walked up to the nearest walls; dimensions were misleading in that shadowless light. I suddenly saw a tiny silhouette appear in the light, stop when I did…A few more steps and at once she was near me, dark and stocky with short curly brown hair—myself. I reached out and touched the hand of my reflection in the wall.

ᴦᴣ

It was a peaceful world, this world underground. There were three different races there, however; the one that lived in the soil, just below the surface; the one that had buried itself deeper, in the layers of rocks; and the third, descended from heretical adventurers, had established itself above.

How they said that word, my peace-loving rock—Ckarias! "Above": a mixture of amazement, reluctant admiration and near religious awe. "Above": in the free air.

Gigantic storms perpetually tore across the surface of that planet, making it uninhabitable: Echneng's climate had entered an unstable cycle a few thousand years earlier, forcing its living species to adapt or perish. The Ckarias had adapted. According to their tradition, the world above was the demon kingdom. But the Dèj Ckarias, the Ckarias of the Above, had dug upward, had dug, dug until they had come up…above the Above: a mountain whose summit rose higher than the turbulent zones. The first explorers had died of asphyxiation. The others, protected by the mountain's inner walls—where most of them still lived anyway—had developed a technology that made life possible at that altitude.

Hundred of years later, they were the ones who'd invented the equivalent of the Bridge, of course. They didn't call it by that name; as is the case in many universes, it didn't work for them as it does for us: they used it for industrial research. Yes, they'd already launched their first manned spacecraft. Yes, they'd contacted other life-forms; no, none of them looked like me.

None?

Why had the Bridge sent me to that particular universe?

I was still very young.

ᴦᴚ

It was a few days after the implanting of the sensors. I hadn't yet gotten used to that deluge of data, especially the radio waves. I walked like a drunken woman. Later, they train the brain to integrate, to sift, not to translate everything into delirious perceptions. But then it was like a drug, every movement triggered waves of sensation that grew wider and wider, and interfered with normal perceptions in the most bizarre ways. I lived in the middle of a vibrant colored sphere, full, full to the breaking point.

Some do break at that stage; I was breaking too: as a chrysalis does. It was the first true step on the Bridge, that metamorphosed body. Egon—I didn't call him Tieheart anymore—shook his head (waves of light, tinkling of crystals): "You've been walking on the Bridge for a long time, Kathryn."

"But it's nothing to just think about it, wish for it!" (my own voice came to me through weirdly-textured distances), "It's nothing even to get here. One has to go through the trials, pass the tests. That's where it all really begins!"

Oh I knew it well, I knew it all! First, the sensors; then all the work on bones, muscles, nerves—surgery, treatments, exercises, all the trainings which turn each Voyager into a survival machine. The remaining part is less spectacular, but that's where many aspirants fail: the remodeling of the brain, its turning into a perfect recorder. Integration of data, eidetic memory…Voyagers leave naked; their only camera and tapes are their eyes and ears; their only computer is their memory, their ability to correlate and their capacity to learn. The perfection of their training will determine the quality of what they bring back to the Center when they return.

That is, those who return to this universe, this planet.

And those who agree to return to the Center

It is said that certain monitors know in advance which ones will return. Egon smiled: "Nobody can know that." His eyes clouded over. "Nobody."

"Haven't you ever felt like going?"

He stretched slowly, like a cat, and I felt a kind of anguish at the perfection of all those smooth curves propagating themselves slowly through space. We had not been lovers long, and with the sensors…

"I thought I wanted to. The Bridge showed me I did not."

Egon, a Voyager? One who'd never left… The desire faded, replaced by a shudder. He must have seen my thought in my eyes: "No, the Bridge doesn't decide, Kathryn. You decide. Your mind does. But sometimes you cannot know before trying the Bridge. I'd guessed it, really. I wasn't very surprised when I woke up here."

"Not disappointed, at least?"

He barely hesitated: "No."

"But you stayed on at the Center."

"I knew where my place was."

He'd been a monitor for ten years, he watched others leave. And it didn't do anything to him?

It took me some time to understand. He did not watch the Voyagers leave: he was waiting for a Voyager, a woman, to return.

⌐⌐

During the two and a half years it took to prepare me for the Voyage, I only saw one Voyager return. She came back at night; it was beginning to snow. We were in the common room. When the bell rang, Egon sat up in his chair; I saw his knuckles whiten on the armrests. Then he relaxed; with a sigh he went out to open the door. When he returned, ten minutes later, he said: "It's a woman Voyager, one of old." A wave of excitement passed through the aspirants. Egon went back to his reading.

The next day, the Voyager was in the dining hall. I watched her with hungry eyes. From afar: I'd been in the Center long enough to know that one does not throw oneself at returning Voyagers. I was disappointed, of course: no halo around her head, her feet touched ground. She was a normal, ordinary woman. Then her gaze met mine and I lowered my eyes to my plate, heart beating. It might take months, years, to learn from her what she'd seen, what she'd lived through. But she'd come back. She'd mastered the Voyage.

⌐⌐

There was a poet among the Marrous…(Actually, their word means "gate"; on my third Voyage, I was beginning to appreciate the finer shades of meaning…Theory, in the Center, is one thing. But reality…So varied, so infinitely complex! And yet, the Bridge does send us to those universes which are most like our own…). Anyway, Mirrn knew of the Bridge only by hearsay: he'd never been to Aïgna, the other continent where a woman Voyager had, centuries earlier, shown his ancestors how to build the machine for traveling between universes—a machine which did not work for them, but Mirrn, the poet, the gate, understood very well.

I was also coming to understand better why they tell us nothing, at the Center. Oh, the functioning of the Bridge itself is no mystery. Everyone knows what it's about even before arriving at the Center. And we're taught the technology of the Bridge in full details, since we must be able to have one built if necessary, to continue our Voyages. In a way, it's very simple: the sphere where we are made to lie down takes us on a brief motionless journey to the heart of cold, to absolute zero. But that is not the Voyage. The Voyage begins when the movement of the molecules stops, and when something called our mind (for want of a better word; would "matrix" be better?) frees itself from space and time and takes along the matter which supports it.

Freed from space and time: from our space and time, here, in this universe. Time is different, perhaps, in other universes, for certain Voyagers, according to the Archives, have come back only a few years after their departure—but a whole lifetime had gone for them; and others, gone for a half-century, had aged only a few months. (And Egon waits for his Voyager, Talitha, who left, and may never return.)

No, the mechanism of the Bridge is not a complete mystery; but that of the Voyage itself…Our mind draws us into other universes. Those universes usually resemble ours; even if we wake up on an unknown planet, there is usually some means there of getting to another Bridge; either it is to be found on the planet itself, or the scientific and technological level of one of the societies on the planet permits the construction of a Bridge; or the planet's inhabitants have developed space flight and can send the Voyager to where he or she will find a Bridge, or can have one built. In some universes, the Bridge-wielding race cannot use it as we do. On the other hand, Voyagers from several other universes have come through to us…

And that's all. That's all they say. Experience has taught them that a more detailed knowledge of the process only confuses it and makes the Voyage more difficult. Voyagers must leave naked, with only one certainty: the Voyage cannot be directed voluntarily. At least, not in the beginning. This is probably why the Bridge's history is so monotonous in those universes where rigid, totalitarian societies have managed to invent it. The only way to direct the Voyage is to kill the Voyager—to kill his or her mind, to rub it out while keeping the body alive, and to reprogram it by impressing upon it only the image of the desired destination.

(Of course, this is what horrified me the most when I consulted the Center's Archives: the thought of those zombies forever deprived of themselves. Yet I always returned to it, with a morbid fascination.)

Why use the Bridge to get richer, indeed, or more powerful? The Bridge is not profitable. There is no immediate benefit to be gotten out of it, the process is too aleatory. The maintenance of a Center is the most disinterested activity in the world. What Voyagers bring, usually, is ideas, different ideas, born of different bodies and environments. The Center is knowledge for knowledge's sake, really. Much more than that, or much less, it's the open door, the constant reminder that something else exists, elsewhere.

Egon listened to me as I preached at the new aspirants, and smiled. I thought it was approval; it was indulgence, tinged with sadness: he knew that was not really why I had come to the Center, why I wanted to leave. At the end of my stay in the Center, I'd changed my tune somewhat. After all, one can't learn nothing in two and a half years. I talked about self-knowledge now, total mastery of one's psyche.

Egon kept on smiling.

"Your mind draws you", Mirrn, the poet, remarked to me. "And you don't really know what it contains. You did arrive in the forest, didn't you?" Towards adolescence, young Marrous leave their family. It is not a socially dictated custom, it is a call which comes from the deepest part of themselves, and which no Marrou society has been able to resist successfully and survive afterwards. They go to the sea and then return, along the lakes, through the forest. And somewhere between the sea and the forest, some young marrous fall down on all four, their teeth and nails grow long, the down that covers them turn into thick fur, and a Marrou family, failing to see its child return, shakes its head and says: "He wasn't able to come out of the sea", or: "She couldn't leave her tree." And on my third Voyage, I woke up in the forest, and lived there like an animal for weeks, having apparently lost all my memory. Until the day when, suddenly, living in a tree and eating its fruits were no longer enough for me. Searching then without knowing what I searched for, I found a village. And I met Mirrn, the gate, the poet, who taught me their language and told me where a Bridge could be found.

As far as the young Marrous were concerned, I thought I understood very well; regression at puberty, recessive genes kicking in, evolutionary recapitulation gone awry, whatever: I had plenty of answers. But Mirrn shook his head gently:"Non, no. It is the water and the earth, the forest, the lakes, or the sea. We are made of the same substance. They are our other faces, our other voices. We must struggle with them to know who we are, to exhaust our childhood dreams. When the old dreams are acted out, we return as Marrous to the villages. Some people remain prisoners of their old dreams, they cannot invent new ones. They stay out there." Was every Voyage, then, for us, and exhausted dream? And when all the dreams are exhausted…we came back? Voluntarily?

At the Center, they only say: It is your mind which directs the Voyage. Your whole mind, not just your conscious will. Thus the Voyage is different for each individual. And each one must learn to know one's mind, one's whole mind, in order to control the Voyage some day.

There are methods for this in several universes: yoga, zen, kaadith, mélenthernë…They take a long time to master and are difficult to put into practice; sometimes they fail. But Voyagers want to Voyage. The quickest way to learn how to Voyage—is still to leave.

And I was so sure I knew what I wished to find.

ᴦ˥

When I left, it was Egon who accompanied me to the hall of the Bridge. Not out of sentimentality but because he was on duty at the Bridge that month. He performed the ritual examinations, declared my physically fit to leave, helped me take off my clothes and lie down in the sphere. He gazed at me for a long time then smiled:"Keep your eyes open to the last", he said. He leaned down, his lips brushed the tip of one of my nipples, and he left. I pushed the button, the lid closed slowly, isolating me in the semi-darkness lit by pilot lights. The liquid began to trickle into the cockpit. It's very strange: by then you are completely desensitized by the drug, you only feel, as though it were very far away, the liquid slowly covering you. It seems you are about to suffocate, but then the drug reaches the brain and everything disappears. A moment before that, my eyes being open as admonished by Egon, I saw, by some curious phenomenon of refraction, my image reflected in the fluid above me, looking down on me. Egon must have learned of this phenomenon through some Voyager, or he may have experienced it himself during his attempted departure. It was his way, no doubt, of telling me that he knew—that he had always known—what I went seeking beyond the Bridge.

It is as if I were always getting closer without ever reaching it. After the universe of the Ckarias, that of the Marrous, and the ten or so others in which vessels of all kinds took me to Earths of all kinds, I now manage to arrive directly at my destination. Sometimes even on the very continent where the Center is located (sometimes it's in Tibet, like on my own Earth, sometimes in France; elsewhere, it's on a continent that was never called America.) And sometimes, more and more often, I meet Egon, older or younger, but his eyes never light up when he sees me: he doesn't know me. The inquiry doesn't take long: not on this Earth either, not in this universe either, will I meet myself.

"Statistically, that's strange", one of the Egons tells me. It is my forty-third Voyage. My father and my mother are here; or rather, the man and the woman who, in my village, live in the house I know well. But the pencil scribblings are not there on the kitchen wall near the door; no child has grown in this house. (Elsewhere, she died at birth, or shortly after; elsewhere, there are other children; once it was a boy, but I couldn't meet him: he was somewhere in the Amazon jungles, getting killed for his country.)

They've insisted on accompanying me to the Center, as they often do. This man who is not my father, this woman who is not my mother kiss me at the threshold of the Bridge: they bid farewell to this tired woman who is their daughter, somewhere, in another universe.

ᴦ⦗

They say nothing to you, at the Center. They open the door, they give you food, drink—it's been a long journey. Someone you don't know takes you to a room; you sit down on the narrow bed. The window is dark, it's winter, night comes early. The door closes and you lie down with a sigh. Another Voyage in sight, tomorrow or in a few days. And another Earth beyond the Bridge, another Center, another Voyage…

Really?

You get up to unpack your bag. The little round mirror hanging on the wall comes to life as you pass. You back up, you look at yourself, half-mockingly: those new little wrinkles, those disappointed eyes, that's you.

That's me.

I turn away, I switch off the light, I grope my way to the bed. Tomorrow, I'll ask them it they'll let me stay here.

ᴦ⦗

But the next day, at breakfast, a tall black man gets up at another table and comes towards me, hesitantly. Egon, staring at me. And a crazy hope flares in me for a moment: this one has seen me before; he may have seen a Voyager with my face, come from elsewhere, my other self, the one I've been seeking for so long in vain!

But Egon says: "Kathryn, you've come back!"

I look around, then—the surroundings, so familiar, of course—and anguish takes hold of me: how can I know? I hadn't thought of that when I was dreaming about Voyagers returning. How can I know if I've come back, or if a Voyager named Kathryn has returned to a Center which another Kathryn, also a Voyager, once left, in a universe very similar to my own? I realize two things at the same time: there's practically no way to know. And it's no longer important.

I smile at Egon, I take him by the shoulders. He hasn't aged much either. I kiss him, I whisper in his ear: "Talitha, did she come back?" He shakes his head, he doesn't seem too sad. (He knows what I'm talking about: a proof? But he could also be waiting for a Talitha in this universe…)

ᒥ¹

The next day, and the following days, they don't press me to tell about my Voyages. I know they won't ask me anything: the Voyager must choose, must speak. In the common room, I idly watch the falling snow: the Center is wrapped in a magnificent blizzard, the sky has vanished, swirls of white obliterate the earth.

"We could be anywhere, couldn't we?" Egon says behind me. I smile at his reflection in the glass-pane: "I could be somewhere else." He purses his lips doubtfully. When I told him a bit about my Voyages, he said, as other Egons had: "Statistically, that's strange." He thinks I have come back. I'd like to believe it too. I've contacted my parents. They're waiting for me in the house where I grew up. At least, they're waiting for a Voyager child.

ᒥ¹

They don't say much to you, at the Center, but they tell you this: the universes that the Bridge opens to us are…like a tree. Born of many roots, its trunks divides itself into many branches. Each knot of causality gives birth to another potentiality, which is another tree, with many branches, they too constellated with knots and branches. It's not really a tree, though; it bears neither leaves not fruits, and it doesn't grow straight: at the ends of its innumerable ramifications, that could be its roots growing. Our universe-tree might endlessly perpetuate itself that way, born of itself and closed in upon itself, since no truly alien, non-humanoïd Voyagers have ever come to visit the Center. How do the universes differentiate? It seems that a law rules their unfolding: the knots of causality are to be found mainly on the macro-molecular level. Sometimes the difference is obvious: on my own Earth there are no infra-terrestrials, and no aquatic humanity. And sometimes it's impossible to say: it's the place of a pebble, the life or death of a butterfly.

"But you were nowhere else", Egon remarks pensively. "You've never met yourself once. I know of no other example of such a case in our Archives. No, Kathryn, you've really come back."

He touches my cheek and goes back to his work with the would-be Voyagers. I lean my forehead against the pane which has misted over, banishing the reflections. I have come back. Why not. Why not stay there, in fact, and meditate upon this possibility: sometimes it is the place of a pebble, the life or death of a butterfly—the knot which makes or unmakes a universe. And this universe exists because it's the one I have come back to. I am the knot.

Of Daedal Skin

Lia Pas

i have this large tattoo kept upon my belly
it dances in shades of orange red & black
it becomes brighter with the moon's dark and with the
    flowing of my blood
it becomes darker as men enter my room and its eyes
    surprise them
following their hungry movements

most times i hide beneath my clothing
but at night i dance in fields
i tear off my shirt and shout and sing
i tear off my skirts and whirl about clothed only in my hair and the
    colors
upon my skin

lately this tattoo has traveled out over my thighs and breasts
lovers stay for one night only
say the tattoo has eaten them

but when my lovers are women
in the morning there are small round marks on their bellies
minute etching of spiders
and i know that these will grow and spread
and that at night we shall dance in the fields together
singing and shouting
laying down tired in the dawn light
embraced in each others intricate arms

THE INNOCENTS

Carl Sieber

It's during a commercial break that my brother speaks up again. This time it's not the cold or wet that gets to him even though he is still full naked in the rain. This time it's not his greed, his deprived childhood or his maladjusted personality that makes him open his big mouth. This time he does it just because he's my older brother and he won't let me forget what happened.

"What happened?" he asks.

I could punch him.

Or I could get up from my log, walk over, put my hands around his scrawny neck, and throttle him so thoroughly that he'd never be able to ask a question again. It would be a favour to the world.

Instead the commercial ends and I'm saved from doing anything. Even so, I remember.

What happened?

We purchased a TV.

⌐¬

Tuesday afternoon. As of Monday my brother and I had been without television for more than thirty years and we needed our next fix of network programming in a big way.

We had lived simple and been sick of it: naked in a driftwood shack by the ocean and it had gotten on our nerves. The tide came in, the tide went out. Then for variety the tide came in and went out again. While the surf thundered. And the surf thundered. And the surf thundered. And it rained.

And no TV.

That was our West Coast paradise for you.

⌐¬

Before that we'd grown up proper enough. A mom, a dad, car, TV, dog, and suburban house: the normal family to all appearances. Only not. Who would have imagined we were faking it? Who could have guessed that behind our front door we were a disaster waiting to happen, a bad piece of business, a ticking bomb?

Certainly we looked normal. William and I worked hard at that; Dad had explained in intense father to son talks what to do, and what not do so as to fit in. "To stay alive sons," is the actual phrasing he used. Occasionally he'd reinforce his survival lessons by sending us off to stay with relatives on the coast. Relatives who definitely did not fit in. Relatives who lived without the basic necessities such as comic books, chewing gum, bicycles, or television. We'd always come back, determined to be normal.

Determined not to ask too many questions.

Ironically I think it was Dad who blew our cover.

I can't say for certain because William and I were visiting the relatives the day the city exploded.

That day, I'm guessing, Dad answered a knock at the front door to find someone who wanted to ask him a few questions. Not the Jehovah Witnesses, no; if it had been them the scale of disaster could have been much worse. I imagine it was the local nuclear protest group trying to enlist a little support from our family. We did live a little close to the nuclear power generator and they must have assumed we'd be an anti-nuke family. They were probably very polite, very well meaning people. I can't hate them for what they did. But they would have asked the wrong questions.

"Sir, have you ever considered the possible dangers of our city's use of nuclear power?"

And Dad would have tried to slam the door in their faces, shouting: "I don't want to think about it!"

But they would have been young, earnest, and eager to educate him. "Just think about it sir. Nuclear Power. At least think about it!"

Well, Dad must have thought about it.

⌐¬

Boom.

⌐¬

There was no home to go back to so we settled down to live with the relatives on the beach. We pretty much had to, the trauma shook us up so much that our "affliction" went into overdrive and we couldn't have passed for normal if we had tried. I had it worse that William but he had it pretty bad too. A wool sweater would start to unravel after he'd worn it for just one week.

We were unmistakably: Throwbacks.

Serious ones. So bad that even our relatives kept us away from their rudimentary possessions: forks, plastic tarps, underwear, and straw sandals. There was never any chance that they'd let us visit civilization. "Cabot and

Will," they'd say shaking their heads, "you two boys are a walking invitation to the stone age."

They did fill in some history for us. Apparently our kind had been around for generations. We'd been known as Luddites and Saboteurs in times past, but "Throwbacks" was the politically correct term now. "Saboteur" implied malice, and "Luddite" implied active resistance, but our kind never consciously wanted to destroy western civilization, it was just our nature to accidentally mangle it.

You see, we were prone to questioning. I mean big time bad QUESTIONING.

Picture a teacher bending over a small boy. The small boy starts to bite his finger nails and stammers, "Sir, I don't really understand..." Slam. Down comes the ruler across the desk.

"Young man, I told you to sit still and listen. I did not ask you to question."

Now before you jump to the wrong conclusion and dismiss that teacher as an authoritarian bastard, consider that he might just have saved the world as you know it.

Teachers, parents and clergy used to be so fierce in their attack against questions not because they were being mean but because they were trying to protect the human race from disaster. Back when the industrial revolution was gathering steam, back before technology had the kind of momentum it now has, any Throwback asking the wrong question could have kept us all in the dark ages.

Throwbacks, as the relatives explained to us, poke their metaphorical fingers into what they shouldn't. "What does this dohicky really do?" Only they do it compulsively, obsessively, relentlessly, unconsciously, probably even telepathically and telekinetically, to such an extent that the poor beleaguered examined thing stops doing its thing.

You can understand the potential for fatal disaster.

Flying from New York to Paris, you get a little nervous, a little preoccupied thinking "What could go wrong?" your fingers start to tap and suddenly, in the moment before the laws of aerodynamics are momentarily repealed, you realize, to your horror, that you have been questioning. What can you say to all the other passengers? Do you stand up and apologize? "I'm sorry everybody that you are all about to die, but I'm a Throwback and if God had wanted man to fly he would have given us wings." Probably not.

ך⁷

It was no surprise that thirty years later the Throwback colony on the coast was reduced to William, me, and a second cousin down the beach who talked mathematics with seagulls. That cousin, by the way, was the reason why calculus occasionally went haywire. William and I kept pretty much to ourselves.

⌐

That last Monday night, the last evening we spent on the beach without television, I occupied myself contemplating the rain. Watching it rain, listening to it rain, smelling it rain, feeling it rain on my head through holes in the roof, and tasting it dribble down my face into my open mouth as I said: "Glub, glub, glub, glub…"

But that was all right. That was life. A typical evening. Sometimes the sun don't shine for weeks.

In my own way I was dealing with the rain.

William though, was letting it get to him.

He was moving. Back and forth, weaving through the rain drips in our driftwood shack, kicking up the sand floor, knocking over the candles, and I was going to clobber him soon.

"Brother, give it up," I told him, "you're dripping wet anyway."

"Yeah, but it's sweat, not rain and besides it helps me ignore your damn 'glub, glub, glub' nonsense."

I closed my mouth and wrung out my beard. "Why don't you go for a walk and cool down?"

He stopped moving and yelled: "Because it's raining!"

I got a kick out of seeing him like that. I considered pushing his buttons as my best substitute for a remote control. "Central heating, electric razors, laptop computers, fast cars, hot fudge sundaes." I spoke slowly, watching him tremble. "Trashy magazines, stereo systems, e-mail, designer drugs, hot showers, espresso machines, credit cards—"

He broke in, spitting out the words: "The Internet, laser tag, assault rifles, plastic surgery, electronic surveillance, international currency speculation, cheap automated mass production…" His eyes rolled back in his head and his hands lifted as if in prayer. "Indoor plumbing, microwave cooking, disposable diapers…"

I slapped him. He'd gone far enough.

"Snap out of it brother. We can't have any of it. That's society and we're not a part of it."

"Cabot," he whispered covering his face with his hands, breathing in ragged breaths, "let's go shopping."

It was his way of being tactful. Offering up an utterly extravagant dare. A dare so stupid, so over the top, so way out of town, so terminally dangerous, that we could both laugh at it and the tension would be broken.

I laughed.

He lowered his hands, and I saw he wasn't even smiling.

So.

I stopped laughing.

You could hear the rain.

"OK William. OK. Let's go buy us a TV."

꒐

You've heard about the "bull in the china shop" haven't you? Well I identified with him. Big, clumsy, and fully knowing that his fetish for fine china was something he ought to vigorously suppress; he went shopping anyway.

And there were disasters. We borrowed clothing from our second cousin but the zippers on the jeans gave us trouble. Standing by the side of the road we were wondering why no one would stop, until we realized our pants were down around our ankles.

"How fast can this thing go?" asked William during our first ride. Moments later the poor trucker's engine quit and we all stood around in the rain poking at the engine.

Then a station wagon pulled up. "You guys want a ride?" asked the driver.

"Sure," answered William, "where you going to?"

Mistake.

The poor driver suddenly didn't know and just sat there, racing his engine and staring at his wiper blades.

The third ride took us into the city but it was very uncomfortable for all concerned since William and I poked, slapped, elbowed and misbehaved in an effort to keep ourselves fully distracted from any questions.

In the seven steps between being dropped off and entering the Mall we managed to set the traffic lights to flashing between red yellow and green, the parking meters to spitting spare change, and almost got ourselves chopped up in the suddenly manic revolving doors.

And honest, we hadn't even asked anything.

We'd just wondered.

Inside the mall the muzak died, the escalators switched direction, and people started looking suspicious so we quickly took cover in a small closet. Unfortunately, two other people were already there.

And then the doors slid closed.

An elevator is a tight place to make a mistake.

You walk into a small box, the doors close you in with randomly chosen strangers, and then you try not to talk, look at each other or fart until the doors open again.

William smiled at the two strangers. "Is this elevator going up?" I fetched him a stunning slap to the side of the head but the damage was done. The elevator shuddered to a stop and the man and woman we were trapped with edged away from us.

I smiled.

She brought her briefcase up and gripped it with both hands, he adjusted his tie and looked away.

I tried to soothe them. "It's OK folks, I'm not crazy and neither is my brother. We're just on a visit to the city, and we're trying hard not to hurt anyone."

The woman stepped further back into her corner and the man hit the alarm button and started desperately prying at the doors.

At least the lights still worked.

The lights died.

"Were you thinking about the lights Cabot?" asked William, quietly, so he wouldn't be heard.

He was heard.

And though I couldn't see anyone's faces, and nobody was saying anything, the silence was suddenly so intense that I knew: they knew.

Mr. Suit & Tie lost it first. "Oh My God. Help me! Get me out of here. Help! Somebody help! I've got a pacemaker, and I'm shut up with a bunch of Throwbacks. They're going to kill me."

"Pink elephants" said William.

"Pink elephants" I echoed. "Pink elephant's, Pink elephants, Pink elephants…"

We tried to centre ourselves, tried to empty our minds of thought. Apparently a man's life depended on it. We tried not to think of pace…whatevers, and whatever they might do or not do, or how they…. enough said. "Pink elephants, Pink elephants, Pink elephants…"

ᴦ⁊

"Throwbacks."

"Pink…" William and I stopped chanting, the man stopped pressing the bell and the word hung there in the darkness.

"Throwbacks." Repeated the woman's voice. There was a certain sound of intelligence along with the word, like she'd suddenly had a brilliant idea.

"I've always wondered," she continued, "just how it is that Throwbacks are able to do exactly whatever it is that they do." Even in the dark I could hear she had her eyebrows raised. Fascinating question.

William slapped me.

But he was too late.

Too damn late.

The lights came back on and the elevator lurched upward.

I felt sick. Violated almost. I was upset, unhappy, and the worst of it was I didn't feel like myself at all.

ᴦ⸀

The purchase of the television was anticlimactic. Both of us were dazed, stumbling through the entertainment department and the desired transaction with only a semblance of concentration. The question, "What happened?" echoed in both our heads and I'm sure that just made the damage permanent.

Getting home wasn't an adventure. "What exactly is an internal combustion engine, and how specifically does it function to propel us down this highway?" William asked, opening his eyes wide and leaning in towards the poor man who'd picked us up. "Explain it to me please. Now," he said, a little sharply, a little angrily, waiting to see if the engine would falter.

It didn't.

"Cut it out William." I told him.

Our driver spoke up. "An internal combustion engine has these small controlled explosions one after…"

"Shut up." I snarled.

ᴦ⸀

The beach seemed empty when we got back. "Hello?" We called to our cousin's shack but there was no answer. After knocking and pushing the door open we found a message he'd left for us. Along with a tape recorder on the table there was a note: "Push play."

Our cousin's voice had some words for us: "This thing works now and I suppose I have you two to thank for that. But I won't. No thank you. No thank you at all. I'm leaving. There's a company that owns this land and has been trying for years to build a resort here. After what you two have done there's no stopping them. Keep the clothes; you'll need them and I don't want them."

ᴦ⸀

Outside I set the TV on a log and started surfing channels.

A few seconds of one program. Flip. A few seconds of another. Flip. Flip. Flip.

William held up the power cord in one hand, tapping the prongs with his fingers. "Shouldn't this be…"

I glanced up from a commercial.

"Shouldn't this be…?"

I cut him off. "Don't ask. Don't ask any more questions."

ALTERED STATEMENTS: #5
SECRETS
AN IMPORTANT NOTICE TO
ALL ENFORCEMENT OFFICERS

M.A.C. Farrant

The terrorist group SPEIV (Society to Prevent the Eradication of Inner Voices) has resurfaced. Printed messages have been appearing randomly on citizens' home entertainment screens, on several of the giant television terminals which line the major freeways, and on work screens at the Department of Silence. Public exposure has been limited because the duration of these messages has been brief and, to date, the public's distress level remains low. This, of course, could change in a matter of hours, erupting into the hysteria and gruesome public flagellations that occurred during previous SPEIV assaults. Officers should therefore be warned that a major SPEIV offensive may be in the offing. The following captured fragment may indicate the direction such an assault might take. It is reproduced and circulated under conditions of strict secrecy and will be the subject of the next departmental meeting. Department members may wish to take a reaction suppressant before reading it.

"…the Department of Secrets says THERE ARE NO SECRETS. But we say there are many secrets. Here are some of them:

1. The idea of the unknown has been obliterated; what's palpable has been made unknowable enough.

2. Your consciousness has been willingly limited; any 'other' reality is now classified as mental illness.

3. Your consciousness has fled; your consciousness is in hiding.

4. The subversive wing of SPEIV operates under the name "The Rules &
   Regulations of an Institute called Tranquillity" in celebration of our
   spiritual mentor, William Hone (circa 1807), the great English satirist
   who pioneered the role of the public informer. Who throughout his
   works said, 'conscience makes cowards of us all.' Who dared to ridicule
   royalty, self-serving governments and all oppressors of vibrant, questioning thought. We are proud to call ourselves Honers, to sharpen our wit,
   to perform our random assaults in his honour. To gather together
   voicing our rallying cry: EVERYTHING MUST BE
   QUESTIONED. We dedicate ourselves to splendour and diversity. We
   are the protectors of the unforeseen, the perpetuators and guardians of
   the novel. Join us. Imagine a strange singing, a mechanical choir erupting from the cities like the whistles and clanking of broken pipes. It is
   still possible for our silenced voices to be heard…"

Song of Solomon

Cory Doctorow

The Christ did me in Chicago, Calgary, Frankfurt, Istanbul and Tokyo, all the while beaming beatitude and beneficence on me.

I can't complain. He's my Lord. Still.

Still, all things considered, I'd rather not die.

ᴦ˥

You're awfully pretty, you know that? Your breasts are very different from Lisa's, the nipples bigger and the aureolae bigger and darker. They look like they should taste like chocolate. They don't. I don't mind.

You know what Heaven is like? I was there, you know, after the Trump, caught up in the Rapture, one of those souls the Lord took on high. Only there for about five minutes but still.

Still, you don't forget the Kingdom of God.

Infinite. That word gets used a whole lot describing heaven. It's big all right. Just a field of white, under the bluest sky you can imagine, stretching over the horizon. The buildings? White. White like His robes. The streets are full but never crowded, quiet and energetic at the same moment, and here and there, niches where lions lay down with lambs, wolves with sheep. You know everybody's name there, and everyone greets you personally. And all you feel is white, white and peace.

I don't feel peace when we kiss. I feel frenetic bloody rushes all over my body, and spiders dance on my nerves. I feel war when your tongue touches mine and my hand slides between your legs, over your cotton panties, as humid as a jungle.

ᴦ˥

I was called to the Christ less than a week before the Trump. I was too hip for religious okeydoke, working the club four nights a week, making eyes at the skinny girls in their spandex covernaughts, sometimes going home with one, sometimes another.

The sound of a club is like the Trump: a fat, funky bassline that makes the little hairs inside your ears shiver, shouted conversations like the allelujahs of the Enraptured.

And one night, I was hauling cases of beer up from the locked store-room, emerging from the bright of the florescents and into the dark smoke of the club, arms straining around the heavy cases. I walked out of the light and into the dark and I knew what Hell was. There's dancing there, twisted angry faces caught in agonized curls. There's music, loud and hammering and full of discord. There's camaraderie, false and treasonous like the worry on a pretty girl's face as her boyfriend's eyes flick momentarily to a go-go dancer.

I put down the case.

I left the club.

I walked into the Christ's loving arms.

ᴦ⁊

You're very smart, young lady. There's never a moment when I don't feel a little bit dull in your presence. You've *bon mots* for every occasion.

You're too smart to have found the Christ. Religion is for the slightly dull, the slightly stunned, the slightly disoriented. Smart people find humanism and say, "There is no sin, only action that can be explained away through upbringing or circumstance." There are no bad people, right Tam?

I'm not putting you down. I never believed, until one day I was too weak not to believe. It was so much easier to believe than to help.

With your lips there, on my chest, and your hands skating nails-first over my arms, I feel like a king. You are more beautiful than any woman I have ever lain with and I can hardly believe you want me. Will you want me in Hell?

ᴦ⁊

Finding the Christ was as simple as finding the nearest soup-wagon and saying, "I need to find God," to the volunteer with the soup-ladle.

She took me by the elbow and steered me within, where it was crowded and stank of old food and bums. There was a bum in the van, too, a pudgy kid without a shirt whose shoes were tatters. He had a string of barbed wire tattooed round his neck and terrible blisters on his chest, and he could hardly breathe. "Shouldn't he be in a hospital?" I asked.

"He won't go," the volunteer said. She wasn't very pretty. She was dressed in jeans that showed me how big her ass was and a T-shirt with a cross over her sagging left breast, and her hair was long and uneven, in a ponytail. She looked like nothing mattered to her but the Christ.

She told me where to find more bread, in a cupboard, and had me sort out the slices and throw out the mouldy ones, and then I buttered each slice and handed them to her on a plate and she gave them out to the skatepunks and squeegee-kids and Legion Hall refugees who stumbled to the van.

The bum stood at sunrise and I saw just how young he was. I would have carded him in a second at the club. He announced that he was going home to his parents. The volunteer found him a pair of beat-up oxfords that were a little big, but in better shape than his shoes, and laced them onto his grimy feet herself.

The she climbed into the front of the van and drove me to the Mission, where my education began.

⌐¬

The sound you make at orgasm is the only thing that reminds me of Lisa. It's barely a hiccough, and so plaintive that it breaks my heart. It's like my erection has touched a part of you that's so secret and so delicate that I've scored your heartmeat itself.

Sex is guilty for you, isn't it? Lisa has no guilt for sex. We were united by the Christ itself, at the Circuses inauguration, and if that isn't a blessed union, nothing is.

We're the best performers the Circus has. Before the Trump, she was the lone Christian in a theatre troupe of degenerate, clever souls like you: too smart for God, using their honed intellects to varnish their sins with reason. I merely had a knack for morality plays: so relieved was I by my salvation, so nearly damnation, that I acted in the Christ's plays with all my heart.

Will you walk with me? The sun is rising here in your city, and the street are washed clean by rain, and they are nearly bare, with only those who work at this early hour, and they are friendly.

Get up. Get up and let me kiss you once more, before your pull over your wrinkled cotton dress. Let me slide my tongue over your chocolate nipple and skate it over the crease of your armpit.

You giggle like a little girl.

⌐¬

The Mission was used to people like me. They knew that those were the end-times. The pastor oversaw my conversion that very morning and drew the cross on my forehead with holy water and I accepted the Christ as my Lord and Saviour and never doubted.

The relief. The end-times, so very near, honed my energies and I was at every prayer-meeting, exhorting alongside of the preacher, testifying to my conversion and warning of the upcoming fires. Every day, my Bible studies revealed a new terror I had skirted and a new joy I had come into. I told the bums who I had been, who I was then, where I was going, where they would end up unless they opened their hearts.

I don't think any did. In the moment of the Rapture, as the Church left earth and ascended, when I knew every soul caught airborne with me, I didn't know any of them. I probably wasn't very good at preaching.

Still, it saved me.

⌐¬

I know that we have walked an entire block and I have kept my distance from you that entire time, but would you take my hand? I miss your touch.

You should be more scared, I think. Your world is nearly empty now that the Saved have left. Wars rage, even here, in your safe land where no war has been fought since the War Between the States and the War for Independence. You have independence in abundance, now.

You should be more scared. You should turn on your television more, and see the eyes of the "Christians" who were left behind in the Rapture, whose faith was impure, who betrayed their love for the Christ by taking false, material idols. See their eyes, as they fight the "Infidels," convinced that they are Chosen, left behind to cleanse the earth for Armageddon. The fucking bastards.

I can say that. I'm saved.

Oh, look! Here they are building a new Tower of Babel, a giant cruciform skyscraper. They can't dispel the rage of the Christ with gaudy industrial baubles. The Christ demands but one thing: slightly stunned and absolute, bovine faith.

⌐¬

I had but five minutes in the Kingdom of God. Then I was called to His throne and His merciful plan was revealed in my mind. And why not? It was my mind only in that I carried it around, but it was His, too. He *made* it.

The Christ wanted me to return to earth with Him. He had a hundred thousand of us there, all of us destined to return. We'd been selected as performers in the Circus of the Lord.

We would go to earth, and we would travel from city to city, performing for the damned during the time of Tribulations, for seven years. During those seven, until Armageddon, we would put on the Christ's morality plays, plays staged with real blood and real death for the players, torment in the service of our fellow man. Each drop of blood we spilled would save a host of souls, strengthen their faith during the Tribulations, midwife their Ascension *cum* Apocalypse.

Lisa was beside me in that host, kneeling at His throne, and her cheeks were streaked with tears. This was Heaven, so I knew her, knew her mind, and it strobed: joy joy joy joy.

It was the most wondrous thing I'd ever felt. I slipped my hand into hers, she hers into mine, and I knew she knew my mind, too. Our minds twined and it was deeper than a kiss.

ᴦ˥

I wonder if Lisa is sad. She is not a very happy person, despite her joy as we received our Mission. She is filled with the Madonna's sorrow for her fellow man, left out of the Light during Tribulations. It's a very soulful sorrow, and that is Lisa in a nutshell: soulful.

She feels very deeply, and isn't very smart.

Don't cry, Tam. It doesn't become you. Your face gets blotchy and crumpled and even if I kiss away the salt of your tears, I still can't really share your pain. I have my own. I've left behind my God for you.

Yes, kick me. Hit me and claw at me, Tam. Strike out and leave a hairshirt of scratched flesh behind. Be my penance.

The harder you hit me, the hornier I get. Come into this alley. The elastic of your panties is shot, and they slide easily over the knobs of your hips. Quickly now, while no one watches, turn around, let me unzip. Oh God, I say, and think of Him, and you give that mournful hiccough.

A child, sticky-faced and dirty-handed, has seen us, looking own from his window high above us. He is all wide eyes as you turn and hold me tightly. Even after I tell you about him, you don't look back.

It's not skin off your back if we spread guilt and sin.

ᴦ˥

The first play is in German. I don't speak German, beyond the lyrics to a Kraftwerk song that the deejay at the club liked too much. Nevertheless, I spoke the words that the Christ magicked into my head with all the fervour I felt, staring at the shrewd, scared faces of the unsaved around me.

I think I was a fat, greedy banker. That's how I dressed, in a comical tophat and sinister moustachios. I know I aimed vicious kicks at my castmates, who scuttled to and fro, heads ducked and bodies bent and oppressed.

I did this throughout the entire first act, whereupon I seized my chest and fell over, tongue protruding slightly from my mouth. I watched through slitted eyes as the other players performed a pantomime of burial with all the generous trappings of Christian forgiveness.

The curtain rang down and then rang up again for the second act. I was centrestage, surrounded by smoky pots of burning brimstone. We played that I was cast into the pit of grafters, where the other players, in the guise of ferocious demons, stabbed at me and burned my flesh with molten gold till the stink of my own meat cooking so filled me that it almost made me hungry.

They burned all of my hair off, and my eyebrows, and then tore my eyes from my face. The burned me at feet and at hands and then worked their way up, reviving me with buckets of ice water when I lost consciousness. I writhed in torment and howled my repentance in German, praising Him and begging for His divine mercy.

The audience was silent throughout, caught in terror and sympathy, and I imagined I could hear their souls being opened to Him and thus saved.

I died with a smile on my bloody lips.

⌐¬

I wonder why you came to the circus at all? You with your clever mouth and clever mind, sweating under the canvas tent, sitting thigh to thigh with desperate sinners on the rough wooden bench, watching the torture of the bad and the elevation of the good. Did you roll your eyes? Did you laugh?

No? Why then?

Scared! You were scared! Fearless Tam, scared of the end-times. That makes me fell better, somehow. When you came to me in the mall, afterwards, so assured and calm, I thought, *Here is a woman who would never be stupid enough to believe.*

Your eyes were so smart, with the beginnings of concentration wrinkles at the corners. I noticed your dimples next, so innocent in a face that was anything but. And then your mouth, for you were speaking to me: "That was disgusting," you said, fearless of the hoots you roused from the crowd.

"That was terrible. What a terrible thing to show the world. What kind of God tortures His creations?"

"It's my choice and my honour to serve him," I said, piously.

"Then you're dumber than I thought. Why does your God need such a big stick? If we were made right—made right by *Him*—then we should be convinced just by knowing who He is and what He wants from us."

The crowd was in no mood to hear this, and was fast becoming a mob. I wondered whether you were stupid or crazy, and I looked deep down into those eyes and saw only outrage and passion. The crowd grew angrier and someone shoved you, and you started to vanish in the press of bodies, stumbling, and I saw the flash of panic in your eyes and, unthinking, dove in after you.

I believe they would have killed us both.

Lisa stood by the Christ as He laid His hands on my broken body and made it live again, truly reborn in Him. She gathered me up in her arms and wept into my shoulder, where only the ghost of the burns and tortures I'd been subjected to ached.

I felt as drawn as toffee, lightheaded and haunted by shades of wounds that the Christ had closed as if they had never been.

She came into my bed and we lay together as man and woman, and she was energetic, almost hysterical. My brush with death had driven her nearly mad. She rode me furiously, as if to shake from me the secrets of the beyond.

And afterward, I got up and left the trailer that we had together and walked to the commissary and got us two waxed-paper cups of ice water, and when I returned, she was asleep. I dipped my finger in the water and let a drop dribble onto her lips, partly open as if waiting for a kiss.

In sleep, her face was as beautiful as the light of the Christ, as He brought me back from the land of shadow.

You've told me a million little stories tonight, Tam. This is truly your city: every storefront and crack in the sidewalk seems to inspire a new anecdote. Your parents, your lovers, your friends. You don't want to go to Heaven, you say, because none of them will be there. None of this will be there.

How easy to say that. You've never been in his light. I also don't want to return to Heaven, darling. Lisa will be there, eventually. She made me so happy and both gave so much for and to each other. And me, who never loved for more than a night, in that place, eternity seemed reasonable.

Do you understand, Tam? In Heaven, I had perfect knowledge of Lisa, her soul and mind and desires, and she mine, and we joined together.

That's a very pretty cemetery. Shall we walk there?

When we fled the mall, I tried to find Lisa's face in the crowd. I couldn't, nor could I spy any of our other castmates. If I could have, maybe I could have helped and we wouldn't have had to run quite so far.

A kiss, here in the boneyard? Why, of course.

Dying didn't get any easier, in the service of the Christ. Death on death, mine and others, under the big top.

The first time Lisa died.

She was a sharpy, a harpy, a smart, urbane woman against a painted backdrop that suggested a richly furnished penthouse. She went to her job every morning with a neat briefcase, a neat suit, her hair neatly coifed and less voluminous than she usually wore it.

She enacted a few kindnesses, change to the homeless, holding a door for an elderly man. But then the houselights dimmed and she delivered brief monologues about the odour of the beggars, her revulsion at the wattles of the old man's neck. In those moments, she acted every bit the sophisticate she loathed: questioning, cynical, clever. Her acting was vicious caricature.

And then the first act ended, with her frightened and alone in a hospital bed, hair fallen out, tubes depending from her arms, cancer devouring her.

And I, as the kindly Christian doctor, closed her eyes and said a prayer for her soul.

The curtain rang up for act two. Lisa writhed in searing, stinking mud as we capered around her, naked, our genitals painted angry red, stabbing at her with pitchforks, forcing her under and then pulling her out before she could drown.

When she did drown, I pulled her from the mud, and, laughing demoniacally, pissed on her, the spray washing the mud from her skin as I zigged and zagged.

ᴦ⅂

I recognise this route. There is the alley we chased through, the shouts of the mob ringing in our ears. Here is the corner where you were nearly run down by a bus as you dashed into the street, pulling me behind you.

There is the mall.

There is the big top.

We've come back to the circus, hurrah.

ᴦ⅂

The Christ appeared over the big top once the curtain had rung down on Lisa's body. The curtain parted again, so the captivated audience could watch as the Christ laid His hands on her and stroked life back into her flesh, closing her wounds, salving her burns, washing the mud away.

A ragged allelujah rang out, whipping through the audience and then back again, thousands of tear-streaked faces and lips parted, enraptured.

Lisa stood, shakily, and came into my arms, and she whispered her love for me in the Christ and I echoed it back to her and then the curtain did ring down.

We made quick, tender love in our trailer, after we'd washed off the makeup. She shivered as we held one another, and shivered still when we went out to walk among the crowds, spreading the Word. I shivered, too, and shrank inside with anger that I had had to kill my love.

ᴦᴧ

There's the trailer Lisa and I live in, Tam. She is surely still abed, quietly snoring, her skin the colour of butter in the light filtering through the flowered curtains. If we went to her now, would she wake and give us tea? Would she weep and hit me? Would she believe me if I lied and told her it was nothing, we'd merely talked?

I've a better idea. Let's get under the big top.

ᴦᴧ

Lisa talks often of Him with me, and His plans. She brings up obscure points of scripture that I barely remember from my brief studies before the Rapture. I usually smile and nod and give her little encouragements. She isn't very smart, but she knows about the love of the Christ. She'll be returning to the heavenly city.

ᴦᴧ

There are the props for our latest play, where a committed political activist suffers and eternity of thousands of hooks piercing his flesh, tugging this way and that, while demons in the guise of foetuses whose abortions he eased torment him.

I've played him. I've had those hooks in my skin, like this. And this. And this.

Don't mind the blood.

I need help, getting them through my eyelids and tongue.

Pull at them, Tam. Let me show you what awaits you if you never repent.

Seven years till the Apocalypse, darling, until we are risen and judged in the Christ.

I die with a smile on my bloody lips.

THE SOLOMON CHEATS

Allan Weiss

The happy ones almost never came.

"You asshole! You're supposed to be so smart, eh? Well, you're nothing but a goddamn ripoff artist!" Don Solomon watched warily as the young man's eyes blazed with rage. Usually it was the angry who came, to put on displays like this. "You told me the goddamn stupidest thing to do, moron!"

The young man—Jay something—half-stood and in that awkward stance pushed Don in the chest. The violent ones always moved through those stages: verbal abuse, then a push, and then....Jay shoved him again, and Don read his expression and body language to see how a few words or grunts of pain would register. He decided on silence.

"Eh? Got nothing to say, eh?" Jay pushed him again, then his leather jacket creaked with the movement of his arms. Don steeled himself for a punch, but it didn't come; as he'd foreseen, Jay had taken his silence as a sign of remorse, and the rage was starting to ease off. With some clients, not saying anything was a provocation, but thanks to his enhancements Don knew Jay better, could read his eye movements and pulse rate. "Fucking moron," Jay said, in lingering hatred and frustration. "She's not coming, you asshole!" he managed in a breaking voice. "She says if I go to Surrey for that job I go alone!"

Jay raised his hand, forming a fist more to release built-up tension than lash out. Then he pushed Don hard into the wall. The pain sprayed through his back and ribs, initiating the internal healing system. Nerve endings froze, and his nanos pumped endorphins through his blood stream and rushed to heal the bruise he must have had on his back. But he didn't want to seem impervious to Jay's actions, so he pretended to suffer the pain Jay was trying to inflict.

Jay showed signs of regretting his violence, though he wasn't quite ready to apologize yet. "What do I do now, eh? She's fucking gone, thanks to you, asshole!"

Don read that it was time to speak. "I'm really sorry."

"Damn right sorry." Jay's rage now dissipated completely, giving way to depression. He also looked a bit sheepish, and perhaps afraid that Don would call the police, something the Solomons never bothered to do unless the violence became truly dangerous. They were a barely tolerated fact of society's life, like prostitutes, and were ready to take a certain degree of abuse. So, Don thought, let him get his money's worth.

Don smiled up at him weakly. Utterly morose, Jay flung his hand half-dismissively, half-shamedly in Don's direction, then turned and walked through the door leading up to the driveway, punching the doorframe on his way out. Don could still hear him repeating his favourite expletives outside, long after the door shut itself behind him.

Don lay on his back for a few moments longer, letting the nanos perform their work. It was hard to tell, but that last push might have cracked his bottom left rib; if so, the nanos repaired it quickly, and muscles reshaped under the skin. Fortunately, Jay Whatever was smart enough to know when to quit. Much further, and Don would indeed have called the police.

He finally got to his feet. The message light was still blinking on his phone. He settled himself into his chair and jabbed the light.

"I'm back," he said.

The face of Nyk Solomon rose again in his head, blocking out the office. "You okay?" Nyk asked, unnecessarily. It was natural for Solomons to worry. Every one of them knew what could happen; one false move by an angry client—a badly aimed punch or kick—and it would be all over for both Solomon and client alike.

"Yeah, okay. I'll let him go."

"What was his problem?" Nyk Solomon's thin face betrayed his deep worry.

"He couldn't decide if he should take a job offer that wouldn't last. His girlfriend was resistant."

"Poor kid. Well, pros and cons." Nyk was a frail, almost skeletal, older man, and it was a wonder he'd survived this long. Every day Don expected to read about his demise, read that some maniac had beaten him far beyond the ability of nanos to do more than preserve him for burial in a North York cemetery.

"Yeah, pros and cons. She ended up dumping him."

"Rough." Nyk transmitted soothing sonic tones expressing sympathy. "Well, the reason I called: I've got a lovely new electrolytes program; very efficient regen stuff."

"Good. But—" As Nyk ought to know, hi-tech solutions could cause more harm than good. You didn't want the regens to be too efficient, because that just made the client feel ineffectual if things got physical. Feeling ineffectual could either dilute the catharsis, or, more importantly, make the client even more violent: If a push won't hurt you, maybe this will.

"No, no, you can slow it down. It reduces toxin release, so you won't have as many long-term effects."

Don smiled, and rubbed at the now-healed rib. "Good," he said, "I'd hate to have aches and pains when I retire."

Nyk laughed. "Yeah."

The real joke was, would they ever really be able to retire? Or would they have to work till they died—which might happen frighteningly soon? Nyk was obviously thinking the same thought as he let his eyes wander pensively for a second or two, then he pulled himself together.

"Okay, Don Solomon," he said, "I'll give you the slow codes. Call me if there are any problems, eh?"

"Will do."

"Helluva way to make a living, no?" Then he transmitted the commands that would make Don's nanos more efficient repair technicians. But you could never really make nerve and muscle tissues as good as new, no matter how many chemicals—enzymes, proteins, electrolytes—you pumped into them. Damage tended to accumulate. Nyk said, "Done," gave a quick, encouraging smile, and exited.

The office reappeared, and Don stood up to prepare himself for the next client, although right now he wanted no more clients, not until he was able to get the image of his own early death out of his mind. Usually he could suppress the fear pretty well, blank it out and renew his faith in the nanos and in the basic sense of self-preservation in his clients. They weren't allowed to beat the bejesus out of him, but they didn't always remember that while in the middle of a serious fit of rage. Fortunately, most who started to get physical were smart enough to hold back. The number of fatalities was surprisingly low (although in the States it was reaching typically American proportions), and the Solomons killed were usually younger, less experienced guys who simply hadn't known their human nature very well. But it only took one out-of-control client; even Don, with all his experience, could end up lying in a bloody heap someday, his nanos overmatched, the police arrived too late, and all his precautions, all his care, would be for nothing.

With a deep breath Don pressed the computer bar, and in a flash was inside the system. He selected "Client Files," ran down the list of pictemes until he reached Jay's, and called it up. Jay Leblanc, 23, musician. Don flagged the file and slid it back into place. "You've had your revenge." He exited and took a deep breath, then covered his face with his hands. His body was back to normal, and all that meant was that he was now ready to be someone else's punching bag.

But he'd served his function, and that made him feel a bit better. He'd relieved someone's stress, and taken on the responsibility that that person had been unable to cope with. Solomons were emotional prostitutes, and like their physical counterparts had to be prepared to be both used and abused.

⌐

As soon as the young woman walked into his basement office, Don felt he knew her completely. She kept her body tight and her eyes lowered, the signs of someone who'd suffered the sort of constant criticism, sarcasm, and domineering that sucks every iota of self-respect and pride out of you. It had probably been going on her whole life. Self-effacing, utterly honest, incapable of deliberately hurting anyone—she was perhaps the gentlest person he'd ever met, or ever would meet.

Her name was Lila Reyburn, she told him with a nervous smile, and she stumbled over her words as she tried to tell him what she wanted from him.

"I just don't know what to do," she said. "I keep thinking, okay, it's just better to get away from Isaac, but then I think I shouldn't because where am I going to go?"

"I understand."

She raised her eyes to his for a moment, with a look of gratitude and pleading, and his heart skipped a beat. Beyond the bent neck, the obvious certainty that he, too, would somehow hurt her, was a grace that touched him. How could somebody that sweet still exist, in a world this cynical and complicated? He admired her for it—or at least that's what he thought he was feeling.

"I go back and forth, back and forth," she said. "Maybe I should wait till I've saved up some money. Otherwise I don't know what's going to happen to me."

"And you want me to help you decide," he said, keeping his voice level.

"Yes. Oh!" She fished in her purse for her moneycard. As her head bowed he saw a ridge of premature gray growing along the part in her straight, black hair. "I'm so disorganized." She shook her head in dismay at her own inadequacy. "Sorry."

"No, no, you're fine. One of my more articulate clients."

She glanced up again and smiled shyly, but seemed to know it was a white lie. She'd probably never had anyone bother trying to compliment her before. Everything inside him seemed to melt at that smile. God, what's happening to me? She caught herself and dropped her eyes again, resuming her search until she found the small red card. She handed it to him with a delicate, slightly trembling hand. "I think I have enough."

"It's okay. Really." But the fact she was here, spending her money on him instead of on a new place to live, told him a lot. He slid the card behind the computer bar, and lasers completed the transaction, then he returned the card to her. When she left he would enter a discount, and might well not charge her at all—he wasn't starving, he didn't need her money—yet he didn't want to make her feel like a charity case, and destroy even more of her pride. Now he felt in need of a Solomon's advice....

He pulled a prepared contract from his desk drawer and showed it to her. She pored carefully over the fancy document with its elaborate "Don Valley District" identifier in Gothic font. She nodded, folded the paper, and jammed it into her purse. "Before I moved in," she said, apparently glad to explain all of this to somebody, "I was living with my mother and brother. My brother drinks, he's crazy, he hit me a few times, and I wanted to get away from him. Isaac was so nice to me, he bought me things, he promised me so much. But then he started yelling at me, too. He criticized everything I did, everything I said, and he didn't want me to go to work but I did anyways."

"Okay." The way she spoke distressed him; she didn't seem terribly bright, or have the life skills she'd need to leave her boyfriend. He read her looking for signs he was wrong.

"I'm good at what I do, they like me at the shop because I never mix up the boxes, they're always on the right shelves. I have to shelve them by numbers, and I think I can do that! I can work. I don't need anybody to tell me what to do."

Good with details but not with anything abstract or complex: she'd have an incredibly hard time surviving without help, but he wasn't sure she'd be wise enough to accept it. It was painful to recognize, but she seemed trapped. Maybe inextricably so.

"Oh, I didn't mean you," she said. "I'm sorry if I sounded...I came to see you because I don't know what to do."

"Don't b—," he began, but didn't dare say, "Don't be silly" because she'd take it literally, think he was calling her stupid. "—worry. Do you have any friends, people you could stay with?"

She shook her head slowly, and he read that she did indeed have such friends, that she'd probably received numerous offers of places to stay, but that deep down she didn't really want to escape. "What if they kick me out?" she asked. "Then where'll I go?" She kept peering down or to the sides, rather than at him. These were all classic symptoms, and unfortunately it seemed to be too late for her. She was hooked on such awful treatment because it was all she knew. She'd need hours with a counsellor, but she wouldn't go to one unless tied up and dragged there.

"What would happen if I said that you should stay with him for now?" The tiny changes in her facial muscles and gestures spoke volumes: that was precisely what she wanted him to tell her. But was it what he ought to tell her? The more he looked at her the more he felt like protecting her, and…he tried hard to deny how he was feeling, suppress it. Did the nanos contain the right chemicals to manufacture a cure for this?

"I could cope with him. All I have to do is be careful. I can handle him. But I want to be on my own!" she said plaintively. "I want to get away. Now!"

"Maybe you should leave right away."

"Yeah," she said, unconvinced. It's what she'd told herself that she wanted (and in a way really did), it's what she needed (or she might end up dead), but it's what she never really would do. She wasn't ready, not yet.

"It's a real dilemma," he told her, trying to keep his voice and words professionally neutral, "and I can see why you've been agonizing over it."

She smiled at him again, pleading silently for help. He saw no guile there, no desire or even ability to manipulate. So often people came to him ostensibly for advice but they were really just trying to foist responsibilities on him—responsibilities other than the ones contracted for. They wanted him to suggest whatever course of action, whatever choice, they already preferred. That way, if things went wrong, they could blame him. "I'm so glad you're there for me," she said.

"Well," he said. "It is why I'm here." It was his job, after all. At first people had put Solomons in the same league as astrologers and palm-readers, out to make money off gullible people, but as Don himself had told a reluctant client who accused him of being no better than a fortune-teller, "I don't claim to foresee the future; I help make it."

"What should I do?" Lila asked simply.

"Are you working full-time?"

"No. But I will be someday. They said they like my work, and they know I'm smart enough, I think I'll get more work, probably become a manager."

Don was dismayed by her self-delusion. The fact was she didn't have enough income or maybe even common sense to survive out in the world, and wasn't smart enough to accept all the help she'd need, from those who could provide it. Except him.

She sat quietly, hands playing with each other on the edge of his desk. She'd descended into a baleful silence, blinking rapidly and occasionally licking her lips; her breathing, too, suggested she was on the verge of crying. If only—despite himself, despite his training and sense of the proper bounds of things, he reached out and put his hand on top of hers. At first she flinched, more out of surprise than displeasure, then let his hand remain there unresisted. She blinked back tears.

"You do deserve better than this," he said in a low voice, trying to slow his heartbeat through conscious effort.

"I know." But she only half-knew it.

If he were smart himself, he'd pull back now. But in a world like this, so complex and full of danger that it needed Solomons, she was something rare, special. Her innocence, her trust, her gentleness drew him in irresistibly. He stroked the back of one of her fingers, and she took hold of his thumb, squeezing it needfully. "Life has gotten so complicated," he told her, wanting her to understand that this was more than a formula to recite to distressed clients; "that's why we're around." Yes, to relieve people of having to make so many agonizing decisions: do I take this job or that? quit this one in case that one arises? leave her for that other one? But as all the Solomons knew, enhanced brains meant responsibilities. What could he do about this situation?

Because now he was becoming one of the complications....

Lila sniffed, and removed one of her hands from beneath his in order to wipe the corner of her eye. But she put it right back under again.

"I think you should leave him now," he said, and as soon as the words were out of his mouth he knew they were absolutely wrong. He didn't need nanos in his head to tell him that this was not right—not yet, anyway—but he couldn't stop himself. The words were right in a way, maybe in two ways: they were what she really ought to do (even if she couldn't), and they were certainly what was right for him. He knew that if he sent her back to Isaac she'd stay there forever, or until another abusive son of a bitch came along. She disappear forever into that pit.

She looked at him hard, panic widening her eyes and freezing the muscles in her cheeks and chin. "Oh! Do you think so?"

He didn't say anything; he couldn't bear to lie to her any more, even though his silence was itself a lie. He knew she'd fail to see the discomfort and uncertainty in his expression, but would read his silence as absolute self-confidence. She was likely thinking, he must be right; I have to do that. She'd come only to hear him confirm and reinforce what she'd already decided to do, but he'd done quite the opposite, and she was in shock. He could see her trying to come up with more arguments favouring staying with Isaac.

"What should I do?"

"Move in with someone who won't kick you out."

"Nobody I know—"

"Find someone. And come back to see me in three days."

"Oh." Her expression shifted with her internal struggles.

"Get your things together and leave him when he's not home. Stay with a friend and come back on Thursday; we'll talk some more then." And by then he'd smarten himself up.

"I don't know what to—"

"You came to me for advice. That's what I've advised." And you could try to beat me up if things don't work out, he thought; I'd certainly deserve it.

"Okay…well. Um."

She stood up, but hardly moved as she tried to absorb what was happening. She hugged her purse to her chest, and Don got up and went 'round the desk to urge her on her way.

"Come on," he told her, "you have to act now or you'll never be happy. You'll be in that situation forever."

"Nooo—"

Don smiled reassuringly at her. I need that kind a smile for myself. "I think I know what I'm talking about."

"Yeah."

"It'll be okay, Lila. Whether you believe me or not, you deserve better than to get yelled at all the time. You deserve better than getting pushed around. You deserve better than to be called stupid all the time, even when you're right."

"How did you know—?" She got over her amazement at his guess and looked very unsure once more.

"Go on. I know you're brave enough." He put his hand on her back and drew her to the door. He was going down a slippery slope, but didn't want to care. Feelings he'd thought dead and buried long ago, when he'd taken over from the previous Don, were resurfacing. He'd wanted to be a professional carer, to help people, see their faces relax as they watched someone else take on the burden of their tormenting decisions. He could do good for people, and get paid well for it, and as for the risk—

—Well, if he was going to die some day at the hands of a furious client, at least it would be from trying to do some good.

Lila finally left, wordlessly, more unhappy than ever. Maybe she wouldn't come back after all, but he'd tried. If she ignored his advice, and did what she should have done—found the strength and sense inside herself to leave, no matter how long that took—then no harm done to his reputation, no ache for his conscience. If she listened to him, though—he called up her file to record a forty percent discount. Maybe that's the only help I can give you, he thought; maybe you'll see you deserve it.

⌐⌐

On Thursday he was sure Lila wouldn't come. He'd spent the past couple of days thinking about her and trying not to, and once called Nyk Solomon intending to ask his advice—but then told him, "No, never mind, I can handle it." Things he hadn't felt for years resurfaced, things he thought had died when his wife left him. He hated himself for it.

That afternoon he had two appointments, the first a young man trying to decide whether to buy another house or rent one instead. Don guided him through the pros and cons, satisfying both the client and himself that they had covered all the possibilities before he would commit himself. He barely concentrated, though, and that made him error-prone. Solomons were the voluntary scapegoats of the age, taking on the duty and consequences of making agonizing choices for overburdened people; but if a Solomon couldn't pay attention, and ooze confidence, he wasn't much good to anyone. The client noticed his distraction once, and Don pleaded fatigue.

"Leave it all up to me," he said.

"Sure," the young man said with a combination of hope and skepticism. Some people weren't completely sure whether a Solomon could really come up with a better answer than they could themselves, but the prospect of having someone else make the decision was enough reason to come. Every year people had to struggle with more and more decisions, thanks to technology and the volatile job situation, until they started to suffer an almost debilitating form of future shock. So many decisions people had to make these days were 50-50; you could be torn over one for months without finding an answer. Such a world of uncertainties was truly a Hell—one that humanity had created itself. So the Solomons had come along, filling the void with their enhanced brains and their nanos and their willingness to accept abuse—even physical abuse, within limits—for a decision gone wrong. In exchange, they got a good living. Society had decriminalized and even licensed, but never fully accepted, prostitution and drug-dealing, and placed the Solomons in the same twilight category.

"It's obvious to me," he told the client, "that you should rent for three years, save your money, and buy then if mortgage rates haven't gone up by more than two points."

What happened to the young man's face then was the sort of thing the Solomons sought above all: every feature softened, every muscle in his body relaxed. "Yeah, that's good! I can't believe I won't have to think about this again," he said.

"You won't. That's one less worry for you." A Solomon couldn't guarantee success, but he or she could guarantee relief from a dilemma. And the options were usually so evenly matched, most clients shrugged off a wrong decision: oh, well, no one could have known for sure.

One or two even showed up afterward to thank him for steering them in the right direction.

"Thank you," the young man said, now smiling as he realized how much of a load had been lifted. Don was nearly as glad about what he'd been able to accomplish. The contract still lay on the desk between them. "Thank you so much. Honest to God, I don't understand why you do this."

"It's a job," Don said, and the young man nodded; people these days understood the need to take whatever came along. Even those with supposedly good, secure jobs knew they were themselves a mere step or two from unemployment. Just as he was always a step or two from death. "I make a good living," Don told him, "and you get used to what happens sometimes."

He'd bought the previous Don's license as an act of desperation, borrowing from friends to buy the nanos, after three years of unemployment, when it became obvious he might never join the ranks of the lucky few with work. His consolation was the pleasant neighbourhood; he was a short walk from the edge of the Don Valley, where he could enjoy the simple pleasure of seeing the fall colours, the rushing cars, and the downtown towers now webbed with aerial walkways.

The client shyly took his leave, obviously feeling he'd pried too much. Don put in a call to Sca Solomon to see if any new pain-suppression programs had come across his desk. Sca was a great source of pain-killers;

he'd once been an anaesthetic technician at Scarborough General. Now, he was letting truck drivers beat him up over bad betting advice.

Another casualty of the times.

Then, to his surprise, she came, and at seeing her he was overwhelmed by a dozen different emotions: delight at her soft looks, shame at his feelings, disappointment in what he read in her apologetic slouch.

"You're still with Isaac," he said as she lowered herself into the chair across from him. No reply, as if he were the one she'd hurt by not following his advice. "Wasn't there anyone—?"

"I told you. I wasn't sure someone else would kick me out."

"I wouldn't ever kick you out." He said it almost before he realized it. He was losing all his professionalism, all his credibility. But right now he didn't care, because another Jay could walk through that door any day now, beat him up over a decision that had turned out badly, and fail to stop himself before that one fatal blow.

"Move in with you?" she asked, incredulous. "What—?"

"It's the only thing to do." His mind raced. "I know your situation better than anyone because I'm a Solomon, so I know enough not to ever kick you out. I couldn't if I wanted to."

She took that as a fact, even though it made little sense and wasn't anywhere near true. No Solomon's mind ever provided incontrovertible conclusions; life itself didn't offer them.

"I live upstairs. There's a separate guest room. You can stay there. Go home, get your stuff together, and take a cab back here. I'll pay the fare."

"Okay," she said automatically, used to having people tell her what to do. But she didn't move until Don rose and held out his hand to her. She let him lead her by the elbow to the door. I've lost my mind, he thought; but he couldn't see her go—and go back there. If he lost his license, so be it. 50-50.

He couldn't believe he was really feeling this way about her. After all, she might well drive him crazy over time, given the gap in their mental abilities. What would they talk about? But his reaction to her had nothing to do with the intellect. Maybe that was why he was reacting so strongly; maybe she satisfied a hunger he'd long denied. And not just physical, either, though that was definitely part of it. She had evoked tender feelings he thought his wife had taken with her when the stresses of life had torn her away from him. He could spend all day making others feel better, but never even wondered about his own condition, never known how much he needed to find that softness again.

Then Lila came along, a beam of uncomplicated purity and vulnerability and honesty in a dark, complicated world. All he could do now was face the consequences, as bravely as he faced the Jays of the world.

An hour later, Lila actually, amazingly, returned; she stood at the door to his basement office holding a giant green garbage bag bulging and in places dangerously stretched with stuff. She looked so lost and sweet that she drove all his reservations from his mind. He took her bag from her; she surrendered it easily.

"How did you get away?" he asked as she came inside.

"Isaac wasn't home today." And that's why you were able to come in the first place, he thought.

"Okay. Let me show you to your room." He led her up the carpeted staircase, and through the open door to the ground floor of the house. He winced at the newspaper and magazine clippings scattered all over his kitchen and living room: articles about economics, politics, sports, anything to help him with his decision-making. Lila would have to get used to that, and was the sort who could accommodate him, no matter what. He'd turned his extra bedroom into a storage room, but he managed to clear away cardboard and bankers boxes of clippings files to make room for his spare futon. When it was fully extended he went to find bedding for it, Lila tagging along helplessly behind him.

"I don't think this is a good idea," she said.

In the linen closet he found an old fitted sheet that he'd never bothered to fold, and drew it together into a lump. "I know. And I can't guarantee it'll work out." He found a pillow and pillowcase, too, and carried them to the bedroom. "But I can guarantee that Isaac will start hitting you soon."

"I could go to a shelter—"

He snickered. No, she wouldn't, and she knew it. Better the devil you knew—and anyway, there were few shelters left these days, thanks to cutbacks. "I want you safe. Don't worry; you'll have privacy. I won't bother you." He tossed the bedding down, figuring she could do this a lot better than he could.

She gave him that smile again. Her smiles were always so real—he wanted to draw her closer, hold her…he blinked the thought away. "Leaving him is the only way to stop his abuse," he told her. "We both know that's true."

"Do you do this for everybody?"

He hesitated. "No. Only when I think it's the best idea." He turned to leave. "You get settled; I still have another appointment today." She stood there, still partly in shock. Just having her in the house warmed it. "The kitchen's all yours; find yourself something to eat."

Concentrate, he ordered himself as he went back downstairs. His next client had asked to see him over a medical question—should she get the genetic test or not?—and he'd have to keep his mind focused. Few questions were more important; few demanded his whole enhanced brain the way this one did. He'd have to try to keep Lila's smile buried somewhere very, very deep.

That night she sat watching TV, flipping through the channels till she found some truly mindless sitcom he didn't recognize, while he tried to straighten up the house and then read in his bedroom. When it was time to go to bed they had some awkward moments over the use of the bathroom. As he tried to sleep he couldn't stand the thought of her being all the way at the other end of the house. He fantasized, childishly, about her knocking on his door. And if he took the initiative himself, told her how he felt (or beginning to feel; surely he hadn't known her long enough), she'd go running in fear back to Isaac.

The next morning he was sure he'd find her gone, but she sat in the kitchen, in a long nightgown and robe, eating toast made from some old wheat bread he'd had in the fridge and seeming right at home. "Good morning!" she said between bites.

"Good morning. How'd you sleep?"

"Okay." Not well at all, he saw. "I can't thank you enough—" Her hand fluttered in frustration.

"Don't say anything."

"Can I make you breakfast? I make a great omelette. Do you have cottage cheese?" She was as desperate to do things for him as he was to help her—although only out of gratitude.

"No. It's okay; I usually just have cereal."

They spent their breakfast together like that, two people reading each other's habits and accommodating them, like a married couple…he wanted to spend the whole morning with her, just talking, maybe slumped together on the couch, his arm around her as he listened to her stories about Isaac's behaviour, the things he could put an end to.

He showered and got ready to go down to his office, and she prepared to go to work. He warned her that Isaac would look for her there; she should stay home, today at least. She was smart enough to know that if she didn't go in, someone else would have her job before the day was over.

"He'll find you if you stay there," Don said. "Try to get another job." But they both knew how likely she was to find one.

Before leaving she said, "I honestly don't know why you do this."

The question again. "People need us," he said, giving her the party line. "Life gives people too many agonizing choices now—"

"I know. I mean you. Why do you do this?"

He didn't know what to tell her. Yes, the money was good—he could charge a fortune for the privilege of berating him, even shoving him. Maybe because it was so damned easy. And maybe, after all, he really did want to help people, do just a little to brighten and simplify the world for them.

"Don't you agonize yourself?"

"Yes." He couldn't tell her how dangerously easy it was to play God. Let the nanos do their work, and sometimes just mentally flip a coin. He wasn't selling right decisions; he was selling an end to worry.

"But do you really know if you're right?"

"Well—" he began. Then he understood why he'd taken the chance of advising her the way he did; he realized that there was a difference between being right and being correct. "As much as any human being can," he said, then went downstairs to lose himself in his work.

The agonizing ones came in a steady stream: financial decisions, medical decisions, work decisions. For some people he knew he was a crutch, not a necessity; they came to him only because he was there, not because they really had terrible dilemmas. If they were willing to pay his fee, he wasn't going to argue with them. The woman who couldn't decide what to serve her guests at her daughter's wedding clearly had more money than she knew what to do with. While dealing with her silly problem he heard his front door open upstairs: Lila come back from work. The thought of her being there made even Wedding Lady tolerable. And fortunately, no one came to complain—

Until later that afternoon when he was on the phone to Nyk Solomon again, and the doorbell rang. His door opened, and a haggard-looking man came in, eyes roving the office and passing lightly over Don. He had a blond ponytail and wore a ratty but clean jean jacket.

"Yes?" Nyk faded, but didn't disappear.

"You the Solomon?" He'd been drinking, but it was clear that alcohol only aggravated his natural belligerence.

"Yes. Can I help you?"

"Where is she?"

Don's stomach dropped. "Who?" he asked in as firm a voice as he could muster.

"Don't fuck with me. I seen the debit."

They had a joint account. Of course they would.

"Where the fuck is she?"

"Even if I knew I wouldn't—"

Isaac's hands were already on him, pushing and whacking with the heels of his palms. The breath was gone, and Don struggled to regain it. The endorphins kicked in immediately, pushing the pain away as best they could—but Isaac was unremitting. Suddenly Don was flattened against the wall behind his desk, spit and fists flying at him. He tried vainly to block the punches. This was what Lila had to deal with, this was what he was trying to save her from....

"What's going on? Don! What's going on?"

And if he let Isaac kill him, the bastard would be put away forever...she'd be safe...but Don would never be with her. Or she might be drawn to another Isaac. 50-50. Don shielded himself and communicated silently, hoping he still had time. "The fast codes! Now! And the cops—"

"Fucking bastard! Tell me where the hell she went!"

Nyk Solomon transmitted the fast programs to his nanos, and Don begged them to hurry. Then Nyk vanished to make the call. The bruises and cuts started healing almost immediately. Isaac, meanwhile, began to smarten up or tire, it was hard to tell which. "You called the fucking cops, didn't you?"

"Stop it! Isaac!"

"Aww, fuck!" Don looked up to warn Lila away, and saw the small knife in Isaac's hand—had he used it, had the nanos masked the pain? He couldn't turn around to check, but felt wetness against his back....

The nanos worked furiously to repair him, but he had so much damage he could hardly move. He could barely see Isaac drag her through the door by her upper arm. She didn't resist. She looked back at him once, with glazed, empty eyes.

"Don! Don Solomon! Are you okay?" Nyk reappeared, eyes wide with fear. Don had come so close, and that fact tore at Nyk, and would tear at every Solomon in the city, every Solomon in the world, when word got out.

"I should be dead now," Don said. The nanos raced through his bloodstream, raced along his nerve endings.

"The cops are on their way. They'll be—"

"I cheated." The pain was still there, buried deep.

"I know." Nyk thought he meant Death; Don couldn't correct him. "You cheated Him good. We all do."

He'd cheated, all right: given advice he'd known was wrong. Or at least incorrect. "I paid for it, too," he said aloud, not caring if Nyk continued to misunderstand him. Maybe he'd still lose his license, even though she hadn't stayed. He'd lose on both counts. Then again, the nanos were pretty powerful devices. They worked wonders on pain. And he could cheat other fates, too. The point was, he'd been wrong, but he'd been right, too.

"Come on," Nyk said. "Your next client. Think about your next client. People need you."

Don stayed there for a moment longer, letting himself not care about bad clients and unhappy customers, letting the nanos work their magic on him, so that he'd be able to face more agonized people. The nanos poured endorphins through his system, and just for a little while, as the siren grew louder, he thought only of why he did this. Because they needed him. Because he needed them.

The cops would come, find him recovering, offer to take him to the hospital anyway, and he'd decline. He'd want to be here when the doorbell rang again.

Heir To the Throne

Jocko Benoit

Vince sat on the throne admiring his work. Another bare bathroom wall gone down to defeat. He read his work with what for someone else might have been pride but for him was simply glee.

"While all you white boys are sitting here I'm giving your beautiful white girls beautiful black babies so me and my brothers can grow strong at last."

What interested him most was not what he had written two days ago, but what so many other people had written in response. As far as he could tell there were a lot of heirs to his throne in terms of cultural politics. He smiled a vengeful smile. He had been called a racist so many times by snobs from his school and yet here was the proof that he wasn't so special. He wasn't perverted and abnormal. He was simply expressing a will more common than anyone would admit. The same went for identical wall declarations he had written on behalf of gays and Jews. One classmate had said to him once that he needed to try to understand people. Vince slammed one of the boy's books up into his face and made his nose bleed. As it turned out, Vince knew people better than anyone knew.

But almost right away the satisfaction of the afternoon went drier than the pens he used for his art. Uninspired by the latest triumph, he left the stall, the washroom and the bus station across from his uncle's liquor store where he had just booked out for the afternoon. There was a screw turning slowly inside him that his mother called indigestion, but he knew was something else. Everytime it turned he thought of his art teacher from elementary school and how she said that all his violent pictures of guns and bombs and knives and people being beaten and body parts all over the page had no place in any art class and that if he couldn't really try to express himself in an artistic way then she would have to make him do something else during her art sessions. So she showed him how to cut out paper dolls. And he would only ever use the white paper because a memory of his daddy saying something long ago before he ran off—something about white being the only cloth that God cuts from.

Vince ran his eyes over the wall mural scenery outside the bus station, passing over much of it without noticing because so much of it was the same old stuff. But today there were a lot of new additions. Somebody had been busy over the weekend. There were the usual bubble signatures and self-portraits of neighborhood artists, as they liked to call themselves, he thought with a smirk, and there were the same old twisted rainbows of abstract design as well as a few fluid narrative murals with some of the same old stories of pride and conquest even he could recognize and understand and truly resent. But someone had, what was the expression these so-called artists liked to use, 'bombed' an old wall-size mural of giant basketball stars and replaced it with a collage of differently stylized bits that Vince recognized from somewhere. Then it came to him. His mother made him watch all that PBS stuff—"cable is important to keep paying for because it's educational," she always argued while she was in the middle of Jeopardy— and he could tell that he'd seen pieces of that mural before. There were Egyptian hieroglyphs, a few gylphs from— who was it?— The Maya? Pock-marked pictures of bulls and antelope and saber-toothed tigers and handprints. Stickmen. The drawings of humans, the solar system, the double-helix he remembered were sent on the Voyager probe. All side by side along with many other drawings he didn't recognize. And there didn't seem to be a point to the collection. It didn't develop into something new like so many of the murals he'd seen. And the pictures, as far as he could tell, were exact copies of the originals. And there was no signature anywhere he could see. It sure wasn't by anyone from this 'hood, he knew.

He would have wondered about the design a little longer except that something else caught his eyes. The design on the side of the abandoned bakery next to the bus station was new too. The flaking white wall facing the terminal was covered by curls and fronds of color. He stopped in front of the new mural someone had painted over the wall and could make out amid the explosions of brown and yellow and green and blue a series of jungle trees and in their crowns a wrecked car, a bus, a TV set and the remains of the stature of liberty. And standing taller than the jungle with its peculiar decorations were a black man and an Hispanic man shaking hands. Both figures were muscled and lean, beads of sweat on their foreheads and collecting at their chins. In their free hands were a pick and a shovel. Vince didn't know what to make of it, but he could feel the anger buzzing inside him. It wasn't the color of their skin just then. It was the hand grabbing hand and the smiles they gave one another. It was a scene that looked so real and yet he had never seen anything like it in real life. The anger, he knew, was because he hated lies.

By the time the bus let him off near the apartment building he knew what he had to do. And by the time the elevator reached the floor of the apartment he knew he would have to do it that night. And when he opened the door and saw his mother checking her lottery ticket numbers against the ones on the TV screen he knew she hadn't bought him the pens he'd asked for.

"Ma," he said, pausing when she shushed him.

The last number flashed up on the screen and she said a quiet "damn".

"Ma?"

"Yes, Vince," she said in a caring but somewhat distant voice.

"Did you get those pens I need for school?"

"I meant to, Vince, but those bastards at work didn't give us our pay on time again," she said perfectly reasonably.

"How many tickets did you buy?"

"Oh these?" she held up two tickets with one hand while her other hand rustled the newspaper on her lap. "Just two, and I bought these a week ago."

"Maaah," he whined resignedly.

"Don't 'maah' me, young man. One day we'll win one of these things and you won't be complaining then. The lottery might just be our salvation one of these days."

"There's no lottery big enough to help people like you and me, Ma." He went into the kitchen and pulled out the jam and peanut butter and four slices of slightly stale bread. "We've got to fend for ourselves because there ain't nobody going to do that for us. The way things are."

"You're talking just like your father, Vince," she let the newspaper slip down her legs to the floor as she leaned around the chair. "And look where that kind of talk gets you. It's either hard word or luck that gets things done— it never helped anyone to go blaming others for your own misfortunes. And God knows I work hard and never get anywhere so luck is bound to be just the thing we've got and ain't aware of yet."

"Mmm hmm," he stuffed a sandwich in his mouth and walked past her to his bedroom.

"Are you going anywhere tonight, Vincey? I want to go to bed early tonight and I can't do that if you're going to be out."

He took the sandwich out of his mouth and turned briefly toward her. "Nah, I'll do some homework with one of my old pens and then watch TV for awhile," he said perfectly reasonably.

The last bus back to the terminal that night came just as he was coming out the back door of the apartment building and he had to cut across the front courtyard and wave frantically, without yelling, for it to stop for him. He staggered breathlessly through the door and spun around so he plopped down in the handicapped seats. He winced as the can in his inside jacket pocket jammed up into his ribs.

He smiled at his reflection in the window as it zipped across the dark city streets. The smile only lasted a few blocks, though. When the bus passed Vivki's place he turned away from the window and stared down at the seat he was on. Someone had taken a black marker and written on the sheet metal in front of him so that the bus driver couldn't see. "L.B. loves K.C." A new one he'd never seen before. But then he didn't sit near the front of the bus much. He didn't recognize the initials at first, but the only people that he knew fit were Larry Bowers and Kevin Chandler. Maybe he would pass that on tomorrow in school, if he didn't sleep in after his mother left for work.

He remembered the time he and Valerie had gone out on their last date. He'd thought about writing something about them on the bus seat they sat in— because, he explained to her, no one would ever know that they had written it because most people only made those hearts to make fun of someone else and embarrass them by pairing them with the ugliest or geekiest person in the school.

"So which one would be which between us?" she cocked her head and asked him bluntly.

"Uh…"

She smiled and he put his pen away.

And that would have been the last big screw-up if he hadn't been trying to find something to say to her while they were sitting on the front steps of her parents' place later on. He picked at the peeling paint on the wrought iron railing and tried to find the right words to tell her how special she was, although he wanted to say something that didn't have the word 'special' in it.

"You know," he said, ricocheting a glance off her curious stare and then looking back at the railing bars to his side, "we've got a lot in common, you and me."

"Oh yeah?" she gave a wry smile and brushed back the hair from his forehead while she leaned down to hear him a little better.

He turned his head sideways and saw her sideways head and thought "KISS", but he turned away and the urge passed. It had to be the right time, he knew.

"Well, we're both the same age and we want the same kinds of things—

simple things." He could see Valerie's slight nod from the corner of his eye. Now, he thought, and he leaned back and snuck his arm behind her so that his back was propped up against the top step and his forearm was just barely touching her back. She inched over towards him on the step almost imperceptibly while she adjusted her dress underneath her. "You and I," he said, "have got the world working against us these days," he put his arm around her warm waist and he felt the warmth move all the way up his arm and right through his body. Valerie leaned into him, her body a new movement that was part of him, surprising him. "Someday you and me maybe will beat those bastards at their game and I'll be happy. Hell, if I could make you happy that'd make me happy right there." Now she had her arm around his waist and gave him a squeeze. "Never mind the jews and the fags and the niggers— look out boys, Vicky and Vince are catching up."

When her arm pulled away slowly and she began to sit up straight a little away from him he at first thought she'd been offended by what he was implying about them having a family together and raising a whole lot of kids. Too soon, he thought, to bring that kind of stuff up. Stupid. Stupid!

"You don't really mean that, do you?" she wasn't looking at him.

"What? Hey, I didn't mean that we'd get married or anything like—"

"No— the other stuff."

"What other stuff?"

"About the great white race and all that crap."

"What's the matter? Haven't you ever thought about why people like us are so poor, why we can't ever seem to get anywhere? Hey, what's the—?"

She was standing up, brushing off her dress. "Look, Vince," she said, still not looking at him, "I just don't want to hear that kind of thing. I didn't know you…Maybe we should think about a few things before we go out again." And she started to reach for his face to touch it but then turned around without another glance and went past the cardboard Santa Claus pin-up her father never got around to taking down until it was time to put up again.

"What does what I said change, Valerie?" he said to the door. "I'm still the same guy. Come on!"

But she didn't come on. She would still look at him once in a while in the hallways at school and she would talk to him whenever he called her after that but she was mostly distant and sometimes even cold or angry. "Can't we talk about this? Can't you let me explain? Or can't you tell me what I could do different?" But nothing he tried broke through the casual careful tone she took with him. The last time they talked she did say he couldn't do anything about it because he just wasn't what she'd thought he was. And he'd corrected her and said don't you mean who you thought I was? She hung up.

He leaned back toward the window and felt the hard cylinder jab into his side again. It was better than walking around with a knife or a gun like some people he knew. It gave him a profound sense of consolation and he smiled again, remembering where he was going.

Hitler was a failed artist too and Vince could identify with that, but it wasn't Hitler he admired most. He didn't need that kind of attention. He just wanted to have some control over what people thought. Not what they thought exactly, but the shape of it, the feel of it, the color of it. Just like Goebbels. He wanted to inherit the mantle of chief propaganda minister. And he didn't even need for people to know his name. It was enough for him to remain anonymous and provoke people the way artists were supposed to provoke them, the way the artists in the past on PBS always did, and not like those other guys with the quiet voices who painted pretty pictures for a half hour on TV.

He slipped off the bus quietly a few blocks from where his target was and snuck through the darkened neighborhood, careful not to look too much like he was sneaking through. When he was sure there was no one around, he climbed on top of the dumpster under the mural and spray-painted thick black swastikas over the groins of the two figures and an even larger swastika right where their hands met in a handshake. He tried to reach up to the smiles on their faces, but when he tried to spray up towards them the spray just drifted off and down, some of it on his face and in his eyes. He gave a short shout and almost fell off the dumpster, but managed to crouch down, regain his composure and slip back to the ground, looking all around him for any sign of movement. He looked back up at his retouching of the mural and smiled a real smile for the first time in days.

When he was walking away for the long trip back home he passed the 'PBS' wall he'd noticed before, but now there was something different sprayed on it. "Busy wall," he thought and wondered why so many kids were interested in bombing only one wall and leaving the others for the most part alone. When he moved toward the wall to get a better look he could see stars, suns, planets, nebulae. The closer he got the more he felt like he was looking right up into a real sky and he had a feeling of vertigo similar to the kind he felt when he went to the Imax shows with planes and roller coasters. He had to step back in an instant of panic to regain the edges of the wall and street. It didn't take him long to pick out something that looked like Earth, bigger than it should have been, he suspected, circling the sun. And there was a long arcing yellow line or white— he couldn't tell even when he squinted. It ran from Earth to something higher up on the wall that looked like a small bright red planet near a spiral nebula. There were numbers in fluorescent pink here and there on the mural and Vince tried to follow them to see if he could figure out what the artist was trying to say. He'd been to galleries and museums when nobody was looking and he recognized modern mural art when he saw it. The trouble was he couldn't tell who had done it and what it was all about. That was enough to irritate him.

But he also wondered why he didn't smell the paint. He leaned in closer and all he got was a different smell that he couldn't quite place. So he knew from what he remembered from another PBS special on smell that he had never smelled it before because then the odor would have brought back memories of when he had smelled it. He moved right up to the wall, swallowing once as the star-studded blackness engulfed him and he touched the wall. It was damp. When he pulled his fingers away he turned towards the nearest streetlight and looked for paint on them. Nothing but moisture. He touched the wall again and slid his fingers across it to soak up some paint. What he noticed was that the wall didn't seem rough at all. Much smoother than a wall, and, he stopped, spongy, almost with a little give where he pressed his fingers hardest.

Vince jumped back, a sudden case of the night jitters hitting him, and he sprayed at the Earth and the nebula and the red planet and as many of the stars as he could, blacking them out. Then he ran off down the street, suddenly sure somebody was watching him. And he made it home with fits and starts of running and walking so that he could get a few hours of sleep before school.

Something made him go to school the next morning— a kind of conscience that made him balance out a prank with improved attendance. Besides, he'd reasoned, he had an appointment with the guidance counsellor and he'd already missed three. It made him angry that a free period had to get wasted like that, but he swung through the doorway of the counsellor on time that afternoon and sat, sunglasses down, eyes peeking over the rims, in the chair opposite Mr. McGreevy. The Guidance Officer, as he liked to be called, was staring at a computer screen to one side of him, tilted just far enough away so that Vince couldn't, even if he had cared, see anything on it. He kept clapping his pen on his desk as if the pen was a paper cutter or a guillotine blade.

"So, Mr. Cameron, I was beginning to think you didn't exist except as a data entry." He smiled without turning to Vince and kept speaking to him while looking at the screen. Vince imagined the man in the turtlneck as a kind of yuppie wizard who was able to look into the glass or through it and see the future. "So, you're about to accidentally graduate out of high school. Have you given any thoughts to what you want to do with your life?"

Vince's eyes lifted lazily up over the dark lenses. "I wanna be an artist," he said.

"I'm sure you do, Mr. Cameron. But there are enough con artists out there already, don't you think?"

"Do I know you?" Vince demanded.

The tone in his voice startled McGreevy so that he almost turned to face the boy. "What do you mean?"

"You and me ain't never even met, so you don't got any right to say anything about me. What the hell do you think you can tell me about my life? Does it say on that thing what I like to eat, who my favorite movie star is?"

"No," McGreevy recomposed himself, "but your little outburst tells me that everything I see here is pretty well true. You've got to settle down, Mr. Cameron, now and after you leave this office. You're not unintelligent according to the files, but you're pretty dumb. Employers don't always care about your grades— especially if they're looking over your criminal record."

"It's just a few misunderstandings."

"Look, you've got maybe one more chance to turn things around. I know it can't be easy growing up without a father, but you've got to rise above your circumstances—"

With one quick motion Vince spun his chair away, got to his feet and gave McGreevy the finger. "Rise above this!"

He squeezed roughly past a secretary and came out in the hallway, right in front of his favorite nerd, Roger. He changed his momentum and bumped into the boy so hard that his glasses flew off and he spun with his books to the floor. "Oh geez, Roger. I'm sorry," he gushed. "Here, let me help you get your stuff." He pushed some papers over towards Roger and made a point of wiping the dirt from his sneakers all over them, ripping as much as possible in the process. Only once did Roger ever get in a last shot. A few months back he had called Vince a "big dumb white trash loser". He had called him that for a long time before, Vince knew.

All the geeks felt that way about him and he was only too happy to play the game they forced on him. And this time, many fists after his last insult, Roger only whimpered once and sat there until he was sure Vince was gone and he could get up.

When he walked up to his uncle's liquor store the next day, Vince couldn't believe what he saw. There were one or two people looking at his handiwork and shaking their heads and walking on, but it was the other wall that had him going. The space mural was gone and was replaced by what looked like a rebus puzzle with all the pluses and minuses missing. He saw tiny symbols from around the world— the logos for fast food joints, banks, gas companies, even the five linked circles of the Olympics. And no signature. He wanted to see if the paint was still wet, but he knew he would look suspicious if he went over there in broad daylight. He decided that he was being in some very subtle way challenged.

So when he got off late and was sure no one was looking he casually spray-painted right in the middle of the design "Beware of" with as big a swastika as he could make without sticking around for too long.

He found his mother asleep when he got home and took the phone into the small kitchen and faced the corner of the room while he talked to Valerie. "Look," he tried to find the right voice without sounding whining. "Would you just let me come by for a bit tonight so I can explain or make it up to you? You're all I think about and I think you feel like I do."

Valerie told him that he could stop by, but that it didn't change anything. Even though her voice was cold, something told Vince that she really wanted him even though she didn't like everything about him. He could feel it on the night when he screwed up and that caring was still there just under the ice.

The plan was to go back to the wall later that night and add "we're watching you" underneath the swastika and then go to Valerie's, but when he went made it back to the neighborhood and turned the corner of the building and stood back he saw a completely different design. He ran his whole palm over the surface and it came up wet, but uncolored. Now there were hundreds of flags, including the Union Jack, arranged neatly in columns and rows covering the wall. He was getting angry. And determined. Suddenly he knew that he was in the first major turf battle of his life and that he was fighting for the right to have his work survive on top of any and everyone else's. There was a crown up for grabs and he was going to win it for the fate of the white race and the world.

It took him a half hour, ducking in and out of shadow between sprays until he'd written over most of the flags he could reach, save the Union Jack. The paint was so thick that there was more dripping than usual and it oozed his passion down in black rivulets to the ground.

He tucked the can back in his jacket that he slung over his shoulder. He resisted the urge to whistle, but he couldn't resist the urge to find a spot down the nearest alley and relieve himself before heading home. When he was done he wiped the last bit of sweat from his forehead and gave a parting glance at the wall.

If he hadn't just relieved himself a moment before he would have when he took in what was there. Everything was gone— his graffiti, the flags. And there were stop, yield, slippery when wet, rockslide, poison, explosive, corrosive signs and many others all over the wall, glistening and fluorescent. It was like the nightmare he had after studying for his beginner's driver's license. The signs in shimmering yellow and red glowered down at him. All he knew was that he wasn't going to see if the paint was still wet.

Suddenly he wondered if the whole wall wasn't some sort of a giant TV screen and someone was playing tricks on him. He picked up a rock and threw it hard at the wall. It sounded a dull thud and bounced away as if from a trampoline, skittering away on the street.

Vince fumbled for his jacket pocket, never taking his eyes from the wall, and came up with the can, dropping his coat to the ground. He shook the can fiercely, slowly approaching the wall. He looked left and right and saw nothing. Then he ran back and forth spraying black paint wildly in a frantic scrawl over the signs and sealed the whole thing with the biggest swastika he could manage until the can fizzled and spuked black only in fits and starts. Then he stood back and waited.

The wall almost immediately shuddered and the colors of the signs and the shape of the swastika rippled and altered until they were replaced by a new design. Vince's hand tightened around the can. In front of him now was a picture out of a horror comic book of a boy who looked exactly like him with his eyes wide and his mouth wide as he was turning to run and behind him, over his shoulder was a graffiti-covered wall reaching out to him with enormous arms and jutting eyeless head and scissor-like teeth. He raised the can up and sprayed as if at a swarm of bugs, shouting in anger and fear until nothing came out of his mouth or the nozzle and he dropped the can and ran.

Vince walked up the steps to the cardboard Santa Claus and rapped gently on the door. No light came on, but he could hear someone coming closer and he stood back. The door opened a crack and Valerie stuck her face out so the streetlight colored and softened it. "Hi," she said, in her best starting-from-scratch voice. "You're pretty late."

"Hi. I know," he said, uncertainly.

"Wait a second," she said, closed the door a bit, took off the chain and stepped outside.

He held her hand and then leaned forward and kissed her without a word.

She opened her eyes and felt like she was seeing him all over again.

"I didn't understand before," he said. "But now I just want to tell you that it's so simple. It's you and me against the world, Valerie. And I want you to be my queen."

She wanted to run away, laugh, sneer and sigh and cry all at the same time, but she couldn't say or do anything except kiss him back. After a moment the warmth between them was too much and when she felt his hand move up under her skirt and touch her thigh she knew she couldn't stop him that night or ever again. And the more she thought how wrong he was for her the harder she kissed him.

The police were called down to invesitgate a building whose owner was fed up with kids plastering it with new grafitti every day of that week. "I mean enough is enough," the old man even stomped once. But when he took the two policeman outside to show them what he meant all the three of them saw was a bare, decrepit wall. "What the…?" the old man just stood there looking up out of the shadow to where daylight was beginning to edge down along the dingy, chipped yellow.

It was only the timing of daybreak that let one of the policemen see something odd on another nearby building. Over a jungle mural with two men meeting in brotherhood and friendship were a handful of swastikas and large words written in a scrawled pastey red-brown across the men's faces. "People of this planet, I understand you I will make more messages"

For some reason the words sent a chill through the morning air. Then the other cop stopped sipping his coffee and threw the styrofoam cup to the ground. "Look!" he half-shouted.

Beneath the mural was a dumpster and both men could now see in the morning light a hand sticking from it. When they opened the lid one of the men turned away and gagged at the sight of the headless corpse inside.

"Goddam!— it looks like he's been practically dipped in blood!"

"Shut up," the other cop gasped between gags.

The first cop looked up at the wall and could see some of the red-brown paint was still bright red in places. "Geeeez," he said slowly, letting the lid shut. "Looks like we've got ourselves another psycho. Goddam— where do these guys come from?"

Franklin Expedition, 1848

Carolyn Clink

April 28

Trapped two years in crushing ice,
our rations
almost gone, we abandon ship.
Captain Crozier leads us across
the jagged frozen floes
to King William Island.

Cinching my belt,
I take my place pulling
a lifeboat filled with tents,
blankets, guns, ammunition, tea and
chocolate. All that we have.

Blinding squalls of blowing snow
Burn my skin, eyes.
Hunger gnaws beyond the cold.
Ahold of the rope, I will not disappear.
One hundred and four men are nearby. They must be.

July

Glimpse in a mirror,
I see my skull.
Everyone's bones are on the outside.

We are on a death march
across a flat, empty landscape
of frost-shattered limestone.

Gray rock blends into gray sky. Twisted dwarf
vegetation, lichen and moss cannot sustain us,
nor do they cushion our step.

The sun brings shimmering visions.
Guns fire. Men fight. I am mad with fear,
and afraid of madness.

Autumn

Falling.
Where are my arms? Sharp stones
cut me. I cannot move.

Hands roll me over. Hazy,
two mates, charcoal on gray,
lift and toss me
                into lifeboat.

Dark
    grabbing me
                bright fire
huddled silhouettes
                approach
                        sharp
knife flickers
                skeleton
                        so little flesh

AMBERS AND GREENS

Eduardo Frank
Translated from the Spanish by
Jean-Louis Trudel

"Kevin…?"

The voice reaches you from faraway, faint, as if coming from the bottom of a well. It seems to you that it's come from the profuse greenery all around, the hundreds of monstrous plants climbing and crawling up the crystal dome like snakes. But you know that, from where you stand, it should be impossible to hear the tumultuous life of this planet in Cygnus, christened Lom by space science.

You will be gazing at the plate and reading it one more time: *IN MEMORIAM - To all the martyrs of exploration who made possible a centuries-old dream*, and the cup, which you haven't yet brought to your mouth, will be trembling between your hands. They've been the cause of everything, the dreams, the damned dreams of this cosmic illness which overwhelmed your will.

It happened step by step. It began during the trip to the lunar station. You could see it all so clearly: how you would assemble piece by piece the complexes of domes, piping, and girders until a new city rose before your eyes. And when the Supreme Council accepted your proposal, it was easy for you to get organized, compute it all to the last digit, and bring the entire project to a happy close. Each time, it happened again: another dream in the middle of the night, of so many nights, all different. The Martian night, interrupted by the hurricane winds dragging along gigantic columns of reddish dust over the endless desert. Night on Venus, caught between condensing aerosols and stations imprisoned beneath ninety atmospheres of pressure and temperatures over four hundred degrees centigrade. Night on Titan, with its tense, calm garrison under the shadow of Saturn. And then it was on Pluto, among frozen methane drifts, that a long dream stretched out a hand to show you what to do on Lom, a planet in a recently surveyed system in Cygnus. And you thought you were the sole creator of it all, that it was only your genius which counted.

So you thought, as if the shape your projects took on in real life did not matter. Back then, your dreams were fully responsive to the impulses of your conscience and never before had they turned into nightmares. Now, they've taken on a life of their own and they no longer bow to your will.

But nobody knows this. For the world at large, you will always be the great designer of the artificial rains on Mars, of the pressure regulators built on Venus, of the medicinal and nutritive plants designed to help humans in various stations and settlements scattered across neighbouring systems…And, most recently, of the erection of the first dome to reproduce the atmosphere and life of Earth in the midst of Lom's teeming, amber mists.

Your eyes lose their faraway look. You set down the cup on the table and strain to listen. You don't know if you will hear the voice again, the true voice, not the one created by your brain. And you discover that, from now on, revelations will not come only in your dreams: they will reach you also in long flashes during waking hours.

You gulp down a mouthful of coffee, though it's cold now, but it doesn't matter. The others are about to arrive. In the central instrument panel, a light will be coming on and the exploration module will begin airbraking. Less than five minutes from now, they will be entering through the airlocks and putting on clothes for work inside, their faces young and smiling, their voices buzzing as they describe their new experiences outside and fill the room with optimism as they reveal long-term and short-term projects. In a nutshell, they will be brimming over with the typical euphoria of missions which exalt the human spirit, adding to the record of efforts and successes compiled by human spacefarers.

And your body shudders. What will you have for them when they come in? Only the reflection of a dark dream soon to become a reality like the previous ones. And this time, there will be no completed projects nor buildings, only destruction and desolation, and unexpected deaths at the hands of bipedal beings, humanoids from the other side of the surrounding crystal wall, from far beyond the sea of reddish tendrils in this hostile environment of a world not yet fully known.

Your chest strains to breathe. It wouldn't be right to shatter the happy exhilaration of the young investigators. How can you tell them that your dreams were revelations of imminent realities, which materialized through the workings of an alien illness? You would have to provide them with detail after detail, to explain how a group of beings as moist and white as mushrooms will burst from their home shores, cross the stands of scabiosas surrounding the station, and tear down the airlock doors. Then how, as the cold and the pressure take their tolls on human bodies, their own skin will crumple into a pale and fragile fabric, not unlike the skin of these aquatic beings. And, in the end, how the bodies fearfully curled-up in tight balls on the carpet will be carried away…

They wouldn't believe you. They would lock you inside the happy-house and bathe you in antidepressive ions. And then deliver you into the hands of a psychiatrist.

You look outside and the glare of the twin stars blinks when the module passes in front of them. The warning light will be turning off. The small craft will have landed on the base's apron. And you will be waiting. You will be expecting the familiar steps, the well-known voices, especially that of Ilona calling you from the pantry in the exact same tones your brain— or what lairs within—reproduced a few minutes ago. And you discover that something has already happened as you'd dreamed it: taking a mouthful of cold coffee and seeing the module slip between the resplendent stars and you. After which will follow the chain of events which awakened you, flooded with terror.

It's too much. You cannot let yourself be overwhelmed by this cosmic illness, that is so advanced now…You cannot allow it to forge reality according to its whims, using you as an instrument. Only on Earth might you obtain the cure through an antidote, but it would take researchers too much time to find it and, meanwhile, who knows if you wouldn't infect someone else?

You have decided. You get up and approach the observation bay. The ship is now nuzzling the ramp.

In a moment, you will be striding hurriedly as you go through the library. You will come to the airlock at the back, open it without activating the seals, and exit into the untouched forests of Lom. For a second, you will be smelling the sweetish and bitter tones, strong and subtle, of the unfathomable jungle where the growths of an utterly alien life twist and twine. Delivered into the power of ambers and greens.

The newcomers will be filing into the dome from the showers and the young woman, rearranging strands of hair still wet, will utter your name as she goes into the pantry. There, on the table, all she will see is a half-cup of coffee. Outside, the cutting drizzle of a blackish and oily powder will be falling vertically onto your body, already white and milky, its fibers melting away under the ferns and the giant scabiosas.

Highway Closure

Aaron Humphrey

Kieran buzzed just as I was feeding my pet rust. I didn't know it was him until he came up, since I didn't bother to find out who it was before pressing the button. Just a waste of time, usually.

"You could get mugged that way," he said when he came in(my door wasn't locked either), lugging a big satchel. "Some drunk thinks it's his girlfriend's apartment and he's come to beat her up, and thinks you must be her new boyfriend or something…"

"Not likely, in this neighbourhood," I said. Or this town, really, but Kieran wasn't used to it. We didn't leave our car doors unlocked or anything, but we didn't put burglar alarms in them, either. Well, some idiots did, but they weren't natives either. The only time I'd ever been locked out of my apartment was when Kieran was staying with me.

"…or worse, it could be Jehovah's Witnesses or vacuum cleaner salesmen or something." Kieran stopped when he saw what I was doing. "Feeding Rusty, eh?"

"Its name's not Rusty," I said patiently, not for the first time, not even just to Kieran. "That's like naming a cat Puss or Boots or Fluffy." I tossed another pin into the water and put the lid back on. The rust's name was Entropy, as Kieran well knew by this time, but he liked needling me.

"Think it'd like one of these?" he said, idly toying with one of Joyce's wire sculptures I had hanging on my wall. "It'd take months to digest, like some snake eating a goat…you'd have to get it a bigger tank, probably."

I didn't rise to the bait, knowing that he'd get to the point of his visit all the sooner that way.

After a short silence, he did. "Wanna go on a trip?" he said.

"Where to?" I said, noncommittally, as if that would help.

He toyed with one of my home-glazed clay knickknacks. "I got a call from Hotch today. He says they're on the last stretch of the highway."

"Ah," I said. I'd forgotten about Highway 40. "I suppose it's too much to ask that he called from the midway point?"

He shook his head. "Nope," he said. "They're at the Grande Cache end.

Which is sorta the midway point, I guess."

"What time did you want to get there?"

"Sundown."

That'd be probably about 7:30-8:00, down there. I looked at the clock. As usual, Kieran had left it until the last minute to even mention this to me. From experience I knew that if I wasted time arguing with him about it, we'd just get an even later start and he'd make me speed, which I was loath to do, car insurance being at a criminal rate as it was. I sighed. "We'd better get going, then. Should I pack some sandwiches?"

Kieran grinned as if, while it had never occurred to him that he might need food sometime, I was an absolute genius for having thought of it. "Yeah, that might be an idea," he said. Not that it was enough of an idea for him to help me put together a few sandwiches, unless criticizing my choices of filling could be counted as helping. Then we went down to my car, where he tossed his satchel into the back seat before we set off.

ґ⁊

I had always found Kieran's tremendous fascination with highways somewhat odd, especially considering that he didn't own a car, didn't plan to, and didn't know the first thing about driving (except, perhaps, that turning the steering wheel Made It Go, as I'd thought at the age of six). The people at the Department of Highways office obviously thought that he spent half his life on the road, judging by his daily calls for updates. He made a point of getting to know people on work crews, so that he probably got even more accurate data than the Department itself, and more up-to-date. When he'd lived with me, briefly, most of the guest bedroom had been taken up with his Alberta-B.C. map, copiously marked. (He'd never said, but I gathered that responsibility for Saskatchewan and the rest of the country, and the world, was in the hands of other capable people that he trusted to discharge their duties adequately. For all I knew, he was part of a worldwide network.)

This wasn't the first of these trips he'd solicited my services on; I was probably his most reliable driver, and almost certainly the only one he was still friends with after using their services for this length of time. But everyone always said I was easy-going.

Now that we'd actually set out, in fact, I was beginning to get curious about what precisely Kieran was going to do. I'd seen him deal with a few repavings, and I was curious to see how different it was going to be when an entire highway was paved for the first time.

I wasn't sure how far we'd be able to go on the highway myself, but Kieran assured me that Hotch had told him they'd be able to get all the way up to the site. Kieran wouldn't let me play music once we got onto the highway, either; I gathered that listening to the sound it made under our tires gave him an idea as to its current health. It was just as well, I suppose, because our tastes in music were only barely compatible; he found most of mine boring, and I found most of his overly raucous and atonal. Luckily my mental stereo system could yield up a near- flawless rendition of "Autobahn", which I had always found admirably suitable.

So we drove along in our respective solitudes. It didn't take long to get to the point where "Grande Prairie" was revealed as the misnomer it was, into the depths of still-being-logged forest (probably the reason why the road was now getting paved). The deciduous trees were at various phases of losing their leaves, depending on their tolerance for cold, but very few were still green, leaving the conifers standing out in a contrast that would only get more marked as winter came. The sun rapidly sank towards the western horizon, which, since we were driving south, meant that at least it would be Kieran who got the sun in his eyes, which were closed anyway as he listened to the highway song.

Of course, as we got closer to Grande Cache, we also got closer to the Rocky foothills, so the horizon and the sun were moving towards each other. I cursed softly as I remembered this, because I'd forgotten to factor it into my sunset calculations; I'd have to speed after all. I tried to do so gently, but Kieran's eyes opened the moment I put on the slightest extra acceleration. He grinned, nodded, and went back into his contemplation.

Going 110, I began to notice that the car was sounding a bit louder than usual. I'd just gotten a new muffler, though, and it hadn't been that long since the wheel alignment had been checked. And this was new pavement, usually the easiest on the ears. Well, at least it was still better than that godawful tar-cracked stretch of Highway 2 that went north through Sexsmith.

The only other traffic we met were big trucks, logging trucks heading up to the Canfor plant back in Grande Prairie, right where we'd turned onto the highway. I was glad that at least it wasn't raining like it had been most of the past couple of weeks, so I wasn't getting my windshield drenched every time they went past.

But I was beginning to revise my opinion of the road's quality. With the sky deepening towards indigo on my side, I'd turned the lights on, and I could swear the road looked totally smooth. But I also swore that I'd rather listen to Kieran's music than the roar coming from beneath my feet. The steering wheel shuddered visibly, making me feel like when I'd had to use the Weedeater on my parents' lawn. I glanced over at Kieran; it was hard to tell against the sun's glare, but it looked like his eyes were still closed, though he was definitely frowning.

It was a positive relief to slow back down to the speed limit when I saw the first construction signs. I figured that I'd probably made up enough time that we'd get there soon enough. Kieran's eyes opened again. "Shouldn't be far now," he said, not even having looked out the window.

We pulled over onto the shoulder of the hill just above the end of the pavement, and munched quietly on our sandwiches. I wished I had thought of getting something to wash them down with, but hopefully we'd be able to actually go into Grande Cache and get some pop before we went back. I wasn't sure yet if this would disturb whatever Kieran had planned, though.

He covered his eyes and peered west into the sun, which was almost touching the line of the foothills. "Now," he said. Digging in his satchel, he pulled out a bottle of some dark substance that looked like oil, a clear plastic bag stuffed with something I couldn't quite make out, and a milk carton. He opened each one in turn, reaching under the car to rub a little oil on the undercarriage, pulling a rubber band(which looked like one end of a long chain of them)from the plastic bag and touching it to the tires, and finally pouring some iron filings out of the milk carton onto the hood. (But of course—barring the nonessentials, what were cars but oil, metal and rubber?)

This done, he replaced the three containers in his satchel and trotted down the hill. I followed a bit more slowly, closing the car doors—which were a lot more creaky than they had been a few hours ago—but not locking them. I hadn't bothered to bring my camera this time, since I figured the lighting would be too poor, though I could've gotten some good silhouette shots. As I walked between Kieran and the car, I could feel a tension in the air, enough to almost make my hair stand on end. I glanced automatically up at the sky, but there wasn't anything up there that would threaten lightning.

Kieran was down on his knees frantically scraping gravel from the short stretch that still had it, and putting it into a plastic peanut butter jar. He stopped just as the sun dipped below the horizon, screwed the top back on, and put it into the satchel. He pulled out the bag of rubber bands and laid one end of the chain carefully on the end of the pavement. I don't know if he found something to hook it around, but it stayed there firmly as he walked across the remains of the gravel, paying it out slowly along the ground, stretched taut, until he reached the far side, where he attached the other end of the chain. There it relaxed visibly.

Then he took out the big bottle of oil and started pouring it, a little at a time, in a continuous line parallel to the rubber bands. As I walked behind him back towards our car I could smell the distinctive odour of burnt oil, but it disappeared as we reached the pavement, where he dumped out the last of the oil(which wasn't much; he'd judged it to a nicety).

Finally, he walked back, sprinkling iron filings from the milk carton in a Hanselundgretelesque path between the rubber bands and the oil. In the dimming light I could see visible sparks as he dropped the filings on the gravel. The carton was still about a third of the way full when he reached the other end, and the sparks stopped.

"There," he said. He grinned and handed me the rest of the filings. "Feed it to Rusty."

We walked back to the car. The tension I had felt earlier was gone, like that of the now-loose chain of rubber bands. I decided I didn't need to cross that last stretch of gravel into Grande Cache after all. I could last until we got back to Grande Prairie. But Kieran surprised me by pulling out a bottle of water from his satchel, quite tepid by now, which we shared.

On the drive back (my wheels now rolling smoothly and almost noise-lessly on the new pavement), Kieran put a piece of tape on the peanut butter jar and, turning on the dome light, wrote "Highway 40" on it in black felt. (I remembered all those jars full of rocks from when he moved in; I'd thought he was a rockhound at first, except for the labels with highway names on them. Another mystery solved.) Then he sorted through the tapecase I had sitting in the car and eventually popped a Hoodoo Gurus tape into my tape deck.

"So you got any more commitments in the near future?" I asked.

He furrowed his brow. "Have to check, but I don't think anything until the Dunvegan Bridge, which should be a couple months."

Dunvegan I could handle. It was only an hour and a half out of town. "Give me a call then," I said.

He grinned, and we drove the west of the way back surrounded by Australian rock music.

ICE

Candas Jane Dorsey

It was a long night's gaze into a sparkling dirty spurt of city. Hong Kong had been pressed long ago into the folds of an island with a spiky intensity which had withheld the ocean's rise. But now spike means something else, I feel it behind the eyes, the safely hidden eyes I've discovered can learn denial as easy as my old ones. Watching the ocean slowly swell up the sides of the highrises and leafing through LiLee's life, the images pressing as seductively against my cortex as the water does against the pitted, algaed metal and concrete. It's a long time until high tide.

Point of view shifts with the melt of the ice. After a while you live in a land of pungent voyeurism, movies on the inside of your skull, consumer products masquerading as spirit. After a while you even get used to it.

⌐¬

LiLee was a little dreamchild when she came down the steps from the Peak past the wall where I lay on my mother's deathbed counting my fingernails. Seven of them then, still had three to go. Every one was a dramatic encounter with destruction, that's how it was in those hungry days, for me even more than for everyone freed when the Chinese army retreated to the mainland and left the island to anyone brave enough to stay here.

She was out of her depth right away, and if most of what would happen next was under the surface, enough was out front for me to reach out and snag her arm. Do I need to tell the rest? She was sleeping in my bed before the week was out, and I quit making plans for discorp, recorp for a while then.

Discorp. Holding her point of view now in my thoughts alongside mine, courtesy discorporation, I never would have planned.

⌐¬

If you push the situation past the verge where it starts the long slide into devasta-tion you start to feel the high. You want me to hurt you when we fuck, I can't quite do that even down here in the dirty streets we end up walking. Walking through past the punk gangs, the wristvid hawkers, the sushi carts and noodle vendors, all the trappings you told me would be here, walking deeper into decadence, that's what you call it, you want me to hurt you, you expect it and you ask me to make it happen.

I'm not made for the streets, not invented by the hackers in their booths of pain. When it hurts it ain't virtual, I think: when I learn how to hurt, and hurt you, I will come back and we can start over. You link your fingers together around my wrist and the tips meld and there is a seamless cuff of your flesh and bone holding me to you.

You want to know what it feels like to be on this end of the story? I saw you on the sunlit stairs and you hooked me, you pulled me down to crowded rooms smoky and sunken, into the trances of spiky professionals taking a break, breaking, breaking down into the world they love to visit as voyeurs.

You spun a good story; you took me home to that cubicle where you planned your invasion. Hands reaching into me before I was ready. Then your cock into me before I was eager. Oh, I was willing, it wasn't rape, but what good did it do me? Do me you said and I filled everything with you, trying to please you so you'd please me.

In the morning it was raining and you had some kind of deal to do so I put on the jacket I borrowed from my sister-lover and we went out on the ferry across the bay. My sister lives down in the night market off that street of dreams; she wouldn't let me go out on the street without some leather to hold off the foreign devils. I didn't know what she meant, then. I thought it was a joke, 'cause I'm from far away.

Okay, so we're in that street of shops, and I'm thinking, will you make love to me next time instead of fucking?, but I feel ashamed of that soft thought, I'm supposed to be on the street, that's what I came here for. And here I've found the glamour boy drug dealer lover I dreamed about in my true romanced comic dreams. What I wanted.

ɼ˥

Hong Kong went to the Chinese in 97, the day my mother was born. Her family's life reflected the times: a prolonged anguish of need that transcended the physical. They sent her to her Canadian relatives as soon as they could sell enough body parts to pay her fare, and she was transplanted like a rare flower into a city where luxury was access to information. Her foster parents wanted her to be a doctor, and so she spent her early life accumulating biotech; nanomen were her only lovers. The day I was born, virgin conception decanted from an artificial womb like a rare vintage, kept in crystal until I could breathe the air unaided, the army gave up on an island raddled with rioting and riddled with sedition, and went home, and my mother bought her ticket back. Packed her babe-in-aspic, packed her medikit, and jetted in to the new HK with a cadre of utopian anarchists looking for a future.

She died on the stairs where we had lived, lying unprotected from the warm rain except by her spiky smile, still believing that when she and her raggletaggle of long-since-broken revolutionaries got their break, they'd create the perfect ungoverned state

"We are the markers of the new millennial consciousness," she said to me as often as she could. "You have a duty to continue the struggle. You must make a daughter, and keep believing. Keep creating."

I was ten. The new millennial consciousness was as old and uninteresting to me as the cohort's stories about the turning of the millennium which had been marked long before my birth: the micro-cohort couldn't hold without its centre, so no-one stopped me when I went wilding.

It was almost a year later when my foster parents rescued me from the Peak stairs, took me back to a drowning Montreal. There amid Asean expats I learned to live in a different kind of utopia as the sea level softly rose. First thing I bought, eight years later, after I'd first found out that my favourite sport could earn me some money, was sterilisation.

I came back again and again like a moth to those stairs, the same step, the same place, the same pipe dreams. I found LiLee in that same place my mother died. She'd been a Peak plaything until she refused her first spike. If she'd known she'd fall so easily later, she needn't have lost it all, but she did, she lost. She was that type. Not a survivor.

Survivor was my e-name.

⌐¬

The Peak is done with LiLee, and for the stupidest reason. She sits on Kowloon side where MahLee lives, on the rail of what used to be the roof terrace of the Cultural Centre, but is now a cantilever over the ever-more-ironically yclept Fragrant Harbour, and thinks, if anybody ever asks me to spike again, I won't be so stupid. Born somewhere else, she doesn't speak the language, any of the languages, and she has run out of money for what might be the last time. She's on her face, except for MahLee, and she can't sponge from her for long: it wouldn't be fair.

He says, "Hey, round eye!" and she turns, relief at the English mixed with irritation. The sun shines behind his head but she didn't think he was God or anything, she'd seen that in too many bad VRs and old flickers, she just thinks, *shoulda bought some sunglasses from Gardner Woo when I had the money.*

"You look down," he says.

"Been better," she says.

"Peak fodder," he says. "Keep climbing, and they'll—how is it? Open-arm you? Welcome you with open arms?"

"I been there," she says. "*Open-arm* sounds like *straight-arm*—how they get rid of you, no subtlety."

"You out?"

So she tells him the story of that last party, how she wouldn't join the ecstasy brigade, feared the drug's name as much as the drug, spike, a stab to the heart? He listened, nodded, seemed to approve, smiled at her warmly.

Suddenly he gets up, grabs her hand, pulls her up beside him. "You coming with?" he says.

"Where?"

"To the Embassy. Perhaps I can get a ticket home…"

She laughs. "Dreamer."

"'Gainst the law to discriminate on account of that."

"Sure, in what continent? This is Hay Kay."

They walk off down the stairs arguing like that. He isn't paying attention really, suddenly lopes off to the side where a vendor's selling oranges. Buys two and throws her one. She's sweating and the orange juice drips off the sharp bone in her wrist. She licks it away, sweet and salty together.

A slim boy in a mesh musclesuit smiles at her when he sees her doing this. The tall blond round-eye she's following is oblivious. She grins at the boy, well, maybe young man, shorter than her but a cute body, she can see almost every detail. Down in the night market she could get one of those if she had the money. MahLee would give her the money, maybe, but ML's saving for her eighth fingernail, so maybe not.

The money from her severance is running out. They won't want to see her at Embassy, any more than they want to see this new boy, but unlike her, he has the benefit of surprise on his side. Still, they only give him credits, but no ticket. He looks at her with desolation in his abject glance.

She turns again to the clerk, begs for a ticket home. "Severance means finished, finito, done, over with, don't come back here no more," the clerk had said last time, but today. although she is required first to cower realistically in the face of bureaucratic anger, gives her the ticket anyway. She gives it to him—but he goes nowhere.

٣

Drowned Montreal looked beautiful in the sunrise light. We had done five buildings that night, rowing into the broken caverns where the plate glass ought to be. We'd never done more than two before, but we were on a dare, and Casse-Tête and Tête Jaune were high, so we planned four. The fifth, Tête Jaune talked us into at the last, because we had some anfo left, though we'd used all the plastique.

But we were late. We'd left the fused anfo in the elevator, so the shaft would funnel the explosion, and were pulling for safety, but the sun was coming up. Casse-Tête was stoned, I said that, and kept stopping to look at the scenery. Then Tête Jaune would say yeah wow and the rowboat would drift. We couldn't put the prop in the water and lever on out of there because of the river riders; we couldn't sail much in the cul-de-sac we were in, surrounded as we were by buildings which sheltered us there from wind. We would have to row out into the plaza and catch a downtown draft on one of the cross streets, and having the starboard oar crew spiked out of their tiny minds wasn't helping.

Mal de Tête was losing her temper, I told them: kept saying, "come on, come on, tête, we gotta move!"

"Lighten up, Mal de Tête," said Casse, but I kept hissing to them, and they kept spiking out, and finally I started to shout, as around the corner came the river police on their jetskis and *we're toast*, I swore at them, they were such fools.

But Casse was a perfect breaker, kept her reflexes even in that state, why we called her that, a kind of tribute really, and she said, "Ashes to ashes and toast to toast," and laughed as she hit the detonators, though we were still only fifty feet from the lobby.

The first three went in order.

One. Fifty four stories above the water, and that one fell into itself sweet as the movies, and almost quietly.

"Tabernac," said one of the cops in awe, and they all turned and watched the shock wave hit the water and travel toward us.

Before it reached us, Two. That was the one we had rigged off centre, but I wouldn't let the others do it again, though they were obsessing on symmetry at that stage of their spike. It was a boxy utility 'scraper at the edge of what had been a freeway, relatively small, and it arced like a falling redwood into a channel of water that would have been empty if we hadn't been late, if the parade of jetski commuters hadn't started with the sunrise. There were only about a dozen in the path, and some of them might have got away, I don't know for sure. The wave, though...

Three, most of the fall hidden behind the wall of wave that Two's knife cut had sliced and turned toward us, so I only heard the twin thumps of the two not-quite-co-ordinated plastique charges and felt the water beneath us quiver as the tsunami from One started to raise us.

Water is slow. Five blew before the wave could lift us more than about two metres. The anfo blast pushed two directions: up through the elevator shaft and out through the empty lobby windowframes. The ceiling low to the water funnelled the force, and the river cops blew away like paper, their jetskis somersaulting into windows still intact forty feet up and across the street.

The boat flew ahead of the wind, skimming the water, down the open street into the lake of the plaza beyond, before the boom hit Casse and vaporised her bone and brain so her body fell through a red cloud across the tiller. We heeled to the left out of the deadly gale. The tsunami had pushed up about ten metres of water in the canyons, and then the water from Two's wave began to fall around us like bombs, and some of it not water, either, ski parts and some red rain too, the water off the deck ran rusty.

I pushed ex-Casse out over the gunwales and pulled the tiller back before we went over. The boat came around as Jaune kicked and cut the sheets loose and the sail unravelled; I was leaning on the loading toggle which had warped somehow so it took a million years in the slow silence of terror for the engine to drop, the props to start and bite the water. We were out in the freeway channel, still surfing on the crest of Two's bow wave. It takes more time to tell it than it took to happen.

Jaune took two steps toward me along the deck then, and fell down like a rag doll. When they rayed his body later, seven of his vertebrae were broken, and the shock of the explosion had ruptured his spleen and his aorta. He'd filled up with blood right in front of me, and collapsed, but not until he'd done what was needed.

I alone remained, to hear Four blow apart, a long time after the others it seemed. I turned to see the explosion fracture the light of the rising sun, and fell back into the boat as the engine kicked into a higher gear. My head hit the gunwales hard.

There are always more jetski cops, and they picked me up when the gas that was left in the holed tank ran out about half a klick later and left me drifting.

After they took the shrapnel out and regrew my heart, the plea bargains started. Finally, I got out on my foster parent's money—they had to endow a hospital, I think—but that's when they suggested I might want to go home, and perhaps might never want to return to Canada.

I didn't care then; I'd had a better offer already.

"*I want you to do something for me.*"

Well, I've heard that before, she thought, *and I'm listening to the replay thinking, well, sure, she should have given some thought to consequences at some earlier point in the process.*

I never did buy that little innocent girl routine, anyway. She came here from Canada sure, but she came on severance, I know what that means. It means, "We want to have it out with you, out of hair, out of here." So tell me she did nada for that? Rien de chien (that's not a doggone thing to you, anglo bitch)?

I knew. I would have been on severance too, but I sent it all back when I started earning my fingernails.

On the way by her memory, I look with my own memories at Tête Jaune—older, and the recorp showed, attenuated him somehow. To me, he doesn't look tall, but I was almost a foot taller than LiLee. How did they meet? Naïve to think it was accident, though she thought it serendipitous. Knowing that he was still alive, body blow, but why I'm not surprised? Recorp serves many goals.

I knew different, knew he'd been streamed by recorp into some revenge mode that wasn't in the original programme. Streamed and sent after me. There were a lot of angry cops when they had to accept my buyout. So what if it took ten years to set me up? Better late than never, and only one worthless recorp to risk.

I don't know if you can crack that kind of recorp warp. If I'd talked with him, would something below the script have stirred and swept away the false history? But I never did, only read him in LiLee's repro. It was too late.

"*Take hold of this,*" *he drawled,* "*it'll put out the night.*" *His skinny form bent over me, how tall was he?, and the thing in his hand was just a shadow.*

I didn't know how to use it, didn't want to admit that so took it into my hand and it seemed pretty clear, how the prickly shape fit across my palm and against my wrist, but his hands helped mine as if we were doing it together, and maybe we were. I felt the penetration, and I felt it drive through my veins, the finest street spike, he got sharp edges, strobed some, I could smell clear sharp pheromones he pumped into stagnant night, smell him wanting me knew he could smell me, cutting toward him in that crowded room. His hand up slow as tar cupped my neck, he lifting me by my head until I half-hung from his hungry mouth, kiss pierced me brilliant, shot dimness an iridescence-edged spear of radiation, hard stuff, seared me, moth flame, I went with him through a sharp beaded flurry, into the back room.

┌┐

I was sitting where I often sat to think, in the spot where I held my mother when she died. I'd slivered my way in beside the bone merchant. While he talked he'd been spreading his stock of what he called ivory on red silk: a hundred years of CITES means all ivory is history, but some of his trade was in human bone out of Tibet. On the other side, secondhand shoes, but not part of our business: we talked low.

I hadn't noticed the new girl stop and hover until she came to ask me if I lived there. In English: she'd heard the bone merchant speaking to me in his contemptuous Oxbridge.

"Might as well," I said, looking over my shoulder at the bone merchant, who was the last of the cadre. Rumour had it he had a house on the peak earned from selling the bones of his friends from the revolution. I don't know about that; he wouldn't have ever invited me home. Even if I was my mother's daughter, you don't eat with the help—and anyway, my Cantonese wasn't good enough any more to pass. Why he wouldn't even speak it with me.

"You have the accent of a missionary," he said to me scornfullly, when I found him selling human bone that the street skinny said wasn't Tibetan holy bone at all, was mined right here on Hong Kong Island.

Utopia was something else in a drowning city, he said to me angrily; utopia would be bought with more money to use to undermine the cartels and crimelords—or to buy a house on the Peak, I didn't care. I didn't care whether he lied or told the truth, if he could afford me.

His dream was to take out seven scrapers, four on Hong Kong side and three on Kowloon side. Below the waterline, look like vandals, scrape a cut of insurance. Same rag as ten other seacoasts, the biggest scam going. Everyone knew it would only work for a little while, until the policies rolled over or the water rose to the no-liability level. I'd been busy around the world: he was lucky to have found me, and he knew it. There were only a few of us, pretty good at it, and I was the best.

I had earned one fingernail per building, worldwide. When I had ten, I'd have a new career, and I figured it would coincide with the old one being made redundant. Seven at once gave me the last three nails *and* the visor: windfall. Last job.

And that's the day I met LiLee.

She went stumbling a little on the end of his hand into the tawdry back room where the strippers changed. She was spiking, clear to see, and him?—by now his body ran on the stuff, made no difference to him.

If it was just about fucking. He promised her a lot while he stripped her, his words hard and basic and—you can see—exciting for her. He opened his tight jeans and she lay undressed of her hard street pride, my leather jacket bunched beneath her hips, her body juiced for him, the milky fluid ran down to stain the lining of the jacket, the red dye running onto her white buttocks like carelessly done laundry. He let her clothe his cock in latex, her fingers hungry, before he entered her, her leg curled around his ass and the other hooked behind his knee, one of his hands on her breast, his nails digging in until he drew blood. If I start to lose it, he said, hurt me a little and it'll be all right. *His thrust hurt, and she shook her head, tried to push aside his hand, while he pushed in on the condom's slick promise, not noticing.*

Then the second wave of the spike hit, and she screamed again, arched her back and cried out. He smiled. He thought it was pleasure. He came fast, spikefast, lay on top of her, and there, his face buried in her flesh so he could not see her eyes tearing up; he told her that he loved her.

He'd held one of her wrists like a handcuff, but with the other hand she felt beneath herself, her fingers came up stained from the cheap red lining of the jacket now soaked mostly with her sweat. Tears tumbled down her temples into her hair, she put her fingers in her mouth and sucked. He saw her with peripheral, smiled, thought it was his pheromones she sucked, but her memory says to me now it was the dye she wanted to taste, my sweat taste burned with hers into the cheap fabric.

He thought she was crying because she had come so hard. She thought it was possible he really thought he loved her. They walked away into the night like that, the crescent wounds his fingernails had made still seeping, staining her white silk blouse, but no-one could see, she was wearing the black jacket again, creased a little across the back, but what was another wrinkle in the street-worn skin? So far, she hadn't been able to hurt him back.

Even though by that time she thought she would do anything for him, she knew already that wasn't going to be true.

I decided to do all seven in one night. It was my last job, might as well echo the job that got me into this, gave me the edge, gave me the reputation. Could afford the silent jetski, could afford the right explosives and detonators, had spent weeks on the harbour junk tours casing the places.

It was all as smooth as the rise of the oceans, and as inevitable, I figured. Set-up for the night of the last of June/first of July. The day the Brits sailed out and the Chinese soldiers came in.

⌐¬

I'm going back still speeded to my sister on the stairs. Bursting with the damage you would always do, walking home under the shadow of the escalator with my last sense of freedom, knowing she was there, walking into our place, her embrace. She's a sister-lover cuz she does me, she does me that morning, she's better than you. Her fingers are shorter than your cock, can't reach as deep but that's okay cuz you bruised me in there anyway.

And she holds me while I cry and then laugh, she thinks it's for her at first, she's gentle as she takes my black boots and my jeans off, I can feel her hands on my thighs, like I couldn't feel you; I am home where I should never have left. Finally I am down enough to come, her hands calming me and I feel the slow, heavy vibrations doppler up my spine.

It's so easy. That's the amazing thing, it's so easy after that to touch her and bring her to coming, me so tired and sick from spiking and still it was easy. Waves in my hands like the tide that comes in under the bridge from some bright ocean I will never see again.

We moved together so quickly that I still wear my stained silk shirt. After, the world starting to come back for us both, she starts to stroke my body under the shirt, and her hands pull the shirt away from the moonmarks on my breast. I flinch. She unbuttons the shirt and looks at the arcs where his fingernails broke the skin. A little dried blood flakes the pale skin around the marks, and where the shirt pulled away from the clot there's a swelling drop of blood held circular by surface tension. "Is that your scene now?" she says, and I turn my head away.

⌐¬

I never asked her why she kept going back. I know how these things happen. When I was younger I got a lot of scars, fighting my way in and out of battles like this. I didn't get all of them fixed, and she used to draw her fingers across them on my body, the shrapnel from Montreal, that stab wound under my breast where the shard found my heart once, only once. I learn quick. She used to tell me the stories of what happened to me, and sometimes she would even tell me what was happening to her. Bruises I couldn't touch; they were inside. Whiter, ever whiter skin I could touch, because she was loosing her blood to him slowly, like a virgin in a vampire novel, the spike giving her its pallour of night, so that she began to fade away so sweet and old-fashioned, just what the customers like. The customers, to earn the credits, because she didn't have the talent for destruction that I do.

And she gave me just what I liked, my mother would have been proud of her, and I bought her paradigm. I thought I could be her centre instead of giving her centre back to her, how could I have been so blind? I began to think I needed my eyes adjusted, after, when she was gone.

But at the time I thought I was being her friend. Friends don't interrogate. And I loved her, the best I could, taking the pain away with loving, trying to take the kinks out of orgasm, trying to bring her back to her past, the place she used to live. If I was not a perfect sister, not a perfect lover, I wish she were in a position to forgive me for it. Now I can see better, I can fight better, I know more.

But that was then. And even if I had known that Tête Jaune was setting her up for the absolute fall, could I have stopped her? After all, she thinks, over and over again in my head, he had told her he loved her. And she had believed him.

ᴦ⁊

"You're gonna like it better this time," he said, and curled her hand around it while she was still standing there mute and angry, standing on the ferry dock with her anger in her hand, wrapped in the black jacket again, that this time she had taken while I was sleeping. Stolen it.

"Where do you get it? Who gives it to you?" she said, meaning the right to take her life out of her hands.

"Around," he says, and she shakes her head.

"I mean, who gives you my permission?" she says, but she makes the mistake of smiling; after all, he did say he loved her.

"You want it bad as I do," he says. "I can get it for you."

"I don't want you, this way," she says, but he presses her hand the spike trapped between their palms, it slides beneath her skin, the drug hits her then, and she laughs instead of crying.

"How do you want it?" he says, and holds her up when she starts to sway, and this time he takes her to some little coffin shop and she watches with drug-clear eyes as he opens the lock, and she says in her recorded thought, I could do that if I had to. I can do anything I have to. But it isn't true, she finds out later. Not everything.

When he gives her the spike it makes her fast enough that he can keep her up. So this time wasn't so bad. They try out some ways he thinks she wants it, and maybe he thinks she is with him, and maybe she does too. And maybe she is, that's the thing, maybe she finds it in her to change for him, and maybe over time she will be able to *give him what he doesn't give her. That's in the recording now. I didn't have to guess about that.*

About what he wanted me to read, his message coming through, that was delivered later. She never knew.

⌐¬

The only tricky one was the Hong Kong Bank. The bone man insisted that the walls had to collapse inward, trap all the bad *feng shui* for which the building had been notorious since it was built. Those charges took weeks to set, only because the building was still in use and security was tight. I spent a lot of human scrimshaw money, but it folded up all right come the night.

The Peninsula Hotel was full of rich tourists. The bone man said he didn't care, but I was three fingernails short of being an assassin, so at the last moment I pulled the fire alarm and all the fire escape Zodiacs fanned out across the old Cultural Centre's undersea shelf, and the rich had a tsunami ride and a view of the prettiest of the seven— it went down in sections, and the restaurant broke open like an egg so that for seconds, before it sank in a cloud of spume, they could see the marble counters of the ladies room tilt toward the sky. I admit: I'd set that one up for last so I could watch from the crowd, and I cheered with the rest of them. Then I went home to my Kowloon-side houseboat which was still rocking from the blast waves.

The bone man loved it. He watched from his living room at the Peak, I think. He thanked me in Cantonese: not *m'goi*, thank you for a service, but *dong jai*, thank you for a gift.

Historic day: birthday de *wo de ma-ma*.

In the accent of a missionary.

⌐¬

So after a while I'm between you, one two and you are still pulling me onto you like a condom and she is still pulling you out of me like sucking a snake bite and after a while we're all feeling the venom.

You're giving it to me, that snaketooth gift, you're shaking with the loss of it, the loss of all you're pumping into me, it's important to you to hear me cry out, you never ask if it was pleasure or pain. I'm riding on the speed, turning pain into pleasure by pulling it through the neural paths backwards. She's sucking that sickness out of me and into herself, she's loving me and letting me too deep into her and I'm too deep into the speed and I'm getting tired of holding you apart.

She goes to the clinic and orders the mods: hands, synthoscreen over the eyes, and I know she's gonna be dressed to kill, but I'll lose her eyes, only thing anchoring me.

By then I'd come to need her on the other end of the lever. She gets on the ferry one night and even if I'm crying she's gone.

␣

I did give back my image of her, but too late. I was just another set of mirrorshades in the making, getting ready to reflect her losses. I wasn't a lover any more, just an antidote. I went back to work knowing that. I got on the ferry and went, and yes, I left her crying. But I left her my jacket in case the drug and the man let her remember she was once whole inside it, with a little help from a friend.

I blew up seven drowned scrapers that night, and not one single piece of one of them penetrated my heart. I had perfectly assured my safety.

␣

I did four customers early. They were numbers by then: I was used to this. Only one of them wanted me spiked: with the others I had to pretend I was flat: innocent, and wanted them anyway. I didn't mind; it costs them more that way. Through it all, he watched me, smiling a little, but not 'cause he was happy.

After number four, as I gave him the credits and he tossed me the spike, I tried to talk to him.

"I don't get it, MaBlond. Why are you angry at me?"

"You are always spiked. You must take these other customers, you sully yourself in the street."

"You wanted me to do it. I did it for you."

"You do it because you are weak and stupid."

I started to cry—stupid, weak, yes, predictable. He slapped me. "Don't do that. Don't snivel."

"Don't hit me either," I said. "You are stupid too. You think you can tell me what to do? You think I want you any more?"

He used to be able to tell I was lying, but I guess I'd learned a lot from him. "That's fine," he said. "We agree on something." Then he walked away.

I was surprised at how I felt, especially because the spike was high in my blood: only a little bit tired, a little bit angry, and with a strange desire to laugh. It was all so obvious.

The Peak doesn't want you if you don't spike, the depths don't want you if you do. The blond boy that walks the stairs between them doesn't know what he wants, and he twists everybody to get it.

Spiky, that made sense.

I did two more clients, not even thinking about it.

The seventh customer wanted to spike together, figured it would be some kind of transcendental bonding experience. I could have told her that it wouldn't work. I should have told her I was already 'way over the limit. But I didn't. So we closed our hands around that hedgehog sensuality, and she started to go up.

Me, I felt something new, something I'd never felt before, spiking or flatlining. I felt myself break through a transparent wall into a sea of calm, and I floated there watching the spike fall like a drowning scraper into the calm water. In that moment which was a lot like orgasm but lonelier, I wished I could be with MahLee, wished I could see her almond eyes that because of the visor no-one would never see again.

Instead I saw MaBlond leaning over me, smiling that little smile. Hurt me a little and it'll be all right, *I thought, and wanted to chuckle at the irony as I saw at last the central fallacy of that request. But because I couldn't tell him—never could have told him—I just watched as he bent closer, as he dropped the net over my head. I'd never seen recorp gear except in the vids: it's expensive stuff. Lay people like me—that's a pun, get it?—can't afford that stuff.*

"Tell Mal de Tête that she killed mine, so I killed hers," he said, which I thought was a little strange, because I didn't know anyone called Mal de Tête—though I seemed to have a powerful headache myself.

I understood then that I had never been Linda Lee to him, I'd been something else.

I went out thinking: well, this is a pain: just when I find out what is really going on, I'm gonna be too dead to tell MahLee.

ר

Their granite and steel spikes fell beneath the surface of the sea the way fingers close over a palm: the way my expensive and elegant fingernails would sink beneath the surface of a kill. I watched them and I thought, I have got to save LiLee from disappearing below the water. I have got to find out who he is and get her away from him.

Perfect timing, as it turned out: in the morning, when I came back to the stairs to find her, she was dead.

That's what happens to the girl in the story who doesn't think of herself first. And my part—well, that's what happens to the well-meaning but procrastinating friend. But I found out soon enough it wasn't that simple. Tête Jaune got her at discorp. Sent me the recording, and recorp gave her back to me. When I woke up in the illegal clinic, with my fingernails and my visor, I had LiLee too.

I had LiLee, edited: from the day we met until the day she first died. So I still don't know where she came from, but I know far too well where she went.

When I thought of her after that—and oh yes, I think of her after that, with a perfect chemical memory impossible to eradicate, a fractal double vision that lets her haunt me more than my own past does—it was of the day she reached for me in the midmorning light and gave me her love without giving me her pain. It was the last time it happened, and it happened a long time before the end. I replay it a lot: it's the last one I have that doesn't have his face in it.

ᴦ⁊

She gets on the ferry one night and even if I'm crying she's gone. Did you know she was there? Did you know how much more I needed her than I needed you? Is that what made you desperate to fill me with all your substances, your substance? Is that what made me nothing but a weapon to you?

And her: did she know it was you she rescued me from? Later when she met you, when she slept with you and you treated her well, did she ever find out whose face was behind the anger she felt? Did she ever leave you and take herself with her? I've always hoped she did, hoped she knew and took another kind of revenge than yours; I've always hoped someone left you properly. I left you, but I wasn't there to enjoy it, my self got saved for something else, something I didn't do, didn't want to do. And all that poison, I remember, all that venom nobody wanted to own. Like a vicious shadow of the spike which ate us all, eventually.

She gets on the ferry one night and even if I'm crying she's gone. She goes to perfect herself in the slow dance of demolition, she goes to get it right this time—and after that there was nothing to balance you, mister destruction, selfish as if you were the protagonist and dangerous because you didn't care if it hurt, you liked it to hurt, you thought I liked it like you.

Hurt me a little, *you said, and I didn't know how.*

Sure I was stupid but that was before I died. I didn't know better then.

Widow's Walk

E.B. Klassen

Running hot and clean, with the prairie summer flowing back like river banks from the edge of my vision. Hot and clean the sky the colour of electricity, of the insides of my fingertips, trying to pull me out through the top of my head and away into that blue. Running high and wide and the dust unable to catch me before I'm gone and crazy down this road, across this prairie, under this sky.

There, at the beginning of vision, rising like a ship against the blue is the house, crawling out of the depths against gravity and death to force the skin of the ocean the skin of the sky to hold it, support it, and let it move free. It does not belong here in prairie flowing summer, summer flowing sky.

The bow of this house, this ship, splashes off the blue and slices through the waves of gold, of grain, heaving on the restless swells of this very summer day. Wallowing through trough and crest like some galleon gorged on treasure, swollen out at the sides until it should split from unsated anguish. But the house's sides are firm and high, banking against these swells of fortune and time, a dam for the ghosts that inhabit her. And it is only these ghosts that can live here. These ghosts and the single hawk pinned against the inevitable dome and depth of blue, blue swelling like some sugar-spun sea bubble. This is a land of heat and light, not life. Life is only condemned to live here, with futures and pasts trickled across golden summer seas. There is no choice, and the hawk disappears into the ecstatic sky.

Riding the eternal swell, the house sails towards me, and I gear down to prevent it passing by. In this land there is only heat, heat and no sound of water. There is only the sound of dry grass singing. Dry grass and the running, the clean scream so pure and thin that the heat and light can swallow it, dissolve it into blues and golds and heat with no sound of water. The wide weight of this wide land pulls at me as I drop down another gear, it pulls me back into the threat of running, threat without action, action without pain. The blue is still uncatchably far away, but the house has moved close enough that I let the long driveway guide me through the ocean to its side. I make fast, tying up with my heel dragging out the kickstand. My shoulders warn me, as I surrender to gravity, that the road lies heavy. I stretch, pulling the helmet from my head. Around me are piles of rust, piles slowly being swallowed by the rising tide of the prairie sea. The bits and pieces still unsubmerged tell me of the ghosts that drift about this place. No dog barks. No cat watches from the barn roof. No bird, no breeze, no sound of water.

Hanging my helmet over the jacket tied on the back of the bike, I leave this ghost to commune with the locals. While the engine and land tick their faith in heat to one another, I try to hear over the sound of the road that still echoes about my head. I don't hear the inner door open. Sea foam has gathered itself together in the doorway and formed this tiny woman in the pale green dress and the invisibly white hair. Her face is a tallow sculpture with the light from within seeming to make her both more visible and invisible simultaneously. When I see her, she is more quiet than the sky, more still than the heat.

"Hi. Didn't know anyone lived here. Just hoping for a well that was still working."

Smiling, she opens the screen door and invites me in. My heels sound hard on the tired steps. Stooping slightly in her direction, I ease past her and into the house.

"Very prairie," I think, walking on the linoleum of a thousand farm kitchens in the grey exhaustion of a thousand farm houses. It is only six steps to the sink and hand pump. The shipwrights who built for these seas all worked to the same plans. The houses all have high sides to withstand the storms. But inside they are a maze of small rooms. The number and arrangement of the doorways is expected to baffle the ghosts that pursue the inhabitants. You can always tell the houses not built to spec. The ghosts of past and future gravitate inward, seeping through the cracks in the corners under the eaves. Like dust on a vagrant breeze they swirl about, pulling the household into their dance. A dance that is at first chaotic, but soon transforms into a whirlpool, spinning cyclonicly through the rooms of the house, ignoring doors and walls. Houses and families that have hosted a ghost dance are instantly recognizable; the houses are empty and always five degrees colder than the outside air, and the families are never again a unit, for some are dead and the rest flung outwards by the force of the dance. They explode like a dandelion in seed hit by a hailstone, erupting outward on a tumult of wind to scatter across the prairie. The next generation too is afflicted, refusing to form an attachment to anything deeper than a cause or ideology.

This kitchen is tired. The counter lists slightly towards the outside wall, and the cupboard doors below no longer close quite properly. The drinking glass is, as always, beside the sink. I work the hand pump and tepid water splashes unconvincingly into the basin. Cast iron aches through the shadow of enamel left after years of hands, and the sound of water is the high cymbal of falling brass. I drink it anyway, and my mouth tastes of metal for days.

"The water is strange here," she says as I turn from the sink wiping my hand across my mouth. "Different currents, I expect."

"Yes, ma'am. Different currents."

"Care for a cup of coffee?"

"Yes, thanks." She takes cups from the cupboard and pours from the stovetop percolator. She is old, the house is old, the coffee is old, the pot is enameled steel, not aluminum.

"Cream or sugar?"

"Black's fine, thanks."

My first sip confirms this is the real thing, the oil of the inner landscape. Never drawn in fine calligraphic hand, but rather painted with the crude and graceless strokes of the untalented amateur. This invisible landscape is fat lines and lack of perspective where sun and sky reduce and erode. The golden sea churns even rock into soil, and only the simplest profiles can remain and be passed on.

These are the over-simplifications spread at the auction sales, the markets, the grain elevators. Like a peat fire, you're never sure where it starts, but it quickly runs underground following veins and deposits to spread invisibly, its boundaries only visible by the shape of the land where winter will not stick. And in spring or high summer the first faint trickles of smoke slide upward through the twisting air until the entire bog is alight. The flames run from bog to hollow to the baby-fuzz poplars, and then it's away from the nurturing ground and into the trees, the air itself. Bog, trees, and prairie join in the ecstatic rush to heat and light and smoke. Across the flats run the flames; down coulees, over hills, ignoring fencelines, creeds, class. Everything burns; fields, houses, tractors, goverments, animals. All that remains is the empty land and aching sky.

Even more than feared, the fires are loved. Loved in that prairie Calvinist way, the love of wrath and new messiahs. For the fire is never set, never planned, but erupts spontaneously, born in the friction of earth rubbing sky with the thin sheen of man caught in the middle. Heat building, combustion begun, the prairie throws up the One, the Burning Man who follows the burn line as a lens, focusing light and heat back on those not yet aflame. Like the Spirit, the flame moves where it will, the most expected and unexpected people flaring into life, running naked in flames through the dry grass and leaving crazy random flame-wakes behind them. As the patterns of fire grow and die, mingle, and are reborn, people begin to gather like accident watchers from the corners, the edges, pulled by the gravity of flame to watch the cities burn. Hoping to be ignited, hoping to be consumed. They stand, shoulder to shoulder, letting heat play over their faces, eyes searching for the heart of the fire. Sometimes the brave ones lean forward to toss a stick on the flames, hoping for greater illumination. The singed pilgrims leave when nothing is left but rubble and ashes and embers quietly talking amongst themselves. The prairie quickly reclaims the black stretches, for the fires destroy nothing important, change nothing permanently.

"Cookie?"

"Yes, thanks." I choose carefully from the faded blue plate. There are the requisite three kinds. I make sure to choose the homemade. This time it's shortbread which crumples wonderfully between my teeth. When I sip from my cooling coffee, the crumbs joyously dissolve, and are washed away.

Carefully she places the plate on an end table that has somehow survived both the prairie and this house. Her fingers keep fiddling, unable to lie still. Quickly her finger sponges up the crumbs from the plate, a lifetime's worth of habit in each stab.

"You've spent all your life here?" An abrupt question, but the hairs on my neck are standing up, and the only charm I know is noise.

Jerking her head slightly, she looks at me, "Here. Lord no. I came over from England when I was thirteen. Moved here from St. John's when I got married. When my husband gets back this time, we're moving away from this horrid ocean. Away to someplace safe and flat." Sipping from her small cup, she turns her smile up a bit brighter. But her eyes shade black.

"The waters certainly can be unfriendly." I am tasting the bitter undercurrent of the coffee.

"I don't understand these people who say they like the ocean." Brittleness edges her voice, fingers weaving about her cup. "Certainly it can be pretty. But you live beside it every day and soon you see just how…" She fumbles for the word, and I see miles of grain bowing before the walking wind. And I know, somehow, that she is seeing water.

"Relentless," I offer, and her eyes jump back to my face.

"That's it exactly. Relentless. The waves always sucking at the shore. So quiet, so pretty. But all the time pulling, grabbing, taking away. Relentless."

I watch her watching the waves. The ocean's hands, reaching out for pieces of the land and pulling them away, out under the waves into the deep places where there is no light. It wasn't the sailors who created the horror stories of the oceans. It was their wives, waiting while the sea claws at the land.

"Has he been gone long?" Perverse sentiment moves me.

"A while," Vaguely. "A while. He's a bit overdue, really. And I am getting a bit worried." Her fingertip traces the rim of her cup. No mountains, no valleys. Just a bit of flat ocean inside and the flat prairie surrounding it. She looks up, eyes suddenly sharp. "What time is it?"

I check my watch. "A little after four."

"Ah." She rises decisively from her chair. "He's been late every time, you know. Every time. But finally that sail lifts over the horizon and the gulls carry him home. Would you care to join me? I always wait until late afternoon. The light is so much cleaner then, don't you think?"

Those eyes lock onto me, pulling me out of my chair. "Yes, certainly," I stutter, getting quickly to my feet. Need has made her much more spry than her age would suggest. Out of form, I take her arm.

All those miles. I feel them washing over us both. All those miles she ran to find someplace safe. Stuffy trains, cars with bad suspensions, and still she brought it all with her. Climbing the stairs slowly, I smell only dust, not age or mildew. The attic boasts an extra set of stairs.

I see her as she was then; travelling alone and a bit scared. Searching for the one place that would save her. And when she saw all this flat land she knew that this was as far as she could come. She never knew that the water once lived here too.

It must have been spring. Spring when she found the house. Spring when she began to do the things they had planned as a couple and now she was doing alone. Then came the summer, and in the late summer the wheat began to reach its full height, green shading off into gold. And all of it moving in the wind. All those miles of it, the endless fields of it waving from the horizon past her house, setting her adrift. Finally she called someone, anyone, and they came out and built the addition to the house.

Opening the door to the roof, even I am surprised at how far I can see. And still nothing but fields of wheat, barley, oats out to the edge of the world. The walk stretches the length of the roof, mahogany rail polished by years of hands.

I feel her going away from me. Away from this house. Away, out to the horizon, knowing that by sheer purity of will she can make the sail appear and bring her husband home. And I, I fall into the forgotten future while she walks straight and firm down the walk, eyes scratching the distance. Bowing under the weight of the sky, I leave her. Stopping only to wash the cups and plate we used—there is no point in confusing her with memories of someone who isn't yet—I leave this house that floats in the middle of the ocean.

On the back of my bike the ghost still waits for me. I draw my past on, and it's back to running, back to beginning again.

The Wheel of Life

Teresa Plowright

Molly's mother, Claire, was a member of the last generation forced to wear out their skin (among a certain class, that is). The Renewers simply replaced the whole organ, holus-bolus. Why, they argued unsentimentally, stay attached to such defective material? Sagging, buckling…"We're not changing our real selves," they declared, "skin is only skin deep, after all." And so they stayed as smooth as billiard balls, right 'til the end of their allotted century.

The Journeybacks, on the other hand, aged more or less naturally, to the half-way point; and then reversed. Molly herself had bravely watched time claw her lovely face until the age of fifty; the last five years were agony. Then (with Tyler, her lifelong spouse), she'd started down the flowery path, to youth again.

At thirty-three—with much champagne—they turned younger than their own beloved twins. During that year, Molly was tempted to give birth again. But after a tear-filled night, Tyler convinced her it would be a selfish act; by the time their new progeneny was thirteen, they'd be only twenty years old themselves. Besides, without children, growing young again would be such a carefree experience.

In fact, the Christmas they turned twenty-eight was festive beyond compare: Charlotte and Edward, their twins, were forty-ish, and run ragged by their own young kids; they loved the peppy help of Gran and Gramps. The only shadow on the occasion was withered, once-luminescent Claire (—who'd long ago pushed Molly on swings with such strong arms—) now sunken into a corner armchair, sucking on irony and peppermints…Claire clung to her ninety-second year, even though she frightened her grandchildren, and hated her full-care Home, and (Molly suspected) secretly sabotaged newfangled home appliances. Where, Molly shuddered, was the nobility in aging that all the Naturalists talked about?

Claire had passed on, and Molly and Tyler had turned twenty-five years young, when their son Edward, now aged forty-four and committed all his adult life to the Journeyback, underwent Renewal suddenly. Virginia, his wife—two years his elder—suddenly, and with no warning, saw her vision of growing young with her beloved incinerate.

But Edward argued that theirs was still the perfect match. For he, (young-skinned as he aged, but wise inside, and all body workings maintenanced), could care for his wife himself as time swept her back to her last, small years; no need for them both to burden their daughter, Grace, in second infancy, or to hire costly caregivers who could not (perhaps) be entirely counted on to cuddle and change diapers at the proper times, despite all the legal devices put in place.

He would cherish Virginia always as she de-aged, moving backward into her teens, retreating forever from his embrace, sinking into giggles and girlish games… He would love her as her understanding dimmed, and her voice flew higher, and her words got cute; he would cradle her as they'd once cradled their beloved Grace, as Virginia grew smaller in his arms until she reached her little grave, two years before he—(his still-firm skin finally burnt to ashes)—was punctually buried at her side.

And even Molly, dedicated Journeyer, found comfort in the thought of her dear son Edward standing like a beacon—(protective, unchanging, tall)—as she and Tyler descended, long before Virginia, through their raucous teens, down, down, to the wild fororests of childhood, to the cathedrals of first consciousness, and beyond.

A Letter from my Mother

Yves Meynard

Yesterday, I received a letter from my dead mother. In an envelope of grayish paper, addressed to "Janosh Kempter". My first name is Jancek, but I immediately recognised the tremulous script, and the uncertain blue of the ink, and I knew immediately from whom the missive had come.

My mother died when I was twelve years old. I remember the funeral, the priest and his habits in six shades of red, embroidered with gold. The bicorn hat, the many chaplets of pearls and semi-precious stones. Yes, the Church has always been rich where I come from. I remember the words he spoke over the coffin-but I recall them in English, not in my native tongue, the tongue in which they were spoken.

Yet I still can speak my native tongue, or at least decipher it. When I crossed the ocean to come here, I brought in my luggage four books from home. I have kept them faithfully, in their assigned place in the middle of one of my shelves. I take them out from time to time, more to sniff at their coarse paper, that has kept its smell of pulp, than to actually look at their contents. But I can read them; if I concentrate, I can understand perfectly what they say. Three are short story collections, thin books you can finish in an evening. Translations from the German. The fourth is an treatise on architecture, ranging from greek columns to Twenties-style skyscrapers; there is not a single reference in it to my native country.

These are books from home only insofar as they were translated and printed there. My native country has produced few men of letters, apart from the token Nobel laureate, a half-blind poet, already senile when the distinction was conferred upon him from on high. It was just before I left. I remember the paper put it on the front page, in huge letters—the end of the war mustn't have rated such a display. My father had allowed his disgust to show; the famous poet's mother was Lithuanian, so how could he be considered a true son of our country?

I have never liked poetry, anyway.

ᴛ⁊

In her letter, my mother wrote:

My dear Janosh,

We haven't gotten any news from you for a long time now. Your father worries a lot about you. Do you need money, because if you do you have to tell me right away, I'll need some time to get some because the State pension was lowered after the Central Committee won the elections.

I lifted my gaze from the sheet. That was the very essence of my mother, this way of attributing her anxieties to others, her desperate attempts to be practical. A perfect stereotype, even better than the Jewish Grandmother.

I had known, even before I alighted from the ship, that I was no more than yet another immigrant from the old countries, badly dressed, more naive than a five-year-old. That I would have to fight to be granted the right to survive on this land, new yet already barricaded against outsiders. With the passage of years, I have learned to be an American, or at least to pretend.

But what I hadn't understood before I left was that our two countries would keep drifting apart. Every passing year worsens things.

There is what is called a "cultural center" three blocks south of my home. I found refuge there when I arrived, fifteen years ago. I was twenty, insufficiently educated, and broke. They found me a low-rent apartment, a job. For years I worked there as a volunteer, to pay back my debt, to help my compatriots. But in the end I stopped going. Every year, the distance between our two countries increases. Every year, fewer people manage to cross over. One evening last Fall, I returned to the cultural center, out of nostalgia. Four young men and a young woman were there, having just arrived. The young men were all dressed in ill-fitting black costumes, smudged with dust and a hint of mildew; all four with thick beards and thicker glasses, the lenses scratched and pocked. The young woman was clad in black from head to foot, her head wrapped in a heavy woolen shawl. No one back home had ever dressed this way.

The young men ate, surrounded by a dozen fellow countrymen who spoke to them all at once. They looked confused, like someone who has shown up at the wrong address. When they were done eating, the men began to talk. Their accent was so strong I had trouble understanding them—and I wasn't the only one.

They talked about where they had come from, why they had left. They said they'd wanted to see the world's modern side. To see planes and cars. Even though my family had never been able to afford one, my whole childhood was filled with the roar of the local-made automobiles that encumbered the narrow streets.

They took out photographs of their families. Blurred images, black and white. Everyone was dressed as they were. These pictures could have been thirty years old, yet they had been taken just before they'd left. All the men wore the same kind of heavy felt hat. I had never in my life seen anyone with such headgear.

I sat at their table, impelled by a feeling of vertigo. I spoke to the young woman, who hadn't yet uttered a word. I asked her what her name was. She looked at me with feral eyes.

She's my sister, one of the young men said. She doesn't talk. She was born at the end of the war, during the air raids. My mother says her little girl understood no one would hear her cries above the rumblings of the bombs, so she gave up on speaking forever.

I asked him, Where did you live? And he answered with the name of the town where I myself was born, five years at least before her. A town that had never been bombarded, I knew for having lived there ten years.

Then conversation drifted to politics, a subject as eternal as it is sterile, as pointless as it is irresistible. The four young men talked of corruption in the regime of the Central Committee; one of them even said, more than half-seriously, that things hadn't been so bad under the dictator Kronst, during the war.

It was then that I left. When I saw my compatriots looking at one another, bewildered, just as I was. They didn't know, anymore than I did, who Kronst had been.

ד

You will never guess what's happening: your brother Boris is getting married! With the Moldner girl but that's true you don't know her, he met her after you left. The ceremony will take place on October 18th. Your father didn't want to ask you, but I can say it because I'm your mama:he would like you to come visit. It's far and it's expensive for you, but he's your only brother.

If you can't come we all understand. But could you write to us and tell us you can't be there? We would all like to see you again and we all send kisses if you can't come.

My mother died when I was twelve; I have an older sister, but no brother.

With every passing year, my native country drifts further away from this one. It took me a long time to understand how deep this truth runs. This America where I have learned to live rushes towards the future, faster and faster. Every year, the rate of progress increases. But my native country regresses. There are no more color photographs there. No more planes, no more cars. Do the peasants starve once more, as they did during the First World War, when they had to subsist on rotting potatoes?

History is only a fiction. It changes with time, like the memories of an old man making his slow way to the grave.

I spent the rest of the day wondering what I should do. How could I not return? See the mother I had lost at the age of twelve, and who is now alive again? Meet my never-born brother.

But I knew that if I came back home, I could never leave again. It wasn't a question of money; simply that the distance would be too great for the return trip. I knew that if I should once more tread the soil that had seen me born, I would not leave it. And I have learned to live in the new world; I spent fifteen years on the transformation. Could I do it a second time? Learn to wear these damp-smelling black clothes, those heavy felt hats? Listen to my parents tell me of Kronst the dictator, the new past of my native land?

⌐¬

Night was falling and still I had not reached a decision. If I wanted to arrive on time for the wedding, I had to leave at once; I did not have the leisure to waver for weeks. I went to bed, to sleep on it.

I woke early the next morning, without help from my alarm clock. I felt freed from my doubts. It was settled: I would not leave. I had become an American, I could not go back. I rose, at peace with myself, prepared my breakfast. When came the time to dress, I noticed I was missing a jacket, two pairs of pants, some shirts. Two ties, also. I looked under my bed: my suitcase was gone.

Then I recalled what had woken me up: the slamming of a door. In the grip of a sudden anxiety, I sought for my mother's letter, but he hadn't taken it with him; he'd left it on the living room table. He must have understood that without this tangible proof, I would have doubted my sanity.

I know he will arrive on time, but not for the ceremony itself. What has become of public transportation? Surely there are still horse-driven coaches, but I feel he will have to do the last part of the journey on foot, wearing our glossy leather shoes, which will be irreparably soiled with mud by the time he arrives at the church. The ceremony will be over, the guests already at the reception. There will be someone there to give him information, and he will set off once more, with the exhausting stride I always fall into when I am nervous. He will arrive at last, his legs throbbing with pain, drenched in sweat, his synthetic-fiber jacket held in the crook of his arm. He will see the guests at the feast, the men wrapped up in their too-heavy black clothes, but bare-headed by exception, the women wearing their finest shawls, with colored embroidery. The bridal couple will be at one end of the table, he in black, she in white lace, looking almost obscene next to these vestments of wool and felt, but nevertheless pure as an angel out of the old illuminated books that were destroyed under the Kronstian regime.

He will remain there, apart, silent and embarrassed. And then my mother will see him, will rise to her feet, screaming, Janosh! And everyone will turn to look at him. My father will run to him, crush his eldest son against his breast, and suddenly he will find himself sitting among the guests, his mother sobbing on his shoulder, a glass of bitter champagne in his hand, Boris laughing unstoppably, the bride blushing, a hand held before her mouth.

And Janosh, among his people, will spare a thought for Jancek, his double left behind, the one who stayed in America. What has he become, Jancek, what will happen to him now, lost in the new world, in a land grown too distant ever to be reached?

Dawn

Karl Schroeder

Maddox sat among the dead, listening to them bicker. The blood of the man he had killed earlier was still warm in his veins, and he wanted peace and quiet. It was raining, so he had returned to Two Houses, seeking the company of his own kind. It was a mistake.

Liam, the youngest of the new brood, waved the limp hand of his victim at Maddox. "Yoo hoo!" He laughed, and his sidekick Henry joined in a second later. Liam sat astride the body of the young woman, whom he had picked up at the bus station. Apparently he and Henry had spent hours killing her, while Minx watched. The two youngest were intoxicated with the kill, buffooning around like drunken college undergrads. Minx, who looked younger than they, still perched expressionlessly on the cellar's heavy oaken table, her torn fishnets inches away from the heavy leather straps mounted in the wood.

"In my day," said Maddox, "we took killing seriously."

Liam sneered at him. He was getting bolder lately. Cocky. "Too much TV, I guess," he said. "The bane of youth."

Maddox sighed. He was tired of this place, these people, but this pair of mansions joined by underground tunnels was the only warren in the city, and he had spent too many decades alone. The warren had a pecking order, and Liam knew it.

"Does it bother you? —Killing, I mean?" Liam mocked. He pretended sympathy. "The poor, poor girl, after all. How she screamed." He dug Henry in the ribs.

Maddox stood up and stretched. "Killing doesn't bother me. It still bothers you. That's why you fixate on it." He heard footsteps upstairs, and took the opportunity to nod to Minx, then turned away from the childish confrontation.

"Well said." Roland had entered, silently as always. Maddox nodded to the warren's leader as Roland settled himself on a divan. The cellars of Two Houses were luxurious by human standards, and the younger vampires revelled in it. Roland and Maddox were indifferent to the setting; Maddox had seen Roland sit with equal poise on a heap of garbage in the sewers.

Roland waved a hand indulgently at the two youngest vampires. "But do carry on," he said. "Don't let me stop you." His voice was deep and resonant, his skin a rich dark brown. The others considered him the absolute ruler here. To Maddox he was a temporary companion, no more or less than anyone else. There was no competition between them.

As Liam self-consciously dragged the girl's body into a corner, three more vampires entered. "Rain's stopped," said Terence, while Lucy patted Henry on the head and the Parson wafted over to the piano to play. As the strains of Chopin filled the warm, candlelit room, the conversation warmed with it, and Maddox began to relax.

He was not so distracted that he didn't notice something odd about the last member of the warren when he arrived. Catcher, so-called because he always dressed like he was heading for the park to play ball, was unusually subdued. Normally he was at least as boisterous as Liam, though he was much older. He had been created back in the days when only natural psychopaths tended to embrace the Dark Gift, so like most vampires he was monotonously unchanging beneath his charismatic exterior. Liam was a bit afraid of him; Liam, Maddox suspected, was not psychotic at all, just morally bankrupt like the rest of this generation.

Tonight Catcher skulked in the background, his face a mask that he pulled into a grin whenever anyone made a joke. He contributed nothing, and he kept wiping his mouth, as though he'd tasted something awful. His eyes met Maddox's at one point, and Catcher looked down quickly, resting his gaze on a neutral object—the dead girl.

Roland had noticed as well. He and Maddox exchanged a glance, but clearly Roland didn't know what was up either. Both chose to wait and see.

It didn't take long for Liam to recover his poise, and by four o'clock he was jumping on and off the killing table, imitating the latest pop star with uncanny accuracy, drawing delighted laughter from Minx. He was getting responses from everyone except the old ones—and Catcher.

"Hey!" He hopped down and walked over to Catcher, who by now was standing near the door. "It's your turn, Catcher. Karaoke night in hell." He reached out.

"Don't touch me!"

All talk ceased. Roland and Maddox exchanged another glance, but neither moved. Catcher backed away from Liam.

"Oh, we're so high and mighty!" Liam pursued him to the doorway. With a lightning-quick move he snatched Catcher's Phillies cap. "Ha!"

Faster than that, Catcher struck back—and suddenly Liam was skating across the floor, blood spraying from his crushed chest.

Roland was at the door before the others could do more than blink, but Catcher was already gone. Maddox leaped over Liam and the others followed him, all talking at once.

The two Edwardian mansions that comprised Two Houses nestled among birch and maple trees at the end of a long sinuous drive. Here near the bluffs it was quiet, though the entire horizon glowed with city light. Maddox paused on the porch, drinking in the newly freshened night air, and looked for Catcher's tracks.

A flicker of movement on the street told him Roland would outdistance him in seconds if he didn't hurry. Maddox launched off the porch and covered the sixty feet to the street in four steps. He was intent on following Roland, and the others quickly fell behind him—all except Minx.

"Where's he going?" Her voice was pitched at a conversational level as she ran beside him; they didn't breathe at all except to speak.

Roland had stopped under a streetlight at the top of the next hill. He whirled, arms akimbo as he looked for Catcher. Beyond him the sky was lightening with approaching dawn. Maddox slowed to a walk and said, "I don't know. If we knew why he did that…"

Minx crossed her arms under her cascade of necklaces. Silver bracelets clinked together. "I saw you and Roland watching him. So I watched him too."

"He was acting guilty," said Maddox.

She squinted. "No…Something else…" Then she brightened. "I bet I know where he went. Come on."

Minx vanished. It took him a second to spot her—she was already vaulting over the back fence of a nearby house, heading for a ravine. He followed without hesitation.

Behind the house the land dropped down into a tangle of bush with a creek at the bottom. Minx could have run straight down and up the other side, and Maddox could have jumped it, but she sidetracked to a chain-link fence that angled steeply into the dark. Mounting it with a nimble hop she raced along the narrow top, down and up the ravine. Probably didn't want to throw a heel on her granny shoes.

The chain-link fence broke for the stream, then continued up the other side of the ravine through trees and into dazzling light. Maddox nearly collided with Minx, who had stopped atop the fence at the edge of a baseball field.

The level green park was empty, but still lit at this hour by tall halogen floodlights. None of the houses nor the school beyond the park showed lit windows; chirping crickets made the only sound.

Catcher was twenty feet up one of the lighting poles, climbing fast. By the time Maddox and Minx reached the pole he was perched atop it by the white lamps.

Roland appeared at Maddox's side. "Catcher!" he hissed. "Come down! Somebody will see you!"

A giddy laugh floated down. "Not by eight o'clock."

Maddox checked the horizon. It was almost five. The horizon was banded with peach and rose. Minx said, "But the sun—" then turned to gape in shock at Maddox.

Roland began to climb hand over hand after him. "What happened, Catcher? Did somebody discover you? Did you lead mortals to Two Houses?"

"No." Catcher's voice cracked. "Leave me. You can't help me."

"But why? What is it?" Roland had vanished into the glare.

"Stay back! I don't know if it's—if…" Scuffling sounds. With a bang!, one of the halogens blew up. Roland hissed in pain, then hit the ground next to Maddox and rolled to his feet. His shirt was smoking. "Bastard!"

"Go away!"

"Catcher?" Minx's voice was low and hypnotic. Maddox imagined this was the voice she used to lure her victims. "It'll be okay. Just tell us what happened. We're your warren. We can help."

Maddox helped Roland to his feet. "Never seen anything like it," he muttered.

Roland shook his head. "They snap sometimes, when they're young. And when they're…emotional. Catcher's neither."

Emotional. Like Maddox, he meant. Not psychotic.

"Push the pole over?" said Maddox. "Or knock him off it with a rock?"

"Neither. Look." A police car was slowing to a stop on the far side of the park.

"Shit," said Minx. "We're going to have to make a mess."

Roland shook his head firmly. "They won't see him among the lights. And we can't have an Incident so close to home."

"We're not just going to leave him!"

Roland nodded. "Yes, we are." Then he was gone. Maddox took Minx's arm and pulled her toward the ravine. The cruiser stopped and its doors opened.

"But—"

Maddox was stronger than Minx. He hauled her to the edge of the park and threw her over the fence. "Stop!" some mortal shouted behind him. He jumped over the fence and into the ravine.

As they neared the warren Roland was far ahead of them, an angry silhouette against the dawn sky. Minx walked beside Maddox and glowered at the pavement. "We can't leave him like that."

"I'm surprised. You sound like this bothers you," he said.

She looked up at him. "Of course it bothers me."

Maddox nodded at the dark figure ahead of them. "Roland is angry. But he's not upset."

"Are you?"

Maddox shook his head, not in denial but in refusal to answer. They were silent for a while, but finally he had to ask: "How did you know where he'd go?"

Minx looked uncomfortable. "You said he looked guilty. Well, actually he was acting like a mortal girlfriend of mine did...the day after she got raped."

He stopped walking. "What?"

"Shame," she said. "It wasn't guilt we saw in Catcher's eyes. It was shame."

⌐¬

A week later Henry disappeared. He had gone to hunt with Liam, who had healed from Catcher's attack. Together they had chased a couple of homeless kids onto the rail lands downtown. They all knew this territory well; Maddox felt he could recognize all the night watchmen in the city's lots and warehouses. By convention they never hunted these solitaries.

Liam and Henry split up and Liam easily caught his quarry. "But when I finished and looked up," he said the next evening, "there was the other one, climbing the fence to the expressway in plain sight. And no Henry. I had to dispose of the body so I couldn't take the time to find the fucker, but he wasn't on the railyard. Thought he might have been run over by a train," he added with a grin, "like I disguised mine. But no. Nowhere."

Henry hadn't returned that morning. They had convened in the upstairs lounge of South House to discuss the situation. Baroque music drifted up from downstairs; Parson was off by himself as usual, but contributing in his own way through the harpsichord.

"He's just left," said Terence. "Decided he had enough of us. Give him a century, he'll be back."

Liam looked dazed.

"No." Roland, seated at his usual spot at the head of the table, steepled his hands and scowled at them each in turn. "We're being hunted. Haven't you felt it?"

Maddox was surprised. For the past three nights he'd felt…something, like the distant presence of another predator. Other vampires came and went, and the older ones could feel one another's auras at a great distance. He'd had some sense of that. "I sensed another vampire," he said. "But why would one be hunting us?"

Roland shrugged. "To set up his own warren. It happens."

"It doesn't feel like that," said Maddox.

"I haven't felt anything," said Liam.

Roland ignored Liam. "Then who is it? A mortal?"

Maddox had no answer to this.

"From now on," said Roland, "we hunt in pairs. And I mean right through the hunt. I know some of you prefer to feed alone," he glanced at Minx, "but I don't want you to let your partner out of your sight during the hunt."

"Do you think this has something to do with what happened to Catcher?" asked Terence. They had returned the night after Catcher ran, and found ashes and scraps of burned clothing at the base of the pole. Catcher had destroyed himself in the sun.

"Maybe. It's just too much of a coincidence that this happens so soon after that. Does everyone understand?"

They nodded. An ironic discord sounded from downstairs. Roland nodded grimly. "Liam, you're with me. The rest of you…" he turned with a dismissive wave, already forgetting them.

Maddox turned to Minx. "Young lady, it would be my pleasure to escort you."

She laughed. "When you put it that way—sure!"

ᵲᵓ

They parked in a seedy neighbourhood and began prowling. The location was Minx's choice. After they had passed several solitary prostitutes and two men walking with guilty quick steps, Maddox asked, "Who do you hunt?"

It was an intimate question—but he would find out anyway.

She had appeared tense as they walked. Now she relaxed a bit. "Pimps," she said. "And pushers. And abusive husbands. They're not hard to find, any given night. How 'bout you?"

"Anyone," he said.

"Anyone? Anyone at all?"

He shrugged, and she shook her head. "I'm surprised, Maddox."

They walked a little further, eyes roving for likely prospects. "Tell me," he said after a while, "how did you know where Catcher was going?"

"He went home," she said. "It's what you'd do, feeling like that. Run home. And he's from Cincinnati, long way from here. The only place around he'd feel at home would be a baseball park."

"You felt empathy," he accused.

"What of it?"

"I'm just curious. I've watched you watch Liam and Henry torture people to death. The two facts don't fit, that's all."

"You think I did Henry!"

"No." He realized what he did think even as he said it. "But I bet you stalked him—both him and Liam. Am I wrong?"

Minx glared at him defiantly. "What of it?"

Maddox met her eyes. "Why didn't you destroy them, if you had chances to? —Or at least stop them from killing innocents?"

She turned away, twining her fingers through the rusted strands of a fence. "I—I don't know." He didn't believe her, but the set of her shoulders told him not to pursue it for now. "I didn't ask to be made," she continued. "Roland came to me, and it was death or the Gift. I was used to men doing what they wanted with my body, so why should this be any different? After I knew, I wanted to destroy myself. Until I figured out a way to feed that didn't eat my guts out."

She whirled. "But I don't understand you. You'll kill anyone? How can that be? You feel for people, too—I know it."

Maddox hadn't expected the conversation to go this far. He was an honourable man—or an honourable monster, he thought. So he said, "I didn't have a choice either. Most of us are killers already before we're made, you know. As you age you discover that the people who dream of being vampires are usually the worst choices. They go mad when you give them the Gift, and they destroy themselves. It's psychopaths who adapt best.

"I was made in the Great War. I and my company arrived from training, all fresh and patriotic, expecting an honourable fight. I remember when we got the front, it was so shocking I just went numb. The cold, the mud, bodies everywhere, men locked inside their own feelings, wrapped around hurts I couldn't imagine then.

"It took two weeks for me to descend from humanity into complete savagery. Finally, one morning, we were ordered over the top. We had to walk slowly across no-man's land, in full daylight. Our own barrage was timed to move ahead of us, you see, we couldn't run. The Germans were shelling and machine-gunning as we walked. One after another I saw my friends blown to bits. One fellow went down with his jaw missing, but otherwise unhurt. He shot himself when he realized what had happened. Then we reached a German trench. It was full of dead and live men, it was hard to tell them apart. But the live ones came at us with bayonets. And at that moment I entered Hell.

"While we fought like animals, something else came into the trench. I didn't clearly see it then, but it passed through the whole mêlée, and killed everyone on the way by. I was thrown against the wall of the trench and landed in a tangle of barbed wire. As I lay there I watched him—the vampire—feeding."

"Two days I spent there among the dead, and all the time he prowled in and out of the trench, talking to me. He was trying to drive me mad—testing me, I know now. I don't know why I didn't go over the edge, but at the end of it he came to me and gave me the Gift." Maddox heard decades of bitterness in his own voice as he added, "He said he thought I could handle it.

"So it doesn't matter who I kill. I'm in Hell anyway."

Minx had turned away, arms crossed. "Liam thinks killing bothers me," Maddox said softly. "He has no idea."

"Liam is an idiot," she said.

"Come." He laid a hand on her shoulder. "You know how to find Henry. Let's go do that. As soon as we've fed."

⌐

"Henry and Liam are boys," she had said. "They like big machines."

Another subway train roared past, inches from Maddox's nose. Minx was pressed against the tunnel wall beside him. She grinned at the startled faces of passengers who happened to be glancing out. Then it was past, leaving swirling grit and darkness in its wake.

"Henry loves it down here," she said. "He thinks this is where we should live."

Yes, of course. It was so like him; if Maddox had given any more thought to it, he would have known this too. He had long ago lost the habit of putting himself in another's place. He frowned.

He and Minx had shared the death of a man whom they had heard beating his young daughter. With the man's blood they had absorbed something of his talents and memory. Neither took satisfaction from it; for Maddox the man's life seemed small and venal, and his death here in the clean and quiet of an urban kitchen was nothing compared to the nightmare Maddox had seen in France. For her part Minx was concerned for the child, not the father; he was merely an obstacle to be removed, his memories a brief sickness to be overcome by force of will.

Each, in their own way, assimilated the life and moved on.

"Look." Minx knelt and pointed. Faint footprints led through the greasy dust, which otherwise had been undisturbed for months. She hurried on ahead.

Maddox gasped and stopped dead. Very suddenly he had felt something turn his way, like the gaze of a vast and intent searchlight. It swept over him, and he couldn't move—and then it was gone.

He reeled. The subway tunnel seemed empty in either direction—but as he gazed to the north, it was as though far down there, at the end of the convergence of dim lines, something looked back.

"Maddox!" He blinked, turning to find Minx gesturing urgently to him. She had found a side opening. "I see him!"

The opening led into a small transformer substation. Henry huddled there under a clutch of humming green boxes. He barely glanced up as Minx and Maddox squeezed in after him.

"Henry!" She shook him. "What happened?"

He looked as fragile as glass. "Hunted," he croaked. He obviously hadn't fed. "It hunted me."

"What hunted you?" Maddox paused as a train thundered past. "A man? Or a vampire?"

"Neither. Something—something that feeds on us."

"How is that possible?" whispered Minx. Maddox barely heard her over echoes from the train.

"You haven't fed," he said. "Come. We must get you some—"

"No!" Henry fought him off weakly. "I can't!"

"What are you talking about?"

"I can't. I—I just can't." He put his face in his hands, and began to cry.

Maddox and Minx stared at one another over his shaking shoulders. Her expression no doubt mirrored his own. He saw fear there.

"Let's get him home," he said at last.

r⁷

"If it wasn't one of us, then what was it?"

Roland stood with Maddox looking in on Henry. A week had passed since they had found him, and he still would not feed. He was hollow-cheeked and weak now, and his eyes had lost their luster. Normally such a fast would not destroy a vampire, but there was something deeply wrong with Henry. Lucy had even offered him her throat, but he had pulled away with a cry. To keep him from wandering Roland had put him in a window-less cell below the cellars. There he lay, too weak now to even hide when dawn came.

When they examined him that first evening, Minx had found two bite marks on Henry's neck.

"You've felt it too, haven't you?" said Maddox. "It's not a vampire."

Twice more he had sensed that terrible, distant scrutiny. Each time he had frozen in place, like a deer caught in headlights.

Roland cursed. "It must be. One of the oldest, that's all."

"No."

"It's got to be an immortal!" Roland walked to the stairs. "If not a vampire, one of the others. They're rare, but we've both sensed them—I met one once, an Ancient."

"They don't hunt. You're sure you've never heard of something like this?"

Roland hesitated. "Sometimes—well, there are stories of impossibly powerful creatures that hunt vampires. Most of them turn out to be older vampires cleaning out a nest to make way for their own. But sometimes a city will lose all its vampires. All gone. Here and there, once or twice a century it happens."

"I've never heard this."

Roland snorted. "That's no surprise. You've spent the better part of your time alone. But I don't believe in monsters. It must be an old one."

Roland looked in on Henry one more time; his expression was that of distaste. Then they went upstairs, and drifted apart. Maddox stood by the half-open French doors for a while, listening to the Parson tune the piano. Then he stepped out into the fragrant night to think.

Summer had a particular sanctity for him. It was too bad the nights were shorter now, but somehow the briefness of the season made it all the more precious. He wished he could see more stars here, but the city washed them all away. It had been many years since he had spent time in the country—it was so much harder to hunt there—and he missed the purity of the deep sky.

Two Houses was beautiful. The Parson and Lucy kept the grounds neat, the hedges well trimmed. The trees were tall and virile. It was good to smell life that had no taint of blood in it. Were it not for green things, Maddox sometimes thought, he would have destroyed himself long ago.

Something moved in the periphery of his vision. Without pausing in his slow saunter or turning his head, he looked in that direction. Their four cars were all in the drive. Whatever he had seen had happened near the Volvo.

There it was: the car's trunk was ajar. The hatch bobbed slightly, as though something heavy were moving inside. Maddox felt an old reflex close his throat, though he had not breathed in minutes. Abandoning pretence, he walked over to the car.

He sensed nothing. No life, no breath. For a second he hesitated, thinking he should call the others. But he had never depended on another being for protection, and he wasn't about to start now. He quickly lifted the hatch.

A shadow swirled around him and hands smooth and cold as metal took Maddox by the shoulders, and pulled him down.

ᴦ⁷

He came to in a long concrete hall. There was no light, but he could see with the vision of the Gift. This was a steam tunnel—somewhere, but where??

Maddox sat up. His neck was sore. When he touched himself there he felt two tiny puncture wounds. He almost laughed at the irony—would have, had he not felt so damned strange.

It took an effort to reach his feet. A day must have passed, for he felt ravenously hungry.

This steam tunnel was part of a warren underneath a hospital. He wasn't too far from home, actually, and it was only about two a.m. It would be easy to feed here; then he could return to Two Houses and tell the others what had happened.

Roland had been right. He mused about this as he moved soundlessly through the wards, looking for a victim. Maybe the presence he had felt was something else—a red herring. Some vampire was stalking them; why, though? There was no benefit to the blood, and the thing had destroyed none of them so far.

The biggest puzzle, though, was why Henry and Catcher had reacted with such a sense of violation to what had happened.

Not that he felt good about it. He entered a semiprivate room and looked at the sleeping faces here. Two women in here for minor surgery; anyone would do. He chose one at random, and bent down.

He stopped. The woman breathed quietly, her face peaceful. He could smell her blood—it was clean and healthy. Left alone, she would recover well, and leave here in a few days.

Why should he care?

Maybe he didn't. But Minx would.

Feeling indulgent, he turned, and headed for the Palliative Care unit.

The Cancer ward was full, as usual. Here he sensed tension, pain, heard laboured breathing and the tapping of a nurse's pen on her clipboard. Yes—it would be virtuous to relieve someone here of their pain.

A young man lay helplessly in a room by himself. He couldn't sleep because of the pain in his belly and legs. As Maddox entered the room his eyes widened. He recognized what had come to him.

"May I?" It had been many years since Maddox had addressed a victim. It felt odd.

The youth closed his eyes. Maddox bent, and sank his teeth into the white flesh of his throat.

He expected the sensation of blood on his tongue, the surge of his own powerful heart pulling the life force from the other. Instead, he jerked in shock as he felt his heart push, and something—not blood, something not quite physical—left him and entered the youth.

Maddox croaked and tried to pull away. The youth's hands came up and clamped behind his head, holding down as Maddox's heart pounded an aether into the veins and heart of the other.

At last he pulled away with a cry. The sense of violation was so deep he gagged, and staggered back to fall against some medical equipment with a crash.

The sound summoned the nurse. "Are you all right, Hugh?" she said from the doorway.

Maddox slipped behind her out the door. He paused for an instant and glanced back. The young man was sitting straight up in bed. His eyes were wide, and his mouth was open in an expression of utter astonishment.

Maddox sobbed, and ran for the exit.

⌐¬

It was such a relief to be back on the grounds of Two Houses. There were the cars, and the lights were on inside South house. He could hear the Parson playing an étude.

He slid the French doors open and stepped in. Conversation ceased as they all looked up.

"Maddox!" Minx ran to him. The others stood as one, grinning in relief.

The smile died on Maddox's lips. The last time he was here he had been surrounded by, if not friends, at least intimate acquaintances. What he saw now was a collection of man-shaped objects, like moving mannequins, who clustered around him now gabbling questions. Only their eyes seemed alive, and of them, Minx's most of all.

A thing that was shaped like a bald black man took his hand and shook it. Its flesh seemed plastic and cold. "What happened? We were so worried about you."

He looked in Roland's eyes. There was no genuine concern there, only an imitation. If there was any emotion behind the act it was only worry for Roland himself, at the whittling away of his warren.

Maddox pulled his hand away. "Get away from me." His words floated like isolated balloons, unrecognizable as his own.

"Shit," said Lucy. "He's gone like Henry."

Roland took Maddox by the shoulders. "Maddox! Tell me what happened! You owe it to us."

They were all around him; if he fought, they would just overpower him and throw him in a cell like Henry. Maddox had not lasted this long by being stupid. He forced himself to smile, and relaxed into Roland's grip. "Sorry. I'm just a bit shocked, that's all. Let me sit down and I'll tell you."

It felt so strange, as though he were alone here and talking to the wall. Or not quite—he sensed other people here, but they were hard to identify with the moving collections of arms, legs, torsos and heads that sat now as he did.

"We are being stalked," he said. Might as well give them that. "It's a vampire. You were right, Roland, it's an old one. He wants to clean out the city, like you said."

"Why didn't he destroy you?"

Maddox shrugged. "He's got no real grudge against us. He'd just as soon scare us away."

Roland sat back; he was clearly unsatisfied, but willing to bide his time to find out the truth. "So what do we do? Hunt him down, I guess."

"Maybe." Maddox slumped back. "I'm tired."

Minx knelt beside him. "Have you fed?"

"Yes," he lied. "But it was quite a chase. And I slept in a tunnel. I'm all wrung out."

Roland stood briskly. "Find your cover and sleep, then. We'll talk about it tomorrow."

Maddox left, trying not to slink. He found his locker and lay back in it, but oblivion would not come. All he could think about was that horrible sensation of being drained as the youth held Maddox's mouth to his throat. In all the years since his creation he had never felt anything like it.

Was this what Catcher and Henry had experienced? Maddox imagined the shock they must have felt, coming home to find their companions transformed somehow. Catcher, in particular, could have had no presentiment that something was going to happen to him. It was no wonder he'd snapped.

Maddox was older—and the events of recent days had prepared him somewhat. Still, as dawn approached and he heard the others enter their lockers one by one, he rose, and prepared to leave. They no longer seemed like his kind.

He waited for silence; it would be dangerously bright out there now, but he could survive it briefly. He slipped out of the locker, carrying a satchel with his few possessions.

Minx was waiting by the door. "Where are you going, Maddox?" Her voice held that hypnotic quality again. He chose not to be offended, and shrugged.

"The writing's on the wall. I don't like Roland's plan to hunt the hunter. I don't think it'll work."

"So you're just turning tail and running? That doesn't sound like you at all!"

"Don't go." She put a hand on his chest, wide eyes boring into his own. "It's dawn, it's no time to be out. I understand you're feeling bad after what happened. You don't have to be alone. Sleep with me today. I want you to."

He felt the pressure of her will. It would have overwhelmed any mortal, and most of the young ones. Maddox shook his head. "I can't tell you why I have to leave," he said. "I—I don't quite understand it myself."

"You're not making any sense!" She blocked his way with her arm. "Maddox."

Angry now, he took her chin in his hand and stared into her startled eyes. "Stand still."

When he glanced back from the end of the driveway, Minx was still frozen in place, like a statue.

⌐┐

He spent that day in a culvert, emerging stiffly at dusk, well before he would normally be animate. The others would still be asleep, except maybe for Roland and Minx. Only Roland represented any threat.

It was strange to think of them that way. A deep and old sense of loneliness began to take possession of Maddox as he hurried away from the neighbourhood where he had so briefly felt at home. So this was what immortality meant—an ever clearer understanding of how ephemeral all things were.

He couldn't face them. Not until he understood what had happened to him.

Thinking about Minx, he had to wonder whether she had ever stalked him the way she had Liam and Henry. Probably, he decided; of them all, Minx was the best hunter, because only she took the time to understand her prey. She probably knew Maddox's safe-holes and typical stalking grounds.

Well then. He would abandon all his familiar ways.

He was hungry. With an unfamiliar dread, he found his way to an abandoned warehouse full of homeless kids. It was a simple matter to climb the outside, slip into a third-story window and find an addict drooling on his knees in the corner of a tiny room with discoloured plaster walls. Maddox hauled him to his feet unceremoniously and bit.

Again—his heart pumped the wrong way. The surge was painful and shocking; with a cry, he dropped the boy, but not before he again felt something leave him, as if a part of his soul had been stripped and given away.

Maddox backed away in confusion and terror as the boy climbed to his feet. Moments ago he had been almost comatose, but now his eyes were alert and he moved with easy grace.

"Hi, man. You're new, aren't you? Did you bring any food?"

Maddox was out the window before he could say anything more.

I'm losing myself, he thought over and over as he walked. Maddox was in a daze, hardly aware of where he was or where he was going. A horrible suspicion was taking hold in him, one he had to deny to stay sane. He felt diminished somehow by his attempt to feed—while his victim had looked....

The strangest thing was that his hunger was gone, as though he really had fed. Fed, and lost something of himself...and been satisfied.

To distract himself he spent some time finding a hiding-hole, and there he settled to await dawn and oblivion. There was nothing in this part of town except the storm sewers, so he finally hauled up a manhole and made himself a nest in an twenty-four inch pipe deep below the street.

Dawn came, and he was still awake. Dots of sunlight from the airholes of the manhole cover moved slowly down the wall of the shaft. Maddox stared at them in fascination. He could not remember such brightness, although at one time he must have lived in it. Gradually as he watched he became drowsy, and slept.

He awoke hungry. Hunting was not an option; he understood Henry now. Giving up wasn't an option either. He had to find a way to fight this.

Remembering his suspicion last night, he realized there was a way to find out whether he was right. He waited until it was fully dark, then left the sewer and ran tirelessly east, toward the suburbs. The warren lay that way, but he had no intention of going there. It was a risk to even enter the neighbourhood, since Roland might detect his presence, but at this hour Roland should still be far afield hunting. If Maddox was gone before midnight he should be safe.

This should only take a few minutes. He stood gazing up at the blazing lights of the hospital where had awakened the other night. What floor had that been? Sixth, yes, that wing there. Silent as a ghost, he slipped through the lobby and, unseen, made his way to the Cancer ward.

Maddox's throat was tight again as he approached the room. It was silent here except for the moans of several of the other patients. Summoning his courage, he stepped into the room of the youth he had bitten.

The young man looked up as he entered. He smiled widely. "You are real," he said.

He was sitting up in bed, and Maddox could sense no pain in him. As the vampire came slowly to stand at the side of the bed, he nodded, saying, "It's gone. They can't believe it. Neither can I. But I can feel it. It's not there." He put a hand to his side, and grinned again at Maddox.

"I'm glad you came back. I wanted to thank you."

Thank me? Maddox couldn't find words to reply. He shook his head.

"You saved my life." The young man held out his hand. "I'm Hugh. What's your name?"

Maddox stared at the hand.

After an awkward pause, Hugh lowered his arm, and cleared his throat. "What are you?" he asked.

Maddox backed away. I don't know, he tried to say, but whether Hugh heard or not he never knew, because he was running again, and this time he didn't think he would ever stop.

It can't be. Maddox sat next to a gargoyle atop one of the towers in the financial district. I'm a killer. I can't save anyone.

There was no question that he had. He was weaker for it, too—both times, he had felt part of himself go into his victim. Catcher and Henry must have felt it too, and for them there could have been no deeper violation, for both of them were vampires of the classic type, selfish and solipsistic. They could only take, to give was impossible.

Before tonight, Maddox had believed it impossible for himself, too. For eighty years now, he had destroyed lives. It was his essential nature, after all; a vampire might be a philanthropist, indulge and cultivate mortals, but all such tenderness was made a lie every night by the consequences of his hunger. Sympathy for mortals had driven more vampires to self-destruction than any other cause, because it contradicted their very being.

Maddox stared down at the traffic. He liked to come to this spot; this particular gargoyle was well crafted, and before he joined Roland's warren he had often sat with it as his only companion after the hunt. He was more alone than ever, and now its cold stone grin gave him no comfort.

Since the horror in the trenches, hope had been impossible for Maddox. Life was no longer possible for him either; he had accepted that. But there was also another aspect of himself he'd thought he had accepted: that he was entirely a killer. Tonight, he was coming to grips with the fact that some deep, stubborn part of himself had never believed it.

"Maddox." He stiffened. Minx had found him.

He looked up to find her standing on the parapet next to him. "I shouldn't be surprised," he said. "I broke my own rule by coming back here."

"Maybe you wanted me to find you," she said.

"Maybe." He gestured for her to sit. They dangled their feet casually over the sixteen-story drop.

"Beautiful spot," she said. "And quite invisible from below. It's nice to know you have your private perches too."

"A common habit among monsters."

"Monsters," she whispered. "Is that what you think we are?"

He was surprised. "What else could we be?"

"Avenging angels. Furies." She said it almost shyly. "Some of us are monsters, true. Like Liam and Henry."

"And Catcher. And Lucy. And the Parson, come right down to it." He shook his head sadly. "And me. Why didn't you destroy Liam and Henry, anyway? They're worse than the mortals you slay every night."

Minx fiddled with her necklace. "They're all I've got," she said in a small voice. "Maybe that's hypocritical, but it's true. All we have, you and me and them, is each other."

Maddox stared into the hazy distance. "You'll get used to being alone. You'll have to."

"Is that why you left, Maddy? Because you don't need us?"

"No."

"Then why did you take off?" She pouted at the skyline. "Henry's gone, you know. He dried up and crumbled. Roland was so surprised."

"I'm not. Henry could never have survived it."

"Survived what?" She put her hand on his shoulder, turning him to face her. "What's happening, Maddox? Are we being hunted?"

He looked at her. He almost felt he could trust her. If he told her what he knew, she might understand—or she might be as deeply shocked as Roland and the others would be. If they had wanted to hunt their hunter before, they would become positively obsessed now.

Somewhere, far out in the glittering landscape, he felt that pulse of presence again. Like a reminder, or a hello.

"It's nothing to fear," he said to her. "I had my own reasons for leaving the warren. You can see I'm okay. Why don't we leave it at that?"

Minx stared at him for a long time. Then she stood abruptly and walked away. Maddox longed to call her back, anything to escape the loneliness he felt. It would be wrong to tell her, though. This was something each of them would have to face alone.

He turned his face back to the lights to the city, and dripped tears of old blood into the sleeping streets.

ᒥᒼ

The next night, he found a decrepit wino, and this time he didn't flinch from the sensation as his heart poured life into the other man. The following night, it was a drug-addicted prostitute, and another one the night after. Night by night he felt lighter, more fragile, but no less strong. Maddox felt he was becoming a ghost.

He deliberately didn't think about it. The experience was the important thing; to dilute it with thoughts or theories would be unjust. It wasn't important anymore that this process might destroy him. If he poured his whole essence into the homeless and damaged of the city, what of it? He was still strong. He might heal thousands before, like Henry, he crumbled.

In some ways, in fact, he was stronger than ever. The sun no longer burned as it peeked over the horizon. By the sixth day he was eager to see it, though at first he could only face it in reflection from the windows of the city's towers. He was still afraid to let it flood into him undiluted. Soon, though. Soon.

Now and then as he worked, he felt the searchlight gaze of the other pass over him. It no longer stopped him in his tracks. His own distance vision was improving; one night he sat in a car by the airport, and saw Roland entering a house five miles away. The other vampire paused, an uneasy expression on his face, then hurried up the steps. Maddox laughed, and turned his gaze elsewhere.

Try as he might, he could not find the other one, the one who had changed him.

On a cloudy morning he stood outside the hospital and watched as Hugh was released. No longer stick-thin and emaciated, the boy gave a whoop of delight and ran into the arms of his parents. Maddox recognized the expression on his face as he breathed the morning air and squinted at the light. Maddox brought his own pale hand up, and examined his fingers in daylight for the first time in eighty years.

At last, in late August, there came a morning when the sun blazed strongly, and Maddox walked out to meet it. He was not sleepy, and the light did not burn him. He stood weeping among the trees of High Park and listened as the birds and squirrels awoke, and traffic slowly picked up on the freeway. The heat of the sun on his face was glorious. He wanted to bathe in it forever.

As he stood there, he felt the other's eyes on him. Maddox turned. No, he was nowhere nearby—but for the first time, Maddox knew where he was. The other seemed to wait for Maddox to find him; then the inner light switched off, leaving certainty behind it.

He hailed a cab. "Mount Pleasant cemetery, please."

At the gates of the cemetery he had to stop again, because he had never seen the place flooded with light. Vampires avoided such places nowadays—there was no life in them, after all. Maddox had walked through it a few times, and he remembered pausing in front of the memorial to the Great War. Then, he had felt only pain. Today, what would he feel? He started forward eagerly to find out.

Dew painted his shoes as he ducked under emerald-laden branches. In the distance he heard a lawn mower. The sun filled him with warmth; he could feel it pouring life into the gardens. A few mortals walked calmly by, meditating, seemingly oblivious to the glory in which they moved.

A marble angel caught his eye. He had seen it before, but never in the golden glow of sunlight. Its eyes were sad and understanding. Maddox laughed in delight, and walked on past.

The cemetery was full of trees, open swathes of ground full of grave-stones, and dotted here and there with ostentatious crypts. The place was huge, and hilly, so after a few minutes he had lost sight of the street. Only the dead and the living trees surrounded him now. And the sun.

A bright flash caught his eye. Maddox turned, shading his eyes.

Atop an Egyptian-style cenotaph stood a glass man.

Sunlight shattered into a million shades and shafts within the figure's body, throwing lozenges and arcs of light everywhere. Maddox found it hard to look at, as though somehow it were brighter than the sun that gave it light.

As Maddox approached, the figure turned its head to look at him. It was hard to tell through the glittering highlights and prismatic light that made up its face, but he thought it smiled.

There was really nothing to say. He stood below the stone spire, as the figure raised its arms to embrace the light. Slowly, then, it began to lose substantiality. The outline softened, the refractions became diffuse. Flickering, it vanished.

Maddox raised his own translucent hand in farewell, and turned to leave the cemetery.

Tonight, he would hunt Minx.

MUMMY BONES

Shirley Meier

Silent highway
Sand drifting
Over cars here
and there

Stopped
Metal tombstones
On grass-cracked
slab

Fallen chunks
Rusted grid exposed

One car
Corpse turned, reaching
to the back seat
Pearls in zephyr
swing inside ribs

Teeth grinning sinew
No lips
Rags rotted leather mummybones

Sealed infant seat
Solar power
"E-Z Ryder never stops rocking"
"Like Mom on the road"

Computer chip playing
Sweet music-box tones
"Hush-a-bye"

Cool wafts, isolated air
Teat reservoir dry
Echoes of hoarse infant screams
Wails ghost wind

Ryder coos,
"It's all right, Mummy's coming"

Mummybones

infant skull sways
Ryder never stops rocking
Lacy bones in a white diaper
Silken hair against blue/pink/green pastels

Sealed tight
"Mummy's coming"

Altered Statements: #6
Experiments

M.A.C. Farrant

The practice of putting old people inside metal cages and placing them in school yards is to be discouraged. There is not one shred of evidence to support the view that this activity will retard the ageing process. Our experiments with caged old people have shown that it is not possible to infuse youth; youth is not a scent that can be worn to dissolve the years. And hundreds of children swarming over such a cage, we have observed, will not result in suppleness in an old person's skin. If anything, under such conditions, old people become even more cranky than they already are; it has been reported that a number of children have been scratched by the elderly trying to grab their arms and legs through the bars.

Side-effects from the caging of old people: namely, they rapidly turn a dull yellow colour—both skin and clothing—which is most unpleasant to view; they become adept at issuing profanities, delivered at the shriller end of the musical scale; if left unattended for longer than two weeks they turn into stone, a granite of little use to the industry

Our experiments further indicate that the youth of children cannot be extracted, rubbed off or otherwise worn with positive results by an old person. Practices such as jumping from school yard roofs into groups of children, smothering oneself with children at birthday parties, rolling in them under Christmas trees, or the wearing of small children on the back like a bulky shawl is of little use as is the practice of maintaining a child-like demeanour.

For these reasons, the Department of Experiments strongly suggests that old people abandon the pursuit of joy and return to their small airless rooms. We find it distressing to witness their mindless capering on the public lawns—old men riding tricycles, old women dancing with each other in wedding dresses. The public lawns should be left to the solemn pursuit of childhood play.

Tremendum

David Annandale

Something came to find Blake while he was deep in REM sleep. It went looking for him beneath layers of unconsciousness, located him, and took over his dream.

It was a good dream up until the take-over. Blake had shed twenty-five years. He was back in his home town, cycling down the highway with his friends. It was a dream of memories: nice, uncomplicated echoes of a last, pre-hormonal summer. Blake was enjoying himself. He wasn't conscious of dreaming. He was aware of having one hell of a good time, and his sleeping self was much more relaxed than his awake one had been for several months. There had been far too many committee wrangles in the real world of late.

So it was too bad when the dream was seized. Blake knew when it happened, if not what had happened, because as of that moment he knew that he was dreaming all right, and he had that premonition of impending shift into nightmare. His bike became difficult to pedal. His friends kept going, and he couldn't shout to tell them to wait, to come back. The sky didn't suddenly fill with clouds, but the quality of the light dropped several notches down from golden to grainy and dim. His friends disappeared. His bike refused to go any further. Blake got off it and stood, gazing down the road, waiting for the arrival. A wind pushed against his face. This was his first real clue that he wasn't alone in his mind, because while he always saw and heard plenty in his dreams, he never felt anything.

He waited, getting scared. He stood at the outskirts of town, a perfect-down-to-the-last-stripmall but utterly deserted reconstruction of home, and stared out to the highway's vanishing point.

Once it appeared over the horizon, it came very quickly. And now Blake knew, right down to the core, that the dream was no longer his, and that his thoughts had been invaded. He knew because, when he saw what was coming, he experienced a brand new emotion. It was like awe, but much more. Awe on a scale he had never felt, had never imagined could be felt. Awe mixed with terror so huge and perfect as to be sublime.

The thing flew towards him no more than twenty feet off the ground.

It was silent. In the first moment it had looked like an airplane, and, in a wrong way, it still did. It was an airplane whose fuselage had disappeared. It was a pair of black wings, perfectly level with each other, separated by just the width of the missing body. The new feeling built in Blake as the wings flew closer. It wasn't their size or their colour or their shape that was the trigger for awe. It was their statement of the impossible, their creation of what should not be, the absolutely wrong. They were aerodynamic scythes slicing through reality's neck. They swooped over Blake, filling the sky. The awe became a god. And Blake woke himself up with his scream.

Eyes wide. Heart bam-bam-bamming, loud enough to be heard. Drenched in instant sweat. Breath held post-scream.

He made himself let the air out, pushed his lungs into a deep, slow rhythm, and his system gradually got a grip on itself.

"God," he muttered, and sat up. He was not going back to sleep. He glanced at the luminous face of his watch. Almost six-thirty. He had to get up soon anyway. He stood, walked to the bathroom, and let the hard blast of the shower wash off the taint of the dream.

But the stain of the invasion, that stayed.

⌐¬

Stubborn as an oil slick, the stain clung to him throughout the day. It was the sense of being watched, from a decreasing distance, by someone with sharp teeth. He was twitchy all through his classes. One of his first-year students asked the "But did the author really mean all this stuff?" question, and he snapped "Yes. Shut up," at her. Unprofessional. Unprofessorial. Unproductive. But he was feeling too frayed to care.

After classes, he sat in his office, staring at the stack of papers to mark, but seeing black metal wings fly overhead, again and again. He wasn't thinking the dream through, analyzing it, trying to work out why it was turning into such a cancer for him. He was simply replaying it on perpetual loop, shivering through the echoes of that terror-awe. And soon it was six o'clock: past time to go home.

He left the Humanities Centre and walked across the parking lot. He was just about to unlock his car when he changed his mind. He crossed the last block of the University of Alberta's campus and jaywalked over to the Library Pub. A little Dutch courage before heading home. It couldn't ward off dreams, but it might hold back the fear of them.

The bar was in the building's basement. Low ceiling, low seating. Armchairs and sofas absorbed sound, smoke, and tired patrons. There were bookshelves along the entire periphery, boasting old psychology textbooks, arcane hardcovers from the 50s, and autobiographies by persons so obscure their own books couldn't remember them. Blake eased himself down into a corner chair and ordered a scotch. He was almost ready for his second when he saw Ford, from Astronomy, come in. He waved. Ford headed over.

"Hi John," he said, sitting down. He stared at Blake for a moment. "If you don't mind my saying so, you look like something the cat dragged in, chewed up, swallowed, and threw up."

"Thanks, Lou. I love you too."

"No, I'm serious. Are you sick?"

Blake shrugged. "Bad night, that's all." My, he thought, but aren't we nonchalant. "Good day?" he asked.

"Wild. You hear what happened at Mount Palomar?"

"Um, let me see, Palomar…Palomar…Oh, that's in the real world, isn't it? I'm in English, Lou. We don't concern ourselves with that vulgar place."

"None of your sarcasm. I'll take that as a no?"

Blake nodded.

"The telescope broke," Ford said simply.

"What do you mean, it broke? Did they drop it or something?"

Ford laughed. "You'd almost think so. No, they didn't drop it, but they must have done something stupid. The mirror shattered. In a million pieces, apparently. They're lucky no one got hurt."

"I don't believe it," said Blake, picturing a five-meter mirror exploding into shrapnel. "What the hell were they doing?"

"Nothing. That's what's so weird. They were just moving it to look at a new quadrant and bam!"

"Their seven years' bad luck is going to be on a pretty massive scale."

"No kidding. It's a shame though. I don't know if they're going to replace it. That's a lot of money, and with the glow of the city getting worse and worse, and the Hubble making the darn thing obsolete anyway…" Ford shrugged. "I think it's the end of an era. We had something of a wake in the department today."

"It is too bad," Blake agreed. He had a nostalgia flash of an astronomy book he'd owned as a kid. Stars, it had been called: basic and to the point. A glossy black cover, showing a comet-streaked night sky above, yes, the Mount Palomar Observatory. He'd fantasized about someday looking through that telescope. The fantasy had pushed him as far as second-year math/astronomy, at which point calculus had performed its Darwinian duty and sent him packing. English had welcomed him to the fold, giving him space to dream, but he still had days—over fifteen years after the fact—set aside for regretting the road barred.

One reason why he liked hanging out with Ford: he could still hear about the wonders, still feel plugged in. It made him sad, in the way of drink-warm melancholy, to think that the image and the exotic, roll-off-the-tongue sound of Palomar wouldn't be triggering the life fantasies of any more generations. He raised his glass. "To a departed friend," he said.

Ford clinked. "Blinded too soon."

ᒥᒻ

He wound up eating at the bar with Ford, and it was past midnight by the time he got home. Stupid, doing this in the middle of the week. He wasn't a grad student anymore. The energy just wasn't around to squander, to say nothing of the time. But home held the necessity and threat of going to bed. Not what he really wanted to face.

The fear of last night had not receded with distance. None of that comforting blurring and disappearing of details that had always happened before, ageing nightmares and killing them off. Fresh and newborn, clear and sharp as a blade, the dream sat in the forefront of his mind. It wasn't the image itself, the black wings, that was disturbing. He was sure of that. The dream was like a Magritte painting: locomotives aren't inherently scary. Nor are fireplaces. But both at once, ah… That violation was what was disturbing, what made the eye recoil and the brain back away. He was responding to the force behind the wings. The force that had come from outside and taken his dream from him.

Blake got out of his car. He paused to look up at the sky as he walked to his house's front door. Late October, pre-snow but crisp, and the stars were out in force. He thought again of Mount Palomar, the putting out of a great and famous eye. Just looking, he thought. It was just scanning, business as usual. His eyes arced up the dome of the night. Aurora borealis shifted, green and queasy. Up, up, to the zenith, thinking of infinity and emptiness and —

The pain was so intense it taught him new things about his nervous system. It shot through his left eye, a white lightning spear that made no distinction between vision and sensation. He fell to the ground, covering his face. Papers scattered over the lawn. His mouth sagged open, but no scream. The pain left no room for anything but itself.

And when it was done, when it had had its way with him, it withdrew, silver, buzzing mercury tide, and pulled the darkness in behind it.

⌐¬

The dream shed its nonessentials. There was no nostalgic preamble this time. No old home setting. No friends. No bicycle. No wings either. There was nothing to see at all. Just void. Or, no. Not void. Utterly black, yes, but...

Not empty. His attacker, the invader, was closer. Too close for his mind to throw up the protective screen, the filter that gave him images he could recognize and deal with, no matter how frightening. Now his system imposed total blackout as the only alternative left.

And a poor one it was. The awe was there again. Even though he saw and heard nothing, the sense of presence, of imminent arrival, was overwhelming, and the awe had a lethal intensity to it.

Wake up, he thought. Wake up. Wake up wake up wake up. A mantra, a prayer, a plea, the only coherent thought he could form, a miracle it existed at all. But he was desperate. Twinned with the awe was the fear that very soon the invader would be too close for the shutdown to handle, and he would be forced to see it. If that didn't kill him, the awe would. And so wake up. Wake up. Wake —

⌐¬

"Mr. Blake?"

— up. His eyes clicked open, but there was nothing to see but grey shapes. A figure was bending over him, shaking him.

"Mr. Blake?"

He gasped, terror and relief in a mortal duel. He was awake, and that was good. But he hadn't woken up on his own, and that was bad. If whoever this was hadn't decided to...Oh. Just who was this anyway? Where the hell...?

"Mr. Blake?" More insistent now.

"Agh," he said, throat parched solid.

"I'm sorry to wake you, but you seemed to be having a nightmare."

"Uhm. Where?" he managed. The word hurt his throat so much he expected to taste blood.

"You're at the U of A hospital. One of your neighbours saw you collapsed on your lawn and called an ambulance. You're all right now."

In a pig's eye. Questions, questions, the prime one being why things didn't look quite right, but first he needed to irrigate the scorched earth of his throat. "Water," he whispered. It came. It soothed. Then he started in on his questions, bracing himself for the bad news.

Eye damage.

He sat in his study, waiting out the last hours before morning, contemplating his victimhood.

Eye damage. Ain't that a treat.

It didn't make sense, but there it was. It was what they told him at the hospital, and he had to believe them, because here was the patch, and his left eye continued to show the nothing of his dream. How did it happen? Well that, they couldn't say. Though the trauma was consistent with a physical wound, there was no sign of penetration. Come again? What does that mean? We're not sure. You're not sure? Do doctors regularly diagnose paradoxes? No. But this is very puzzling. Were you hit by anyth— No. I was just looking at the stars. I see. (Oh great choice of words, great bedside manner.) Well, we'd like to keep you in for observ— Not a chance.

He could still see with his right eye, and the prospect of staying in a place where they would make him be horizontal, and try to get him to sleep, was three or four steps beyond unbearable. He discharged himself, over doctors' protests, and cabbed it home.

Where he sat, pumping coffee into the system, thinking and waiting. Thinking about why's and who's and what's. Waiting for the sun to clear the sky of night and stars, and protect him for another twelve hours.

He thought about the telescope at Palomar, blinded for the innocent act of looking. And it was innocent, not malicious prying, not voyeurism. Voyeurism implied being in a position of power. It meant violation. But looking up at the immeasurably larger and more powerful than you? The most tentative attempt of the insignificant to reach out and understand? Where was the power, where was the crime in that?

He drew parallels between himself and the telescope, animate-inanimate, and ascribed intent to the cause of his injury. Not the most logical, or even rational, of arguments, he knew. At least under normal circumstances. But the circumstances…Well, his dreams changed the equation radically, took it to a whole new plane. The dream linked the events. A certainty. It was the centre, as far as he was concerned, the point of condensation where those events and worse ones to come entwined and birthed something noxious. Something was coming.

All right, he thought. We're agreed on that. But what? What's coming? Why is it hurting me? He didn't know. He went through the steps of his brooding again, knowing he wouldn't get anywhere, but it was something to do until the sun came up. And then what? It didn't matter. One bridge at a time. First he wanted to see daylight again. (And oh, John, aren't you lucky your left eye hit that bad point in the sky first, and you jerked away. Otherwise, no daylight ever again. Lucky man. Lucky man.)

Finally: dawn. He sighed, relaxing, as if he had accomplished something. He watched his window turn paler and paler shades of grey, and then the world appeared, and then the sky turned blue, and then at last it was bright, and he didn't need his study light on anymore.

He got up. Breakfast first, then see if he felt he could manage classes today. Distraction would be good, but physical collapse in mid-lecture would not, especially if it happened with the first-years. That would be a fair lethal loss of face. He didn't care to lose any more of his face than he already had, thank you very much.

The joke fell flat. Tone deaf whistling in the dark.

As he stood up, a book spine caught his eye (the right one, the good one, the only one to catch). No particular reason for him to notice the book. Not sticking out, just sitting there, minding its own business, third shelf from the top, a dozen books in from the end. But it wasn't hidden either, so he saw it. Rudolph Otto. The Idea of the Holy.

The epiphany hurt. The light that went on wasn't the prayed and thirsted for illumination of day. It was the cold silverflash of attack that had stilletoed him last night. He put a hand on the back of the chair to keep from sagging. Should have known. Oh, you poor fool, you bloody well should have known. What kind of professor are you? Can't make the simplest links.

He made them now, though. Good old Otto and his pinned-butterfly faith. Analyze it and dissect it and still can't quite explain what makes it tick. Oh well, guess that's the nature of faith. Blake hadn't thought about the book in ages. Had read it, what, ten years ago? At least. More. Must have still been an undergrad. Hadn't been overly impressed. Dry, earnest, a bit passé. But a few interesting and, yes, influential concepts. Otto doing his best with non-rational emotions. Trying to express the inexpressible. Like what causes transcendent sensations of rapture, reverence, awe. Oh yes, and impotence, nothingness, and bladder-release horror. Holy terror. Sounding familiar, isn't it?

Blake shook his head. Must have been wilfully ignorant to forget until now. Otto and his mysterium tremendum: the wholly Other, the unknowably gigantic, the utterly alien that overpowers and reduces you to a quivering, shaking, blasted collection of fear and awe. So there it was. That's what he had been experiencing all along. Maybe he hadn't made the connection because the gap was too huge, a Grand Canyon, between the dry abstract and its seismic reality.

Something's coming, Blake thought again, and felt a cold loosening in his gut. Something big, and, sorry Otto, I don't think it's holy in the least. This isn't your numinous at all. Whatever it was, it didn't seem to be God or the Devil or their appropriate stand-ins. There was nothing of the immanence of a force of absolute supernatural Good or Evil about this. It had been far away. Now it was closer. Physical, not metaphysical, distances.

It was coming. Was it bad? Oh yes. Easy decision. No millennial hope here, oh no. This is really going to hurt.

He had to talk to Ford. He needed to know if something more had happened last night, something that would tie his wound to Palomar's. Something to prove that it wasn't just him. That it wasn't just his mind gone worse than his eye.

He looked at his watch. Getting close to eight. Time flies when you're running scared. Ford should be up by now, might even be on campus already. Breakfast a fading idea, Blake picked up the phone and dialled Ford's home number. Three rings, then click and "Hi. I've got my superstrings tangled and can't come to the ph-"

Blake hung up. Bad astronomy humour. Not in the mood for it. He tried Ford's office, on the off chance.

Busy.

Hmm. Early day. He waited two minutes and tried again.

Busy.

There's that chill getting worse. Easy now, no reason to freak. Everyday occurrence. Calm down.

He didn't. He hit redial, hung up at the signal, redial again, and like so, repetition compulsion. Not going anywhere, not doing anything else, until I get through. Come on, Lou, get off the damn phone.

Ten minutes. By this time the gestures so automatic he almost hung up when the phone did ring. Once.

"Yeah?" Ford abrupt, what is it now? in his tone.

"Lou, it's John."

"Hi John. Look, this isn't a really good time right—"

"Only take a minute, Lou. Sorry, this is very important." For whom? "Um. Did...did anything happen last night?"

Brief, telling pause. "Happen?"

"Like the Palomar thing. I'm not sure—"

"God, John, what didn't happen. It's going to be all over the news by tonight. It's not just Palomar. It's everything. Reflectors, refractors, radio, satellite, you name it. All being wrecked. Glass breaking, fuses blowing, hard drives being wiped. Hell, we don't even know if the Hubble's still up there. We're being blinded."

"How?"

"Who knows? There is a pattern: it moves west, and happens when it's the middle of the night wherever the observatory is. We're telling people on the other side to shut the damn things down before they get wrecked, otherwise by the end of the day we're not going to have any eyes left at all."

You're telling me, Blake thought. "Sabotage?" he asked. Yeah, right.

"You'd think so, but it's happening to everybody. I can't think of a single likely reason for this to be going on, but it is. Listen John, I've got to go. We're at panic stations across the field. I'll call you later."

"Okay Lou, good luck."

"Thanks." And click. Connection severed.

Blake phoned the English department. Sorry, not well, cancel classes. No point cloistering the poor buggers in a classroom on the last day of the world.

Then: oh, stop it, you don't really believe that, do you? Well…

Tremendum.

He walked into the living room, turned the TV on to CNN. Updates on Bosnia. The usual stuff. Just wait boys, big story coming. This one'll kill you.

His stomach grumbled. All right, he thought. Meal for the condemned. He went to the kitchen, got himself some cereal (and more more more coffee), and came back to sit down and watch the news.

He came close to falling asleep as the hours ticked and The Same Old Thing paraded by on the screen. Then, at noon, the story broke. Not in the form he had expected, but he recognized it just the same. Should, in fact, have predicted it. There was nothing about telescopes. At least, not in the lead item. Palomar and company were three stories down. Connection hadn't been made yet. What the lead-off was about was a sudden epidemic of blindness spreading across Asia, Africa and Europe. Blindness and hysteria. Details sketchy, but victims reported to be in the thousands.

Nightside, Blake thought. Night there, and it's like what happened to me, only worse and widespread. Now why is that? Obvious, really. It's closer.

He imagined something cruising the universe, bearing down on Earth's little neck of the woods. At first so distant, only a powerful telescope aimed at just the right sector could see it. Palomar victim of a lucky fluke. Then close enough to hurt the naked eye. Himself also fluking it off, maybe called by the dream to look at the exact spot. And now? Close enough, big enough, to fry anything and anyone looking that way.

Fair enough and scary enough, his theory worked as far as it went. But there were just a few almighty questions. What was coming? Why? And oh, the Hows: How big? How many impossible multiples of the speed of light fast? And how how how is it hurting us? Hurting me?

He didn't know, couldn't expand the theory to embrace the questions. Speed? Not the slightest idea. But it must be happening. Size? I truly do not want to know. How? He thought about non-causal quantum events. Particles that affected each other without being connected in any way. But that was quantum, after all. And the hurting was taking place on a physical plane of a hugely different scale. How bad is this thing that we can't even look at it?

At one o'clock the news went from bad to spectacular. Estimates of the number of blinded were in the millions. But it was hard to know. Communications were iffy. Civilization on that side of the world seemed to have come to a halt. Imagine that, Blake thought, the humour appealing to him in a necrophile sort of way. Just because most of your population goes blind is no reason for order to collapse. Millions. He snorted. Try billions.

CNN tried that number before the hour was up. Blake noticed that the anchors were sounding edgy. He'd never seen that before. A world of wonders. Too bad it has to end.

Once again: do you really think that? And this time: yes. It was over. Even if the approach stopped now, the jig was up. Blake, cynicism as survival mechanism getting into high gear, had to admit he was impressed. Neat trick: terminating a civilization just by coming near it.

By two o'clock, the news was in full-out hysteria. By three, when it was six on the east coast and evening had come, the Emergency Broadcasting Network took over, and the entertainment was done. No more updated body counts. No more shrieking, blinded and half-mad correspondents. ("Hello, Jeffrey? Are you still there, Jeffrey?…Uh…We…We seem to have lost the feed in London…") Instead: black screen, scrolling words, and the Voice of Doom reading them out. "Stay indoors. Draw your curtains. Do not look at the sky. We repeat: do not, under any circumstances, look at the sky." Keep watching the skies, Blake thought. Wasn't that what they had yammered on about at the end of The Thing? Guess they were wrong.

That was a mistake, thinking of The Thing. Humour can get you killed. It was a mistake, because it cracked open the What Is Coming? question and let out the more dangerous one that was hiding underneath, the question he'd stopped asking as soon as the scale of the badness became obvious: Who Is Coming?

He'd done it now. Genie out of the bottle, Pandora's box opened, all that nice stuff. Time to face all the facts now, and no more abstracts. Yes, this was a Who, not a What, coming. A What didn't have malice. And malice had been present the instant the dream had been taken from him, turning him into a prophet who couldn't even make himself believe. Cassandra in denial.

Until now. Now, as night crawled onto the continent's eastern shores, he stared up at the ceiling, thoughts aimed at the sky, and wondered Why? A pleading, close-to-tears question. Why me? Why come after me first? Luck of the draw? Something I did? Why? Beyond the horizon, something smiled, but it didn't answer.

And the other Why: Why do you want to hurt us? Why do you even care? It was like a truck driver deliberately running his windshield into insects. Pointless. So far below petty it belonged to subatomic physics.

Why? Because you can?

From somewhere, the sense came that the answer would be: Because we are. He closed his eyes, shrinking from the thought of beings whose immensity and mean spiritedness were correlates.

His mind shut down for a bit after that. He sat in his chair and watched the day get old and slink off to die. Every so often he tried to pray. Our Father, Who art in Heaven, so hopelessly far away…. There didn't seem to be any point in that, either. Evening, sky going down from blue to orange as the sun said its farewells, and then the dark. Blake had gone through the rest of the day on automatic, moving only when his body told him he needed to eat or go to the bathroom. When it went full black outside, though, he felt himself wake up.

He turned off the television. He knew what he wasn't supposed to look at, yes got the message thank you, but so what? What possible difference would it make now?

He got up, went to the door, and walked outside. He wondered when it would hit. Intuition said tonight. Very soon. Well, he thought, after missing out years ago, now's your chance for some real hands-on astronomy. Going to meet you head-on, whoever you are.

He stood on his lawn, waiting. Back in that first dream again, little boy bracing himself for the blow from the sky. He looked up.

The pain again, expected, but so much worse it was a difference in kind, not degree. Sight was an instant memory. But he didn't pass out. Blessed or cursed, he hung on to consciousness. He kept his eyes open, thinking (through the magnesium glare of agony) maybe, maybe...

And yes. Something that huge could be seen without eyes. It couldn't not be seen. Blake's mind threw up the last line of defense, and the filter lasted just long enough to make him see the wings again: blacker than the sky, silent, surreal, bigger than God. Then the reality punched through the image and there, there, a shape too huge for any geometry, an Other vaster than the full scope of evil.

Blake waited out the last, frozen, unscreamable moment, no questions answered, no quarter received.

He hoped he wouldn't feel the arrival.

But he did.

Altered Statements: #7
Paper

M.A.C. Farrant

That's right, Mam, we have only one piece of paper left and when we get another one we'll let you know. In the meantime you'll have to try working with empty spaces. There's much to be done with those. No, we don't know when to expect a second piece, these things aren't subject to any known predictions. Paper arrives when it will but we have our people working on it. The last paper storm was some years ago, on the Prairies, but because of the rush, much of it was ripped. And you know we can't predict the storms. As for free paper, it flutters from the heavens at odd occurrences, so there's no predicting that either. Why don't you try sitting under an oak tree at full moon and see what happens? It could be some time before we get another piece in. Yes, we know it's difficult; our people suggest you try silence instead. Or if you're desperate, what about the margins of old books? Many have tried pasting margins together with some success although we agree it's not the same because of the flaking. Yes, we're sure you've used up your allotment of cardboard boxes but that's no reason to start crying. What about walls? Many are doing that now. The series of novel houses, each room a chapter. It's brought a revival of reader participation for those so inclined. Yes, we realise the electronic screen is useless, there's no taking it to bed and, no, you can't have this last piece of paper. Something of importance might have to be said. In the meantime, take a number and wait in line.

QUERY
Bob Boyczuk

September 20, 19—

Dear Mr. Poyntz:

Thank you for your query of September 11. I have just returned from a short (but long overdue) vacation in the southern climes, and am afraid I am somewhat behind in my correspondence. Yes, we received your manuscript; a detailed log of all submissions is kept and it clearly shows your manuscript (Hipshot by Alfred Poyntz, 437 pages in length) arrived on April 14 of the previous year. Indeed, I recall the manuscript in question, for, if I am not mistaken, it was printed entirely on pink paper. Though this is not as unusual as one might imagine, it was the only one (pink, that is) that I had received in the last year (canary yellow and powder blue leading the way amongst those who favour colour). Over the past months I watched it advance from shelf to shelf, slowly making its way across the bookcase reserved for submissions, until it achieved the final shelf. From there I moved it to my desktop two weeks ago. You should have had your reply already were it not for an urgent editorial matter that required my immediate attention. Unfortunately, this matter arose just before my vacation, and occupied all my time until the moment of my departure, and so I am somewhat embarrassed to say I did not manage to read as much as a single page of your manuscript. I did, however, resolve to tackle it straightaway upon my return.

Life, alas, is uncertain at best.

No doubt you've read about the troubles we've had out here? About the series of seismological upheavals we've suffered? When I returned from vacation on Monday morning it was to find the building which housed our publishing offices had suffered extensive structural damage as a result of the latest series of earthquakes to strike our already reeling city. The building in question, or parts of it to be more exact, had tumbled into one of the many fissures that have opened up in the earth and now dot the landscape like open wounds. Remarkably, half the building still towered above the lip of the abyss as if untouched; the other half had vanished completely. Perhaps you can imagine my shock, my incredulity, as I stood on the street outside this once impressive edifice, only moments earlier looking forward to closeting myself with your manuscript.

Naturally, I was appalled.

Hastening to my office (no mean feat with the elevators still out of service and the stairwell littered with debris and twisted cock-a-hoop), I chanced upon Trevor Marchman, a colleague in the Literature division, who advised me against proceeding. His face was streaked with dirt and his tie askew. Placing a trembling hand on my shoulder he explained we had lost the entire Children's Literature section, most of our genre fiction (Romance being the sole exception) and our latest Self-help Guides; on the plus side we had retained our highly successful Cookbook and True Crime lines. The Nature and Acts of God divisions (he continued breathlessly) had fortunately suffered only minor damage and were rushing to get first-hand accounts of the disaster published as soon as possible. Though he had not been to the Literature office yet, he feared the worst, as it straddled the line along which the building had been bisected. I shrugged off his hand and pushed forward, seized by a renewed sense of urgency. If the worst had happened, then I knew I must see it for myself.

When I emerged on the seventeenth floor there was little evidence of the catastrophe itself. The reception area looked much as it had for the last two decades, the patterned carpet worn and dusty, the solid oak desk still manned by the ageless Philip, the chrome and vinyl chairs of the reception area occupied by the usual gallimaufry of writers (albeit more nervous and bedraggled than usual), clutching their usual assortment of boxed manuscripts and large manilla envelopes.

"Good morning, Mr. Gardner," Philip said with his customary aplomb, and several heads bobbed up, eyes looking hopefully in my direction.

I nodded curtly at him, still too breathless from my exacting climb to essay a more congenial response. Then I spun on my heel and hastened down the corridor. I passed the offices of proofreaders and junior editors, their names neatly stencilled on the frosted glass of the windows. Several doors were ajar, and within I could see young men and women seated amongst tottering piles of paper, diligently poring over galleys and manuscripts, the soft glow of computer terminals warming their backs. The air of normalcy gave me hope. I moved towards the corridor in which my office was situated. A few more steps, I thought, and I'll know the tale. My heart thudded fearfully in my chest.

My door was where I had left it.

I cannot convey to you in mere words the relief I felt. I thought briefly of Marchman whom I had passed on the stairs, how I had always considered him foolish and fanciful; and how I'd forgotten this in my moment of panic. He was an alarmist, I now recalled, frequently berating Literature. "There's no future in it," he had said more than once. "Get out while the getting's good!" I chastised myself and vowed in future never to pay him the least attention at all.

Stepping up to the door, I grasped the handle and pulled it open.

A gasp escaped me.

Opposite the door, where a panelled wall hung with framed photographs normally would have stood, was an expanse of blue sky. It was as if the wall had been swept cleanly away, leaving the rest of the room intact. I took a step forward. Outside, gulls circled against a backdrop of brilliant cerulean streaked by ropes of black smoke from the various fires that still burnt unchecked about the city. The low, keening ululations of sirens sounded distantly. Looking down, I could see the dark rents where the earth had split open into gaping maws, all roughly parallel, like furrows made by a monstrous plow. Occasionally, the top of buildings poked above the lip of these crevices, as if they had been lowered there gently, on purpose. More often, the ruins of others were visible, some reduced to anonymous piles of rubble. In the deeper fissures, nothing but an ominous, impenetrable black was visible. Everywhere, tiny human figures were busying themselves about the edge of the crevices, lowering ropes and ladders and cables, swarming into the ruins to rescue those that might still be alive or perhaps to recover what they could of their lives.

While I gawked at the carnage below, a sudden gust of wind blew through the office, riffling the pages of the topmost manuscripts that were still arrayed on the submission shelf. Loose sheets, hidden until now behind my desk, blew about the room in frenetic circles, two fetching up against my legs and fluttering there like wounded birds. Then one was torn free and scudded past the splintered edge of the wooden floor; it was snatched by an updraught and spun out of sight.

I know of no way to soften the blow so I'll give it to you straight: the pages were, as you may have guessed, pink. I glanced at my desk. Other than a blotter and a modest pen and pencil set (a gift marking my twentieth year of service), the desktop was empty, your manuscript gone, scattered by the wind.

Bending over, I carefully peeled off the sheet still coiled about my shin. It was page forty-seven.

I moved as close as I dared to the edge of the room and caught sight of that other page, still dancing like a leaf in the wind, but drifting lower and lower now, falling inexorably towards the fissure. Eventually I lost sight of it as it sunk into the dark reaches of the abyss.

I stood there for a time staring after the lost page.

Mr Poyntz, let me not bore you with the rest of the mundane details; suffice it to say we recovered only two more pages from your manuscript (page fourteen behind a radiator and page three hundred and twelve caught up against a leg of my desk). The rest have vanished.

Perhaps you may think it unfair to judge a manuscript on three disjoined pages, orphans as they were from their extended family. Yet, we often give a manuscript only a few pages in which to catch our attention; after that it is returned, the greater bulk of it unread, with a rejection slip. So I presumed to judge your work, prepared to return the three remaining pages with this letter of apology and a somewhat gentler than usual rejection.

However, this was not to be the case.

At the risk of swelling your head, I saw in those brief, disconnected scenes a spark of promise. And the Senior Managing Editor (to whom I conveyed—with great excitement—pages 14, 47, and 312 shortly afterwards) agrees. No doubt you can understand how distressed I was to read in your query letter (dated September 11th) about the misfortune with your hard-disk. The entire novel gone! A head crash is, as you point out, "very unforgiving." If nothing else, perhaps this will serve as a lesson to you about the usefulness of making backups!

As you may imagine the rescue teams have been extraordinarily busy in recent days; recovering manuscripts, sadly, is not one of their priorities. However, the Senior Managing Editor has authorized me to undertake an expedition to recover the entire text of your submission—or as much as is humanly possible. Tomorrow I will begin the descent into the fissure, taking along with me as many junior editors, proofreaders and text entry clerks as will volunteer. I will endeavour to keep you informed of our progress.

Once again, please accept my sincerest apologies for the delay in our response.

Yours Truly,

Roland Gardner, Managing Editor, Literature
Cameron, Blaylock, Fulsum and Hui

ד

September 21, 19—

Dear Mr. Poyntz:

This morning I stood for the first time at the edge of the abyss. The fissure is a long tear in the earth, seven kilometres in length; the chasm measures one hundred and fifty meters at its widest. Where I stand now it is roughly a hundred meters from lip to lip. Along its brink are office towers and commercial establishments, forming an eerie canyon of half-human, half-natural design. Those building that haven't collapsed entirely, leaving sad, gap-toothed openings in the wall, are similar to our own: it is as if the structures had been neatly sliced with a scalpel of extraordinary proportions, laying bare their innards like those cut-away models of car engines and hydro electric plants one often finds in museums. In several, the day to day activity of commerce has resumed, and the figures of men and women could be seen working at desks or edging along the narrow lip of half-corridors with a briefcase or file folder tucked beneath their arms. Occasionally, the trilling of a phone or the hum of a fax machine echoes from above.

Nearest us, the crevice is steep, a sheer face that drops precipitously out of sight. Further along, a series of ledges of varying widths can be seen in the depths, some supporting the remnants of buildings—others littered with unidentifiable rubble. At our feet, however, nothing is visible save a blackness as thick and impenetrable as that of a child's nightmare.

It is nearly noon now, and I am typing this note into my laptop as we are making last minute preparations for the descent. The party I've assembled includes two mountaineering enthusiasts among the volunteers, only too eager to have a go at the face of the fissure. As I write this they have already set off, and I can hear the ring of their hammers as they fix pitons in preparation for the descent of the main party. In total, we number seven. We might have had a nice round ten, but only moments ago, Marchman (whom I mentioned in my previous letter) sent word that he was recalling two editors and a proofreader, citing the loss of two other assistants—who were unfortunate enough to be working late the night of the quakes—and the rapidly approaching fall launch deadlines. Though I am in fact his senior (he being the Assistant Managing Editor, Literature), this seniority has always been nominal, eroding over the years until its only manifestation is an office with a window. Beyond that, we work as equals. Reluctantly, I must allow them to return. Yet, I continue to be optimistic. I believe the remaining members to be sufficient for the job.

But let me not dwell on the bad; there is good news also.

Searching near the lip of the abyss, we have already recovered half a dozen more pages of your manuscript (73, 121, 160, 344 and 349). I admit I was somewhat apprehensive when I read page 160, for the prose there is unlike that of any of the other nine pages. If I may be blunt, it stumbles along in an awkward, uncertain manner, poking about like a blind man with a cane in an unfamiliar room, leaving the reader to surmise from these faltering sentences its significance. This sudden change so unnerved me that for a moment I reconsidered the entire project.

But then, pacing back and forth near the edge of the fissure, chin cupped in palm, I was struck by a thought. What if the words were purposefully awkward. What if this halting, muddled prose is intentional, reflecting the distracted state of a character's mind. Recalling the passage, I imagined a withered old man, soured by repeated disappointments in career and love, his outlook jaundiced by the accumulated bile of years of disillusionment. As if someone had adjusted a projector lens, he snapped into focus for me. Taken as such, his rendering was masterful. The more I thought about it, the more I realized this could be the only explanation.

Trust, Mr. Poyntz. I should have trusted my author....

It is the first and foremost lesson of being a competent reader—and one I'd somehow forgotten. Thank you for reminding me. In future I promise to give the pages of your manuscript the latitude they deserve.

Yours apologetically,

Roland Gardner, Managing Editor, Literature
Cameron, Blaylock, Fulsum and Hui Publications

ᴦ⁊

September 21, 19—

Dear Mr. Poyntz:
Six of us began the descent in earnest this afternoon.

The seventh, a pallid data entry clerk fearful of heights, remained at our base camp on the edge of the fissure. Earlier, we had attached a pulley to the top of an A-frame constructed of two-by-fours. Running a lengthy rope over the wheel of the pulley, we tied a bucket to its end. We wound the other end of the rope around a windlass. Then we fixed the whole contrivance with cement blocks so that it projected out over the fissure. The clerk who remained behind will man this contraption, passing down such supplies as we need and pulling to the surface any pages we recover. He will work as if he were at a well—although he will be drawing words instead of water. Through this crude device (and the clerk's diligence) I also hope to send you letters (such as this one) to keep you apprised of our progress.

The first hours of climbing were uneventful. We rappelled down a featureless surface, the lights of our helmets crossing and criss-crossing in the chasm as we worked the ropes. The granite wall was smooth and surprisingly warm to the touch, as if it still retained traces of the heat produced during the upheaval. Looking to my right, I could just make out where the two walls came together in a sharp V a kilometre or so away, closing off the fissure; in the other direction the end of the chasm was invisible, the light of my helmet fading into the darkness. As we descended, the sounds of our progress bounced off the opposite wall and were returned, through some trick of acoustics, magnified; at times I heard only the echo and not the sound that had engendered it, creating the illusion that there was another party, like ours, on the other side, also working its way towards the bottom. It was an unnerving sensation, and one I suspect affected the others as it did me: conversation, brisk in the earlier stages, ceased altogether, as if no one wished to make any more noise than was absolutely necessary.

Several hours passed in this manner.

Bit by bit awareness of my immediate surroundings slipped away, for there was nothing to fix my attention on save the endless wall and the darkness. What I thought of instead was my office and the manuscripts still patiently waiting for me there. Of how, in all the years I'd been Managing Editor, Literature, the pile has never once diminished. Read one and two more would appear. Read those and the afternoon mail would bring half a dozen additional submissions. Everyone in the world, apparently, has decided to become a writer. Now this might seem a cause for celebration, heralding a new golden age of literature. But, curiously, as our submissions increased, so our sales in the division have plummeted. Given this, I began to suspect that several of our regular correspondents wrote more novels in a year than they actually read!

Being a writer yourself, Mr. Poyntz, you may not find this strange. But for me, first and foremost a reader, this notion was disturbing in the extreme. It was a love of reading itself that impelled me to become an editor. I had no writing aspirations of my own. Nor do I now. I was—and am—a bibliophile in the truest sense of the word: I read gently, lovingly, losing myself readily in those landscapes of the imagination. When I was younger I thought there was nothing more exciting than the smell of a new book. Ah, how I remember those days! I'd sit in my favourite wingback chair, my reading lamp on and ready, the unopened book in my lap, anticipating that moment, that glorious, orgasmic moment, when the spine of the book would at last be cracked and the doors to an undiscovered world flung wide!

Alas, there are few true readers left. And, sadly, altogether too many writers. What will happen when the scales have finally tipped? Will writers be forced to pay their readers for the privilege of having their novels read? Will I, and others readers like me, be courted by authors anxious to be read by someone who understands their work? I fear things may come to such a pass.

Even in my division, the bastion (or so one would like to believe) of reading, we no longer attract readers of quality. Take, for example, young Trevor Marchman. To him reading is merely a job, no better or worse than selling vacuum cleaners or making car parts on an assembly line. It is a convenient rung on the corporate ladder. I know he eyes my position jealously, seeing it as stepping stone to the rarefied heights of "upper management". Though he does a competent job, it is performed passionlessly and without commitment. To him, the only thing that counts is the bottom line (of which he tirelessly reminds us).

But I digress. I have left you (and me) hanging.

Our progress down the wall of the fissure, as I have already said, was uneventful. At least until the end of the day, at which time we encountered an obstacle that caused us to halt our descent. For there we came across a series of small, regularly-spaced ledges jutting out from the wall. Swinging wide on the end of the line, a flashlight clutched in her hand, our lead climber reported that the ledges continued to mar the face of the fissure for some distance down, and estimated their number to be in the hundreds—if not the thousands—all ranging from half a meter to two meters in width. The bottom, she reported glumly, was still out of sight.

One would think that we'd be grateful for any horizontal surface after countless hours of rappelling down sheer wall. Yet, when we finally decided to make camp (our party splitting into three separate groups to fit comfortably into the limited space of adjacent outcroppings), the momentary pleasure of shrugging out of the constricting loops of my climbing harness gave way to a feeling of dismay. These cursed ledges would, I realized, only make our job doubly difficult. Not only would they impede a speedy descent by taking away our direct line to the bottom, but we would also be forced to investigate each and every outcropping lest we miss a single page of your manuscript. Such an undertaking will require days.

But what else can we do?

I have spent a lifetime chasing words and know no other way.

Yours sincerely,

Roland Gardner, Managing Editor, Literature
Cameron, Blaylock, Fulsum and Hui

ⲧⲁ

September 24, 19—

Dear Mr. Poyntz:

It took the better part of two days, but we've completed our inspection of the ledges. We sit here on one of the last sizeable outcroppings as we patiently await our daily rendezvous with the bucket. Below, the wall drops away, now black and featureless, into the depths. Our efforts, though taxing in the extreme, have yielded twelve new pages, more than I could have reasonably hoped. I read them all with great interest, saving for the last four consecutive pages, 212-215, stuck together along their edges by a dark, gummy substance (cappuccino, if I were to hazard a guess).

Bravo! Bravo! Bravo!

I must say Nell is a completely (and unexpectedly) delightful creature. Her name, like her idiosyncratic way of speaking, is at first distracting, but within the space of a few hundred words becomes wholly natural and familiar, leaving us feeling sheepish for not having realized sooner—as you clearly did—how truly suitable it is. To use such a name and make it work as well as you have is not an inconsiderable feat. It reveals the hand of a master. Though I am a jaded reader, I was absorbed by your description of her, and found myself watching Nell with fascination. With a start, I realized that, in the brief span of four pages, I had come to care a great deal about her.

You may understand, then, why I was disturbed by the scene on page 331, where a child, who might or might not be Nell, dies. Could it be her?

No, don't answer.

I must find out for myself.

Your Besotted Reader,
Roland Gardner

p.s. A curious event to report: yesterday, without warning, a building dropped past narrowly missing us, the screams of its occupants clearly audible above the building's own complaints. Perhaps it had clung to the edge for as long as was possible, then gave up hope and tumbled into the abyss. The experience left me somewhat shaken, not only because of what might have happened if the building had chosen to tumble upon our party, but also because I had thought it to be our building. But at the last moment I caught sight of a flash of red, the telltale banner of the neighbouring Insurance Firm. Why, one wonders, do people (and I count myself among their number) continue to inhabit edifices on the brink? Is it force of habit? An irresistible love of their work? A way of confronting their fear? Or do they just have nowhere better to be? If it is the last, I sometimes wonder why they do not leap themselves and have done with it. But then, that kind of courage is a rare quality amongst men and women of business.

ר⁷

September 25, 19—

Dear Mr Poyntz:

Today we reached the beginning of the end.

That is to say, we encountered a series of flat shelves that descend, like a gargantuan staircase, to the floor of the chasm. We decided to strike a base camp here from which we will explore the steps more fully. After assembling our tents (the blue fabric incongruously bright against the black and dark grey in which everything else down here is expressed), we gathered stones to ring a fire. The overall effect is, surprisingly, cheery. As I write this my back is to the camp and I am sitting on the edge of the first step, my legs dangling two meters above the next. Here and there the debris of buildings can be seen. Not five meters from my perch (and two steps down) is a crumpled hot dog cart, its decaying contents spilled over the hard, unforgiving ground. Scattered throughout the carnage are pink sheets. It was all I could do to keep myself from clambering down a rope to the next level so as to collect more pages. But we are exhausted from the day's work. And we have already gathered twenty-three pages from the first "step".

I still have not learned any more about Nell. Though the pages we recovered span a broad range (7, 23, 29, 68, 101, 128, 145, 155, 170, 221, 224, 226, 256, 289, 303, 314, 367, 368, 390, 395, 400, 416, 421), there is nary a mention of her. Could she have only been an ancillary character? A convenient figure who carries out her role and then is casually discarded? Somehow, I cannot bring myself to believe this….

The writing is, as usual, impeccable, the voice authoritative and refreshingly new. Peach is a fine foil for the Colonel, and his antics make for what I assume will evolve into an interesting subplot. The arcane practises of the sisters (introduced on page 68) hint at a sense of foreboding that is skilfully rendered. And when the Harrisons came over and disported themselves on the lawn—well, I laughed aloud! A few of the finer points bothered me, however: when did the Colonel acquire his scar? Have both the sisters seen it?

Yet, as entertaining as these others are, they are still mere shades next to Nell. I cannot get her out of my head. You may think it foolish, but I've offered the lion's share of the rations to whomever finds the next reference to her.

I'd best go now. All the others have turned in and we make an early start of it tomorrow. I can hear the assorted sounds of their sleep—wheezing and snorts and restless shufflings—from directly behind me. The only other sound one hears down here is the occasional stone clattering down the side of the fissure or the wind howling far above, like it is blowing through a troubled place we've left behind. Down here, though, nothing stirs. Everything is calm. All the countless distractions of the waking world have disappeared without a trace.

In a way, I am growing to like this.

Still yours,

R. Gardner

p.s. A bit of disturbing news: when the bucket descended at its appointed time yesterday it contained (along with the usual rations of sardines and bread) a brief, hand-written note from a junior editor on my staff. In it, he worries that our expedition might be recalled. There are rumours, you see, that Marchman has acquired the ear of the Chief Managing Editor in my absence. It is widely known Trevor has opposed our purpose from the start. A reliable source reports that during a discussion of your manuscript he was heard to mutter, "There are plenty more where that came from." I'm afraid he can be a rather insensitive bastard at times. But I should be more gracious. If only he had read, as I have, these scant pages, he might not be so pigheaded. But one of the great tragedies of life is that you cannot force people to read what they ought, as good as it might be for them.

ᴛ⁊

September 26, 19—

Dear Albert:

A major find!

I can barely contain myself. After we returned to our base camp on the first step, I collated the pages we had collected today (fifty-three in total from the first seven steps). My hands trembled uncontrollably when I realized we had recovered the longest continuous section thus far (pages 231 through 254). Perhaps this will satisfy them upstairs. Although I am certain Marchman will be unimpressed, I believe the Chief Managing Editor to be a perspicacious man. He will understand the importance of this find.

Yet in my elation, a disappointment: nothing about Nell—unless the first sentence on page 231, in its elided phrase ("knew he couldn't get her out of his mind…nor out of his house") refers to her. Yet I fear not.

As for the rest of it, the writing is top-drawer. Though I don't quite see how these pages relate to the rest of the novel, they are brilliantly conceived. Until this moment, I had supposed this was a coming of age tale, but this new section calls my assumptions (presumptuousness?) into question. One moment I was happily immersed in your story, the next I realized I'd misread large parts of it. But then, isn't that what the best writing does? Throws you a curve when you least expect it?

I shall have to rethink my approach to your work. It will be difficult now that the bulk of the manuscript has been sent up top. But, as I often said, patience and doggedness are the hallmarks of a good reader.

Roland G.

p.s. I apologize for the brevity of this note, but the bucket fell early today surprising us and nearly breaching my skull. No sooner had we placed the pages of your manuscript within it than it was jerked back up, as if that junior editor working the line is growing impatient with his job. Perhaps I will find him something better suited to his temperament when I return!

ꓩ⁷

September 27, 19—

Albert:
Disaster has struck.
This morning, shortly after breakfast, the earth groaned, a deep guttural thing that vibrated in our bones. Everyone froze; we stared stupidly at one another, not sure what to make of this preternatural noise. For a moment there was a silence as profound as the one at the beginning of the world must have been. Then, without warning, cracks appeared in the walls, each accompanied by a report like gunfire. Stone moved upon stone with ear-piercing wails. The ground heaved, scattering editors and proofreaders like nine-pins. Large chunks of earth, torn loose from the lip of the abyss, crashed down amongst us, shattering with thunderous reports and throwing off shards like shrapnel. Preposterously, I found myself lying on the ground, staring upwards. I was not frightened; I suppose I was in shock. Waves of dust, accompanied by small stones, rained down around me. Above the din, a voice in my skull spoke clearly, urging me to find shelter. I looked around.

To my immediate left was the wall of the fissure; rising from its base was a narrow crack. Calmly, I regained my feet and walked, somewhat unsteadily, towards the small protection it offered, catching my right thigh on a jagged edge and tearing both my khakis and the skin beneath as I angled my body into the opening. Absurdly, I had wedged myself facing in. Behind me, the havoc continued unabated.

I cannot say how long the entire episode lasted. To me it seemed to be upwards of half an hour; in reality, it could only have been a few minutes. When it did finally end, I backed out from my refuge to find the landscape altered beyond recognition. A thick cloud of dust hung in the air; shattered stone was everywhere; the shelves of rock leading downwards, once smooth and regular as stairs, had buckled and splintered; our camp—and all its equipment—had disappeared, save for the single tongue of blue tent fabric that flared out from beneath one of the larger boulders. Overhead, barely visible through the narrow channel that leads back to that other world, dark clouds roiled, but whether they were thunderheads or an accumulation of the blackest smoke I could not have said.

The long and short of it is that our party has been decimated.

Our lead climber lies unconscious, a fragment the size of a finger embedded in her forehead. Two others have disappeared, either buried in the new debris or panicked and run off. The remaining members—a lad who clutches his knees and rocks back and forth while emitting a low moan, and a woman who stares sullenly into the darkness, refusing to answer any questions—are covered in bruises and numerous cuts.

Our situation is not good. Our supplies are gone. We have no tents, no food and only two functioning lamps. Nor will there be any chance of replacing them. Earlier, searching through the rubble, I came across the corpse of that hapless editor who I had stationed on the edge of the abyss. He lay jammed between two boulders, his thin body folded over like a sheet, his vital fluids collecting in a sticky puddle beneath. Curiously, a crumpled piece of paper lay caged within his lifeless finger. Swallowing back my distaste, I managed to pry the note free. It was from the Chief Managing Editor and addressed to me. In no uncertain terms, we'd been recalled.

I wadded the note up and buried it deeply in the debris.

How things can change in the space of a few moments! I had thought us safe from that other world, too distant to be touched by its vagaries and inexplicable whims. But, Mr. Poyntz, when the very ground heaves beneath you, what certainties are left?

The others wish to return to the surface. I tried to explain how I need their help more than ever now that several pages of your manuscript may lie buried in the debris. How this is what the Chief Managing Editor would wish. But my pleas fall on deaf ears. Nor would they hear anything of Nell. Ignoring me, they have begun rigging a litter in which they hope to raise their wounded comrade. Leaving now would serve no purpose: can they not see she is already as good as dead? But explaining this to them has no effect, and only seems to infuriate the sullen lad. He has taken to throwing stones at me when I approach.

Tonight, while they sleep, I will slip this letter into the pocket of the lead climber. I do not know how (or when) I will be able to apprise you of my further progress; I do, however, believe the Chief Managing Editor will come to his senses and renew the search. But that may not be for some time.

For now, I carry on alone.

R. G.

ᴦ⅂

A:

Please forgive me for scribbling this note on the back of your manuscript, but it is the only paper I have.

Two (or is it three?) days have passed since my last letter. I cannot be certain of the time, for my watch is gone, its strap severed in my mad scramble down the broken shelves of rock. Nor can I say if it is day or night—at this depth the opening to the upper world is no longer discernible. For all I know, the fissure might have resealed itself, leaving me forever trapped.

Yesterday, I reached bottom. A cold, steady breeze winds like a river along the bed of this lowest level, trapped in a narrow channel between the steps I descended and another set climbing the opposite wall. Lowering myself from the penultimate shelf to the floor was like slipping into icy water.

In the last days I'd recovered only half a dozen new pages; now, on the lowest level, I found but two more, caught against rocks. The bulk of the missing pages, I surmised, had been carried off by this gelid breeze. Perhaps you can understand the momentary dismay I felt: I had thought my journey near its completion, only to discover yet another ending in store for me.

Now don't misread me. The pages I found I'd consumed with the same eagerness a starving man might consume a single celery stick—I was grateful, but it was only enough to sharpen the edge of my hunger. So I set off, the wind at my back, the weakening beam of my flashlight marking my way, determined to go the distance.

I walked slowly, doubled over, searching carefully for any stray sheets. The wind increased, its icy fingers snapping the cuffs of my pants with loud cracks and causing me to shiver uncontrollably. I ignored it as best

I could, hunkering down into a small shape, continuing to sweep the light back and forth across the floor. So great was my concentration that it wasn't until some time later, when I paused to stretch, that I realized the walls of the fissure had drawn in and the channel had shrunk to half its original width. Pointing the light ahead, I discovered I was no more than fifty meters from the point at which the two walls met. At the base of the conjunction was what appeared to be an incline of scree, like one often sees at the foot of a retreating glacier, though it was hard to be certain, the weakening cell of my flashlight now incapable of clearly illuminating anything that distant.

I hurried ahead, pushed along by the mounting wind.

When I reached the base of the scree I stopped, clinging to a large rock to be kept from being blown over. The wind tore past me, howling up along the incline of rubble and rushing into a black, man-sized opening at its summit. It looked as if the gap had, at one time, stretched from the floor of the fissure to its present height. But the last upheaval must have sent this rubble down to partially block the opening, constricting the passage through which the wind drained, increasing its velocity fiercely near the mouth. Weighting my pockets with as many stones as they would hold, I began the climb.

Twice, in particularly vigorous gusts, I felt certain I would be plucked from this loose face of rubble and swept in; but somehow I managed to cling to the heap. Small objects, pebbles perhaps, stung my back and arms as they shot past. The scream of the wind deafened me. I gritted my teeth and edged upwards until I could shine my flashlight past the lip of the opening.

The scene made my heart stop.

Beyond and down was a mammoth cavern, filled with a forest of stalactites and stalagmites painted in breathtaking colours; overarching all, the roof was covered with a dark, lush growth that glittered in the beam of my light like the heavens on the clearest of country nights; at the cavern's extremes were countless passages twisting out of sight, each coloured in its own unique hue. And here and there, scattered throughout, were hundreds of pink pages.

I scrambled back down the windward side of the slope.

You may consider it foolish, Alfred, but I have decided to go into the cavern. I can think of nothing but Nell. In my present state, it may well be impossible to struggle back out through that narrow gap against a wind which I can barely keep from dragging me in. You might argue, as my colleagues would, that these last pages are better left consigned to darkness. However, I am a faithful reader and could never contrive my own ending. That would be false, a gutless betrayal.

No, it will be your ending or none at all.

I must finish this note now, for the bulb in my flashlight grows dimmer yet; I fear it will last no more than a few minutes. But do not be dismayed: I've armed myself with a stick of wood I found lodged beneath a slab of granite. When this light fades altogether, I'll use the stick as a blind man would a cane, tapping about darkness until I've found those final sheets.

I leave these pages beneath a cairn of stone here at the foot of the hill of rubble. In the event I should not be able to return, I can only hope that this note (and your pages) will be found and conveyed back to the surface.

Wish me luck—and good reading.

R.

ך٦

September 29

Dear A. Pointz:

Thank you for letting us see your manuscript. Unfortunately, it doesn't suit our needs at present. Please forgive this form letter, but the volume of manuscripts that we receive makes it impossible to reply to each submission individually, as we wish we were able. Good luck placing it elsewhere.

Trevor Marchman, Acting Managing Editor, Literature
Cameron, Blaylock, Fulsum and Hui Publications

THE DEPARTMENT OF HOPE

M.A.C. Farrant

If the public has been confused again, we're sorry. We know it happens each morning at daybreak with the unearthing of the Image Store and, like most citizens, we're concerned with the eruption of unsanctioned images which can appear at that time, particularly those images of sickness and death, and of phantom landscapes emitting a strange and haunting beauty. Our early morning radio newscasts which break into sleep have been designed to subvert these rebel images and we urge citizens to make use of them.

We at the Department understand your distress but again remind you that it is dangerous to indulge in independent dreaming and fantasising or in exotic reading of any kind. Indeed, we actively discourage these seditious practices. Our aim at the Department is the eradication of the unknown and we're confident that the citizenry endorses this goal.

A machine which will program your imagination for you is in the developing stages. In the meantime, continue with your imagination suppressants.

Afterword

Paula Johanson

"Now it is a strange thing, but things that are good to have and days that are good to spend are soon told about, and not much to listen to; while things that are uncomfortable, palpitating, and even gruesome, may make a good tale, and take a deal of telling anyway."

J.R.R. Tolkien, The Hobbit

These stories and poems didn't come out of thin air.

We read stories and poems by dozens and hundreds, one for every day of the year, before choosing these particular ones. We believed that good things as well as gruesome may make a good tale, and found a great deal of telling to sort through while proving it.

Each of the Tesseracts anthologies has come to be looked for and looked through like cargo; we sort things rare and precious among the staple goods we depend on so much. But I wonder whether this latest volume is really a boat coming into harbour with all that you've looked for from far away. These works don't come from "away" if your idea of "here" includes every region of Canada.

The return addresses on these stories and poems were from cornflake-plain placenames like Summerhill, Hearthstone and Townsend. They came from streets so crowded that instead of names, it takes eleven numbers to place an apartment in the north-west quarter by the river. And they came from wide-open places where the postal codes are full of zeros, like my own T0G 1L0, where the postmaster once said to me in all seriousness that of course I got the letter addressed with merely my given name and the small town eight miles away—there's only one other person in twenty miles with the same name, and she doesn't get letters from far away.

If there is anything more than thin air and a few barbed-wire fences between us and the North Pole, postal code H0H 0H0, it must be a few stories of things that are good to have and days that are good to spend. And, of course, palpitating tales.

ZERO VISIBILITY

Eileen Kernaghan

the wind howls in the eaves
snow-laden, apocalyptic

Guy Lombardo on the radio
grey confetti on the TV screen

torn scraps of history
sucked through the storm's eye

outside, the horizon shifts, tilts
there are no more signposts

About the Authors and Editors

David Annandale, a resident of Edmonton, has just completed a PhD in horror fiction and film. His fiction has appeared in *Northern Frights* and *100 Wicked Little Witch Stories* and his plays *Alpha Male* and *Revulsion* have been mounted at the Edmonton Fringe Festival.

Since 1991, Natasha Beaulieu has published a score of science fiction, fantasy and horror short stories in various magazines and fanzines. In 1995, she won the *Prix Septième Continent* with *La Cité de Penlocke*.

Jocko Benoit is a Cape Bretoner currently living and writing in Edmonton. His poetry has appeared in magazines in Canada, the U.S. and Australia and his first published story appeared in *ON SPEC*. He is also the author of a poetry collection titled *An Anarchist Dream*.

Everything you need to know about Bob Boyczuk can be found at: http://pandora.senecac.on.ca/~boyczuk/writing.

Carolyn Clink of Thornhill, Ontario has published SF poetry in *Analog, On Spec, TransVersions, Tesseracts4,* and all four volumes of the *Northern Frights* series. She is still recovering from editing Aurora-Award-nominated *Tesseracts6* with her husband Robert Sawyer.

Cory Doctorow is an up-and-coming young fiction writer living in Toronto whose work has been published in *SF Age & Northern Sun, Asimov's, Odyssey, Amazing* and *On Spec*

Candas Jane Dorsey is a writer of short fiction, poetry, novels and non-fiction. Her latest book is *Black Wine* (Tor Books, 1997) which has won the 1997 Crawford, 1998 Tiptree, and 1998 Aurora awards. She is the publisher of two imprints in The Books Collective, and lives in Edmonton, Alberta.

Scott Ellis is a Winnipeg freelance writer and editor.

M.A.C. Farrant is the author of five collections of satirical short fiction, most recently *What's True, Darling* (Polestar, 1997). Her work has been dramatized for television, appears regularly in various magazines (including *Adbusters* and *Geist* as a correspondent) and has been nominated for national and international awards. In 1998 she spent two months in Australia on a reading tour which included appearances at three major writing festivals and stints as a writer in residence at two universities.

Eduardo Frank, originally from Cuba, lives in Newfoundland and writes in Spanish.

Wendy Greene is a translator and simultaneous interpreter, born in Toronto, who has lived in Montréal for the past twenty-two years. She lives with her sons Sam and Daniel and her husband John Dupuis, who is the SF addict of the family.

Aaron V. Humphrey reads, writes, listens to music, occasionally acts, writes computer programs, plays Nomic, and has lived in Grande Prairie and Edmonton, in a two-SF-writer marriage with novelist Nicole Luiken.

Jan Lars Jensen lives in Chilliwack, BC. His stories may be found in *The Magazine of Fantasy & Science Fiction, Interzone, Geist, On Spec, Grue, Aboriginal SF* and the anthologies *Synergy 5, Tesseracts5, Tesseracts6* and the forthcoming *Northern Suns*(Tor).

Paula Johanson is a freelance writer and market gardener who spends summers on a farm near Edmonton and teaches part of the winter in Victoria. She has published one book, *No Parent is an Island*, and a number of speculative fiction short stories. Her speculative novel *Copper Lady* is due out in 1999, and she also broadcasts non-fiction radio commentaries.

Nancy Johnston has published fiction in *The Girl Wants to*, *Tessera*, and *Bending the Landscape*. Her PhD on Emily Dickinson's poetry probably has nothing to do with her interest in science fiction. She currently teaches SF and American literature at Ryerson Polytechnic University in Toronto.

Eileen Kernaghan's work has appeared in many magazines and anthologies, including *The Year's Best Fantasy & Horror* and four of the *Tesseracts* anthologies. Her novel *Dance of the Snow Dragon* (Thistledown Press) appeared in 1995, and a new YA, based on the Snow Queen story, is forthcoming next year.

E.B.Klassen lives near Edmonton where he earns his living as a market gardener and his reputation by making bad puns.

Dora Knez was born in India and lived in other distant places as a child, but did most of her growing up (to the extent possible) in Montreal, which she considers her home town. She lives there with her husband and son, writing short stories and perpetrating the occasional poem. Her work also appeared in *Tesseracts6*.

Lydia Langstaff's poetry appeared in *Senary*, *Midnight Zoo*, *On Spec* and several small-press publications. Her first short story, "Nightmares of the Pat", was published in the US anthology *the Magic Within*. Lydia passed away in 1994 at age 28 and is survived by her husband Jeff. The Lydia Langstaff Memorial Poetry Prize has been established in her honour.

Joy Hewitt Mann has been writing for nine years with genre work in *On Spec* and *The Rosewell Review* (New Mexico). Literary work appears in *Malahat Review* and *Event*. In 1997 she received the Leacock Award for Poetry. Joy lives with her family in Spencerville, Ontario where she runs a junkstore.

Judy McCrosky has published two collections of short stories and one novel, and currently focuses on speculative fiction. Two of her books were shortlisted for major awards. She lives in Saskatoon with her husband, teenage children, and too many small rodents, some of whom had cameo roles in her story.

Shirley Meier's published works include *The Sharpest Edge*, *The Cage and Sabre* and *Shadow*, all co-written with S.M. Stirling;and short stories in *Magic in Ithkar IV*, *Tales out of the Witch World*, *Northern Frights I and II* and *Bolos at War, Vol. II*; *Shadow's Daughter*, her first solo novel, and *Shadow's Son*, co-written with S.M. Stirling and Karen Wehrstein. She has published three volumes of poetry. She lives in Muskoka, Ontario.

Yves Meynard lives in Montreal. He won the1994 *Grand prix de la science-fiction et du fantastique québécois*, is a five-time Aurora Award winner for the best short work in French, and has won the *Prix Boréal* four times. His stories have appeared in several English-language magazines in Canada and the U.S., and in *Tesseracts* anthologies *4, 5* and *6*. He has published over thirty stories in French, mostly in the magazines *Solaris* and *imagine...*, and also works as an anthologist and editor. He has a Ph.D. in computer science from the Université de Montréal. His novel *The Book of Knights* was published by Tor in 1998.

Lia Pas is a composer, musician, and writer living in Saskatoon. Her poetry has appeared in *Grain*, *NeWest Review*, *Filling Station*, and *Tesseracts6*.

J. Marc Piché is a poet and journalist, and only his wife has a better sense of humour. They walk their dogs together in Lloydminster.

Teresa Plowright is the author of Dreams of an Unseen Planet (Tesseract Books) and *Into That Good Night*. She lives on Bowen Island in British Columbia with her husband and sons.

Mildred Tremblay of Nanaimo, British Columbia, has had a book of her short stories, Dark Forms Gliding, published by

Oolichan Books. She is currently working, with the help of a Canada Council grant, on her first book of poetry. She has been published widely, and has won many awards including The League of Canadian Poets Award and the Arc National Poetry award. Recently, she placed first in the Canadian Poetry Association's competition.

Jean-Louis Trudel is the author of a number of books published in French, and many short stories published in French and English. If encouraged, he will also claim to be a translator, an ex-astronomer, a historian of science, a literary critic, an editor, and a world traveller.

Gerald L. Truscott has been an editor and publisher for more than 15 years. he was cofounder or Tesseracts Books and co-editor of *Tesseracts3*, with Candas Jane Dorsey. He has also published several short stories, including "Cee" in the first *Tesseracts* anthology, and more recently, "Transit" (*Transversions #7*) and "In the Court of Crimson King" (*On Spec*, Spring 1998). He live in Victoria with his wife and three duaghters, and is publisher/editor at the Royal British Museum.

Karl Schroeder lives in Toronto where he is a member of the Cecil Street writers' group. His work has been widely published, including in *Tesseracts3* and *Tesseracts 4, ON SPEC* and *ON SPEC: The First Five Years*. He is co-author with David Nickle of *The Claus Effect*.

Carl Sieber writes, rappels from helicopters, and walks at first light.

Michael Skeet is a writer/broadcaster living in Toronto. He has written hundreds of articles on film and music, and has been a syndicated CBC film critic. He co-edited *Tesseracts4*, and his fiction appeared in *Tesseracts2* and *Tesseracts3*.

Pierre Sormany has a background in physics but he is a career journalist, who has taught at the University of Montreal and worked for Radio-Canada, where he is currently in charge of the weekly science magazine *Découverte*. He has written a guide to journalism and technical papers (including a study on the future of biotechnologies in Canada and a report on the development of Information Society in Quebec). He has five published short stories and the compulsory yet to be published novel.

Richard Stevenson lives in Lethbridge, Alberta, and teaches at Lethbridge Community College. He has published 10 collections of poetry, including, most recently, *A Murder of Crows: New & Selected Poems* (Black Moss Press, 1998). A collection of young adults verse, *Nothing Definite Yeti*, is forthcoming.

Élisabeth Vonarburg was born to life in 1947 (France), to reading in 1952 (myths, fairy tales, comics, adventure), to writing in 1958 (poetry), and to science fiction in 1964 (at last!). She has won many awards for her witing in France, Quebec, Canada, and the United States. Previous Tesseract titles include *The Silent City*, *The Maerlande Chronicles*, and *Reluctant Voyagers*.

Andrew Weiner has published over 50 short stories in magazines and anthologies including *Fantasy and Science Fiction, Asimov's, Science Fiction Age, Interzone, Amazing, Twilight Zone Magazine, Quarry, Prairie Fire, Tesseracts* and *Full Spectrum*, some of which are collected in *This is the Year Zero* (Pottersfield Press) and *Distant Signals* (Tesseract Books).

Allan Weiss is a Toronto writer and bibliographer whose fiction and criticism has appeared in numerous magazines, and who was co-curator of the National Library of Canada's *Out of This World* exhibit celebrating speculative fiction in Canada.

Melissa Yuan-Innes is a newlywed in her third year of medicine at the University of Western Ontario. Coming soon to a hospital near you. Her short fiction has been published in *Parsec* magazine.

TESSERACTS ANTHOLOGIES
AVAILABLE FROM TESSERACT BOOKS

Tesseracts (1985)
edited by
Judith Merril

Tesseracts^2 (1987)
edited by
Phyllis Gotlieb and
Douglas Barbour

Tesseracts^3 (1990)
edited by
Candas Jane Dorsey and
Gerry Truscott

Tesseracts^4 (1992)
edited by
Lorna Toolis and
Michael Skeet

Tesseracts^5 (1996)
edited by
Robert Runté
and Yves Meynard

Tesseracts^Q (1996)
edited by
Élisabeth Vonarburg and
Jane Brierley

Tesseracts^6 (1997)
edited by
Robert J. Sawyer and
Carolyn Clink